The Rush

The Siren Series

Volume One

Sadie
The rush
is the best part!
Rachel
Higginson

Rachel Higginson

The Rush
The Siren Series
Book One

By Rachel Higginson

Copy editing by Jennifer Nunez and Carolyn Moon
Cover design by Caedus Design Co.

Other books by Rachel Higginson currently available

Love and Decay, Season One
Love and Decay, Volume One (Episodes One-Six, Season One)
Love and Decay, Volume Two (Episodes Seven-Twelve, Season One)
Love and Decay, Season Two
Love and Decay, Volume Three (Episodes One-Four, Season Two)
Love and Decay, Volume Four (Episodes Five-Eight, Season Two)
Love and Decay, Volume Five (Episodes Nine-Twelve, Season Two)

Reckless Magic (The Star-Crossed Series, Book 1)
Hopeless Magic (The Star-Crossed Series, Book 2)
Fearless Magic (The Star-Crossed Series, Book 3)
Endless Magic (The Star-Crossed Series, Book 4)
The Reluctant King (The Star-Crossed Series, Book 5)
The Relentless Warrior (The Star-Crossed Series, Book 6)
Breathless Magic (the Star-Crossed Series, Book 6.5)

Heir of Skies (The Starbright Series, Book 1)
Heir of Darkness (The Starbright Series, Book 2)
Heir of Secrets (The Starbright Series, Book 3)

The Rush (The Siren Series, Book 1)
The Fall (The Siren Series, Book 2)
The Heart (The Siren Series, Book 3) coming November, 2014

Bet in the Dark (An NA Contemporary Romance)

Striking (The Forged in Fire Series) This is a co-authored Contemporary NA

To Miriah,
My dear friend.
Here's to honesty and the F word.

Chapter One

"Are you sure you're up for this? You know after everything that happened last time?" asked the blonde haired sexpot dropping me off. My best friend, one of two of my only friends, and she was not even going to let me pretend this was okay.

Which was why I loved her.

Even if my blood pressure could not even handle this situation.

"Obviously not," I snapped. I took a breath, and then another one and then counted to five in my head to calm down, or attempt to calm down. I didn't need to apologize to Exie; she would know she wasn't the reason for my temper. Well, at least this time. "But what choice do I have? *He* says I have to go back to school, so *she* is making me go *here*. God, I can't wait until I'm eighteen."

"Like that will make any difference," Sloane, the final third of our threesome remarked bitterly.

"Focus on the trust funds ladies; we have a plan," I repeated our lifelong mantra softly, knowing it would soothe all of our nerves. Only two more years to go until that money became mine and I planned on taking full advantage of the dearly departed biological father I never got to meet. He stayed married long enough to my mother to knock her up, take care of my future and then give up his fight with cancer.

Thanks a lot Daddy Dearest.

That's what made him such a phenomenal fatherly candidate. The cancer that is, and all of the money of course.

And it didn't hurt, I'm sure, that before his illness had nearly finished the job of murdering him slowly and the chemicals had taken away his hair and stripped him of his dignity that he happened to be a very attractive man.

Or so my mother says.

I've never even seen a picture of him.

"I need to get out of here," Exie grumbled, flipping her waist length blonde hair over her shoulder. "I feel like I'm going to catch something."

"You're such a snob, public school is not contagious," I laughed.

"Are you sure about that?" Sloane clarified, narrowing her big brown eyes on the downtown campus.

Since I actually wasn't sure, I didn't answer. It could be contagious, what did I know?

"You guys better go anyway. We're going to get mobbed if you don't and I am really not in the mood for a pack of rabid high school boys this early in the morning. Or worse, jealous girlfriends." I twirled a loose auburn curl around my finger absentmindedly, trying to remain casual. I didn't like to get worked up about things. I mean, sure I was probably a little bit feisty with my temper, but other emotions bothered the hell out of me and I preferred to avoid them all together- yep, *all* emotions.

"What are you going to tell them, Ivy?" Exie asked with just the tiniest tone of sympathy. I turned to look her in the eyes, knowing both these girls hated feelings just as much as I did. I couldn't say that's why we were best friends. Honestly, we were friends because we had no other options, but it did surprisingly bond us together in a way that didn't make much sense.

"I'm not going to tell them anything. I'm going to let them believe whatever rumors they want to and just focus on getting to graduation day." I sighed, knowing that whatever rumors were being spread were not kind or flattering, but it was a routine I was familiar with.

"If that's what you want," Sloane sympathized. I had been down this road before, but a six month absence from school would only intensify whatever was being spread around about me.

"If you have a better idea S, I'm all ears. But I can't tell them the truth, the girls will hate me no matter what, and the boys will keep being boys. So it doesn't really matter what story they believe as long as they leave me alone in the process," I snapped again.

Sloane let out a very long, exaggerated sigh and nodded her head in agreement with my argument. "You're right."

I sighed feeling guilty for my irritable behavior and gave her an apologetic smile. She raised a slim shoulder casually and sent me a small smile so I knew she didn't hold it against me. We were all nervous about my return to school, all on edge. At least she understood where I was coming from.

"Hey, Ivy," a teenage boy approached confidently. Oh, great here we go.

"Oh hey, um..." I gave him a little head nod and prompted him for a name.

"Uh... I'm Chase Merrick, we had a, uh, we had chemistry together last year," Chase's confidence started to fade under the scrutinizing gaze my friends and I were subjecting him to.

"Oh, yeah, I remember," I lied, and forced my lips into a smile. It was almost painful. "How are you?"

"I'm good," he smiled one of those charming smiles that popular boys reserve for their next conquest.

Lucky for him I was easy.

Okay, not easy... I kept my legs together.

But I was looking for a boyfriend. I know that sounded trashy, but to be fair it wasn't like I was some jungle animal on the prowl. It was just safer to be committed to someone. Plus, he was cute in that all-American way with his floppy sandy brown hair and perfect, white teeth. He even wore a letter jacket which was a major bonus for him even if he didn't know it yet. A letter jacket meant that if I could tolerate this relationship longer than this school day he would at some point offer it to me and in turn I would wear it every day to support my awesome new boyfriend. That all led to effectively branding me as "taken" for the whole school to see.

On closer examination he had dimples.

Another point for... um... Chase?

Yes. Chase.

"So you're back?" he asked breaking the silence and my tally of his better qualities.

"We're going to go, Ivy, before you know, we need a prescription for this or something," Exie interrupted in her best valley girl impersonation.

"Alright, pick me up?" I asked, turning to receive the light hug each of them would give me. It was moments like this that we were perfect imitations of our mothers. And that annoyed the *hell* out of me.

"Oh, do you need a ride?" Sloane asked barely containing her smirk.

"I could give you a ride if you need one," Chase gallantly offered.

What a gentleman.

"Really? I don't live far. Thank you. That would be such a life-saver," I played up my enthusiasm, but everything inside me felt dead.

"Sure, it's my pleasure," Chase smiled again, popping out his identical dimples.

"Ladies, I'll call you later," I told them. I turned to face them while walking backwards up the long set of stairs that led to the school building.

"Just breathe, Ivy," Sloane called out knowing I needed some last minute advice. "Two years, that's all, just two years!"

I continued walking backwards, taking each step in stride and watched Exie and Sloane climb into Exie's brand new, silver BMW. She gunned the engine and then cut across traffic dangerously.

Central High School was located exactly downtown Omaha on one of the busiest streets, Dodge, which ran almost exactly down the middle of the city. It was also the most traffic jammed street, especially at this time of the morning. Exie was lucky she didn't nick her brand new car in the onslaught of oncoming traffic. She got off lucky with a few honking horns and a confused but angry homeless man who screamed obscenities at her from the sidewalk.

I cringed for her and her lack of driving ability. But then again, she probably didn't even notice.

"So, Chase, are you a junior or a senior?" I asked, dropping my gaze to my future boyfriend as he followed me up the stairs like a loyal puppy.

"A senior," he smiled. He answered everything with a smile. His happiness was going to a problem. I really hated breaking the happy ones' hearts.

"Oh, exciting!" I gushed, and this time I almost meant my enthusiasm. He only had nine months left until he could write his own ticket out of here.

So jealous.

"Yeah, I guess," he laughed, probably surprised by the sudden energy in my voice. "I still have to figure out where I'm going to school next year though."

"Undecided?" I asked and he nodded in response. "I'm sure you'll figure it out. You seem like a smart guy."

I said that generously because I seriously had to wonder why we would have been in the same chemistry class if he were such a genius. Although maybe chemistry had been one of my AP classes.... I couldn't remember. Last year seemed so long ago and I really hated remembering it anyway.

He chuckled at my way-too-cliché compliment and mumbled a "thanks."

Chase actually seemed like the kind of guy to be put off by obvious flirting. He was the type of guy that could probably pick and choose his girls and didn't need them to throw themselves at him for attention. Ugh. It just wasn't fair that he didn't really have a choice when it came to me.

"I like your hair this color, by the way," his smile turned shy.

"Not a fan of the black?" I forced myself into a conversation about my past. Really, seriously, truthfully.... I *hated* thinking about anything from last year.

"I mean, it was pretty. You could do anything to your hair and you would still be gorgeous," he offered thoughtfully, like I didn't already know that. It was all part of the curse. "But I like this red color; it goes better with your freckles." He reached up and brushed his pointer finger along the bridge of my nose to emphasize his point.

I crinkled my nose in reaction and blushed a deeper shade of red than I felt comfortable with. I hated my freckles. *Hated* them. Granted they weren't excessive, just a smattering of light brown on the bridge of my nose, and no doubt designed to make me some kind of more beautiful than the average girl, but they drew every eye and boys were constantly making comments about them.

Like now.

"This is my natural color," I offered that piece of personal information free of charge and wildly out of character for me. It would be the only one he got. "After everything that, uh, happened last year, my mom made me dye it back. Believe me when I say I desperately miss the black. I preferred the way it washed me out."

Oh I was wrong, he would get two pieces of personal information.

It must be his lucky day.

Except he would disappointingly not do anything with it. He may be smart, and now that I noticed the pins on his letter jacket weren't all sports related but actually included some academic endeavors, I started to believe that maybe chemistry was an AP class last year, but he wouldn't be smart enough for this game we were playing.

And that was just disappointing.

He laughed, thinking I was joking and I sighed, hating that I was right about him.

We reached the top of the stairs. Finally…. that was seriously a long walk from Dodge Street upwards to the entrance. "Grrr" to my mother and her refusal to let me get a driver's license.

She didn't believe in driving, if you could believe that. Like driving was some weirdo religion. Or like you could actually choose not to believe in it.

But she claimed that was what boys were for.

Yep, I just threw up in my mouth.

She was like the anti-feminist. She was sexist, but in the opposite way.

I was still walking backwards, you know in that flirtatious way that only really coordinated girls can pull off, giving Chase my undivided attention and choosing to believe the busy hallways of the ancient and decrepit school would simply part for me. They did, with no doubt every single eye watching my every move.

This was high school after all. And I was something of a legend….

No, that wasn't the right word.

Hot topic.

I was something of a hot topic.

I was like the definition of notorious; famous but with negative connotations- *very* negative.

Or at least I had been when I took my little six month sabbatical at the end of last year, over the summer and part of this year. I was banking on coming back, amping up the gossip mongers material and adding mystery to my ever growing nefarious reputation.

"What's your first class, Chase?" I asked as I slowed down near the office doors.

"Calculus," he answered, slowing down with me.

"Not slacking off in your last year? You must be undecided about good schools then," I remarked, narrowing my eyes on him.

His cheeks reddened just a bit in response.

"What about you?" he asked while coming to a complete stop with me in front of the long set of glass windows sandwiching the door that led into the school office.

"I'm not sure yet," I nodded in response to the office. The bell rang and he was officially late for class. Not that I thought he would mind. "I'll see you around."

"You'll see me later," Chase clarified boldly. "Ride home, remember?"

"Oh, I remember," I smiled coyly and then turned my back on him.

The glass door closed behind me with the tinkling of bells overhead and I visibly shivered against that interaction. Breathing deeply and counting to five again, I promised myself that the minute I graduated high school and had access to my trust fund I was so beyond out of here.

But the worst part, the part outside self-disgust and recrimination, outside the monotony and easy simplicity of all this was the guilt. The guilt that crept up slowly in the shadows of my heart and spread like a black sickness through my veins.

The only thing I knew about Chase at this point was that he was smart, good looking and way too easily impressed. Nothing about our interaction should have him enraptured by my every word, not even my looks, which were, unfortunately way too pretty for my own good. It so wasn't his fault and I felt bad for that.

He didn't really get a say. And I got absolutely no say.

In the end, I would leave him heartbroken and he would leave me shattered just like every single guy before him.

And believe me when I say there were a lot of guys before him.

It was my job.

Chapter Two

"Ah, Ms. Pierce, I wish I could say I was happy to see you," Mrs. Tanner, the evil witch of a secretary, acknowledged me with a smug smirk that seemed to confirm the fact that yes, in case you were wondering, high school *is* the ninth ring of hell.

"Oh, Mrs. Tanner, I wish I could say the same thing," I replied as sweetly as I could. I met her halfway with a long counter in between us.

She was not amused with me.

"You can't miss anymore school Ivy," Mrs. Tanner warned and I realized it was practically painful for her to give me advice to heed. This must be coming from the principal, the *male* principal Mr. Costas. "At least not this semester, unless you have a written note from your doctor. Mr. Costas would like to remind you that you are going to have to work hard enough to catch up this late in the quarter and that skipping, ditching or taking unnecessary sick days will not benefit you toward your goal of graduation."

"Tell Mr. Costas, I appreciate that he's looking out for me," I answered in that same sickly sweet voice I used to annoy the hell out of her.

She ignored me. "Here is your class schedule."

"Thank you." I snatched it from her hand and turned on my heel before she offered any more unsolicited advice.

"The faculty of this school would also like to ask that you not send any more of its students to the hospital," she called out snidely to my back.

I tensed immediately, my back ramrod straight and my nerves shot to sudden hell. "I'll do my best," I ground out and picked up pace.

I just needed to get to the glass door, push it open and get to class. Fifteen more seconds.

"If you have any extra cash on you, that canister by the door is for Sam's recovery fund," she finished on a high note.

I couldn't help myself. I should have bolted, and not just from the office, from school, from Omaha, from America.... I should have just gone.

But instead of listening to the sound voice of reason my inner conscience was screaming at me, I let the rotting guilt spread its ugly, vicious wings and glanced down at the canister. There he was. Sam. Smiling and happy in his senior picture that was not at all indicative of what he looked like now.....

The canister was covered with construction paper asking for donations to help with his physical therapy and explaining that he used to be a senior at this school, that he used to be a basketball star and that he used to be able to walk.... The same life he never got the chance to live before a car accident changed his world forever. The plastic cover had a slit cut out of the top so you could drop money into it, long enough for coins and wide enough for folded up dollar bills.

I couldn't do this.

I didn't want to do this.

I felt my breakfast lurch in my very upset stomach. I lunged for the office door knowing even a second more spent trapped in the same room as that canister was going to send me into another breakdown.

Only this time there would be serious consequences to pay.

I threw the door open without seeing. I mean literally I couldn't see anything. My mind had slipped into the horrific memories of the past and I was pretty sure I could make a solid plea for temporary insanity at this point.

So when I shoved the door with as much force as I was capable of and met shouting resistance and then found myself tripping, toppling over something on the floor, I was completely taken off guard. The situation was made worse when in the middle of my fall I was drenched with severely hot liquid and landed painfully on my back, soaking wet.

I lay there for several moments sprawled out awkwardly on the hard tile before the clearest, deepest gray eyes I had ever seen hovered over me. His thick brow line and hard edges to his tanned face prove he was male, definitely male. Our gazes locked together and I felt uncomfortably immobilized as the liquid I could now identify as coffee started to cool on my shirt and against my skin.

And then those eyes narrowed on me. My eyes flickered to a face that was completely unreadable, in that I couldn't identify his expression except that it wasn't good. Like.... he was mad at me. Like, he was *pissed* at me.

"Let me up," I growled, confused by his less than stellar reaction.

"Excuse me?" he asked politely, schooling his expression and realistically sounding polite, like he hadn't heard me correctly.

"Let me up," I slowed my speech down, thinking he just hadn't heard me, probably because he was so disconcerted from staring into my eyes.

I'm not being stuck up here. That's just usually what happened. I was speaking from experience.

"No problem." He scooted back from me and I scrambled to my feet. He joined me seconds later with two empty coffee cups in his hand.

We both side-stepped the spilled coffee puddled in the hallway and I thought for a second that I heard him huff an impatient sigh, but I knew that had to be wrong.

The halls were empty now, and we were left to stare each other down in front of the office. I prayed Mrs. Tanner had gone back to hiding in her hole of a break room; otherwise I needed to be concerned with her swooping down at any moment to haul my ass to the principal's office. If I was lucky she would demand a detention, but more than likely she would be petitioning for a suspension. She would use this or any other thing she could find against me.

Like I assaulted gray eyes with his hot coffee in an attempt to end any promising future he might have. Like this would be related in some way to Sam.

Realizing that could be the case, I looked down at my shirt hoping to have evidence that I was actually the one assaulted. And then hope turned to irritation when I noticed that it was completely ruined, and uncomfortably sticky and cold. Not that it was a designer shirt…. but the tight fitting, scoop neck black long-sleeved tee looked great with my gray bubble skirt and knee high charcoal boots. And the only extra piece of clothing I had with me was my favorite hoodie that I wasn't supposed to wear.

"What am I going to do now?" I bit out, while mystery man watched me from a few feet away.

"Excuse me?" he asked politely again, only this time I heard the faint tones of aggression and confusion.

Not possible.

"You spilled coffee all over me; I don't have a change of clothes, what am I supposed to do for the rest of the day?" I asked not at all politely.

"I spilled coffee on you?" he asked slowly, his patience growing thin.

I stopped then, in that moment and lifted my eyes to meet his again. He wasn't looking at me though, his arms were crossed and he was looking around the hallway as if he couldn't actually believe what was happening and he needed someone else to clue him in. I took his distracted second to look him over.

He was all bad boy with thick layered dark brown hair that was clearly not styled and left messy and sexy from sleep. He had the thick kind of eyelashes that made most girls go crazy, with tanned skin completely in contrast to his silver gray eyes. His gray t-shirt that was just a little too tight, stretched over his biceps deliciously. His low slung jeans completed what might as well have been the uniform for all things wicked.

17

"Are you seriously going to blame me?" he asked in disbelief, drawing my attention away from the hollow of his throat.

"You spilled coffee on *me*," I pointed out, pulling my shirt away from my skin mostly because it was so uncomfortable but also and a bit calculatingly because I knew it would expose my stomach and I was dying to see his reaction to a little skin.

"You came flying out of the office like a bat out of hell and ran into *me*," he laughed unbelievably. And not once did his eyes fall to my exposed skin.

"Listen, I don't have time for this, I'm already late for class," I ignored his potentially valid point and waited for the part where he would shake off his disbelief and ask for my number.

"You're seriously unbelievable," he continued to sound irritated with me and honestly it was a little disconcerting.

"Me?" I gasped. "*You're* unbelievable!"

Only I really meant that. Something was wrong. Like maybe I was broken.

Maybe I was broken....?

I had to test this theory, which meant swallowing all of my pride. My entire life thus far had conditioned me to think that nothing was ever my fault and there was always someone else to blame. Usually a man. An apology would take some effort on my part.

"You are one snide little-"

"Wait a second, before you start calling names," I interrupted him, holding my hand up before he could get any naughty words out of that beautiful mouth of his. "You caught me way off guard. I may have been a little defensive," I relented, not feeling a single word I was saying, but knowing if I wanted to get to the bottom of this I would have to play his game.

"You are apologizing for being defensive?" he clarified, not looking at all pacified.

What the hell?

"Yes, um, that and for running into you," I mumbled in a rush.

"What was that?" he stepped forward, tightening the arms that were folded across his chest. I knew he heard me.... cocky bastard.

"I apologize for running into you, I was in a hurry," I offered magnanimously.

"Obviously," he narrowed his eyes on me again and rocked back on his heels. "It's fine, I mean, you took most of the hit anyway." He nodded to my stained shirt and that's when I realized he was completely dry except for the hem of his t-shirt.

I hesitated for a long moment, feeling irrationally vulnerable under his scrutiny. Which wasn't fair, because I was usually the one getting to do the scrutinizing. He looked me over for all of three more seconds before seeming to come to an indifferent conclusion.

Which, let's be honest, confused the hell out of me.

"I can write you a pass," he offered out of the blue. *This was it! This was him showing his true colors!* But his tone of voice was not anything like the doting, fawning boys I was used to.

"You can?" I squeaked while still feeling exposed for some strange reason.

"I'm the office aide this hour, which is why I had coffee in the first place," he motioned to the still wet ground.

"Oh."

"What's your name?" he asked as if he didn't know.

"Really?" I laughed.

His expression turned confused. "I can't write you a pass without it."

"Oh." I couldn't tell if he really didn't know my name or not. He looked confused, but really I was the one that was so confused I couldn't even make a sentence.

"Uh, your name?" he asked impatiently.

"Ivy Pierce," I struggled for confidence. Who was this guy?

"Come on Ivy, what class are you going to?" He motioned toward the office, but there was absolutely no way I was going back in there. Not to mention, the minute Mrs. Tanner figured out he was trying to help *me* out, she wouldn't let him go through with it. And for some unexplainable reason I didn't want to get in it with her in front of him.

Whoever he was.

"Um, I have," I gave my schedule a quick glance before answering, "Mr. Taylor for creative writing." He motioned me to follow him so I had to call after him before the door swung shut, "I'll just wait out here."

He nodded his head without turning around to acknowledge me. Huh. He jumped up, so he could reach over the chest high partition and grabbed the yellow late slips before settling back down to the floor and filling it out. I watched him through the glass in kind of a state of disbelief. He hadn't looked back at me, not even once.

Obviously my self-confidence was used to more petting, but I had legitimate reasons to have always thought of myself as desired. I was desired- always. And it wasn't something I liked or ever hardly tolerated, but still it was the truth. The male species as a whole couldn't resist me and suddenly I smashed into someone I didn't know, get splattered with hot coffee and my mojo was gone?

"Ivy Pierce?" a girl's voice made me turn my head away from watching the mysterious office aide.

I turned to meet Kenna Lee as she approached the office. I forced a smile that I didn't really mean and realized how hard it was to keep my focus on her. She was nice enough, or as nice as a girl could be around me and we had known each forever, but as far as friends went.... she didn't like me. At all.

And I didn't blame her.

Plus it was hard to keep my eyes off the office aide writing me a pass. What if he turned to check me out and I missed it? Or even better, what if he *never* turned to check me out?

Kenna's smile seemed halfway genuine though so I had to wonder if girls would also be affected by my loss of mojo. Maybe I would start making friends.

"When did you get back?" she asked. She was one of the more attractive girls in our junior class. Her dad was Japanese and her mom was Italian American so she had the good fortune of beautifully mixed genes with long, silky straight black hair, and pretty tilted eyes that were a shocking shade of green.

"Today is my first day," I answered, wondering what to make of her friendliness.

"Good luck," she smiled knowingly, but friendly enough.

"Uh, thanks," I mumbled while she left me in the hallway and entered the office.

Office Boy turned at the sound of the door bells tinkling and his gray eyes lit up as soon as they landed on Kenna. He stopped writing my pass to pull her into his arms and smother her in a kiss. She threw her head back in laughter and he went for her neck playfully.

It was kind of gross, in that sickeningly gross happy couple way that makes everyone around want to vomit. Really blissful couples always made me uncomfortable anyway and I felt the need to avert my eyes.

The office door opened again and a tan, long-fingered hand was thrust through the space. I followed the sinewy muscles up to a perfectly toned bicep along his shoulder, collarbone, and throat and up to those clear gunmetal eyes staring at me with nothing more than complete disinterest.

"Sorry, again about the coffee," I apologized more sincerely for that spill than I had anything else in my entire life.

Okay. Almost anything else.

With one giant exception.

"No worries," he replied without even a smile before the door was shut on me and he, whoever he was, went back to flirting with Kenna in the office.

That was honestly a first for me.

Chapter Three

After a mind numbing morning, I needed a break from the world of academia but could truthfully say I was not looking forward to lunch. Seriously, there was nothing more intimidating for a teenager than starting school well after everyone else and facing the death chamber known as the lunch room.

And I was not even thinking about the food.

I was pretty sure I would have preferred lethal injection.

Or at least the lame therapy center my mom sent me to for recovery. Nobody judged you there at lunch. In fact, lunch usually came in the form of an assortment of rainbow colored pills in Dixie cups.

Mmmm. Delicious.

I had no friends at my school- none. Exie and Sloane, the only people in my life I could use that term even loosely with, went to private school. Why? Because their moms loved them. Well, maybe love was too strong of a word, but they cared more about their reputation than life experience, unlike my mom.

I had nobody here. I mean there were guys I had dated, or used or whatever. But girls in general hated me and I usually tried to avoid all past relationships. Using ex-boyfriends for friendship instead of making out usually tended to confuse most guys and I didn't have the patience to deal with that.

But I hated feeling intimidated and I hated it even more when I wasn't brave enough to face my fears. So I took a deep breath and stepped into the stale smelling cafeteria and hoped for the best.

The best being me making it to the end of the period alive.

And with no more food spills or stains on my now pathetic outfit.

I got in line immediately so I could scope out the room under the pretense of boredom and started filling up my tray with various healthy options, like an apple and bottled water. Lunch could not get more exciting than that....

"Hey," Chase came up behind me, startling me a bit.

"Hey," I offered back and then resettled the bottle of water I had tipped over in my jumpiness. "So, that's cool, we have lunch together."

"Looks like it," he smiled, his eyes twinkling with interest.

Ok... so my mojo still worked with him? I didn't get it.

What was going on with the mystery-coffee-spilling office attendant then?

"Where are you sitting?" I paid for my meager lunch, hating that I couldn't stop eyeing the cheese fries. I mean they were products of a high school cafeteria; they were going to be awful. Still... they didn't look awful, they didn't smell awful and they're nearly neon yellow processed cheese topping practically had my mouth drooling.

"Is that all you're getting?" Chase looked down at my mostly empty tray.

"Uh, no?" I gave into the cravings that were haunting me and grabbed a granola bar without paying for it as I followed him through the lunchroom. It wasn't cheese fries, but I hoped it would at least tide me over until dinner. It would be just me and my mom tonight so I had a super yummy bare as could be salad to look forward to.

Yum. Lettuce.

A fresh wave of utter hatred for my life washed over me.

And in a new form of self-loathing masochism I gave one last longing glance back at the cheese fries.

"I'm over here," Chase called, pulling my attention from the greasy, fattening food I wasn't allowed within smelling distance of.

Exie and Sloane were so much better at not missing junk food than me. But ever since I hit puberty and had to give up virtually anything that couldn't be bought in a hundred calorie snack pack, I decided my very first purchase with my trust fund would be a candy bar. Okay, probably it would be a plane ticket, but then definitely a candy bar.

Maybe two.

I was awesome at dreaming big.

I followed Chase to his table, nearly groaning at how many girls were sitting near or around him. This was going to be an interesting lunch.

We wedged in between two of his friends. I knew they were friends because of the guy fist pump thing they did when we approached and how they scooted out of his way so we could sit down on the narrow bench seat.

"Ivy Pierce?" The guy sitting next to me asked all surprised and shocked.

"Yep," I nodded, peeling open the wrapper of my granola bar. I realized then that if the entire table kept staring at me like that I wasn't going to be able to eat any of my lunch. Damn it.

"I didn't think you were coming back, like ever," he so eloquently explained his disbelief.

"Well, I'm here," I clarified shyly.

I was not shy. Actually the farthest thing from shy, but along with the feral attraction the boys at this table were watching me with was a mixture of astonishment and confusion. It was super distressing and I kind of just wanted to find a quiet place and die.

That wasn't too much to ask for was it?

"So they wouldn't let you transfer to another district?" A snotty girl from across the table asked innocently. I knew boys, but I knew mean girls better and this girl had an agenda. Her overly big brown eyes watched me with excited anticipation and I could almost feel her punch line hanging in the air.

I just shook my head.

"Oh, they didn't want you either, then," she sighed with mock sympathy. The girls around her tittered away their approval of her joke and I shrunk into Chase, using him as a shield against the open hostility.

Last year I would have snapped back with something that was both witty and cruel. I would have easily put her in her place by simultaneously hacking away at whatever façade of self-esteem she had and planted seeds of doubt that would plague her for years to come. I would have shut off every emotion and trickle of potential guilt and acted in a way I was raised to. I would have made my mother proud.

But since nowadays I could barely look at myself in the mirror, I had nothing for Amber. I couldn't even level her with one of my death glares. She was right after all; no other district would let me transfer into their school. Not even my mom's own power of persuasion could get me in. I mean, that was *a lot* of fear and rejection.

"Geez, Amber," Chase muttered disapprovingly at my persecutor.

"What? It's the truth," Amber narrowed her eyes on me. She was really pretty with her short, rich brown bob with red highlights. Her face was pixie-like with a cute nose and full lips underneath her huge eyes. She was definitely pretty enough to get all the attention of the boys at this table. She shouldn't have had to fight me for it anyway.

But she did.

We both knew it.

Only I was the only one who knew why.

"I'm sorry about my rude friend," Chase sighed, shooting Amber a look. Her eyes narrowed infinitesimally more and I recognized the pain she was trying to cover up.

She *liked* him.

"It's alright, she's right." I had to stop with the pity party or I would never be able to keep my stone-cold-bitch rep up. I went through the

25

routine I always did, the one where I stripped away my real feelings and replaced everything about me with what was expected of me. I sat up straighter, and pulled my wavy red hair over my shoulder where I knew it would look the most attractive, I put on an amused smile and then laughed. "Guess you guys are stuck with me."

That was met with a murmured chorus of "We don't mind," from the guys around me.

Amber did not like that and with a snort of disgust, got up from the lunch table followed by her posse of high school socialites.

"She's kind of annoying, right?" a guy from across the table asked.

I shrugged in response, but his amused tone made me lift my eyes to meet his and when I did I almost audibly sighed. He was one of those adorable kind of high school boys with curly, way too long shiny brown hair and a once-upon-a-time broken nose. He was scrawnier than most of the guys around me and endearingly disheveled.

On closer inspection, he was less scrawny and more…. gangly. Like really long and lanky, which was my favorite type of guy, but only because they always seemed so cartoonish and I was oddly fascinated by very tall people.

"When did you get back?" tall guy asked casually.

Chase shifted next to me. This was an uncomfortable road we were about to walk down, he probably didn't want his friend pissing me off and ruining his chances with me. If only he knew he had absolutely nothing to worry about.

"Uh, yesterday," I mumbled.

"Whoa, and you're already in school?" tall guy blurted in disbelief. "I would think you should get at least the rest of the week off."

I laughed at his nonchalance about the whole thing. Good for him. "I'm pretty sure this is just all part of my mom's never-ending scheme to punish me until the day I die."

"Ah, I have parents like that," tall guy nodded knowingly.

"I doubt they're as bad as mine," I sighed.

"Really? My name is Phoenix," he laughed and the rest of the guys around him laughed too.

"Phoenix?" I smiled. He was kind of contagious.

"Yep. Phoenix. They're total hippies. My little sisters have it worse than me; their names are Sparrow and Wren. But the baby, as in the newborn baby my forty year old parents *conceived* and then *birthed*… at *home*…. In the *bathtub*…. they named him Buzzard."

I gasped loudly. It couldn't be helped. "No they did not!"

He just nodded, laughing at my reaction. "It's true. My sisters and I have already decided we are only ever calling him Buzz, but still, can you imagine my hippy mom with her dreadlocks and marijuana perfume chasing after him in the grocery store wearing all of her hemp clothes yelling 'Buzzard you get over here!'"

I giggled at his story- giggled. The sounds felt strange and jumpy in my chest, but still they flowed out, exercising my ribs in a way that had been atrophied for way too long.

"I can totally see your mom doing that too," Chase laughed with me. His hand had slipped to my lower back as if protecting me from falling backward off the slim bench.

"You're right," I gasped for air, this time in a good way, "six months of banishment and public school hardly seem bad at all compared to a lifetime of Buzzard."

"So you see my point," Phoenix nodded.

"Where were you banished to?" the guy next to me asked.

"Uh...." I stuttered. I was prepared to not deny rumors, but I hadn't exactly prepared myself to come up with my own explanation. "Rehab," I choked out in a lie.

"Really?" He couldn't stop himself from the shock and I couldn't blame him.

"Yep," I looked away, not wanting to meet his eyes.

I felt him shift toward me on the bench. Oh no, he was going to ask more questions.

And then I felt the cool gray eyes of the mystery guy on me. I couldn't explain how I felt his stare before I saw him approach the table, it wasn't like we had a connection of any kind or I knew him at all. But then Kenna's laughter floated through the air and drew my attention before I could stop myself.

They were joining us. His arms were wrapped around her waist and she was looking up at him, laughing with careless grace at something he had said. She rose up on her tip toes and pressed a sweet kiss to his jawline before taking her seat next to Phoenix. Mystery guy followed suit and since I could apparently not stop watching the two of them interact, his cold gray eyes found mine in a look of disgust? Or maybe pissed off disbelief?

Please let it be something neutral like just surprise.

Ugh. I shouldn't care either way.

"Ryder, what is up?" Chase asked next to me, all happy smiles and friendliness.

"Same," he shot back.

He was pissed. Damn it and it was because of me. Seconds ago Kenna had his face lit up like a freaking Christmas tree. One look at me and all happiness faded from the room.

What is *up* with him?

"Who's your friend, Chase?" Ryder nodded in my direction and I gulped back more of those irrational fears.

"Ryder this is Ivy. Ivy Pierce, Ryder Sutton and his lovely girlfriend Kenna Lee," Chase offered politely. "With the exception of the lovely Kenna, no offense," he nodded to Kenna and she just shook her head at him, "we are every important part of the soccer team. "Keeper," he pointed to Phoenix. "Striker," he pointed to himself. "Midfield," he finished with Ryder.

"I know Kenna," I said quickly before things got even more awkward.

"Didn't you guys meet this morning?" Kenna asked, her pretty slanted eyes narrowing on me cautiously.

"Uh, not formally," I practically whispered. Ryder hadn't taken his cool gaze off me and I felt like I was shrinking under the weight of it. But there was no attraction there, no undressing me with his eyes or even less than admirable thoughts floating around in their gunmetal depths.

"I dumped my coffee on her this morning," Ryder explained with a small sarcastic twist to his lips. "I, unfortunately, tried to tie-dye her shirt the color of coffee and French Vanilla creamer."

I sat stunned, frozen by this sudden inside joke we shared. Luckily Kenna interrupted with an inside joke of her own, "Mrs. Tanner's fave."

Ryder broke his gaze with me immediately to stare into his loyal girlfriend's eyes. They shared a secret laugh and the hollowness inside me spread from the hole in my heart to my fingertips.

"How's your first day back?" Kenna asked politely. I knew she didn't like me. She *couldn't* like me. But she was a nice enough girl to pretend in front of other people.

"Same," I sighed. I felt like I was folding into myself, becoming my own version of a black hole. Soon I would be completely sucked into the void of darkness that was my soul, pulling in everything and anything around me.

Guy next to me felt like this was a perfect opportunity to jump back into our earlier conversation. "So what was the stint in rehab for anyway?"

Classy.

All conversation stopped at our table and every eye slid cautiously to me. This was a lie. This was a lie. I wasn't an addict, except to maybe hope. Yes, I was only addicted to hope for life after my eighteenth birthday.

"Everything," I muttered. I didn't feel up to the task of picking out one of the many reasons to go to rehab. I had lots of vices; I didn't want to give any one of them up just to prove a fake addiction. "Seriously, you name it."

The table was quiet for six entire seconds as the heavy information sank into all those around me.

"Sex," Ryder said clearly in the wake of the awkward silence.

"What?" I sputtered.

"Sex, were you addicted to sex?" he clarified. He settled his gray eyes on me again, their depths becoming pools of liquid silver. But still, he was mocking me, calling my bluff. There was nothing sparking in the air between us and I couldn't help but be intrigued. What was different about him? Why wasn't he pulled into the same bullshit every other man on the planet had to suffer from?

"Absolutely," I sat up straighter, my confidence gaining with each moment he held my gaze. "But I refused treatment; I prefer to live in denial." I laughed.

"You're basically like the female version of Tiger Woods," Ryder stated but his eyes danced with amusement.

"Exactly," I nodded, offering him an amused smile that lacked any of its usual flirtatious traps. "But it's my cross to carry."

"Nuh-uh," guy next to me grunted in complete disbelief, like I was the holy grail of damaged daddy issues. He scooted closer to me on the bench and I couldn't help myself, I clung to Chase. I was destined to this sort of depraved, user lifestyle, but nothing could make me willingly give myself over to creepers. I had standards.

Not very many standards....

But there were some levels of crazy I just couldn't mess with.

"Back off, Hayden, she's not serious," Chase barked at him. I was really beginning to like Chase. He tossed his floppy hair out of his eyes in disgust and then turned his deep blue eyes on his friend. "And it's disgusting that you would be attracted to somebody else's real problems."

"I'm just messing around, man," Hayden laughed. "I wasn't serious either."

"Right," Chase rolled his eyes and his hand went from my lower back to all the way around my back.

29

He was strong and protective and I melted into him. But it was all fake. He was under a spell, nothing more. This would fade....

And I would be left with an attachment that meant nothing.

"Hey, want to go with me to the Biology Lab? I have to drop off some extra credit," Chase leaned in so he could ask me quietly. He held my gaze in his searching blue eyes, looking for something, making sure I was okay.

"Yes please," I whispered, trying to show him that I was fine. I wasn't. I wasn't anywhere close to being fine, but it didn't really have anything to do with sleazy Hayden or even the fact that I had been sent away for treatment, just not of the addictive-behavioral type.

It did have a lot to do with the behind the scenes of my life, the ones that nobody could see, the ones that hurt and cut the deepest and screwed me up until I was a walking disaster of bipolar emotions and feminine insecurities.

But mostly it had everything to do with the gray eyes staring at me across the table like they knew me, like they saw through all of the pretty façade of my life and cut to the empty, lost part of me. But most of all it had to do with the fact that he saw me; Ryder *saw* me and didn't care.

What the hell was I supposed to do with that?

I followed Chase from the lunch room, letting him lead me by the hand and I decided that I had to find out. Even if it meant that eventually I would turn on the glamour and he would be sucked in just like everybody else and all of his appeal would crumble around him.... still, I had to know.

Chapter Four

"Ivy, is that you?" My mother called from her bedroom.

"Yes," I called back wondering if she was expecting someone else. I walked over to the windows that looked out at the busy downtown street and watched Chase pull back into traffic. I half wondered what had taken him so long to leave. I lived with my mom in a trendy midtown loft and because of the busy one way streets, Chase couldn't park and walk me to the door as he had originally planned.

That was fine with me. We weren't on a date; he was just taking me home from school. Although I wondered if my nonchalance about the whole thing hurt his good-boy ego. The stress of that thought had me glancing at the cherry wood upright piano that sat three feet to my left, pleading with me to play it. To take out my nervous energy on the ivory keys and unforgiving demands of Tchaikovsky.

"How was your first day back?" My mother asked as she walked out of her bedroom. She looked stunning in a short black cocktail dress and six inch stilettos. She was fastening a diamond chandelier earring with two well-manicured hands and perfected the concept of elegance.

"It sucked," I sighed and then turned my back on her.

I walked over to our immaculate eat-in kitchen and grabbed a bottle of water out of the stainless steel fridge. I noticed a note on the counter from the cleaning lady and had to grip the counter to keep from rolling my eyes. I hated everything about this apartment, about our clothes, about our possessions.... about our lifestyle.

It was honestly disgusting.

"Ivy, ladies don't say 'sucked,'" my mother chastised.

"I apologize," I mumbled. I forced myself to turn around and face her. It took a huge effort on my part and an even greater effort to look in her forest green eyes without cowering. I was her spitting image, it was our strong genes that kind of took over any mixing of DNA and molded us into replicas of each other. One day if I had a daughter of my own she would be just another carbon copy of me. Good thing I would never, ever, ever have children. That was so not in my life plan.

"So, tell me about your first day back," my mother asked with way too much enthusiasm.

"Why are you so dressed up?" I deflected. We were supposed to have dinner together tonight. I wouldn't be all that upset about the loss of mother-daughter bonding time, but I was terrified for whatever man had to put up with my mother for the rest of the evening.

And possibly through the morning.

"Oh, right," my mother sighed looking down at her ensemble as if she just realized how dressed up she was. Her eyes darted around the room never quite reaching my face. "Uh, Nix is in town. He has some sort of business thing tonight and we're going to dinner first."

My fingers found the edge of the granite counter again and I instinctively dug in, gripping it tightly until the pads of my fingers started to tingle with numbness. I concentrated on my breathing, steadying my ragged breaths and forcing myself to remain calm. I had to remain aloof; I needed to keep the perfect disguise of cool indifference. I couldn't let her see my fear, or my anxiety, or any of the other hundreds of emotions spinning like a self-destructive tornado inside me.

"Are you meeting him somewhere or is he coming here?" I ground out, barely keeping the bite of anger out of my tone.

"He's coming here," my mother said slowly. She was watching me carefully, her eyes sweeping the length of me, waiting for me to fall apart again.

But I would *never* fall apart again.

I learned my lesson the first time. I couldn't be real anymore. I couldn't show anything beyond the plastic casing I wrapped myself tightly in or they would know; they would see something immediately.

And I would have to pay.

Eighteen. Trust fund. Two years. Breathe. Just breathe.

"He wants to see you," my mother continued. Her smiled tightened just a fraction into a practiced ease that meant that she felt the volatility of the moment as acutely as I did.

"Good," I breathed carelessly. "I want to see him too."

My stomach started twisting in the aftereffects of my lies. I felt lightheaded and dangerously close to trembling. I could not let her see me struggle for calm. She had to believe I was relaxed, or at least as resigned to the situation as she told me I had to be.

"Good," she smiled wider, her expression becoming natural once again.

The twisting got worse until bile was rising in the back of my throat. I turned my back on her, my fingers instantly finding the counter again and digging in until the edge cut into my skin and I could have winced from the pain.

"Why don't you change then, he shouldn't see you so…. disheveled," she remarked callously. "What did you do? Spill on yourself today? I saw a

32

boy drop you off earlier, I'm surprised he took any interest while you looked like that."

I held in my gasp of indignation. It was just my shirt, my dark shirt that barely showed any signs of stains, that was ruined. Something in the room was slowly sucking out all of the oxygen leaving me lightheaded and disoriented.

I gasped for breath.

I needed to hold it together.

I couldn't lose it.

Not again.

"I spilled coffee," I explained in my practiced patience. "I'll go change. When will he be here?"

"Soon, sweetie. Why don't you wear that new red dress I bought you?" she suggested.

I paused for a moment near tears. "I don't have to go with you, do I? I'm just really tired from school today and I have a lot to catch up on from the quarter that I've missed so far."

"Oh, no, you're not going with us. I just know Nix would appreciate it if you put some effort into yourself when you're around him," she explained like it was the most obvious thing in the world.

She was my mother. *My mother.* Why was this okay to her? Why couldn't she see how wrong this was?

A million different responses flashed in my head, all of them intending to get me into trouble. "You're right," is what I said instead. "I'll go change now."

"Ivy," she stopped me before I could get to the sanctuary of my bedroom. I turned to acknowledge her and faked a yawn, just in case she noticed the glassiness to my now tear filled eyes. "I'm glad you're home, sweetheart. I missed you."

"I'm glad to be home too, mom," I answered, avoiding any accolade that had to do with her.

She rewarded me with her most charming smile, the one that would get millionaires to sign their wills with her as the sole beneficiary and make ordinary men melt into whimpering piles of stupidity. I mimicked the smile, knowing I looked like the mirror image of her and that it would on some level, drive her crazy.

The buzzer sounding near the door drew both of our attention. She waved me off to go get ready while she answered the door. I fled to my bedroom, not even waiting around to find out who was there.

I knew who it was.

Nix.

A shudder slithered down my spine; I felt it all the way to my toes and fingertips. I stopped from choking on the disgusted nausea that had wrapped around my stomach in a heavy blanket of warning and reminded myself that they were leaving.

This interaction would only last a minute, maybe a few minutes and then I would have the entire evening to myself. I would finally get to be alone and have precious moments to breathe.

I could do this.

I heard the door open outside of my room and the deep tones of a melodic male voice greet my mother. The voice had goose bumps rising quickly all over my skin in more forewarning. I shook my head out in a desperate attempt to get out of the fearful fog I had conjured around me.

I walked over to my closet and stared into the depths of cluttered clothing packed in tightly together. There was no way I was putting on the paper napkin my mother considered a dress. I needed something in between mega-slut and carelessly cute.

I threw myself into finding the perfect outfit. It wasn't something I enjoyed doing, but after years of studying the art of dressing to impress, it was something I could do almost blindfolded. I picked through my massive closet that took up an entire wall of my large bedroom, tossing several pieces on my four poster queen-sized bed.

When I was satisfied with a few different options, I laid them out carefully on my robin's egg colored down comforter and decided from there. I went through the checklist before I came to my conclusion: spray tan, check; shaved legs, check; pedicure, check; tattoo concealer.... probably needed a touch up.

I settled on a pair of mostly white with black pinstripes shorts and a silky black cami: sexy but casual. I pulled my wavy reddish-gold hair into a side ponytail, letting the length of it hang over my shoulder and expose my neck. Then I reached into the deepest depths of my closet, into a mostly empty Louboutin shoe box where I retrieved my tattoo concealer. I applied it on the inside of my right wrist and then on my ribs, underneath my cami just in case.

I shivered again at what "just in case" could imply.

I looked myself over in my mirror, deciding that everything was in place and then returned the concealer to its hiding place. I practiced breathing with several deep breaths in and out and then turned to face my doorway. I could hear them out there, laughing and talking. They were so at ease with each other, with their whole lives.

It was insane.

They were insane.

And I was insane for putting up with this whole bullshit life.

I opened my door quietly, hoping they wouldn't immediately notice me, but I was an idiot for holding out any kind of optimism. Their eyes fell on me at the exact same time and I had to stop breathing completely to keep from cringing as they both eyed me hungrily. My mother's gaze was deranged pride and satisfaction and Nix looked me over with a ravenous desire he didn't even try to conceal or downplay.

"Hi, Nix," I greeted casually, leaning my hip against the doorway.

"Hi, Ivy," his perfect lips spread into a gorgeous smile that even I couldn't be totally unaffected by. But it was part of his charm, part of what made him who he was and even if physically I couldn't stop myself from being attracted to his sexy-as-sin mouth, I could at least mentally remind myself of the price it came with. "Happy to be home?"

"Of course," I shrugged one shoulder and then walked over to the couch just for something to do.

"Ava, why don't you go check the account we were just talking about," Nix addressed my mother. She paused for a moment too long, as if waiting for a better reason to leave the room. "We'll leave as soon as you're finished." Nix turned his reassuring smile on my mother and lifted his dark eyebrows expectantly.

"Of course," she agreed, obeying him. There had never been any doubt in my mind that she wouldn't do exactly as she was told. She lived a complete subservient life, in the utter will and command of Nix. The same life I was supposed to embrace and walk willingly into, as well.

Not happening.

Eighteen. Eighteen. Eighteen. Eighteen.

Once she was gone, Nix walked over to the couch. I fought the defensive surge to pull my knees to my chest, knowing it would give away the physical signs of needing to protect myself and crossed my legs instead. Nix let his dark eyes float over my exposed limbs appreciatively; he cleared his throat letting his gaze linger way too long on my thighs. I resisted the urge to fidget when his eyes moved to my hands. He couldn't see the tattoo; I had checked it out enough to know that it was perfectly hidden. Still there was a part of me that believed he could see through anything.

He was just a man. Nothing more. Nothing more than a man.

Okay, maybe something more.

"How was your first day back?" he asked, his deep, gravelly voice caressed each word and floated in the air around me like music. He looked god-like in his immaculately tailored navy blue suit, with starched white oxford and red charcoal tie. His tan skin was the exact color of caramel and because I was crazy I stopped to notice how delicious his large hands looked hanging casually at his sides.

"Same as it always is," I answered, not fooled at all by the cocoon of safety he was trying to wrap me in.

He was not safe. He was not anything but absolutely dangerous.

He sat down on the chic, mustard colored coffee table in front of me and rested his elbows on his knees so that he could lean forward and meet my eyes at an even level. He let his fingers trail up my bare calf before he reached for one of my hands and took it gently in his. I couldn't hide the goose bumps that covered my skin, all I could do was hope that he thought they were good goose bumps and not the result of the paralyzing fear pumping desperately inside of me.

"Ivy, I am happy you're home," he admitted. He ducked his head as if with sincerity before looking up at me through his thick, black eyelashes. It was a practiced move, a move meant to make any girl puddle at his every word. I was not fooled, but I had to be somewhat sneaky about it. "I was so worried about you. You can't do that to me again, alright? I need to know that you will be okay, here. If you don't think this is a good environment for you, or if you feel even a little bit like you could relapse I need you to tell me."

"Thank you, Nix," I answered in a barely controlled voice. "But, I'm fine, really. I'm happy to be home with my mom again. She needs me."

He sat there pensively for a few moments, drinking in my answer. His eyes darkened suddenly and I couldn't stop myself from wondering if it were from lust or anger. I hoped anger, but flipping a coin would have given me more insight than trying to read his expression.

"But what about what I need?" Nix asked playfully. His full lips tipped up into a smile and small creases appeared near his eyes, making it seem like he was a regularly happy person, that a smile was part of his constant facial expressions.

I swallowed quickly, my throat working overtime to keep from puking. I buried whatever thoughts sounded like *What about what I need?*

"Nix, I'm only sixteen," I chastised playfully. *Where* was my mother?

"Now, now, that's not what I meant," he backtracked when we both knew that was exactly what he meant. But I wasn't his property. Not yet. "I only meant that I'm very concerned about your well-being. I understand that your mother can't leave Omaha, but you aren't under the same obligations. I need to know that you're safe, that you're well taken care of and that you're protected."

"I am," I assured him.

"I know that you think you are, but let's not forget what happened just six months ago. I could have lost you Ivy. Do you know what that has done to me?" His expression seemed so sincere and if I were a weaker woman I would have melted in the intensity of his feelings for me. It didn't matter how old he really was, he looked like he was maybe mid-thirties.

"I can't apologize enough for my stupidity," I threw myself into this moment as a character in a tragic play. I had to convince Nix, my mother…. I had to convince everyone. And I would do whatever it took to get out of here. If Nix took me to live with him, I would never see freedom, never see my trust fund. I had to push through the fear and vile hatred coiling inside of me and just pretend. I scooted to the edge of the couch and slipped my other hand in his. I rubbed my thumb nail across the inside of his wrist slowly and gently, a move that usually got me anything I wanted with men. "I was confused and not thinking right. I won't ever let that happen again…. I won't *ever* behave like that again." I shrugged one of my shoulders, hopefully drawing attention to the curve of my neck and collarbone and then used his own trick against him by looking up through my lashes.

"Promise me, Ivy," Nix whispered through a thick voice. "Promise me you won't ever get like that again and if you even think you might be slipping you'll come to me immediately."

"I promise," I responded with enough sincerity that even I almost believed I was telling the truth.

"Mmmm, good girl," Nix murmured, his gaze settling on my lips. He leaned forward and I sucked in a quiet gasp, preparing for his touch. One of his hands lifted to cup my chin and he tilted my mouth upwards to meet his sensual lips. He kissed me lightly, gently, his lips never opening but lingering a little longer than I could stand.

When my thumb slipped out of nervousness and grazed over his wrist one more time, he groaned against me. His hand gripped my neck firmer and even though he pulled away instead of deepening the kiss I knew it took all of his willpower.

"You're exquisite," he whispered. "And if I didn't love your mother as much as I do, I would demand you come live with me right now."

Well, at least I could thank my mother for something.

He laughed gruffly as if he were trying to gain his composure and then stood up and moved away from me. I bit down on my bottom lip to keep from saying anything that would get me into trouble and slid back into the deep recesses of the couch.

My mother came out of her bedroom wearing a designer coat over her designer dress and a beaded clutch in hand. She gave me an excited smile after glancing at Nix as if I had just won some kind of championship game.

I broke out in a cold sweat.

"I'll be in town for a while," Nix told me, his eyes still smoldering. "Do you already have a date for this weekend or will I be able to take you out one night?"

"I, uh, I," I stammered, loathing the idea of a night out with him. "I met a guy today; he gave me a ride home from school. We don't have anything set up, but I'm positive he'll ask me out this weekend."

"Good," Nix murmured and I could see the confliction in his eyes. He was happy there was a boy but disappointed all the same. "Maybe Sunday, then?"

"Maybe," I answered noncommittally. "Will you be back tonight?" I turned to my mom.

She looked to Nix for the answer, he shook his head negatively. "I guess not," she giggled. "Will you be Okay?"

"I'll be fine, have a great time," I gushed, so ready for them to be gone.

"Alright, bye sweetheart," my mom walked over and kissed me on the forehead.

"Goodbye, Ivy," Nix's eyes swept over me appreciatively one more time and then he winked at me.

I waved from the couch and then held my breath until the door clicked shut behind them. As soon as they were gone I leapt from the couch and rushed to the bathroom. I barely made it to the toilet before I started vomiting up every single thing I ate today, which wasn't all that much. I shuddered even against the violent heaving as I emptied my stomach.

When I was finished I sunk to the floor, leaning my back against the bathroom wall.

Two years might as well have been an eternity. If I had to put up with too much more of this, I would never make it. I would crumble... shatter... I would explode into the million broken pieces I already felt like composed me. I was already wrecked. Completely fragmented and I wasn't foolish enough to believe that freedom would fix me.

But it would let me breathe.

And that's all I needed. I just needed to breathe.

Chapter Five

They were gone for ten minutes before I let myself move. I had to be sure they were gone. I had to know they weren't coming back and I was free to do as I pleased.

So when I was sure, I tore from the bathroom floor and ran to my room. It was still early in the evening, but Wednesdays were a bit of a ritual night for me and since I would be taking the bus I needed to get my ass moving.

In my room, I changed again. I was in what I called my "Mom-approved-skanky-casual." This included nice, expensive clothes that were at the same time subtly revealing and not at all age appropriate. I was a sixteen year old girl that rarely got to act sixteen except on Wednesday nights when I was in Omaha. And this was my first Wednesday back in over six months.

I ripped of my cami and shorts and shot to the very depths of my closet, the depths on the opposite side of my tattoo cover up, because both secrets were very closely tied to my heart and I couldn't have one giving away the other, just in case of worst-case-scenario-secret-exposing-Armageddon.

Which was obviously the worst kind of Armageddon.

And could happen at any time, day or night.

People get ready.

I pulled from the bowels of my clothing sanctuary the most depressing, most soul-baring, most emo clothes I had been able to stash away over time and grinned like an idiot. I peeled, tugged, yanked and scooched my tightest black, faded skinny jeans on and paired them with depressingly worn out Chucks.

They were worn out because, in my entire short-lived life, I had only ever had one opportunity to sneak a pair of black and white Chuck Taylors into my wardrobe. And I knew, without a doubt, if something ever happened to them I would never get that opportunity again.

I pulled on a faded to gray Johnny Cash t-shirt and inhaled the musty smell that came with being tucked into a hole in my closet for too long. And then to finish my glorious ensemble, I zipped up my plain black hoodie. I almost squealed with delight. A hoodie. A freaking hoodie!

It had been six months since I'd been able to wear something as comfortable as a hoodie.

I always carried one around with me in my backpack, but I never wore it. It was like a security blanket for me. And maybe something more, something like the Promised Land.

I pulled a hair-tie off my vanity and wrapped my hair into a knot on the top of my head. I darkened my eye-liner to Goth-gorgeous and painted on some bright red lipstick. I stepped back so I could approve of my look in the full-length mirror.

Then I really did squeal.

If I had complete freedom, as in the ability to choose small aspects of my life without having to answer to anyone other than myself, this would not be the wardrobe I would choose. I wasn't some closet monochromatic safe dresser or even someone that belonged in a Goth sub-culture, but I also wasn't the glamorous uber skank I usually dressed up as either. I was somewhere in between.

And in my daydreams and all the thoughts I had that centered around two years from now, I pictured myself one day having the opportunity to discover and explore what my real tastes and opinions were. I could not wait to try something on in the dressing room, decide I looked great only to hate it the minute I got home. Then, in these pipe dreams, I would complain about having to return it, go to the store anyway and purchase something as equally unflattering. Rinse and repeat.

As it stood now, I didn't get to choose my wardrobe. I barely got a say in what I wore on a day to day basis. And then I very secretly rebelled by going in the exact opposite way I lived my everyday life just because it was rebellion. I had no attachment to these clothes other than memories of concerts made of horrible music and boys not giving me even a second glance. I didn't care for the way the pants clung to me and when I got sweaty they really clung to me, the shoes were well beyond their good years, hell they were way beyond retirement and my t-shirt and hoodie were just meh. But they were something my mother and Nix would disgust and even possibly not even recognize me in. And even better they made me feel, even if it was just for one night…. they made me feel alive.

And I desperately needed to feel alive.

Because if I didn't feel alive, then I would feel…. dead.

And dead was unacceptable, because dead would mean giving up hope.

I shook my head to free myself of those thoughts and grabbed my ID, my regular, real school ID, not the fake ID from Nix, and a wad of cash and stuffed it all into my pocket. Yep, not even a purse. And then I took off for the long journey across downtown Omaha to NoDo, North downtown, via bus for my Wednesday night ritual.

The sleek, trendy concert hall was packed with bodies, both underage and of-age. Partly because Wednesday nights were huge at the Slowdown with the under twenty-one crowd and also because the main stage was curtained off and the band was positioned at the back of the room on a mini-stage.

Sweat, beer and the faintest hint of weed wafted through the air. The space was almost completely dark, with every overhead light in the exposed ceiling turned off. Only the stage lights and dim bar lights over a large selection of alcohol illuminated the room. Tables were spread out in between the t-shirt stands in the back and the space in front of the stage where standing fans congregated. Board games were stacked unceremoniously on a cluttered bookcase near the front door and the stairs leading to the balcony were roped off. Welcome to the Slowdown.

The opening band was blasting on stage, their drums beating so loudly my heart was forced to keep quick rhythm and I felt the reverberation of the bass guitar to my very bones. I didn't know their name, and really I didn't need to. I just wanted to sport my under twenty-one wrist band that declared under no circumstances should I be served alcohol, even though the bouncer tried to convince me I looked twenty-one and would totally get away with a real wrist band.... come on.... what will it hurt?

His words not mine.

I said, "It will hurt *me*, damn it! I will obviously drink cheap tequila until I'm obliterated, then leave with some random, way-too-old-for-me-stranger, get knocked up, get into a drunk-driving accident *and then* I will die! And then you will be responsible for the death of a sixteen year old minor! Damn it!"

My exact words.

Then he shrunk back on his stool and gulped, "Sixteen?"

And then I walked into the music hall completely satisfied with how that went down.

Despite my aversion to certain libations tonight, I was still thirsty after two and a half hours on and/or waiting for various public transportation. So I pushed my way through the pressing crowd and to the bar. In the trek over I had to weave through lots and lots of bodies and then in order to get a place at the bar I had to stand near the back of the room where the t-shirts were being sold, and elbow my wait to the chest-high counter.

I didn't mind it back here. The air was fresher and cooler and it was decidedly less populated since most of the crowd was currently trying to press into one solidified organism, like the human centipede, against the stage. It wasn't going to work, but there was no use telling that to them.

"Water!" I yelled when I caught the bartender's attention. He gave me a questioning look so I waved my wristband his way and he nodded in a disappointed but resigned way.

Once upon a time, before I could hold my liquor, Nix had taught me to order a Blue Dolphin when at a bar, which was essentially water on the rocks. He said ordering it that way would make me sound more sophisticated. When I ordered water now, I did it with a smile and hoped to God it made me sound as immature and pathetic as possible.

I gulped the deliciously cold tap water down in two huge swallows as soon as the bartender handed it to me. Before he could get the chance to walk away I made a circle motion with my pointer finger and yelled, "Keep 'em coming!"

That earned me an amused but slightly predatory grin from the college-aged bartender with floppy black hair and neck tattoos. I had a thing for tattoos, it was like a weakness of mine, but I was so off the clock tonight.

So I turned my head away from Mr. I Dig Minors bartender and out to the riotous crowd. This was it; this was why I loved Wednesdays. There was too much adrenaline pumping in the shared air for people to really notice me. I mean, if I was talking one-on-one to someone they got the vibes, but usually people were so absorbed in the music I was hardly noticed at all. And the smells of cheap liquor and vomit helped put them off the scent.

Not to mention I had a deep and abiding love affair with music.

All music.

It didn't really matter what kind or how good. If it, whatever it was, was put to music I could easily lose myself completely. Seriously from bad pop to heavy rock to my favorite classical composers, I loved it all.

Well, maybe except the jazz flute. Regular flute was fine. But jazz... that was an entirely different circle of hell as far as I was concerned.

An ugly, confusing, shrill sounding circle of Hell.

Just don't tell Ron Burgundy I felt that way.

It was during this perusal of my environment that my eyes fell into, not to, but *into* the gray depths of Ryder Sutton. I felt my mouth fall open;

literally my bottom lip detached from the firm hold my top lip had on it and my jaw followed.

He glared at me from across the room. *Glared* at me. He had his back to the far wall and one foot propped up with his knee bent. His arms were folded across his chest and even from here I could see ripped biceps tensed and flexed. He was in the same outfit he wore earlier today, the only difference was his hair was slightly bigger. It wasn't like his hair had multiplied or anything, but it just stood out from his head a bit less controlled…. crazier…. no…. sexier. Like he had his hands in it, or someone else had their hands in it.

Like Kenna Lee, who had just walked by me without even noticing I was here and straight to her cliché-rebel-boyfriend. Ryder then proceeded to take his eyes off me, put them on his girlfriend and then rock her world by pulling her into the most disgusting display of public affection I had ever seen.

Gross.

I so did not get people kissing in front of other people.

Hell, I didn't even get how people liked other people enough to like kissing them.

Romance was weird.

In my life, romance didn't even exist.

The bartender handed me my second glass of water and when I was finished with that one, I slammed it down on the bar like I had just finished the proudest kind of awful-tasting-shot. This earned a throw your head back kind of laugh from Neck Tattoos, to which I had to agree, I was hilarious.

It was amazing how escaping my life for even just three hours took the weight off my shoulders and allowed me to have some fun. If I could let this loose after three hours, imagine ultimate freedom in two years.

I winced in anticipation. I could make it. I could get through two years.

"Ivy?" someone yelled from behind me.

I gave the bartender a desperate look for more water to which he shook his head, amused at me, and then turned around praying it wasn't Ryder and Kenna.

Some prayers are answered with a "yes."

Some prayers are answered with a "no."

This was a "no" kind of situation.

"Hey!" I shouted over the music. "What are you doing here?" I forced myself to keep my eyes on Kenna and not look around for Ryder who seemed to have disappeared. He hated me that much he couldn't even stand to have awkward small talk with me?

I seriously had to get to the bottom of this.

"My boyfriend is playing tonight," Kenna shouted back. She was dressed for the girlfriend-of-the-band part in a fifties' style red wrap around dress with black polka-dots. Her long, black hair floated around her shoulders in silky straightness that remained perfectly unfrizzed and untouched by the humid atmosphere of the bar. She was wearing a proud smile and bouncing in her vintage ivory pumps showing off her extreme excitement.

"Ryder?" I clarified.

Instead of trying to beat the volume contest she nodded, flashing a smile full of affectionate pride.

"Cool!" I offered back and then turned my own attention to the stage. I wasn't sure if she wanted to hang out or not and it was way too loud to try to carry on a conversation. Plus, I didn't really have anything to say.... so there was that.

We bobbed and swayed in the general vicinity of each other for twenty more minutes, rocking out to some grass-roots kind of blues sung by college aged boys with underdeveloped voices and wardrobes straight from the Kurt Cobain catalogue.

Perfection.

Kenna didn't exactly engage with me, but she didn't walk away either. I didn't know what to do, or say, so I stayed near the bar and slammed another shooter of water. I didn't have to look back at Kenna to know her eyes were on me and my tumbler full of ice and clear liquid. She would assume the worst.

I would let her.

The opening band finished up their set and the loud music was replaced by a quieter but none the less angsty speaker sound. I finally turned back to Kenna to force myself into small talk. I was out of excuses and some irrational part of me wanted to prove to her that I was still lucid despite the three supposed shots of vodka she assumed I had taken. I sucked in a breath, prepped myself with a faux mental face slap full of cocky self-assurance and opened my mouth to make a comment about the last band but the menial opinion died in my throat because Ryder was standing next to her now.

With his gray eyes watching me intently, I lost the nerve to say anything and instead my attention fell to the toned arm he had wrapped around Kenna's waist. I grunted when I noticed the green and black tattoo marks snaking up his forearm. Didn't I just say I liked tattoos? But his... he was so cliché. I swear he had read some kind of bad-boy handbook and followed steps one through twelve to pull his dangerous rep together.

Plus a band? Seriously.

"You here for an AA meeting?" Ryder asked from the other side of Kenna.

"Obviously, those are anonymous," I retorted, with attitude. Let the record show, I answered with attitude.

"Right," he smirked. And for a moment, for like a moment and a half, I thought he was flirting with me, but then his hand squeezed Kenna's side and she giggled happily before swatting his chest.

"Dedicate a song to me?" she asked in a cute pout I would never stoop to.

"Of course," Ryder smiled down at her. This was his get-lucky-later-play. And Kenna was eating it all up. I, of course, rolled my eyes. I had to. The situation demanded an eye roll. "I'll dedicate one to you too, Red."

"I'm a recovering sexaholic, be careful with your promises," I shot back snidely.

"No worries," his smile turned genuine and he looked down at his girlfriend again. "I'm faithful to the girl I love."

Holy hell. It was a warning. He was warning me! *He* thought *I* was into him!

I rolled my eyes. Again. And he disappeared to go start his sound check after another agonizingly long public display of affection with Kenna.

She had to fan herself when he finally walked away.

But true to his word, she did get a song dedication by him and his band Sugar Skulls. So did I, it was a song called "Crash and Burn," and he dedicated it to me and Folgers Dark Roast.

Chapter Six

Ryder and his band were good. Like, really, really good.

Their sound was something in between a soft indie-alternative like Snow Patrol and something a little bit harsher and more rock and roll like the Black Keys. The blend was solid with all the basics of a garage band: bass guitar, second guitar, drum and at times a harmonica. Ryder held it all together at the mic- with vocals and lead guitar.

Was anybody surprised that Ryder played lead guitar? Anybody?

Nope, not me either.

But he looked good doing it. I couldn't fault him there. His vocals were perfection, deep, rich and sexy. He caressed the sound as it carried across the room. He connected the enraptured audience as if he was singing a personal ballad for each individual fan. I believed his love songs, I felt emotion in his lyrics. Hell, I even danced.

And then there was the guitar.

I really, really hated how good he was at the guitar.

No boy should be that good at something. Especially not a high school boy.

"He's amazing, isn't he?" Kenna shouted in my ear, probably noticing the drool running from the corner of my mouth to my chin.

Uh, amazing didn't begin to cover it.

"He's alright," I admitted with a shrug of one shoulder.

Kenna gave me an incredulous look that doubted the nonchalance of my answer, but didn't press me to say anything more. Having no more conversation between us, she returned her attention to the stage. She watched Ryder with a rapt attention that left me with little doubt the girl was in love with him.

My chest tightened at the thought and I rubbed against my heart. Suddenly I was really hot and cranky and I had no idea why my lungs felt like they stopped working. I unzipped my hoodie and slipped out of it, setting it on one of the tall stools lined up in front of the bar. I signaled to the bartender I was ready for more water and he chuckled at me from where he stood. I couldn't actually hear him chuckle, but I watched his shoulders bounce up and down in a chuckling motion.

"I've never heard them play here before," I announced to Kenna in between songs, while Ryder was exchanging his electric guitar for the acoustic variety.

"Um, they've had a pretty steady gig here for a while now," Kenna explained and then her eyes got big with realization. "Oh, probably while you were away. Ryder moved here right before…. uh…. right before Sam. So, maybe you guys just didn't cross paths before?"

I whipped my head back to the stage not able to come up with any kind of response. I tried to focus on Ryder's fingers gliding across the strings of his instrument and the way he started the song softly and alone. This was the song he was dedicating to Kenna. This was an intimate love song that made innocent girls blush and not so innocent girls horny. But it was all lost to me while Sam's name bounced back and forth in my brain inciting the kind of drowning panic I was becoming too familiar with.

I didn't want to talk to Kenna about Sam. I didn't want to talk to Kenna about *anything* anymore. My hands started trembling, freezing up into stiff joints and unusable fingers, so I shoved them deep into the pockets of my jeans. But no matter how hard I fought against the spreading ache in my chest or tried to ignore the quickly spiraling thoughts leading me into very dangerous territory, he was still there, still heavy in my head. Sam. Ugh, *Sam*. Heat prickled against the back of my eyes and I felt my nose start running in a sure sign tears were on their way.

Damn it.

"I'm going to the bathroom," I shouted sharply against the soft smoothness of Ryder's acoustic solo and then left Kenna alone.

I left too fast to know if she replied; I just hoped she didn't try to follow me. I was so not in the mood for sympathy or worse… pity. I pushed into the equally dim bathroom and immediately turned on the faucet. I ran my hands under the hot water and scrubbed at the invisible germs I felt caking my skin, clinging to me like grease and filth. I tried to scrape away the guilt and self-loathing.

I took a stuttering breath and allowed one tear to slip from my right eye. The lonely drop made a trail down my cheek, ending at my jawline and falling to my t-shirt where it left a small wet spot. A screech of frustration followed, echoing in the long tiled bathroom. I slammed my hands against the wet counter, splashing water on my jeans and bare arms.

One more tear was allowed freedom, landing on my shirt where it was lost in the other water spots left from the counter splash and then I decided to get ahold of myself. I slowed down my scrubbing and inhaled deeply. I counted to five and then I forced my eyes to the mirror.

It was easy to avoid mirrors usually. Most of the time I wished I never had to look at my face ever again. I didn't care what I looked like. I didn't want to care what I looked like. And I really didn't want to see the accusing, hate-filled eyes that I knew would be staring back at me.

But I still made myself do it.

I had to get through this with my mind intact. My soul was shot to all hell, and my emotions were one tear-fest away from a doctor-recommended Xanax prescription. But I had my mind. My mind was my savior, my ticket out of here, my future. I had to stay sharp.

That meant facing my demons.

At least some of them.

I turned the water off and gripped the sides of the sink basin. I slid my eyes upwards and readied my nerves to face myself.

Rich auburn hair streaked with brighter reddish gold highlights pulled up high on my head. Deep, disturbingly green, emerald eyes. Plump, perfectly bowed red lips. Flawless skin. And that small smattering of freckles across the bridge of my nose.

Mine was the kind of face that guys didn't forget and girls hated on principal. I was a genetic mistake. A freak of nature and fate and a curse.

My face was a curse.

I stared myself down and dared my heart to give up now.

Sam. Sam didn't die. Sam is alive. I am alive. Sam will get better one day. Sam *has to* get better one day. And *I* will be better one day. One day, I will leave this all behind.

One day I will be free.

It was a practiced mantra, one that I said constantly to myself. And it worked. I molded my mouth into a smile, tightened my hair-knot and rubbed at my bottom lip since I hadn't brought ChapStick with me.

I shook my hands of leftover water and then reached for a paper towel. This was my night of absolute reprieve from my life. I could put up with Kenna and Ryder for a little while longer if it meant I didn't have to be home alone, or worse with Nix and my mom.

I turned for the door and decided that I was done wallowing and needed to get over myself when it was suddenly thrust open and Ryder came strutting inside. My hand flew to my neck instinctively and I took a few beats to steady my breathing. My pulse thumped wildly against my fingers and I tightened my grip against my throat. Ryder and I assessed each other from a few feet apart, his eyes were cool and calculating, mine were wide and frightened.

"You scared the hell out of me!" I finally yelled at him.

A small smile tugged at the corner of his lips, and his eyes softened into careful amusement. "Sorry," he finally relented. "Kenna was worried about you. She asked me to check on you."

"And that meant storming the girls' bathroom?" I snapped.

"I was waiting outside, but you were taking so long I started to wonder if Kenna had a right to be concerned," he explained. His gray eyes were heated in the low lights of the bathroom but full of excited adrenaline from being on stage. The ends of his hair were damp from being under the hot lights and curled around his neck and over his ears, slick with sweat. His shirt clung to his body, sticking to him from the performance. He was full of feral energy; his presence was completely intrusive and demanding. His energy was infecting the room, reaching every molecule and atom around me, making the air bounce off the walls in an excited frenzy.

He was overwhelming.

And for once in my life *I* was the one pulled in.

"Kenna's sweet, but as you can see, I'm fine," I broke the silence that had settled between us. It was in no way comfortable. Being alone with Ryder felt dangerous and explosive.

"Yes, I can see that," Ryder nodded, pulling in his bottom lip with his teeth.

After establishing that I was fine, I expected him to escape. I could tell he wasn't comfortable being around me, which only made me want to explore this phenomenon all the more. He was dominating in the doorway, he took up so much space. But it wasn't just physical, it was like his presence hovered in every empty space in the small bathroom, pressing against me, crowding me. Pushing *me* out of the way.

I sucked in a breath, needing to break the silence, "You guys were...." I paused, not sure what to say. Any compliment I could give him didn't feel like enough, there wasn't a word for how great he was. But at the same time, saying something nice felt like a betrayal of everything that I was. He didn't even like me! I couldn't give him that.

I was saved by a pack of girls stumbling into the bathroom and directly into his back. They burst into giggles when they realized he was a boy and then glanced between us with knowing looks.

"Sorry," one of the girls announced on a laugh. She was petite and tiny, with a short blonde bob highlighted with pink and purple streaks. "We didn't mean to interrupt."

"It's no problem," Ryder announced benevolently, but his eyes had yet to leave mine, making me feel like they actually were interrupting something.

I just didn't know what.

"Oh, my gosh!" another girl announced. She had red hair not at all like mine, vibrant, blindingly red and obviously from a bottle. "You're Ryder Sutton! You're from Sugar Skulls!"

And then the three girls squealed in unison.

"Oh, my gosh, you're *Ryder Sutton*!" I intoned obnoxiously, taking a step forward and laying a hand on his chest bravely. I was annoyed with the girls, both for their intrusion and the way they were ready to drop their panties for him. "I didn't know it was you!" And I went to move by him. I pushed through the crowd of groupies but left my hand on his chest. His skin was hot and muscled underneath my hand, holding me to him like an intense magnet, locking my skin to his.

He turned with me, apparently not minding that we were causing a scene. His hand wrapped around my wrist, his strong fingers closing tight against my bare skin. A lone butterfly flapped distantly in my belly, and a charge of electricity shot straight up my sternum into my heart. What the hell?

"You know me," he stated simply. His silver eyes bore into mine and his tight hold on my wrist kept my hand to his chest, when I thought for sure he was going to remove my touch.

"I don't know anything about you," I replied, just as simply, just as sincerely.

The redhead let out a burst of rude laughter breaking into the bubble of intimacy Ryder had created around us. I snapped my head her direction, reminded that we were still in the bathroom, that Ryder still wasn't affected by my charm judging by the cold look in his gunmetal eyes and that his girlfriend was waiting outside for us.

"Fair enough," Ryder admitted and then released my hand. My arm dropped to my side and I worked my hand into a fist and then relaxed it trying to find the strength that had been there a minute ago. But my hand was useless, completely zapped of motor function and usability thanks to the weird spell Ryder put on me.

I was never affected by men. *Never.* That was the key to my voodoo.

I did the affecting.

Not the other way around.

Ryder needed to learn that.

Or I needed to get the hell away from him.

Probably both.

I pulled the bathroom door open a little too violently and it swung at me with a rush of hot, humid air from the concert hall. I jumped out of the way and tumbled out of the bathroom. The gaggle of fan-girls erupted into laughter and I felt Ryder immediately behind me, escaping before they asked for autographs on their boobs.

Kenna was waiting at the bar for us, holding my sweatshirt in her hands, probably to save it from the exiting masses. The concert was officially over and save for some last minute t-shirt sales the crowd en masse was pushing their way through the door and out onto 14th street.

"Thanks," I offered to Kenna, reaching for my hoodie. "He's all yours." I threw out as a candid acknowledgment of Ryder behind me.

There was a long moment of awkward silence before Kenna looked me straight in the eyes with a pinched expression and declared, "He's always been all mine."

Yikes.

I didn't know how to respond to that. I hadn't meant to issue a challenge, but Kenna was looking at me like she was deciding which hand to slap me with.

"She is well aware, Ken," Ryder saved me by pulling his girlfriend to him and nuzzling into her neck.

Ugh. More PDA.

I looked longingly at the door, determined to flee. My night of freedom had been trampled and tainted by these two love birds and now I was being accused of poaching. Kenna's claws had come out to protect her valuables and I was caught in between the product of my heritage and the uncomfortable third wheel.

"Seriously, Kenna," I started, forcing an apology from my lips. This was not in my nature, but something deeper than my instinct to run whispered that I needed to protect this relationship. Or at least protect Ryder…. from myself. "I don't know what you've heard, but I'm not like that. I mean, what's yours is yours. I didn't mean to intrude tonight. You came up to me…. I'm not interested in… I mean, you have nothing to worry about."

Ryder looked up at me from his hold on Kenna and could barely hold back his laughter. "You've given her a hard enough time, Kenna. She gets it, yeah?"

"Yeah, she gets it," Kenna answered Ryder and her eyes narrowed on me further.

"I get it," I repeated and then backed up toward the bar. I needed another drink before the bus ride home. I turned my back on the happy couple and called out to the bartender. "One more for the road," I flirted a little, flashing him a smile, since he was already cleaning up and I knew I was being a pain in the ass.

"I'm just not sure the vodka gets it," Kenna sniped, not even trying to soften her voice or disguise her disgust.

"Hey, give me a break," Neck Tattoos held up his hand in a gesture of surrender. "It's just water. I don't serve minors." And then he went back to scrubbing down the bar. That was the last shot of H2O I was getting tonight.

Thankfully the bartender had been defensive enough that even I believed he wouldn't have served me. I turned back to Ryder and Kenna not really wanting to meet either of them in the eye. Water was bad for my rep.

I ignored the part of my soul that felt relieved somebody else had seen this part of me. The part that preferred water. The innocent thirsty part of me.

I didn't know what that meant and now was not the time to try and untangle the mountains of screwed up I was.

"Uh, recovering addict and all," I mumbled. I didn't exactly meet their curious stares, but I did notice Ryder's lips curve into a barely there smile. "Well, good talk. See you two tomorrow."

I maneuvered around them during their simultaneous goodbyes and finally fled into the cool night. I immediately threw my hoodie on, zipped it up to the top and pulled on my hood. I had a trek to get back home and chances were homework was completely out of the picture. But I had gotten my night of freedom.

And there were parts of it that actually felt.... free.

Chapter Seven

"Hey," Chase met me on the sidewalk in front of the school the minute I stepped out of Exie's silver Lexus. I gave a fast wave to Exie and met him in front of the long set of stone steps leading to the front door of the antiquated school. Once upon a time Omaha was the capital city of Nebraska and Central High School the capitol building. When Nebraska moved the yellow star to Lincoln, Central became a high school. It was a really pretty building, but a super crappy school... at least in my opinion.

Chase was football-star-studly today in his letterman jacket and swoopy hair that fell across his forehead. He two-strapped his backpack and rocked back and forth on his heels while waiting for me. I was the recipient of a very confident smile this morning. His two dimples were like some kind of magical force, drawing out my own smile I thought had died sometime in the night.

"Hey yourself," I replied without any edge in my voice. Yay for me. "Were you waiting for me?"

"Yep," he grinned down at me. "Walk you to class?"

I wasn't sure what to do with his chivalry so I just nodded. I was used to boys and boyfriends and all that came with them. It was like my after school job. But in reality I hadn't had a boyfriend since last year, since.... Sam. And I felt awkward trying to get back into the pattern. There were instincts buried inside of me that would let me flirt freely and command attention with practiced skill. But right now I felt alien in this role, I couldn't remember how to toss out smiles and demand flattery. Right now I just wanted to go back home and go to bed.

We took the long walk up the stairs in silence. I could feel Chase radiating with an excited energy that should be contagious, that should reinforce my self-esteem and pride. Instead, I sludged along next to him, holding back an epic sigh that would signify my utter dread for the day ahead.

Ugh. I was so messed up.

"So Calculus again?" I asked at the top of the staircase. We were as reluctant as most of our peers to actually enter the building, so we hung out collectively with the rest of the student body in front of the two story-stone façade.

"Nope," Chase cut me a side glance as if he was surprised I had paid attention yesterday. "Applied Physics."

"Even more fun," I smiled at him, happy to have his full attention. There was something about being near Chase, having his eyes on me, standing in his shadow. He was like the sun, bright and happy and warm. He was exactly what I needed right now. Even if I didn't feel a spark from my end, I could still breathe when I was near him.

And I needed to breathe.

Besides, when were there ever sparks from my end?

He opened his mouth to say something, but we were interrupted by a gangly arm that reached out to clasp hands with Chase. Phoenix emerged from the crowd around us all smiles and long limbs. He was wearing at least three different shirts all layered in chaos, a short sleeve, a long sleeve and then another short sleeve. His loose, low-waisted jeans were ripped at the knees and tattered at the cuffs and his hair was curlier than yesterday but I suspected that had something to do with the October drizzle this morning. He was also wearing big, pink-framed, plastic sunglasses that I was sure were purchased in the junior's section of Target.

"What's up, Phoenix?" Chase asked him, breaking out into a friendly smile.

I was surprised I had never run into any of these guys before this year. Although Central was a very big school, several hundred to each graduating class. Still, they were good looking enough and seemingly popular enough that they at least should have been on my radar last year. Then again, when I actually read the badges stitched to Chase's letterman jacket I remembered soccer was his sport of choice and last year had been all about making my way through the basketball team.

"Not much," Phoenix returned and then his attention fell to me. "Ivy," he acknowledged happily.

"Phoenix," I replied back in a mock imitation of his deeper voice.

"Kenna tells me you were at the show last night. You should have stuck around, you could have chilled with the band," Phoenix's smile widened with pride and I realized he must have been part of the band.

"You're in the band?" I asked bluntly, a little disturbed that I hadn't noticed. It wasn't like I was into Phoenix for more than friendship, if that could even exist for me, but I still should have noticed him. Then again I couldn't place faces to any of the band members.

Save for one, the stupid lead guitar.

Freaking Ryder.

He was seriously throwing me off my game.

"What? Yes! I'm the drummer!" Phoenix defended himself as if I really hurt his ego.

Oops.

"Sorry," I gushed with a little bit of laughter. "I guess I couldn't see you beyond the egomaniac in front."

Phoenix nodded in agreement and gave me a look that said he forgave me. "So you'll stick around next time? Hang out after?"

"Sure," I conceded, hoping to avoid any future Sugar Skulls concerts and if at all possible run-ins with Kenna or Ryder in general.

"You went to see Sugar Skulls last night?" Chase asked. His eyebrows had drawn together and he seemed a bit confused and a bit more hurt. "I would have gone if I would have known you were going to be there." His lips curved into his signature charming smile and the hurt was washed away and replaced with easy flirtation.

"It was a, uh, last minute decision," I lied. "Plus I didn't know I was going to see Sugar Skulls. I didn't even know who they were until last night. I was just getting out of the house and I like the Slowdown on Wednesday nights." That was more like the truth, but not common information either and I felt a chill of fear run through me. I wasn't used to sharing this much, revealing this much about me.

"Right?" Phoenix agreed via question. "Slowdown gave us a pretty steady gig for Wednesdays, so there will be plenty of chances to hang. You can be like our groupie!"

"Ugh," I groaned. "I met some of your groupies last night. I didn't realize you thought so little of me."

"We have groupies?" Phoenix asked, genuinely surprised.

"Well, I don't know if they could be applied to the whole band, but um, Ryder has groupies."

This got both Chase and Phoenix to laugh. "Of course he does," Chase grinned. "Speak of the devil."

Kenna and Ryder appeared from the thick mob of students climbing the steps to the school building. Ryder had his arm draped across Kenna's shoulders and they were smiling and laughing and drooling and making googly eyes at each other and in love. And I wanted to vomit. Chase slipped his hand to my lower back in a move of possession and I sunk against his body, thankful for a place to go. I pressed against his side; half hoping he would just absorb me inside him. Gross, right? Still the desperation to disappear weighed consuming and suffocating against my lungs.

Chase wasn't home, but he could at the very least be a shelter from the storm of my life.

"Morning love birds," Phoenix called out to them.

Suddenly I was surrounded by people..... by friends? It was very confusing. I didn't do friends. And what was more confusing was me.

"Hey, Kenna," I called out as a way of greeting.

She had the good grace to only hesitate for a second before responding, "Hey, Ivy."

She eyed me over like I was ready to attack her precious boyfriend at any second and I shuffled backward out of the tight circle we had created. My eyes flickered to Ryder instinctually, but not in the man-eating way Kenna assumed I meant, more in like the.... I didn't know what kind of way! The kind that felt like a gravitational pull, the kind of way that made it feel as though I was helpless to stop the slide of my eyes. The confusing kind of way. He was watching me with careful amusement, like I was his entertainment, like it was possible for him to look anywhere else, but he chose to look at me. I had to get out of there. Chase's arm dropped from my back and he turned to face me, confused by my retreat. I struggled for an excuse but then my phone rang, some miraculous intervention by the gods, and I reached for it quickly.

I held it up in apology, waving it around and letting the loud ringtone pierce the conversation that surrounded us. I walked into the school building away from all those impossible but bourgeoning friendships.

"Hello?" I asked into the speaker without checking the caller ID first.

"Nix is here? Why didn't you tell me?" Exie screeched from the other line.

I waited a beat, hoping she would forgive me in the silence of the airways. No such luck. "Who told you?" I sighed into the phone. This is why I didn't do friendship.... I wasn't any good at it. But I did like to protect my girls. They were the closest thing I would ever have to real relationships.

"Sloane made the announcement this morning. Her mom is throwing some kind of shindig for him tomorrow night. You should have given us the heads up." She sounded hurt. "You should have told me this morning in the car."

No. She sounded terrified.

And she was right.

I should have given her the heads up.

I should have texted them both last night.

"I'm sorry," I breathed into the phone, finding my locker and stuffing my backpack into it. "I was hoping you wouldn't have to deal with him. I was hoping he was just here for me and mom."

"Apparently he rented an apartment. I guess he's going to be here for a while," she grumbled and I could feel her freaking out through the airwaves separating us.

"How's Sloane doing?" I asked, taking some of the pressure off Exie.

"She's freaked. Evaleen turns twenty-one in two months."

Shoot. I hadn't thought about anyone other than myself. "Your sister's already twenty-one," I reminded her on a whisper. Not that she needed to be reminded. I felt despair settle over me and pushed my forehead against my open locker door, pressing my skin to the cold metal. Ridges in the metal, vents that kept the locker from smelling like dirty socks, pressed into my cheek, indenting my skin with the harsh edges.

"Anaxandra wants this life," Exie replied and I could tell she was near tears. Her sister was no different from anyone else in our circle.

"Anaxandra's been brainwashed by Prada and European vacations," I bit out harsher than I intended.

Instead of getting defensive Exie let out a tired sigh, "So has Evaleen." There was a long moment of silence while we digested the exact meaning of those words before Exie asked in a shaken, weak voice, "Will that be us one day?"

"No," I answered immediately, my voice steady and full of conviction. I took a breath and fortified my resolve, "Never."

More silence on her end. She wasn't so sure. Damn it, we were stronger than designer purses and expensive cars. Stronger than our sisters. Stronger than our mothers.

So much stronger.

"Talk more later?" Exie asked.

"Give Sloane my love," and then I hung up.

I stared into my locker full of books and notebooks and loose papers unseeing for a long time, long after the warning bell rang. Students and teachers rushed by me, the overwhelming noise and bustle of the morning faded away. And only I remained. The hall was empty behind me, everyone else carefully tucked away in homeroom.

Eventually, I pulled myself back to reality and picked out my American Civilization book and the corresponding notebook.

Crap. I was late. Again…. Mrs. Tanner was going to have my ass for this.

I slammed my locker shut with as much force as I could muster and then kicked it for good measure. A string of curse words flew from my mouth before I could stop them and my hair came loose from the effort I took to attack my locker. I threw my books down in another attempt at getting rid of the stifling anger boiling inside of me, none of it having to do with tardiness. My pen skittered across the tiled floor and bounced into the opposite bank of lockers.

It was too much. All of it.

Breathing was suddenly difficult, the world fading out around me. My vision narrowed to pinpricks and a high pitched ringing pierced my ears. I was so frustrated. So, tirelessly frustrated. I hated it all…. Nix, my mom, this stupid world I lived in, that my hair had gotten messed up, that I had to care about my hair at all. And now a party? I couldn't do this.

Some days, after everything I had been through in my life, some days eighteen didn't feel that far away.

But then there were days like today when eighteen might as well have been eighty and the end was nowhere in sight.

"You alright, Red?" a voice asked from just a few feet away.

I hammered my head back against the lockers before I opened my eyes to meet the voice.

Ryder.

Chapter Eight

"Just fine," I answered Ryder, not trying to hide the despair choking the life out of me. He wouldn't care anyway. Actually, he'd probably ignore it completely.

Thank God.

"Sure about that?" He asked with a sarcastic edge to his voice that grated across the space between us.

Today Ryder was wearing a long sleeved gray thermal shirt and dark washed jeans over leather flip flops. His hair was layered carelessly at least a good inch off his forehead, pushed out of the way by an obsessive need to run his hand through it. His gray eyes were gunmetal with concern and he was holding a stack of papers divided up with yellow sticky notes labeling them.

"Yes, I'm sure." I snapped.

"That's why you're at war with your locker instead of in class?" he assessed me judgmentally from where he leaned against the opposite wall. I wanted to think he was joking, but there was nothing light or teasing in his eyes. He was radiating worry and it was driving me crazy with the need to prove I didn't need him to care about me.

I gave him half a smile anyway for his attempt at humor and then turned away from him so that I could stare down the long hallway. Light from the arched windows skittered across the floor, breaking up the dull florescent lighting that buzzed with the effort to stay on.

"It's just that... this locker really pisses me off," I finally admitted.

Ryder choked on surprised laughter and I turned back to face him. His expression had relaxed into amusement and I could finally suck in a much needed breath. "You two should probably get couples' counseling then, since you have to put up with each other for the rest of the year and all." He bent over to retrieve my pen before he crossed the hallway in three strides so that we were just inches away from each other. He remained calm and cool, my presence doing none of its usual tricks. So I was even more irritated by how unfair it was that I was struggling to remain indifferent. He was just fine, completely freaking fine. He was like this presence that penetrated every last bit of my consciousness, even his shadow weighed heavily on me, pressing me back into the bank of metal lockers. And his smell, maybe his cologne that clung to his clothes and floated in the air between us was surprisingly delicious and maybe a bit peculiar... like coconut and cookies. It infiltrated every one of my senses until I could barely suppress the need to lean into him and nuzzle against his neck. His smell threw me off. Way off.

"You smell like a girl," I blurted out a little bit too loud.

Ryder paused, giving me a look of complete confusion, before his lips slowly turned up into an amused grin. "Shut it, Pierce. It's my shampoo."

An unexpected giggle burst from my throat and I smacked my hand over my mouth to stop any more foreign sounds from escaping. "Your shampoo?"

"It's coconut oil," he admitted, dipping his head as if embarrassed.

"Why?" I asked simply, shaking my head at him.

"Don't ask questions you're not prepared to hear the answers to," Ryder growled ominously, but I could tell he was being sarcastic.

"What does that even mean?" I shook my head at him, laughter bubbling up inside me again.

"I don't really know," he laughed too, mimicking the side to side motion of my head. "But I was trying to sound manly again. You know, most girls like it. I usually get complimented." He finally defended himself with an air of self-importance, crossing his arms across his chest and pulling his t-shirt tight across his pronounced muscles.
My eyes dropped from his silver pools of eyes to his chest for just two and a half seconds before I popped my gaze up hoping he hadn't noticed. The narrowed slits of his eyes told me there was no chance in hell I got away with checking him out. Shoot.

"I'm not most girls," I grumbled. I bent over to pick up my books that were strewn in a messy pile at my feet and Ryder held out my pen to me, waiting for me to stand up again.

I heard him mumble, "That is the truth," under his breath and I whipped up into standing to launch a full-fledged attack on him when I found him grinning at me, completely disarming my intentions. "It's supposed to be healthy…. like good for me. I was told that it would reduce my uh…. issues with my hair. I'm starting to think the girl who cuts it might actually hate me though."

It took me until the word "hair" to realize we were talking about his shampoo again and not my issues. When I finally caught up to the conversation I couldn't stop myself from laughing again. Real laughter, the kind that expanded in my lungs and bubbled out of my mouth like a fountain. The expansion in my chest felt foreign and underused and my lungs ached with the effort, but in a good way…. a really good way.

"Your hair *is* kind of awful, actually," I admitted lightly. My fingers were tangled through his coarse locks before I knew what I was doing. My hand slid through his thick, unruly hair, brushing it back from his forehead and testing the rough, bristly texture between my fingertips.

"What?" He gasped with faux defensiveness, his eyes going wide with pretend horror. "You're not turned on by the sexy bedhead look?" He leaned forward and shook his head roughly so that my fingers fell from his hair, displaced and instantly missing the touch.

I only had a second to take in my feelings though when he lifted his head and was just inches from me, closer than we were before.... closer than we had ever been. "I had no idea you were so vain," I whispered, trying to find the good natured humor that was with us seconds ago.

"I'm not vain," he narrowed his eyes, but didn't put any more distance between us. "I'm just.... afraid I will hurt someone if I don't take proper care of it."

"Good point," I agreed, taking a big breath and speaking with more volume so our close proximity didn't feel so intimate. "Why is it so scratchy?" I laughed at him. "It's like horse hair!"

"It is not!" he defended himself animatedly and then punched me very gently in the shoulder, pushing my back against the locker, but not in an unkind way. He was gentle but firm... detached but oh so sexy.

Holy hell.

My breathing was suddenly very shallow.... shaky, pathetically hitched. I ran my tongue along my bottom lip, so aware of every piece of his body and how close we were standing. His hair was lifted from where I ran my fingers through it, casting a shadow over his too pensive eyes. His gaze was smoky and penetrating and I was frozen beneath him in confusion and lust.

"It is," I argued, but my voice was a shell of its former lightheartedness. "But I understand the coconut now." I smiled, secretly praying he wouldn't kiss me.... secretly pleading that he would. And then to force myself into distance, "Probably safer for Kenna that way. Plus, you kind of smell like cookies."

"At least now you understand," Ryder smirked, arrogant and cocky, and the spell was broken. He stood up to his full height, towering over me and resonating dispassion. "I suppose you want a pass for class now?"

I gasped as hope and the thrilling feeling of ease swelled in my chest. "You can write me a pass?" There was almost a desperate quality to my voice, I was kind of pitiful. But I had to get my act together here and now, I *had* to make it through this school year and the next. I couldn't afford to mess up.

"Office aide, remember? Yesterday you spilled coffee all over me, yelled at me and then out of the very goodness of my heart I wrote you a pass? Any of this ringing a bell?" He was teasing me now, in the same way that made me feel like he planned on keeping a very wide measure of space between us.

Maybe that's why my heart had relaxed. Ryder was complicated. Too complicated. It was like our powers were reversed. And I didn't like that at all.

"Oh yes, now I remember!" I grinned at him, snapping my fingers as if in time with the memory. "You will save my life if you can write me a pass today though. I promise if I ask Mrs. Tanner to write one, she'll expel me instead."

"Expel you, huh?" Ryder asked from over his shoulder as we made our way down the hallway and to the office.

"Okay, probably not expel me. But definitely try to burn me at the stake," I mumbled, trying to keep my tone light. Ryder shot me a confused look. "You know, like a witch trial?"

"Ah, but she could probably make a valid case." Ryder turned his head again, shooting me a very amused grin, but something didn't quite reach his eyes... like he almost believed I could be a witch.

I shook my head. It wasn't possible. Even if thinking I was a witch was completely off base and totally in the realm of crazy, there was no way Ryder could tell I was different. It just wasn't possible.

I waited outside the office while Ryder ran in to drop off the stack of folders he was holding and retrieve the small yellow notepad that would excuse me from missing nearly all of my first hour class. I watched him, discreetly, or what I hoped was discreetly, while he leaned over the tall counter and wrote some lame and untrue excuse down. This view of him was perfection with his back to me and his head bent furtively scrawling in sharpie across the notepad. His shoulders were broad and muscled, his hair just a little long at his collar and the heels of his feet hidden beneath long, tattered hems. A sigh escaped me before I could stop it and I slammed my back into the cold stone wall that lined the halls in between banks of lockers, completely wrecking my view of Ryder and the office.

Grrr.

What was going on with me?

I stared off into space, focusing my gaze on the windowed front doors so that I wouldn't be tempted to check out Ryder or his delicious ass anymore. Ugh...

Voices and commotion drew my attention to the other end of the hallway when a classroom door banged open and students filed into the corridor. I squinted in an effort to recognize any of them as they walked excitedly in my direction. Chase was somewhere in the middle of the crowd, with Phoenix right at his side and my heart stuttered a little with anxiety. I shook away the feeling of being caught, and tried to convince myself that not only was there nothing going on between Ryder and me, but Chase didn't really have any claim over me anyway.

If I were my mother or any of the other women in our circle, I would be practically bursting with pride and a reason to make both men jealous. But I was so not them and sickening guilt and shame flushed through my blood like a fast rush of self-loathing.

I put on my best smile and willed my eyes to look happy when Chase and Phoenix slowed down to talk to me. Chase cast a curious, worried glance in the office and I wondered if it was aimed at Ryder or the potential trouble I could be in.

"Hey what are you guys up to?" I asked, drawing Chase's gaze back to me.

He held up a paper airplane that was being carefully grasped between his thumb and index finger and waved it around. "Physics project," he explained.

"We're taking it to the hill," Phoenix cut in, and nodded with his head toward the front doors of the school that would lead out to sprawling, steep hills on either side of the long staircase and down to Dodge Street.

"Fun," I drawled unenthusiastically.

"What are you up to?" Chase asked, taking a step closer to me.

I hesitated while Ryder walked out of the office handing me the pass. It burned in my fingers, painting me as guilty. Ryder exchanged greetings with his friends completely unfazed with what I was going through. Of course, he wouldn't or shouldn't feel any of the stirrings of guilt or remorse; we really had done nothing wrong.

"My phone call went long," I explained not telling a lie, but not exactly telling the truth either.... my specialty. "Ryder was nice enough to write me a pass so I wouldn't get marked for being late."

"Aw, that's nice of you, buddy," Phoenix crooned at Ryder and tried to pinch his cheek.

"Back off, man," Ryder laughed, smacking away Phoenix's long, gangly arm.

Their exchange was followed by thirty very awkward seconds of silence while Chase sized Ryder up and shot me a nervous glance that let me know to some men, I still had power. Chase took another step toward me, like he was marking his territory and a flash of panic heated my belly. Not wanting to examine it for too long, or analyze if my reaction had anything to do with Ryder's watching gaze, I raised my hand in a wave goodbye.

"Well, thanks for the pass Ryder," I started walking backward, clutching my books to my chest and the thin yellow paper between my fingers tightly. "I better get to class, since I've missed so much already. See you guys at lunch."

I didn't wait for any response, but turned on my heel and high-tailed it out of there. Okay, weird morning. But at least I had been sufficiently distracted from thoughts of Nix, my mother, or what was waiting for me at home tonight.

Chapter Nine

"Thanks again for the ride," I offered for the fourth time. Chase sat across the armrest in the driver's seat of his tan Honda Civic sedan and smiled at me. It was obvious I was stalling, but I was hoping he thought it was just because I wanted to spend time with him.

Which I kind of did. Chase was easy to be around, there was no hidden agenda, no evil plans for my future or even my pants. I could breathe. And breathing was the most important thing in my life right now.

"We could go do something if you're not ready to go home yet?" he answered back intuitively.

"No, I'm ready," I whispered weakly and then realized how lame I sounded. "What I mean is that it isn't that. I just.... um, this is nice." I motioned back and forth between us with my pointer finger. He grabbed onto it yanked my arm forward playfully. His fingers grazed the inside of my palm slowly, barely touching but capturing all of my attention.

"This is nice," he gave me his charming smile, the one that melted normal girls' insides and then somehow, through tricky moves only boys can pull off, his hand was now holding mine. "So tomorrow is Friday...." he started suggestively.

"Finally," I breathed out in relief because I was supposed to, because it was expected. Every sixteen year old looked forward to the weekend. It was the way of life. But truthfully, with Nix around I preferred to be in school over the freedom of the weekend, not to mention the cocktail party tomorrow night that was bound to leave bone marrow deep scars and painful emotional trauma on my psyche.

"And I thought maybe I could take you out...?" He spoke his words slowly, carefully, like he was nervous and unsure. He was adorable, I couldn't deny that.

"Tomorrow night?" I gulped, wishing more than anything I could say yes. He nodded while his deep blue eyes begged me to say yes, not to let him down. "I can't," I groaned and there was nothing but sincerity behind my tone. "I have this family thing and there's no way I can miss it." I pushed out a playful pout and moved my thumb back to graze across the inside of his wrist.

"Oh, bummer," he replied, equally as sincere.

Chase was so sweet, so super sweet. If I had to suffer through all this dating, I was lucky there were guys like Chase out there that made it easier. God knew I had dated some absolute tools in my short lifetime. Chase was an exception to the rule and one that I wouldn't be able to hold on to for long. And I hated to disappoint him, but our reasons for wanting to go out tomorrow night were completely different. I wanted to escape the crazy, f-ed up world I lived in and he couldn't help himself but be attracted to me. It wasn't his fault, but it wasn't totally sincere either.

"But I'm free Saturday night," I offered with a small smile. My thoughts flickered to Sam and how sweet he had been at first. I couldn't let that happen with Chase, I couldn't ruin his life because I was selfish, because I was fundamentally and forever screwed up. My throat started to close at the memory, my heart pounded painfully against my aching chest, echoing loudly in my ears. Damn it. I shouldn't have even thought his name.

"Saturday works," he smiled but with less enthusiasm. "Do you care though if we go to a party? I promised Phoenix I would stop by at his thing Saturday night while his parents are at some bizarre-o nudist colony."

"Nu-uh," I laughed. Chase nodded, his eyes glittering with the gossip. I had to meet Phoenix's parents sometime. They sounded kind of awesome. Just hopefully they weren't nude all the time.... "No, that will be fun!" I threw as much enthusiasm into my voice as I could and leaned forward to brush Chase's cheek with a kiss.

"Yeah, fun," Chase agreed but I could see a hint of disappointment in his expression. "If you don't want to go though, I can always make an excuse. I mean, if you want our first date to be special. I hate that it's just going to be a house party." And that's why he was disappointed, he wanted to woo me and a high school kegger didn't exactly scream romance.

I smiled again to hide my relief. If he put effort into this, I was in danger of another breakdown. I was in danger of ruining someone else's life. A party would be perfect. Just enough distraction without any romance or intimacy.

"You'll get your chance for special," I murmured coyly. "You can save the fireworks and champagne for our second date."

Chase's face lit up with my suggestion, his blue eyes shining with future promise. "Deal."

"Deal," I repeated and then moved for the door. I was dreading going upstairs, completely opposed to the idea of putting myself in the lion's den, but I had run out of excuses to sit in Chase's car. "Thanks again for the ride."

"Anytime, you know that," Chase said seriously.

I gave him one last wave as he pulled out of the circular drive that rounded a string of midtown apartment buildings and businesses and a sprawling park that tumbled down in front of the modern architecture. The park used to be the home of every homeless person in the city, but when the city remodeled this part of the downtown area, they kicked the bums out and made this section classy and upscale. The bums scattered further east to the heart of downtown and the no bigger than two bedroom condos filled in with rich couples and eligible bachelors. My mom loved this area because she felt hip and important. I loved this area because I felt like it was hiding a filthy, dirty, secret past.

Just like me.

With a deep, fortifying breath, I walked into the modern elegance of my building and took the elevator to the top floor, preparing myself for the worst. The shiny elevator doors opened and I crossed the quiet, empty hall to our sprawling two bedroom apartment that overlooked the park and downtown Omaha.

I let myself in quietly and set my keys in a porcelain bowl designated for keys and other junk on the kitchen counter. Mom had decorated the apartment completely modern chic, which meant that every room of my home was cold and unwelcoming, but expensive and looked nice.

I hated it.

Not that I would have ever expected my mother to pick out an overstuffed couch and comfortable throw. She wasn't one of those women that could curl up in front of the fire with a nice book. She never stood still for more than two minutes at a time and the designer heels that were permanently attached to her slender feet would have poked holes in any such couch by now anyway.

Plus it's hard to relax when you have a giant stick up your ass.

But I did wish that my house felt a little bit more like a home. Everything was ivory and robin's egg blue or some shade of gold. Everything was breakable and easily stained. The appliances were expensive; the electronics were state of the art, the windows were floor to ceiling and the thread counts high hundreds. And everything, every single thing was bought and paid for with some other schmuck's credit card, including my once upon a time father's and the string of lovers stupid enough to fall for her charm and long legs.

Once the door was closed with a final click behind me and the lock had slid into place, I struggled for a big breath; I was slowly suffocating in this posh prison, slowly fading away into the slavery I had been born into. I set my backpack down on a narrow, Tiffany's suede bench by the front door, and tossed my trendy pilot's jacket on top. I straightened my shirt, and fidgeted with the hem of my short jean skirt doing my best to delay walking fully into the apartment.

I could already smell him here, his cologne permeated every inch of air around me. He was man where there was usually only female, he was musk and rich earth where there was usually just floral and fruit. Suddenly my feet felt cemented to the bamboo flooring, my back magnetized to the front door. He was everywhere and I couldn't make myself walk forward and meet him. Every instinct inside of me cautioned to get the hell out of here, to run. But I was conditioned to repress those feelings, raised to ignore instinct and reason. Hot tears pricked at the corners of my eyes, my nose twitched with the effort not to cry hysterically. I was a wimp.

"Ivy," Nix purred as he rounded the kitchen cabinets and came face to face with me.

I smiled at him, forcing my feet forward, forcing my legs to move. I was a coward and a hypocrite and a terrible, awful person. But I couldn't do anything but move toward him and step into his open arms. I kissed his cheek, once and then twice on the other side. He held me close to him, his strong arms encircling my biceps and his hard, chiseled chest pressing against me inappropriately.

"Hi, Nix," I greeted in what I hoped sounded like a chipper, welcoming voice. I mean, I heard the unmistakable tremble and crack in every word.... but I just had to hope *he* didn't.

"How was school?" he asked. He took a step back and I relished in the space between us. I sucked in a sharp breath, but he was still everywhere, his scent, his cologne, his essence still clung to every bit of air around me, choking the life out of me.

"It was, um, the same." I met his emblazoned gaze and tilted my chin for an added illusion of confidence.

"Despite what your mother has told you, I could get you into a different school if you wanted me to. I know you're unhappy where you're at. Just say the word, and you can join Exie and Sloane wherever they're at. Enough money will always get you what you want." He finally released my arms to walk into the open kitchen and poured himself a drink from my mother's intense alcohol collection.

"Not necessary," I said quickly, too quickly. He glanced back at me over his shoulder and his dark eyes studied me for way too long. "It's just that I don't want to go against my mom or anything. She wants me at Central, so at Central I will stay."

Nix turned around and leaned back against the granite countertop, arms crossed against his chest, his tumbler of Scotch resting in his hand.

70

He was classically handsome with a tall, lean, muscular frame and broad shoulders. His dark hair was perfectly tussled and cut exactly business-man short. His even darker eyes were framed with long lashes and were as intense as they were sultry. He was the perfect specimen of man, enticing, alluring, sexy as hell and absolutely terrifying. Women were drawn to him without reserve or caution, men feared him, my mother worshipped him and I had to hold back my gag reflex. He was vividly evil, the worst kind of human being.

And he controlled my life. He controlled everything about me…. every little thing past, present and future.

"I like that, Ivy," he paused to take me in again, his gaze raking over my figure from head to toe. I stilled the shudder that threatened to rip through me, repressing it into the deepest, darkest part of my soul, the part he couldn't touch. "I like your obedience." His voice was low and seductive and I didn't even want to think about what he could be referring to. I couldn't think about it. The fear of what was left unsaid haunted my nightmares and every waking thought that spun around tumultuously in my head.

"Where's my mom?" I asked in a breathy, child-like voice. I wanted to stand up to him so desperately; I wanted to shout at him to stay away from me, not to touch me or even look at me. But I couldn't. He was all-consuming and demanded respect and I had been conditioned to react to his every breath since the moment I was born.

"She went to see Honor," Nix explained turning his gaze to the floor to ceiling windows across the room that led out to our substantial balcony. The look of pure, unadulterated hate flittered across his face, and his eyes turned to pools of malicious energy. Waves of aggression rippled through the room as he let his emotions fill up the apartment.

Finally, even amidst his overpoweringly negative energy, I found some solace in my situation. I was a prisoner, trapped and held without permission. But my sister, my little sister had an actual chance at life. Nix hated that, hated her. But without much of a choice, him and my mother tolerated Honor's dictator of a father, with the hope that one day Honor would come into full custody of my mother.

My mother, the renowned and somewhat notorious Ava Pierce, had followed her routine with Honor's father to the last ounce of successful practice she did with every one of her conquests. She found rich men on their death beds, exploited their loneliness and her exceptional good looks and then wiggled into the last will and testament moments before their final dying breath. It was her way of securing our wealth and my future.

Securing children took an entirely more complicated approach, however, and there was a ton of work that went into the process. She couldn't just pick anybody. The sperm donors had to pass an entire gamut of criteria and qualifications in order to be considered a viable candidate and then they had to be near enough to death so that they weren't an issue for much longer, but healthy enough to father a child. It was a disgusting mess of deceit and sin. And somehow my mother pulled it off with me. But with Honor's father, things didn't go exactly as planned. He made a last minute miraculous recovery and when he came back to himself it was like my mother's spell was completely broken. He divorced her and somehow managed to keep custody of Honor. His gobs of money and the female judge overseeing the case saw to that. Now my mother was only allowed supervised visits with his permission.

This was what kept us in Omaha. My mother had to get Honor back. Her pride, not her motherly love, demanded that she win. Plus, she was a huge embarrassment to our circle because of her failure and lack of ability to secure her offspring. She was biding her time until Honor became her possession. Nix was making sure she followed through. Honor's father was securing a separate future for his daughter. And Honor was sheltered and protected from it all, while I was caught in the middle, a jaded, shell of a human being.

I would do anything in my power to protect Honor from this life. I loved her probably more than myself, even though we weren't that close. I wasn't allowed to visit her without my mother and it was almost impossible for us to have a conversation with *her* hanging around. But I adored her, she was my sister, the only person in my life that had no expectations for me, had no hidden agenda or was captured under the curse. No matter what it took, I would always make sure my mother had absolutely nothing to do in Honor's life. She was eleven now, too young to see what an evil wench her mother was, but still blissfully adoring of her doting father. I prayed it stayed that way. I prayed that she never met Nix and the circus of demented hell he brought with him.

The silence that fell between us after mentioning Honor was expected. Nobody knew what to say about her. Her father keeping her was unprecedented. Her father denying my mother something that she wanted was absolutely unparalleled. And it drove Nix mad.

"We're meeting her for dinner in an hour. Go get dressed, Ivy," Nix commanded, taking a sip of his forty year old beverage. He continued to stare out the window, his expression a mixture of hateful, concentrated emotions. A trickle of fear slid down my spine in the form of a single bead of sweat and as much as I wanted and needed to protect my sister, I said a silent prayer that none of the feelings swelling inside of him would ever be directed at me.

I nodded my acceptance of his demand and peeled my feet off the floor, where I swore they had started to grow roots. As soon as the promise of escape from Nix and his ominous presence was offered I took off like I was in a race for my life, practically sprinting to the solitude of my bedroom.

His deep, melodic voice followed me down the hall and before I could escape to the sanctuary of my bedroom he threw out one last command, his voice no louder than it would be if he were standing right next to me. I heard every word as if he were whispering in my ear. His words snaked around my insides, coiling them tight with revulsion and hopelessness. "I want you on display, Ivy. Wear something that I can appreciate."

The door closed behind me, like the door to my fears and feelings. I bottled them up, shut them away and locked everything tightly inside of me. I ignored the trembling of my hands and the ice cold feeling of dread that washed through my stomach like acid and foreboding. I was sixteen years old. How the hell was I supposed to deal with that? Process it? Tonight there wasn't any choice but to obey Nix, his word was absolute law in my life, no matter how much I hated this life or him.

I just had to get through the next two years. Just two years.

Someday soon he would have no say in my life…. or in my wardrobe.

And I would be able to breathe.

Chapter Ten

"Ivy," Nix called out from the other side of my door. I stood frozen in front of my closet in only a lace bra and matching underwear, undecided on what to wear. "Can I come in?"

Fear, cold and shrill, chased my blood through my veins. He could come in if he wanted to and there wasn't anything I could say. I was not really wearing any clothes, but that wasn't even the most frightening part of this. Nix had seen me like this before, hell, Nix had seen all of us like this before. My terror originated in the fact that my tattoos were completely exposed and I would be so dead if Nix found them.

"Uh, I'm still getting dressed," I called back in a quivering voice. I walked over to the door on my tip toes, making as little sound as I could. My breath felt hurried and deafening as I tried to be as quiet as humanly possible. I desperately wanted to disappear, blend into the carpet or dematerialize into the stagnant air of the apartment. I placed two shaky hands against the solid wood of the door and held them there as if I could stop Nix from entering, as if I could stop Nix from doing anything that he wanted.

There were several beats of silence and I wondered if Nix was processing the real reason I was keeping him out. "Do you need help?" he asked in an almost exasperated voice. There was no perverse anxiousness or even inappropriate curiosity. My mother would be waiting and Nix hated to be late, even for her. My stalling cost him time and money, that was all.

I exhaled a small breath of relief. A small, tiny one, almost insignificant. But it wasn't. It wasn't trivial. Just a little bit of release, that was all I needed, that was all I wanted.

"No, I'm just finishing up. I'll be ready in five minutes," I answered more confidently than before. I slid one hand down the smooth wood, enjoying the cool, flat feel under my fingers and as quietly and slowly as I could manage I double checked that the door was locked and secured. Another miniscule breath of relief.

Not that a locked door had ever stopped Nix from getting what he wanted, but tonight I had the desperate hope that what he wanted was not me.

"Five minutes," he echoed in a surly command.

I moved back to my closet and slipped inside, digging out the tattoo cover up from my secret hiding place. I rubbed it generously on my ribs and wrist and then took thirty seconds to stare at myself in the mirror and make sure everything was hidden. Even though I hoped these parts of my body would always stay hidden, there was no denying the fear I lived with daily of being found out for these small acts of rebellion. I didn't even want to think about the price I would have to pay. Thank God for Kat Von D and her miraculous cover up products.

Once the cover up had dried and done its job, I moved back to my closet and selected a nude long sleeve, off the shoulder mini dress with a pretty lace overlay. There was no cleavage exposure, which I preferred, but the dress was short enough and tight enough Nix would be pleased.

I shuddered involuntarily at my appraisal.

My red waves were swept over one shoulder in a fishtail braid that seemed complex, but wasn't and my makeup was fresh and clean. I slipped into some nude, studded pumps and added a long, dangly necklace. I stared at myself for two more minutes, giving myself the pep talk, pumping myself into handling the next four hours and then grabbed my phone before meeting Nix in the living room.

He was staring out the window, taking in the city skyline. His reflection was mirrored in the clear pane, his expression intense and serious. He didn't turn automatically to greet me and so I stood awkwardly leaning against my doorframe, waiting for him to notice me. His broad shoulders were covered with a perfectly fitted navy blue suit, and his hair was expertly styled. I studied his profile more from raw hypnosis than conscious desire. His jaw line was chiseled and strong, his nose the perfect accent to his striking face, his dark eyes penetrating and always passionate. He was gorgeous, that much was undeniable. He screamed masculinity, testosterone and dominance. A shaky breath and nerves that felt like tiny grenades setting off inside my blood reminded me that evil could easily be deceptively and blindingly beautiful.

That was Nix.

Dazzling.

And wicked.

The worst kind of wicked.

He finally turned to face me, fiddling with one of the four buttons on his cuff. He wasn't wearing a tie and had left the button open at the collar of his crisp white oxford. My nerves calmed some at the sight of his perfection and the feeling of how he commanded every room he stood in, how he stood out from the rest of humanity like a god sent from Olympus. That kind of outward perfection was inherently flawed on the inside.

He had to be.

Or I would never survive.

My hand instinctively flew to my ribs and where the scrawled words I had picked so carefully were etched into my skin. His eyes bore into mine from across the room, the intensity of his entire aura stealing my breath, hazing my vision.

"I'm ready," I announced. I met his gaze and defied logic by holding it.

"I see that," he murmured, stepping towards me. He took the room in four confident strides and was only two inches in front of me before I could even regret the bravado I tried to pull off. "You're lovely tonight." His voice floated around my ears with a deep, rich sound, one that demanded melting and fawning. But I couldn't give in, not even a little bit. His voice was dangerous.

"Thank you," I replied because that was what I was taught to say.

"Your mother is waiting," he whispered regretfully. What he was regretting I didn't even want to speculate, so I took the arm he had offered me and let him lead me out the door and down the elevator.

His sleek Jaguar C-X75 was waiting for us in front of the building. He opened the door for me and helped me slide onto the luxurious leather seat. I hadn't bothered with a coat and I had forgotten my purse, so I fiddled with my cellphone idly while I waited for Nix to climb into the driver's seat.

Nix put the car into drive and eased out of the circular driveway in front of our building. We headed north, away from downtown and toward Dundee, a quaint section of Omaha with expensive bistros that served uniquely world class food. It wasn't that long of a drive, and silence filled the space between us. Nix was intense while he drove. Nix was always intense and never tolerated idle conversation unless he absolutely needed to. I was intimidated and anxious, so silence was fine with me.

My phone buzzed in my lap, but I ignored it. If Exie or Sloane were texting about Nix or really anything right now, I didn't want him to get curious. I was more afraid that it was Chase though. We exchanged numbers yesterday and I didn't want to have to explain too much about him to Nix. There would be too many questions, too much investigation and if Nix asked me to do anything in regards to the relationship I would have to say yes. And I wasn't ready for that.

Nix found a parking spot directly in front of the restaurant, which I thought was lucky, but probably normal for someone like him. The very best of life just fell into his lap, he was used to it, expected it even. I stayed put in the car while he climbed out and walked around to open the door for me. Years of training had taught me how to behave properly; I was a prisoner to manners and tradition.

And the curse.

Just like Nix was.

My mother was already seated at a table inside the dimly lit French restaurant. She stood when we walked in the door, greeting us each with a gentle hug and a kiss on both cheeks. Her eyes flitted over me from head to toe and I forced myself not to cringe from her scrutiny. She was of course, above reproach in stylishly cut, high waisted black tailored pants and a soft pink silk shirt. She looked more like a movie star than a mother. That was always my thought about her. She was stunning, completely elegant, poised and absolutely untouchable and distant.

Eventually, the beauty would fade, she would develop wrinkles, and her hair would thin and gray and her body would begin to sag. It happened to every woman, we were without exception. But my mother would never lose her allure; men would always be drawn to her.

And to me. No matter how I detested this outward beauty, men would always worship it.

"How's Honor?" Nix asked first while we settled behind our menus, and they sipped their wine.

My mother paused for too long. She made a show of drinking her wine and looking around the restaurant impatiently for our waiter. I clenched at the napkin in my lap, dreading whatever had my mother so nervous. Her eyes flickered everywhere in the room, except to Nix and this only made me more anxious.

"She's very devoted to her father," she finally admitted.

A rush of air expelled through my mouth and I felt myself visibly relax into my seat. Nix shot me an intolerant glance, but I smiled brightly, hoping to avoid an explanation. I loved that my sister had a father and they were so close. I loved that she had been saved from our world, from my mother…. From Nix. But obviously I couldn't explain that to them.

Nix slid his wine glass between his thumb and middle finger slowly. He didn't have very many tells, his ability to mask every emotion was one of his greatest skills. But his fingers were white with the effort to stop himself from crushing the glass between his fingers.

I wiped at the corners of my mouth to keep from smiling at his frustration. "So she isn't willing to go back to trial?" I asked in a meek voice.

My mother's sharp green eyes found mine with such intensity that it felt like she slapped me. "No, she doesn't want to dispute custody. She says she's happy with the way things are." My mother's words fell off her tongue like malicious drops of acid. How dare one of her children be happy...

Nix's gaze bore into my mother like he could change the finality of her tone with a powerful look. His lips had formed a tight frown and I watched, practically mesmerized, by the pulsing, angry vein in his neck. When he finally spoke, his words were carefully controlled and measured. This was Nix with barely concealed anger management issues; this was Nix just at the verge of losing control. Terrifying. Captivating. Deadly.

"She doesn't know better, Ava," he finally relented. "She's been with that man for as long as she can remember, she doesn't know life differently. Continue how things are, we'll work on the details together."

My mother nodded curtly, as if she were in complete agreement. It was only the tremble of her fingers when she reached for her glass that gave away her internal fears. I found her quiet terror comforting, even though it meant that if my plans failed in the future I would be imprisoned to a life of fear.

"But I will not tolerate this for much longer," Nix continued, "Your failure to possess your own offspring is not acceptable. Her father is an anomaly, I understand that, and I'd rather not risk exposure by pressing him too hard. But there cannot be loose ends, there cannot be...." Nix cleared his throat, pulling himself back from the hateful monster he was becoming.

"So you don't think that could ever happen again?" I asked before I could stop myself. Ryder had felt like this giant impossibility ever since I met him, but I had forgotten Honor's father was also completely resistant to my mother's spell. Maybe there were men alive that could resist us. Maybe there was hope!

"Ivy you have nothing to worry about," Nix answered, misreading my curiosity. "What happened with Smith was a fluke. It won't happen again, especially not to you." His eyes settled on me appreciatively and I could almost feel my mother's bitterness radiating between us.

What he didn't know was that I thought it had already happened to me.

My mother wasn't alone. And I could solve this new gap between us caused by Nix's implications if I were honest with her about Ryder.

But I never would be. Never ever.

"Smith and Honor are extenuating circumstances," my mother defended herself. "Who knows what those chemo drugs did to his mind, to his brain. Nobody expected him to survive those treatments or his disease, not even his expensive team of experts." We sat in silence as my mother's unnecessary argument settled around us. I didn't have an opinion that could be said out loud about her situation and no matter what my mother said, Nix had his own ideas that would not be dissuaded. "Maybe I should talk to my lawyer about that. Maybe it just wasn't his relationship with me that was affected. Nobody knows the long-term effects those drugs could have on his mental capacity."

Nix made a noncommittal sound and gestured for the waiter to come over and take our order. Nix proceeded to order for all three of us without asking our opinion, and then dismissed the waiter just as abruptly. I was used to this. It was annoying, but I was used to it. And at least I wouldn't have to eat dry lettuce, my mother's favorite food.

We sat in silence for a few more moments, lost to our own thoughts. Nix's concentration never softened, and if anything he grew more agitated with each passing moment. He was wound tight with powerful energy, his eyes burning holes into the table as his fingers worked his wine glass in small twists back and forth. My mother seemed to shrink under the force of his intensity and I could only watch with sick fascination, hardly knowing what to expect.

"Ava," Nix looked at my mother over the small candle in the middle of the table, the dark lighting of the restaurant casting a shadow over half of his face. He pinned my mother to her seat, leveling her with the concentration of his dark eyes. Before he said anything else I knew she would agree to whatever he was about to say, she couldn't help herself. When faced with a force of nature like Nix, one did not say "no," one simply shook her head and quivered in promises to carry out his wishes. "It's important that Honor is put in your custody soon."

"I know that, Nix," my mother crooned confidently, but I saw the way she pressed her lips together to hide her nerves. Her attempt at hiding her anxiety was slipping quickly. She needed more wine.

"Honor needs to be your legacy, not Ivy," Nix continued and I choked on a piece of ice I had been crunching on. Literally, I choked. I flailed my arms, chugged my water and made an entirely unattractive spectacle of myself. My mother and Nix waited for me to gain control of my motor functions and breathing with disapproving glares.

"Sorry," I squeaked, looking intently down at the beige table cloth and wishing I could crawl underneath the table and hide or find a gun. A gun could solve a couple problems right now.

"Why not Ivy?" my mother asked defensively, showing the first sign of backbone I had ever witnessed. And the first sign of a possessive connection to me. "She's grown into a stunning young woman. She's everything you want in your legacies and more."

"I'm not arguing with you," Nix was quick to respond, waving his hand in the air for effect. "You've done a fantastic job with her; she's everything I could ever hope for."

Except for my mental instability, I thought dryly.

"Then-" my mother started to ask, but Nix interrupted her.

"I want her for me. I want her in my collection," Nix explained as if this were typical dinner conversation, as if my world hadn't come crashing down around me at his words, as if I could still breathe.

My mother looked over the table at me, beaming with pride. Her green eyes sparkled and her shoulders bounced a little relishing the news. I realized too late that she was never defensive of Nix's opinion of me, her pride had been wounded. She was soaring now, what with a daughter handpicked for Nix's *personal collection*, how could she not be? This was what every mother wanted, what every mother dreamed of her daughter becoming....

But what about the daughters? What about what *they* wanted?

And my heart stopped beating. I stopped living. I stopped existing.

"Nix, I had no idea Ivy had made such an impression on you," my mother gloated.

"When?" I croaked. The word tumbled from my lips in a hoarse, desperate plea for time.

"When you would have come to me anyway," Nix explained, his eyes drinking me in with a calculating indifference. He wasn't happy with my reaction, with how my face had paled, and my hands gripped the table to keep myself from falling out of my seat. But this was the best I could give him; this was my last desperate attempt from falling apart. "I won't ask you to leave your mother just yet. But you will be mine, Ivy."

His words sunk into my skin like deathly sharp daggers, cutting and slicing open every vestige of hope I held. I bled despair and anguish from every pore, and cried invisible tears of defeat. Eighteen was more important now than ever, but never more unattainable.

The dinner continued on without me present, at least intellectually. Nix and my mother moved onto different, less life-changing topics. But I remained in the soul-wrenching limbo of suffocating hopelessness.

There was no point to breathing anymore. There was no need for air.

Chapter Eleven

You will be mine, Ivy. You will be mine. You will be mine. You will be mine.

"Hey are you, okay? Ivy, are you okay?" Kenna's voice cut through the memory of last night and shook me into the present.

Breath.

One full breath.

"Um, yeah, I'm fine," I smiled at her, hoping I looked fine. Obviously I didn't, but to be fair, she caught me in the middle of reliving the worst nightmare of my life. And I had lived a lifetime of nightmares. "I was just thinking about something."

She smiled back, but I could tell she didn't really believe me. I relied on our acquaintance-only-status to keep her from prying further and with one more fortifying breath I turned my attention back to Chase as he inhaled his pizza. I reached over and stole a pepperoni before he could consume everything on his plate and then ignored the instinct to lick his plate clean for him.

"I tried to share with you," Chase scolded. He wiped his hands on a napkin and gave my lonely orange and bottle of water a depressed once over. "That is so not enough food for lunch."

"It's plenty," I argued, savoring the taste of the greasy pepperoni on my tongue. "I'm just not a big eater," I explained. I wasn't a big eater, but not by choice. It was part of the rules I lived with. I wanted to be a big eater. I wanted to weigh four hundred pounds and eat ice cream all day long and drink soda by the two-liter.

I wanted to wear elastic pants.

Chase made a noncommittal grunt that sounded like he didn't really believe me either. I ignored him and dug into the orange in front of me, my fingernails sinking into the soft flesh causing juice to squirt out everywhere, speckling my hands with sticky spray.

"So who's coming tomorrow night?" Phoenix asked by way of greeting. He sat down directly across from me, flashing a goofy grin and waggling his eyebrows. "Ivy, you in?"

"Yeah, I'm in," I grinned back and nudged Chase with my elbow. "Chase invited me."

"Nice," Phoenix's smile grew bigger and he reached out with his gangly arms to steal my water bottle and take a drink. Apparently our lunch table was more like a communal buffet.

"Wait, is this the first date?" Ryder asked, squeezing in between Phoenix and Kenna. He threw his arm around Kenna and placed a quick kiss against her neck before waiting for an answer. I watched them helplessly, feeling something hollow open in my heart but not understanding it.

Kenna giggled loudly and then wiggled out of Ryder's arm so that she could finish her lunch. She really was pretty, even today when she wasn't really trying. Her stick straight hair was thrown up into a messy bun, but it was so straight that it fell limply on top of her head. She was wearing a simple V-neck t-shirt and tight jeans with a loose scarf around her neck, but she was still eye-catching, still beautiful.

I found myself jealous for a moment. Not because I didn't think I was pretty, I knew I was. But each one of my outfits had to meet the approval of my mother and anything less than perfectly styled hair was completely out of the question. Even the ballet flats I wore today with skinny jeans took hours of convincing and negotiating. My mother was under the impression that unless I was in at least four inch stilettos I just wasn't trying.

I tore my eyes off Kenna to stare at Chase, expecting him to answer Ryder's question. He blushed just barely, his cheeks pinkened and his eyes averted me completely.

"This is the first date," I acknowledged, saving Chase from having to answer.

"F for effort," Ryder goaded. "Don't get too attached to that one, if the best he can come up with is a lame-ass party at Bates' house."

"It's my fault," I felt the unexplainable need to defend Chase from Ryder's judgment. "I'm busy tonight and he had already promised Phoenix he would go."

Ryder gave me a skeptical look and I wasn't exactly sure what it was for, but Chase jumped in and saved me from asking. "Like you're any better Sutton. You're taking Kenna to the party, yeah?"

"Yeah," Ryder agreed. "But tonight I have big plans."

"Oh yeah?" Kenna nudged Ryder with her elbow gently. "What kind of plans?"

"Big ones," Ryder smirked at her, and the innuendo was clear.

I felt my cheeks get warm and I had to avoid any eye contact at the table while everyone snickered and laughed around me. I didn't know why I felt so embarrassed by Ryder's comments; it wasn't like my life was protected from sex, or sex-related activities. In fact, it was more inundated with them than anything. But I didn't like to think about whatever Ryder had planned for Kenna tonight. For whatever reason those thoughts made me extremely uncomfortable.

"Hey," Chase lowered his voice and leaned into me. "We don't have to go to the party. We can always do our own thing."

"No, you can't," Phoenix jumped in, shaking his head and giving Chase a stern look. "No, you can't do your own thing. Ivy's never been to one of my parties. They are seriously epic. There will be no ditching my party." This was the most serious I had ever seen Phoenix, and he was still glaring at Chase.

"Geez, eavesdrop much?" Chase complained, shaking his head at his friend. "And you can't peer pressure Ivy into going, she makes her own decisions."

"Very true," I laughed at the two of them going back and forth. And it was true. I was completely immune to peer pressure. Parental pressure was a whole different category however and in my case, so, so much worse. "Don't worry, Phoenix, we'll be there." I turned to Chase and smiled at him. "I don't want to disappoint him, he seems so pathetic."

Chase just shook his head. "How do you always get your way, man?"

"Boyish good looks and infinite charm," Phoenix offered seriously. "Oh and my parents have good weed."

I let that sink in for a minute before declaring, "Nope, sorry, so not into recreational drugs." I shook my head, my auburn hair whipping around my face, hammering in my point. I didn't know what made my confession so absolutely vital, so important that I needed to say it out loud with loads of conviction. But I had to assume it had something to do with Kenna presuming my drink the other night was vodka. I had a reputation, and I couldn't stop the rumors, but this group of people was different from anyone I had ever hung out with before. They were better.... more wholesome or something. And I felt myself wanting to prove my virtue. Which was totally lame....

"Oh, no worries," Phoenix threw out immediately. "The weed is just there, I mean available. Personally, I never do it either, but my parents leave it where all my friends can find it. They think that makes them cool parents. I think it makes them irresponsible, but what can you do?"

"I don't believe you," a snide voice called from down the table. I lifted my eyes to meet the same girl that was mean to me before. I couldn't remember her name. Initially, I thought she was accusing Phoenix of lying, but by her pinched, hateful face I had to assume her statement was directed at me. "I've heard you're into *everything*," she continued, letting her ambiguous innuendo slide over every one of her words.

"She doesn't do drugs *anymore*. Rehab, duh, Amber," another voice from down the table scolded but with a fair amount of amusement in his annoying voice.

Hayden. Ugh.

"Oh, that's right," Amber laughed like a hyena at my expense. Her chin length hair bobbed around her face and got stuck to her overly lacquered lips. Her eyes glinted maliciously at me.

That wasn't the reason I didn't do drugs. I would never do drugs. Ever. But those were reasons I had to keep private, reasons I couldn't even admit to myself out loud. Plus, I still had to perpetuate the whole rehab lie anyway. In only three days, I had almost completely forgotten that I was supposed to be a recovering addict. That was one lie that was going to be hard to keep straight. Goodbye wholesome. Hello, nasty rumors.

"Yep, the twelve steps and all," I mumbled half-heartedly. I didn't even know what any of the steps were after the first one. Admit you have a problem. I knew they involved forgiveness, but that was the only other one I could come up with. I should have probably googled the rest for obnoxious moments just like this.

"What does that even mean?" Ryder asked in an amused tone, drawing my attention back to our smaller group.

"Come on, don't be a douche too," Chase pleaded, saving me from answering. It was a good thing too, since I had no idea what I meant by that and I should have known better than to think Ryder wouldn't call me out on my crap. "Are you alright?" Chase looked down at me and I felt enveloped in his protective care. His hand slipped to my lower back and I instantly felt better in his bubble of white-knighthood. It was really nice to have someone stick up for me, to say something on my behalf. Even if he was a victim in all of this too.

"I'm not trying to be a douche," Ryder said a little bit softer and he drew my attention back to him. I met his gaze from across the table and couldn't help but fall just a little bit into his silver depths. "Sorry, Ivy. I wasn't trying to pick on you." He held me motionless from where he sat; I was more than a little bit paralyzed by the look of sincerity in his eyes. I could see that he felt bad for calling me out, but that was it. There was nothing else there, no hidden desire, no blatant interest, just apology. He was completely immune to me and suddenly every single one of my thoughts was wrapped up in Ryder Sutton and how the hell he could resist me.

"Hey, it's fine," I shook my head, breaking our stare down and searching for anything else to look at. Chase's hand warmed my back, setting off anxious feelings of guilt and embarrassment for letting me get so sucked into the vortex of Ryder's self-control. I settled my gaze on one of my orange peels and began shredding it between my fingers, shrinking a little from these unfamiliar emotions.

"Sam Evans doesn't think it's *fine*," Amber half shouted from across the table.

My head snapped up with her accusation. Instantaneously I was consumed with every negative, hateful emotion possible. "Shut your filthy mouth," I growled, not caring that there was a captive audience surrounding me. "You don't know what you're talking about. Don't you ever say his name again with that much disrespect."

Chase's hand became stiff and still on my back, his whole body rigid next to me. I felt wide eyes burning into me with intense surprise and curiosity. But I couldn't explain. I couldn't explain how it was my fault what happened to Sam and that I would have to live with the guilt and sin of that night.

"Did I hit a nerve?" Amber smirked pompously.

"You have no idea what the hell you're talking about. So I suggest you stop talking now," I threatened in a low voice. My hands had started to tremble so I clenched them together and hid them beneath the table. My breathing stuttered and staggered in a worthless attempt to draw in oxygen. Black spots prickled my vision and I could only fear the impending breakdown that was swooping down on me between the flashes of horrific memories of that night.

"God, you're such a bitch," Amber's voice bit out from somewhere beyond the craziness playing out in my head.

I felt Chase whisper against my ear, asking if I was alright, but I wasn't capable of answering him at this point. It was all caving in on me, my control was slipping, and my future was fading away...

"Who's the bitch?" a strong voice cut through my haze and called Amber out on her bullshit. "Don't start shit you know nothing about just because you're jealous."

I lifted my eyes to Ryder who was very effectively putting Amber in her place. Her face had paled and her eyes filled with tears at his admonition. I felt the shattered pieces of my soul start to mend themselves back together and I worked to pull in a full breath, filling my lungs and expanding my chest. Ryder turned back to me, his gaze softening, his eyes searching.

"She's been trying to hook up with Chase for two years," Ryder explained in a loud enough voice that I knew this was still directed at Amber. "She's jealous of you."

I nodded because that was all I was capable of. Ryder held my eyes for half a minute more before turning back to a stunned Kenna. He went back to engaging her in conversation, giving her every ounce of his doting attention. Slowly quiet chatter grew around us and everyone at our table seemed to move on. I leaned into Chase, enjoying the strength of his chest against my back, relishing in the warmth of his body pressed against me.

I would survive this.

I had to.

Chapter Twelve

"Finally!" Sloane called from the top of her staircase when my mother and I walked into her midtown French Beaux-arts design house. Her mother had drastically different taste than mine. Where my mother worshipped at the altar of modern chic, Sloane's mother was all classic French doors and imported antique tiled floors. The house was a magazine spread waiting to happen, with expertly decorated classic French furniture and a drool worthy backyard grotto complete with a cozy fire pit and sunken fifteen-person Jacuzzi. "Up here now!" She snapped her perfectly manicured fingers impatiently and I couldn't help but smile.

"Geesh! You are so bossy!" I called back, feeling a weight lift off my shoulders. I hated being here tonight. I loathed being surrounded by these people, by these women who had sold their souls to the devil without putting up any kind of fight. But I loved my girls. And it was good to see them.

"Ivy," my mother stopped me before I could hang up my coat and disappear into Sloane's bedroom for the rest of the night. Her voice was poised and authoritative, her glassy green eyes narrowed and expectant. "I expect you to put in some face time tonight. You heard what Nix has planned for you. He won't want you to hide away. You need to remind him and everyone else why he would pick you. It's not public knowledge yet, but when he makes his claim to you I don't want there to be a shadow of a doubt for why he would pick you."

She leaned forward to straighten the neckline of my mandarin collared sheer shirt dress. She brushed invisible lint off the shoulder and then adjusted it so that it layered over the dress-length slip perfectly. I willed myself to be still underneath her ice cold fingers and intense scrutiny.

"Mom, nobody will notice," I argued doing my best to keep the pleading tone I desperately felt out of my voice. "It's not like Nix is going to announce his intentions tonight."

"Don't argue with me," she chastised immediately. "And please, Nix's affection for you has never been anything but common knowledge. Do you think anyone else could have pulled that little depression stunt last spring and gotten away with it?" My mother laughed derisively, completely and effectively putting me in my place. "Hardly. So don't you dare seem ungrateful tonight. Get your act together and give Nix what he wants."

"Yes, mother," I ground out obediently sounding like a Stepford robot. I knew there was no point arguing what might as well have been a command straight from God in this circle of delusional people.

She gave me another head to toe dissecting glance, pausing a little too long on my solid black leggings like they were an eye sore. And then she turned her back on me to greet her.... colleagues. I looked around the elegant rooms of Sloane's house, each one exquisitely designed and furnished. The house cost the same as our condo which could have reflected badly on Sloane's mother Thalia. Our circle was entirely wrapped up in price tags and paychecks. But where Thalia had been frugal with the house she had made up for with extravagant pieces of art and design.

The first floor of Sloane's mother's house was filled with women just like my own mom, gold-diggers all vying for Nix's desired attention. Not that Nix would ever be an end all for these rich bitches, but he had his own charm and appeal that was absolutely intoxicating to these women.... to every woman. Nix floated between clusters of beautiful but conniving females, dazzling them all with his charm and wit.

I had a sudden urge to vomit all over the antique ottoman to my left, just to cause a scene. Obviously I squashed the urge, but the bitterness stayed firmly lodged in the back of my throat.

I took one more brave look around the first floor from my vantage point in the foyer, swearing to myself that I would never become these women, that I would never let myself get swept away in the shallow-possession-coveted existence that poisoned them. I lifted my chin in mild defiance and let the promise to myself weave a protective layer around my cynical, jaded soul, and around my broken, malformed heart. I was better than this. I was better than this life.

Nix caught my eye from across the room, his dark eyes hypnotizing me, his allure calling to me, asking me to stand by his side. He hardly acknowledged me other than the way he kept his gaze tightly locked with mine, not even a head nod or incline of his chin. But it was because of the subtlety of his authority that I felt the call to him stronger than even the oxygen in my lungs, more intimately than the blood pumping through my veins. I held my ground and fought with everything I had against the intense desire to walk over to him. His lips quirked into a perceptive smirk, and I felt his expression turn to knowing. It was like my defiance only spurred him on, only encouraged him. More afraid of that truth than anything else, I broke our gaze and bounded upstairs and to the safety of Sloane's room.

"There she is," Exie squealed. "Shut the door behind you, Ives."

I followed her directions and plopped down on Sloane's oversized bed. Her room was decorated in the same style as the rest of the house, light and airy with touches of eighteenth century France. Every piece of her ivory painted provincial bedroom set was occupied in some way by Sloane, Exie or their sisters Evaleen and Anaxandra.

Exie was at the vanity curling her sister Anaxandra's hair. She had long golden curls, just like Exie and icy blue eyes framed by impossibly dark lashes. They were big-boobed Barbies with tiny waists and perfect manes of hair. Anaxandra watched disinterestedly as Exie arranged her hair in a perfect mess that would appear casual even if it had taken several hours to accomplish.

Evaleen, Sloane's sister shared her pale complexion and deep, dark brown eyes, but her hair was more chestnut than Sloane's rich almost black hair. Evaleen was definitely Snow White's older sister, and *not* the fairy tale princess that Sloane was, but she was still breath-taking, still heart-stopping. All of these beautiful girls could give anyone an inferiority complex.

That is if you weren't equally as beautiful and acutely aware that this kind of splendor came with an insipid, disgusting price tag you would have to pay for the rest of your existence and never, not once, not even in your outspoken fantasies or most private hopes and dreams have the opportunity to be free.

"Hey, Ivy," Evaleen greeted in a falsely casual tone. She lifted her eyes from a gossip magazine and pinned me with an accusing stare. "It's been a while. How was the…. what are you calling it? The mind-vacation?"

I gaped at her. She was speaking to me with barely hidden cruelty like she was accusing me what happened was my fault. She should know better. We were all brought into this together, the same way. We used to be in this together. But apparently Exie was right, these two girls that I used to look up to as heroes had bought into the lie.

Everyone in the room was waiting for me to say something, staring at me with jewel-like eyes and practiced expressions of curiosity.

"Rehab," I finally whispered, my own voice failing to stand by my side. "I've just been telling everyone I went to rehab."

Anaxandra snorted her disapproval. "Not a very flattering lie. Fat camp would have been better than *rehab*."

I swallowed my righteous rage at her callousness and decided to save the "beauty is on the inside" fight for when it actually aided my case. In fact, all of my beauty was on the outside. *All of it*. So it didn't really matter if I wanted to argue with Anaxandra or not, she would clearly win this argument.

"But rehab isn't really a lie," I replied pathetically. "At least not if you hear Nix or my mom talk about it."

"What was it like?" Evaleen asked, sliding down from her perch on Sloane's long gilded dresser. "Was it really intense?"

"Yes," I admitted. I hadn't even had this conversation with Sloane or Exie yet. I preferred never to think about my time in the posh brain-washing camp I had been sent to. Most of the time I believed my soul was still intact, well, small pieces of it, but there were moments of weakness when I wasn't so sure they hadn't penetrated my mind. "Lots and lots of therapy. And Nix had several veterans visit and share their *success* stories with me. I guess he was trying to sell me on this whole thing." I gestured around the room lazily, as if Sloane's room summed up our entire existence.

"Spa time?" Anaxandra pushed, probably noticing my glowing skin and manicured nails, both of which I had chosen to neglect before I went in. I nodded my answer. She sighed enviously. "It sounds like vacation. What I wouldn't give for Nix to pamper me like that!"

Evaleen squealed with laughter, "No kidding. Six months of constant relaxation and spoiling. It sounds amazing! Was it amazing?"

"No, *obviously* not." I looked at these two girls that had just as much influence in raising me as my mother did and could not believe how far gone they were. They were five years older than me, which was an insane amount of time in my life. It was the difference between fighting fate and accepting it. They were almost finished with college, about ready to enter our society completely and they couldn't stop going on and on about *spa time*? Everything in their lives already replicated a vacation from reality and still they wanted more? I wondered who they were at the core of their beings; how far down the morally deluded path to hell had they really fallen?

Evaleen once pulled me aside at a garden party when I was thirteen and slipped comfort inserts into my four inch pumps when she could tell I could barely walk straight anymore. She whispered in my ear when I turned fourteen and had to go to dinner with Nix for the first time by myself that I would be okay, that I was strong enough to handle a four course meal and when dessert was over to simply tell him that I was exhausted and had school in the morning and couldn't be out any later. She had shown me one of Nix's greatest weaknesses, that he was a gentleman to a fault in public and nothing would come between him and keeping up appearances.

And Anaxandra had been the closest thing to an older sister I ever had. She tweezed my eyebrows for the first time, taught me the tricks of well-placed duct tape and Band-Aid placements and never let me cry in public. Never. She would somehow see tears form in my eyes from across entire ballrooms, race to me, scoop me up and hide me in the nearest bathroom until the tears stopped and she could reapply my makeup. I was gone six months and came back to *Invasion of the Body Snatchers*. I came back to sell-outs. The reality of that epiphany was like a slice to my already battered heart. What if that was me one day? What if I forgot all my moral high ground and coveted convictions and allowed the idea of spas and vacation to completely cloud my judgment? That was the scariest question of all.

"I was still processing Sam... It was kind of the opposite of a vacation." I breathed out in a shaky whisper.

"Oh, my god, Ivy, get over it already. It's not like he *died*. You are being so dramatic about the whole thing!" Anaxandra rolled her huge blue eyes in an exaggerated circle and then removed her attention from me completely, looking down at her nails as if they held the solution to world hunger.

Exie smacked the back of her sister's head with a sharp satisfaction. "God, Ana, that is the ugliest thing you have ever said! What is wrong with you?"

"Ow!" Anaxandra rubbed at the back of her head and scowled at her little sister. "What is wrong with *you*? And you know that Ivy is the only one upset about the accident. Everyone else seems to think it's a good thing... a sign of things to come!" Her face lit up with an expectant smile. "You're a good omen, Ivy. Stop worrying about Sam and enjoy what this means for you!"

The bile rose higher in my throat and I lunged forward, throwing myself in Sloane's bathroom. I didn't have time to reach the toilet, so I stood at the sink, dry heaving the non-existent contents of an empty stomach. A weighty pressure landed on my lungs and my vision blurred at the edges, threatening my consciousness altogether. *I couldn't breathe. I couldn't breathe. I couldn't breathe.*

Sloane appeared behind me and turned me away from the mirror where I had been unconsciously staring daggers into my own, hated reflection. She pushed roughly on the back of my head until the top half of my body hung upside down and my face was awkwardly placed between my knees.

"It's okay, Ivy," Sloane murmured sweetly to me. "Inhale. Exhale. Inhale. Exhale. Slowly, that's it, slowly." Sloane's voice held a gentle authority that I responded to immediately. This wasn't the first time we had been through this routine.

The world started to come back into focus even as all the blood rushed to my head and my neck flooded with warmth. Breathing became easier; the sick, venomous feeling slowly receded back to the depths of my black, toxic soul.

"Ivy sooner or later you're going to have to get over this cry for attention," Evaleen taunted from the other room. "If Nix loses his patience with you, you're only going to have yourself to blame."

"There is something wrong with you two," Exie scolded as she joined us in the en suite bathroom. "You're just like everybody else. It's like you've turned into *them*." Exie gestured toward the floor, indicating the party downstairs. She hit them with an insult that once upon a time would have really riled them up. "You've been drinking the Kool-Aid."

"Grow up, Ex," Anaxandra snarled. "Some of us like drinking the Kool-Aid. One day you'll get it, you'll accept what every single one of us eventually comes to accept. It's easy to be judgmental from where you're standing, but one day you'll have to stand in our shoes, one day when they offer you the proverbial Kool-Aid you're going to drink it. Just like we did, just like our mothers did, just like their mothers did. Remember that." Anaxandra finished her speech by returning her gaze to the oval vanity mirror and preening for three more seconds before nodding her head to Evaleen. Both girls gave us one more pitying stare and then left to join the party downstairs.

The three of us stood silent and frozen in the safety of Sloane's bathroom processing Anaxandra's ominous words. Sloane was the first to move and when she did it was with an icy frigidness. She turned around and leaned forward on the bathroom's marble countertop, gripping the edge until her hands became white.

"What if she's right?" Sloane whispered, avoiding her face in the mirror. "What if we turn out just like them?"

A hundred different answers spun and twisted in my head but when I finally spoke it was with hope. "What if we don't?" I paused, letting the question settle in the air around us. "Sloane, what if we don't?" Each word was spoken with solid intension and earnest strength. There was so much hope in that seemingly impossible future that it was too tempting to set aside without further examination.

Exie looked up when I spoke, shaken from her fearful trance. There was a lighter spark in her deep blue eyes, a glisten of miniscule hope that hadn't been there before. "Sloane, what if we don't?" she squealed and pulled me to her in a tight hug. She bounced up and down and then pulled Sloane into our circle of affection like we had already conquered this life and moved on to greener pastures.

I let myself get caught up in her excitement, feeling real hope bloom as the first flowers of spring after an endlessly frozen winter. There was no reason for it, no explanation for why this time my voice sounded confident and sure. But there it was all the same and the three of us were suddenly infected with as much hope as we were once diseased with despair.

Chapter Thirteen

"Alright ladies, it's time to make an appearance," Sloane admonished after several minutes of hugging.

Exie and I made simultaneous groans of frustration, but let Sloane lead the way out her door and down the staircase to the main floor. There weren't that many women gathered tonight, less than fifty. But each room was packed with competitive estrogen and enough ego to suffocate an innocent bystander.

Caterers floated from room to room carrying trays of bite-sized canapés or flutes of champagne and soft jazz drifted through the air barely heard over the steady conversation. Men had joined the ranks of women since I was upstairs, dates, husbands, lovers, Nix's apprentices…. There were not as many of them as there were women, but the crowd was diversified and it put me back on edge.

We waved and smiled at everyone important, at everyone we were supposed to pay notice to. But each of us avoided Nix's authoritative eye and the expectation-filled expressions of our mothers. Exie and Sloane were as uncomfortable as I was dealing with these people and we shared a mutual acknowledgment that a quick walk-through constituted a legitimate appearance. With a sad, soul-crushing kind of despair, I noticed Anaxandra and Eveleen mingling with the veteran women in the crowd, sipping vodka martinis and discussing current events.

Another one bites the dust.

And another one and another one, and another one bites the dust.

We ducked into the den toward the back of the house. The room was unoccupied, but we knew it would be. Personal offices are always off limits at these things, hence the reason we use them as our safe haven. Technically we were still apart of the party.

We squished together on a rich, chocolate suede sofa surrounded by floor-to-ceiling bookshelves. They were artfully stacked with volumes of intellectual books that had probably never been opened. Snuggled together and somewhat tucked away, we began our ritual of making fun of everyone we could remember seeing in our brief sprint from the bottom of the staircase to this room. We pulled our cell phones out and multitasked by trash talking and texting. This was the procedure for us, years of routine and tradition.

"So did that guy ever work out for you?" Sloane asked with a sly lift of her eyebrow.

"Guy?" I clarified. A surge of irrational panic slid through my veins leaving sticky residual anxiety congesting my blood vessels into immovable blockage.

"That one from your first day back? The one that offered you a ride?" Sloane clarified as if I was especially slow tonight.

"Oh, right. Yes, actually. We have a date tomorrow night. Some house party thing..." I trailed off and then felt the need to defend Chase's choice of the first date. "He asked me out for tonight first, but obviously I had other plans. So we decided to do this thing tomorrow night because he already told his friend he would be there," I rambled nervously. "His name is Chase." For a moment I assumed she meant Ryder, which sent off all kinds of panic alarms in my head. I realized then that I held a fierce desire to protect Ryder from this life, from me... and I didn't understand where it came from. I didn't even like Ryder. He was more like this phenomenon in life where everything had become far too predictable. But maybe that was why I wanted to protect him. Maybe because he was all but invincible to my curse, I wanted to protect him from every potential female that could hurt him.

Which was kind of messed up since he was already saved from being a victim.

It was all the other boys that lay in the wake of my war path that I should really be concerned about.

Except I tried that once... I tried that with Sam and things did *not* end well.

"I remember," Sloane grinned, lifting her second eyebrow to join the first. "But a house party? Seriously? I thought I raised you better than that." She threw me a saucy grin to let me know she was kidding.

"Well, if it makes you feel any better, he had this whole wining and dining event planned but when I turned him down for tonight he was already locked into this party thing. It should be fun. The guy who's throwing it is super sweet and funny. And Chase's whole circle of friends will be there, so...." I trailed off not really knowing where I was going with that or why I was defending the night at all. It was a party, so what? We went to parties all the time.

"Aw, I think our little Ivy is nervous," Exie elbowed me in the ribs from where she sat in between Sloane and me. "You're rambling a little bit, sweets. Are you scared to go to the party?"

I thought about that for a minute and decided I was more than scared, I was petrified. It would be my first high school event since the accident last spring. I had plenty of reasons to be nervous, but I was raised to believe that kind of anxiety was a weakness.

And I wasn't supposed to have any weaknesses.

"Maybe just a little bit," I smiled, hoping my nerves would be misinterpreted. "I kind of like Chase. He's adorable in that soccer-jock-I'm-so-I-laid-back-I-should-be-a-surfer-way. You know?"

"Sure, we know," Sloane giggled, turning her attention back to the text message she was sending to her boyfriend of the month. "Surfers in Nebraska where there aren't even any noteworthy lakes, make complete sense."

The three of us dissolved into laughter.

At that moment, my phone lit up with an incoming message and I smiled down at Chase's name and short note. *Having fun at the family thing?*

Chase was a good choice for a first boyfriend back in the game. He was low maintenance and extra sweet. He would be careful with me, even if I would eventually break his heart. He didn't know it now, but even if he was the best thing for me, I was definitely the worst thing for him.

"Speak of the devil," I mumbled.

"And he shall appear," Nix finished the phrase from the doorway. A chill slid down my spine at his reference and I couldn't help but picture his dark mess of hair with red horns and his perfectly sculpted hands holding a pitchfork. "It's hard to enjoy the party when you're hiding back here, ladies." He smiled casually at first, slowly, as if he were in on our private joke, but then his expression grew more serious and he hit us with the intense severity of his dark eyes that only Nix was capable of. "Your mothers are all looking for you."

We responded without talking, jumping to our feet in trained obedience. I tried to get to the door first, hating the idea of being the last one in the room with him. Not that I was abandoning my friends, but either of them would be safe. Nix wouldn't try to detain them. Not yet anyway....

He caught my eye though and with an infinitesimal shake of his head I knew I had been trapped regardless of my efforts. I moved to the side and let my friends through the door. They gave me a discreetly sympathetic look before slipping into the hallway in search of their mothers.

"Ivy," Nix greeted smoothly, piercing me with his concentrated gaze, like a knife in the gut. His expression sliced open my belly, hemorrhaging my insecurities and fears.

"Hey, Nix," I replied smoothly, confidently, casually and with any other positive adverb I could convey. I forced myself to remain the picture of aloof ease, proud and relaxed. With my chin tilted just a fraction higher and my shoulders held back I faced the monster in front of me, silently pleading he would believe my act.

"I thought I made it clear at dinner last night my intentions for you," his voice was velvet and silk, assertive and authoritative, enthralling and tempting. It took an expert to notice the thinly veiled threat and strain of pure evil pulsing with each syllable.

"You did," I smiled up at him, letting a hint of confusion show through my carefully constructed mask.

"I want you by my side, Ivy. That means tonight. That means every night," Nix growled out, letting all pretense drop away.

Forget acting 101, my heartbeat took off in a rapid flutter of nerves, my palms began to sweat and my careful mask of control shattered in front of him. I took a step back, my ballet flats sliding against the polished wood floors with a swoosh sound that cut through the silence of the room like a knife. I hated that my fear showed through, that Nix's face lit up with satisfaction and predatory delight, but I couldn't stop the reaction. Even me, a girl who had been raised in this world since birth couldn't stop the innate fear from rising up like a revolt against my actions when Nix was around. "I-"

"Don't," he cut me off not even allowing an excuse. I should have known better than to believe I could deceive Nix. He leaned against the door jam, tucking his hands into the pockets of his perfectly cut black trousers. "I'm not in the mood for your games. I'd be a fool not to see how you feel about this…. lifestyle. But I'd be an even bigger fool to let you go. You're mine, Ivy. I'm not expecting you to embrace the idea, but I'm not going to do anything about it either. I will break you over time, I'm not concerned. And until then I plan on enjoying every bit of your free spirit."

I opened and then closed my mouth, only to open and close it again. I had never really been under the impression that I was fooling Nix, but to hear everything laid out so honestly, so openly was more than I could deal with.

He continued so I wouldn't have to flounder. "I don't expect you to feel good about anything I just said. When you're as determined as you are, words like mine can only damage your pride. That feeling will fade, I promise. You just need to trust me. And if I were you, I would leave your friends out of whatever rebellion you're planning. They will be the ones getting hurt, not you. You will only be the one left to carry more guilt around. After Sam, do you really think you can handle two more lives to add to your list?"

"Are you threatening me?" I whispered in a raspy voice. The heels of my feet hit the wall with an empty thud and I realized Nix had me right where he wanted me. I was the trapped baby gazelle, while the experienced lion stalked his naïve, helpless prey. This was his plan all along, fear as motivation, friends as incentive, threats and promises to perpetuate the cycle.

"Hardly," he sighed, taking a step forward so he towered over me. I felt small and weak next to his intoxicating masculinity. "I don't have to threaten you because you're not going to let this get out of hand. You're going to bend to my will. You're going to obey me."

A loaded silence dragged heavily between us. I wasn't going to agree to Nix's outrageous demands and he wasn't ever going to back off. Not ever.

Eventually, he changed the subject. "I don't like the idea of you going to a party tomorrow night. I think it's too soon."

More silence on my part. This was my job: parties, boys, drunken revelry.

"Ivy, I'm not trying to offend your pride," Nix wisely pacified me. "I'm concerned for your well-being and nothing more. A party…. after the accident last spring, could trigger all kinds of-"

"Nix, I'm fine," I interrupted, a sharp, determined edge to my voice. "I know what you're going to say, but I'm better. The depression, the breakdown… that's not going to happen again. The crash was just… unexpected. I'm better, Nix. I promise." I pushed as much commitment and feeling into my words and body as possible. I couldn't go back to treatment; I couldn't, even for one second reveal how just *not fine* I really was. Nix could see through anything, every single one of my lies, but I was hoping this was a lie he wanted to believe. Or at the very least believed he could make true.

Nix's eyes narrowed in thought, his laugh lines making a pronounced appearance as he looked me over and waited for me to recant from my knees in pleading supplication. "Ivy, the accident… The car crash… I know you had a soft spot for Sam, but what happened wasn't necessarily a terrible thing. You could look at this like a sign of great things to come, you could look at this like a-"

"Nix, don't," I whispered desperately. I overstepped my good graces when I dared to interrupt him twice, but I could not bear to hear him put a positive spin on the accident. I destroyed someone's life, *destroyed* it. There was no sign, or omen, or great thing to come. There was only me, the destroyer of men's lives and ruiner of promising futures.

"One day you'll understand, Ivy. One day you'll see," Nix promised, his eyes softening with sweet adoration. "Now, come along, you're by my side from now on." He held out his elbow for me and I took it obediently. The exposed skin of my forearm slid easily along the silky fabric of his expensive suit. The hard lines of his body were pressed against my side as he led me out to the rest of the party.

He was dominant strength to my fragile obedience. He was entertaining and lively to my submissive silence. I participated only when directly engaged but played the part of his pretty bobble in every way I was taught to. For now, I was allowed to be sixteen, or as sixteen as any other woman in our circle was ever allowed to be. But if I didn't do something, if I didn't escape, I had a lifetime of this to look forward to and worse.

Sam's drunk driving accident would only be the beginning of a never ending list of lives demolished by the notorious Ivy Pierce.

Chapter Fourteen

My hand shot out from under me with surprisingly fast reflexes since the rest of my body was complete dead weight. The alarm buried in the clutter of my nightstand refused to stop blaring and so with expertly placed force I batted at the snooze button until the incessant bleeping stopped. I squished my eyes closed as tightly as I could and retracted my arm to the snuggled position underneath my tired torso, but it was no use... I wouldn't be able to fall back asleep.

Thoughts of the party last night tumbled around in my exhaustion addled brain. And when I was finally able to push those depressing thoughts aside they were replaced with hope for tonight, for a little bit of escape from my reality. Even spending time with Chase ignited an excitement inside of me I didn't want to admit to.

I rolled over in bed, taking the thick, down comforter with me. My hair followed, tangled and wild across my face. I lay there for a few minutes more, letting the early morning light from my wall of bedroom windows seep into my skin and wake me slowly into consciousness. The warmth of the blanket cocooned me in safety and for those few, uninterrupted minutes I felt protected from the rest of my life. I felt safe.

But it was a fleeting feeling that drifted away like the forgotten memories of dreams.

I needed coffee, desperately.

It was that mundane thought that brought reality crashing in around me. My mother was the farthest thing from domesticated as one woman could be, so there was never food in our house, let alone caffeinated necessities. Plus she was a pushy, indoctrinated anorexic. Like those avid PETA supporters that threw cans of red paint on anything fur, my mother looked down at food on my plate with a condescending eye that was almost palpable.

She only ate enough to support her exercise-addiction and fill out her size two cocktail dresses. She expected me to have the same infatuation with non-eating and treadmills. I expected myself to not faint in the middle of the morning because of hunger and add something to my tiny little b-cups.

So this Saturday morning I was going to rebel with a latte and a pastry.

Maybe even two pastries.

I lived a dangerous life.

Damn the man.

Or in this case my mother.

I crawled out of bed and rubbed at my still sleepy eyes. I had taken my makeup off late last night and even though it was a pain to go through the beauty regiment my mother had strictly laid out for me, I was thankful now to have a scrubbed face. I tossed my boy shorts and cami on the floor and wiggled into some gray skinny jeans. I grabbed the first bra I could find and then slipped an off the shoulder soft pink cashmere sweater on before pulling my hair into a ponytail without bothering to brush through it. Later today I would take the time for a shower, and blow dry and all that, right now my mind was firmly set on a twenty-four-ounce caramel macchiato and a cream puff. I had tunnel vision and that prompted the single swipe of mascara and lip gloss that constituted my make-up and the ballet flats I left near my bedroom door on my way in last night.

Not my best effort at looking good, but the coffee shop was only across the street and it was still too early for my mother to have skulked from her own bed and joined the land of the living. She stayed out later than I did, and where my drinks consisted of water on the rocks, her drinks were filled with Grey Goose and Bombay Sapphire. She wouldn't need coffee. She needed an injection from the fountain of youth to recover from that kind of licentiousness. To be fair though, whenever the women of our circle were gathered together in small quarters like they were last night, they all needed copious amounts of alcohol to forge through the fake friendships and plastic pleasantries. These women did *not* play well together.

I grabbed my apartment keys and wallet and slipped out of the house unnoticed. The entire condo complex was quiet and still as I walked to the bank of elevators and waited for one to take me down to the lobby. Our complex was one of many brand new pieces of trendy architecture in this part of Omaha. Sleek, modern and artfully chic, this living arrangement fit my mother's personality perfectly. I walked out the front doors of our building and through the drive up circle that included a hotel, a posh gym and a fancy restaurant. Across the street stood a three story dine-in movie theater, one of a kind in this city, and a coffee shop recently transplanted from downtown.

I crossed the street without waiting for the walk sign; there was virtually no traffic this early and not even the shadows of the building fell on the empty street. The autumn sun was bright this morning, warming the chill in the air and igniting the crisp smell of leaves falling from the trees that lined Farnam Street in decorative pots.

Delice was a European bakery with simply the best orange and raisin scones ever, in the history of scones, and even better fruit tartlets. The small gourmet coffee shop used to live in the epicenter of downtown but when midtown started to rebuild so did Delice. The shop migrated a little west, upgraded their rent and opened for business directly across the street from me. It was love at first sight between the two of us, we were young and lonely and couldn't get enough of each other. Well, until I was banished until my brain got better…. my long six-month absence stretched out between us like a tragic Shakespearean play.

But I was back now, and walking through these doors felt more like coming home than well… coming home did.

The small shop was all but empty, save for an elderly couple cuddled together over the morning World Herald in the corner. I walked straight to the counter so that I could eye the case of pastries up close. The racks were filled with elegant, precisely decorated goodies that triggered my taste buds into an immediately hungry frenzy. Yesterday I had 87 ounces of water, a snack sized bag of pretzels, a banana and one arugula and ricotta cheese canapé.

Oh and a half glass of champagne that went straight to my head.

I deserved to eat this entire case of unnecessary calories as far as I was concerned. I wiped my thumb against the corner of my mouth, discreetly checking for drool and then lifted my head to address the cashier. I hadn't been here in a long enough time that I didn't recognize the college-aged hippy across the counter. But then most of the girls that worked here were imported from the local universities and so job turnover flowed with the school schedules and breaks.

"Can I help you?" the dread-locked twenty-something girl asked, but her eyes moved from mine to the door that opened behind me. A smile lit up her face and she gave a tiny wave to whoever just walked in.

"Yes," I announced, drawing her attention back to me. "I'll have a caramel macchiato and an orange scone." The girl started to ring in my confident order and suddenly I felt panicked to add onto it, desperate to break the rules and fill my empty stomach, "And a chocolate croissant." I cringed at how frantic I sounded, treating this breakfast like my last meal before the electric chair, but that didn't stop me from throwing in another pastry, "And a cream puff!"

I reached forward, clutching at the counter until my knuckles turned white. I didn't want to give up one of the pastries or even any of them, but even as she pushed the right buttons on her computer screen the unwanted guilt of eating such an extravagant breakfast started to sink in through my skin like acid eating away at my resolve. I looked down at my wallet on the counter as if it would have the answers for me, either enough guilt to make me change my mind or enough solace to wipe away the remorse completely. Meanwhile the girl behind the counter rattled off my total without noticing my internal struggle.

I decided that I really only needed the chocolate croissant and was just about to tell her that when a deep, recognizable voice from behind me spoke up first, "I'll get that for her Tarryn, just add it to my total."

I spun around on my heel, shocked more than I should be to stand face to face with Ryder Sutton. "I can pay for my own breakfast," I snapped quickly. I trained my eyes on his gunmetal grays, refusing to take in his sleep-mussed hair, morning scruff that outlined his chiseled jaw or the thin black t-shirt and loose jeans that hung on his body deliciously. I simply refused to notice all that.

Besides he was just wearing jeans and a t-shirt. There was absolutely *nothing* special about his boring outfit. In fact, allowing myself one, tiny, insignificant glance, it looked like he had dug them out from underneath his bed, *everything* was wrinkled! There was so nothing attractive about that....

"I never thought you couldn't buy your own breakfast," he sighed, already agitated with me. I couldn't really blame him, but that didn't mean I dropped my defenses. "I'm just trying to do something nice for you, Ivy."

"Is this for here?" Tarryn asked from behind me.

"Yes," I replied without turning around. My eyes stayed narrowed on Ryder, not really sure what to do or what to say next. "Thank you" seemed drastically out of the question.

"Excuse me," he strong-armed me out of the way, his sharp elbow connecting playfully with my ribs. A jolt of electricity zinged up my spine and a lone butterfly flapped its nervous wings in my stomach. "You know what, Tarryn, why don't you hold off on the two regulars and just make my Chai. I'm going to stay and eat breakfast with my friend here."

I whipped back around to face the counter, mouth hanging half ajar at Ryder's announcement. I was assuming he meant me since there was no one else in the café, unless he meant the elderly couple but then I was pretty sure he would have said "friends." "We're not friends," I defended on instinct, more for his sake than mine.

"Fine," Ryder agreed never looking at me. "Then I'll be right over there," Ryder pointed for Tarryn's benefit, "with my arch-nemesis."

My mouth dropped the rest of the way opened and I stifled the hysterical giggle that was bubbling up inside of me.

"Come on, Dr. Evil," Ryder called to me, and then took a seat at a secluded table with a view of the street. He had my plate of pastries in front of him and was busy tearing the corner off my chocolate croissant.

I watched him for a moment as he placed the stolen piece of food in his mouth and chewed on it thoughtfully. His jaw worked at the food, his throat moving once as he swallowed. I tore my eyes from his Adam's apple just in time to watch his eyes lift under thick eyelashes. He just stared at me, waiting for me to do something, waiting for me to make the next move. Obviously he planned on eating everything on my plate. And obviously I couldn't let him do that. I settled something in my heart, something that felt like warning, and decided that I was obligated to eat breakfast with Ryder after he paid for it…. and before he could eat it all.

"Why am I Dr. Evil?" I followed him over, wondering if I had ever wanted to put up a fight. "I should be Inspector Gadget and *you* should be Dr. Evil." I sat down heavily on the chair as if I was being held there against my will and forcefully pulled at the plate so that it was more on my side of the table than his.

"Inspector Gadget?" Ryder's face clouded in confusion and then cleared just as quickly. "You're thinking of Dr. Claw. Dr. Evil is from Austin Powers."

It was my turn to be confused. "I've never seen Austin Powers."

"Are you serious? That's kind of like a crime against humanity," Ryder shook his head at me and then reached for my croissant again.

"It's not a crime against humanity," I announced obviously.

"It's kind of a crime," Ryder argued. "I can't believe you've never seen Austin Powers. It's like your life isn't even complete right now.

He had no idea.

I rolled my eyes at him and then made room when Tarryn brought over our hot drinks. I took a long sip of my macchiato, suddenly realizing what I looked like. I brushed at hairline, pushing back nonexistent frizz. "I think I'll survive."

"Well, just to be sure, we can watch it at Phoenix's tonight. He has the complete set," Ryder finished decisively. "Really, thinking you'll survive and knowing you will are two totally different things."

A thought occurred to me, an ugly, horrible, awful thought and before I could talk myself out of it I had to find out. "Why are you being nice to me?" I blurted out with no tact whatsoever.

Without even a second to digest my question, Ryder answered, "I'm not being nice to you. We're arguing about a movie."

I slumped back in my chair, completely dizzy. He was right of course. But arguing also kind of felt like flirting…. not any kind of flirting I had ever done before, not the kind that guaranteed a boyfriend that same day or the kind that would help groom me for my future career… but still, maybe this was a different kind of flirting altogether? A more normal and safe version. Or maybe Ryder was right; maybe we were just fighting over an obscure movie.

"You look confused," Ryder noted. He was staring at me over the rim of his Chai Tea. I could smell the strong spices from over here. I felt my insides melt a little at the picture of Ryder, holding his coffee cup with both of his absurdly masculine hands. I imagined his fingertips calloused from playing his guitar and his palms rough like sandpaper. His gray eyes were depthless silver, intense but playful. His lips twisted to a soft smile. This was Saturday morning Ryder, this was relaxed and playful Ryder and my heart started beating double time on instinct.

Because relaxed Ryder couldn't be more dangerous.

Good thing he had Kenna.

Good thing I had Chase.

Or anybody else I wanted.

"I was just wondering what you were doing here and how you know the staff so well," I improvised, dropping my gaze to the pastries in front of me.

"I know Tarryn because I work here too. I *am* the staff. I usually work after school though and Sunday afternoons. I'm here now because my dad has been in love with this place since we moved here and even though we live downtown, he makes me bring him coffee every Saturday morning…. and every night after work…. and every Sunday afternoon…. and every time we are in a ten mile radius." Ryder's face lit up into a huge smile while he talked about his dad. His home-life happiness was infectious and I couldn't stop the smile that turned my mouth. I took a big bite of scone to hide my reaction and stared down into my drink.

"So does your mom like the coffee here just as much, or is this strictly Mr. Sutton's addiction?" I asked with a mouth full of food.

"Dr. Sutton," Ryder corrected gently. "My dad's a music theory professor at the University of Omaha. A *doctor* of music theory."

"Dr. Sutton," I corrected in a soft voice. "And mom?"

"My mom passed away when I was little," Ryder explained a bit roughly. "So it's just me, and my dad and my Uncle Matt."

"My dad died when I was a baby too," I announced and then immediately regretted the casual proclamation. I meant to sound understanding but it came out like I was bragging. Or maybe not bragging, but definitely not remorseful. Ryder stared at me from across the table, taking me in. He didn't offer a reply but his brow furrowed together between his eyebrows like he was seriously thinking this conversation over. Ugh. "Your uncle lives with you?" I asked just to change the subject.

"Yeah, he's my dad's much younger brother. He's only ten years older than me and he's living with us while he goes to college." Ryder explained, the light returned to his face and I relaxed a little bit into the comfort of having an interesting conversation.

"So your house is like a bachelor pad? Three guys living together? I can only imagine what your laundry situation is like," I joked even though my own laundry situation was currently a nightmare. My mother insisted on leaving everything for our housekeeper though and since I didn't even know how to turn the washing machine on I was inclined to follow at least that edict.

"Hey, it's not so bad. My dad has all the chores divvied up. Uncle Matt cleans the house, dad does the laundry and I do the cooking. We make it work," Ryder's grin widened and I couldn't tell if he was joking or telling the truth about the division of work.

"You do the cooking? Like on a regular basis?" I almost choked on scone. I did not like knowing Ryder could cook, not at all. The knowledge did funny things to my bones, making them clack together at the same time they felt like they were melting into warm puddles inside my skin.

"Don't look so surprised! I can grill a peanut butter and jelly sandwich with the best of them," Ryder laughed, reaching for what was left of my chocolate croissant.

"Did you say grill?" So obviously he was joking.

"Yes ma'am," he answered seriously. "Are you telling me you've never slathered your PB&J's in butter and then fried them?"

I shook my head quickly at the disgusting idea. I wasn't allowed to eat peanut butter ever, let alone slathered it in butter....

"Ivy, you haven't seen Austin Powers, you've never had a fried PB&J.... I'm starting to seriously worry about you. What kind of life do you live anyway?"

"You don't even want to know," I mumbled unable to keep the depressing truth out of my tone.

"Speaking of food, this is the most I've ever seen you eat. Hangover cure?" Ryder eyed the crumbs on the plate, the only evidence left of my delicious breakfast.

"Mmm-mmm," I contradicted. "I was just hungry. I'm six-months sober remember?"

"Yep, how could I forget? You act like *such* a desperate drunk usually," Ryder sounded unconvinced and skeptical of my alleged stint in rehab and for some absurd reason his cynical tone made my heart swell in my chest, pushing against the cage of my breastbone, flaring hope in the darkest places of my soul. When I didn't say anything though, Ryder continued in what could have been considered an attack. "But seriously, you never eat at lunch. I thought you were one of those girls with an eating disorder or that thought you could impress boys by how little you consume. Because here's a piece of advice, boys like girls that can eat entire meals."

"I don't need you to tell me what boys like. And I'm not one of those girls," I rasped out in a defensive whisper, knowing I basically did have an eating disorder but not because I didn't see myself correctly or was worried about weight gain. It was my mother and her completely f-ed up view of reality. "I love to eat." I said that part louder; confidence was easier with truth behind it.

"So why not at school?" Ryder pressed. "Are you trying to impress Chase? Because I promise you, he could care less what you eat for lunch."

"It has nothing to do with impressing any boy," I argued, feeling myself bristle at his ridiculous accusation.

"Then other girls? Kenna?" His voice dropped to a concerned whisper. His gray eyes pinned me to my seat no matter how desperately I wanted to bolt from the café. This conversation was awkward and intrusive and there was absolutely no way I could open up to him. Even though suddenly, desperately... I wanted to. For the first time in my life I wanted to explain everything to someone outside of our circle. Those kinds of feelings were stupid and dangerous and yet there they were anyway.

"Not Kenna," I forced myself to hold back the sarcastic bitterness that came out of nowhere. Ryder really thought I would compare myself to perfect Kenna Lee? Not a chance.

Like his girlfriend was this icon of everything I wanted to be in life. *Psht.*

Still it kind of bothered me how much it bothered me.....

Ryder looked at me expectantly. He sat waiting for me to open up to him about some fake disorder, like a random breakfast was enough to appoint him my sobriety sponsor.

I had enough of counselors during rehabilitation. If you could even call them that.... droves of women constantly coming to Nix's defense, singing his praise and bragging about his bedroom prowess. God, it was disgusting. And then when we did get down to business, to my issues, there was no real help offered or solutions given. They were sponges that absorbed every last piece of information and sent it right along to Nix. Six months in intensive therapy was merely a tool to uncover every last one of my secrets and scoot me right back to the assembly line with all the other mindless Stepford robots.

I had every reason to distrust Ryder's concern and even more so his "listening ear." Still, the silver in his eyes glinted with honesty; his mouth was pressed into a sincerely grim line. He cared. He actually wanted to hear about my problems.

What was even more, it seemed like he truly wanted to help.

And I wanted to let him.

I could have compared notes all day long, but Ryder was not one of those brain-washed women that would go running back to Nix the minute I spilled my guts. Ryder was safe.

Following a morning of firsts that was the first time in my entire life I had thought that. Never before had I believed someone or something was completely safe.

A part of me was wholly and utterly shattered by that knowledge and the hope that sprung up with it. The other part of me cowered in fear and shame, just waiting for me to blow this up, to destroy it just like everything else in my life.

The words were falling from my mouth before I could stop them, "My mom is really strict about what I eat."

Not a lie. And probably the most honest thing I had ever said to a boy.

"So strict you can't eat *anything*?" Ryder tried to joke, but the expression in his eyes never relaxed and his hand slid forward on the table as if he were getting ready to grab mine.

Whether to run or to hold I didn't know.

"Sometimes," I admitted, hoping it wasn't too much. I felt myself still underneath his calculating gaze. He was trying to sort truth from my reputation for bullshit. And I didn't blame him. But I also couldn't look him in the eye and silently plead with him to let it go, but to also believe me. He was too perceptive, too wise and with one long look at my face I would give away too much. I would open up about everything, about how eating was the least of my problems and that there was so much more to the twisted home life of Ivy Pierce.

"Ivy, do you want to come home with me for breakfast?" Ryder asked in a soft, sincere voice. His question landed on the table out of nowhere; hitting me hard with a longing I didn't quite understand. Suddenly his body relaxed into his chair and his hands rested casually as he crossed his arms over his chest. "My uncle always makes a big thing of eggs and hash browns on Saturday mornings. In fact, they're probably waiting for me now. It's like his one meal that he can make, and I get the morning off." I looked up just in time to watch Ryder gesture to Tarryn that he was ready for his to-go coffees. The small café had filled in around us, the later time drawing in all kinds of diversity in the crowd. Some people were clearly still working, despite the weekend, some were family-types on their way to kids' activities, some were couples in love, some were merely picking up coffee on their walk of shame home, and some were just enjoying their Saturday morning with nothing better to do than sip lattes and eat fruit tartlets.

I thought about Ryder's offer, wondering where it came from. Was he taking me home because he thought eggs and mushy potatoes could solve an eating disorder I wouldn't even talk about with him? Or was he more interested in solving other problems of mine? Because by the way he was staring at me from across the table I could feel how his concern spread roots far deeper than intense dieting.

A guy at the counter interrupted his order to let out a low whistle and soft cat call. I turned, distracted from Ryder's question, but the truth was I felt thankful for the three seconds I was gifted to think this over. "That is one nice car," guy at the counter remarked, his voice a hushed reverent purr.

And just like that I snapped back to the depressing, no-win reality that was my life. Without even laying my eyes on the car I could feel the identity of the driver in the deepest marrow of my bones. A few more manly catcalls sounded out from over the mellow vocals of Over the Rhine playing softly in the background café sound system.

Despite the ominous intuition sitting at the base of my spine, I reluctantly gave into curiosity and turned my head just as Nix exited the driver's side and slid the valet an absurd tip before ducking into the building. I couldn't actually see the tip, but I knew from experience it would be enormous.

"I can't, Ryder. Thanks for the offer though." I wanted to investigate Ryder's reason for inviting me over. Pity? Concern? Actual interest? But with Nix so close my skin started to crawl. I hated the idea of Nix sharing the same city block as Ryder, let alone the same oxygen. And if Nix spotted me over here, no doubt he would make some excuse to spend time with me. Or maybe he wouldn't even bother making excuses anymore. Maybe we were beyond that.

Something deep and innate warned me to keep Ryder as far from my evil godfather as possible.

I stood up abruptly, anxious to put some space between us and get back home where things were ugly but predictable. "Alright, Sutton, thanks for the coffee, but I have things to do."

"Sure you do," Ryder grinned at me as if I was some kind of semi-entertaining side show.

"See you later tonight," I smiled winningly and turned my back on my breakfast date.

"Later," he mumbled.

I escaped out the door, but my thoughts immediately leapt to the night ahead of me. I should definitely not be as excited about the party as I suddenly was. Ryder was so off limits and not even interested.

Plus there was Chase.

Ugh. I needed to get my life together. Forget them both. And focus on just surviving the next two years. Focus on my trust fund and how it would change my life.

Somehow I knew that was way too much to ask.

Chapter Fifteen

"Hey, gorgeous," Chase called.

I practically ran from the door of my building to meet him at the passenger side door of his car, which was not easy in heeled boots. Nix and my mother were watching from way above us, I knew it instinctively and I was in a hurry to get out of here, to get far, far, far away from them. I gave my most charming smile when Chase opened the door for me and threw my arms around his neck in an exaggerated show of affection.

"Hey, yourself," I whispered against his neck.

I felt his surprise when our bodies collided, but it took no time for him to return the gesture and wrap his arms around my waist. He stayed the perfect gentleman however and released me exactly on time. I gave him one more happy-grin and then slid onto the cool leather seat.

The warm autumn day had turned uncomfortably chilly once the sun went down. If only the full moon offered as much heat as the sun. My pleated, high-waist shorts did nothing to prevent the cold from seeping into my skin, despite the thick charcoal tights I wore underneath them. I hugged my oversized purse to my chest, trying to fight the chill that had seeped into my bones, but it wasn't until Chase pulled out onto the main street that I felt capable of finding warmth again.

"It's good to see you," Chase breathed a little self-consciously. My gut clenched in frustration. The curse worked fast, I knew that from too many years of experience, and I hated that he was already starting to feel attached.

At the same time what choice did I have?

Or he have?

"It's good to see you too," I replied. "I'm excited for this party! Last night was so awful; you have no idea. I need to get away for a while."

"Oh yeah? My family's kind of crazy too," Chase laughed.

"Not as crazy as mine, trust me," I sighed. "But what makes your family crazy?" I asked because I genuinely wanted to know; even though I knew I would win a who-has-worse-problems debate, I couldn't imagine Chase having actual issues with his parents. He seemed way too stable and adjusted.

"Ugh, mostly my parents," he groaned. "They are so stressed out about college, it's out of control. My older brother went to Northwestern on an academic full-ride and they have equally high hopes for me. But recently I was thinking maybe instead of division one traditional, I would pursue something smaller, something liberal arts focused...." Chase trailed off as if waiting for me to completely reject the idea or at least try to talk him out of it. Since I was basically obsessed with the idea of college and knew I would never get the chance to go I generally tried not to judge other peoples choices. I wasn't going to start with Chase's, he knew himself better than I did and besides all that small-liberal-arts-college-thing kind of sounded cool. When I stayed silent he continued, "So anyway, my parents are pretty flipped over that. They don't think I can get a decent education and especially not a decent job. Last night they bribed me with this insane spring break trip if I would burn all my unapproved-by-them letters of acceptance."

I laughed at the absurdity of his parents' incentive, "What is an insane spring break trip anyway?"

"Cancun, no questions asked, limitless allowance," he ticked off as if each idea were more ridiculous than the last. "I don't want any of that. I want to go to school for something I like, something I'm passionate about. Besides, I don't believe for one second that my mom could actually not ask any questions. It would be the third degree as soon as I got home and probably an appointment to test for STD's."

"Which would, of course, be smart after an *insane* trip to Cancun," I laughed and Chase joined in.

"You have to know I'm not like that," he grumbled and I did know. No way was Chase the one night stand with Random Girls kind of guy. Which was going to make this so much harder than I wanted it to be. He had one week left.

"I know," I agreed softly. "So what is it that you want to do? What's at a liberal arts college that isn't anywhere else?"

"Uh," Chase stalled a minute while playing with the dials on the radio. "I'm thinking about Carleton College. It's in Minnesota so not so far from home, and they have a smaller campus, small classrooms and all that."

"Okay," I smiled patiently at him. "And what would you be learning in those classrooms?"

He gave me a crooked smile, staring at me with those deep blue eyes of his and flashing his dimples before turning his eyes back to the road. It was like he was deciding if he could trust me or not.

But the thing was.... he couldn't.

Or at least he shouldn't.

"Social science," he finally admitted, sounding completely embarrassed.

I fumbled with thoughts of how to turn that into career and came up completely empty-handed. "No wonder your parents are concerned for your future," I joked.

"Hey now," he shot me a playful glower and then explained "I want to run campaigns, like political campaigns. Start at the city and state level, like mayoral and state senators and then eventually work my way up to larger scale elections."

"One day, presidential?" I guessed. I admired his ambition, his quiet dreams that were held with such obviously fierce resolve.

"Maybe," he answered quietly, his cheeks heating with an embarrassed flush. "One day."

"I love that," I whispered. And I did. We were silent for a full minute before I announced decidedly, "Don't take the trip of debauchery. You *need* to go to Carleton."

His cheeks returned to their natural tanned tone and he nodded his head enthusiastically, "Well, when you put it like that... and just when I had decided to sell my soul for a week of cheap tequila and hookers. Mom will be so disappointed."

Laughter burst out of my mouth and Chase joined in. He reached out subtly and grabbed my hand, holding it gently in his. My breath caught in my throat at the super sweet gesture and I relaxed into the leather seat. We drove through a neighborhood close to Creighton University in north downtown Omaha. The houses were big and old here, some pathetically run down, and some immaculately taken care of. Poor mixed with old wealth, multicultural diversity mixed Mexican restaurants, specialized hair salons and ethnic markets. College students layered the area that surrounded Creighton's brick academic buildings and their brand new soccer stadium. This area was an intense mixture of culture but still it felt exactly like home, like everything that made up Omaha.

"I'm sure your future still holds plenty of opportunity for reckless debauchery. No need to worry." I teased.

"Oh, I'm not worried," Chase assured me with mock gravity.

He pulled the car over to the side of the street in front of a Victorian-inspired two story house. Phoenix's house had a long front porch painted pastel yellow with a white porch swing that swayed in the cold night breeze. The yard was neatly trimmed where grass was allowed to grow, or in this case die with winter coming soon; but most of the yard was mulched and made into flower beds that held the remains of withered stems and dilapidated plants. There was a short, knee high picket fence that lined the property and didn't really make much sense to me. It seemed too short to be of any real purpose and too tall to just be decorative. The front door was open, letting light spill out onto the front porch and cast shadows along the curving sidewalk that led to the house. I could see lots of movement just beyond the screen door, rowdy teenagers making the most of a no-parents-around scenario.

Chase's hand gave mine a squeeze and I exhaled suddenly. I hadn't realized how nervous I was for this party until just now. Excited, anxious, even a bit hopeful, but the peer pressure and teenage revelry that waited just beyond the door weighed down my constricting chest. Memories of my last house party, of Sam and our breakup... of everything that happened that night rushed at my emotions like a speeding train while I stayed trapped and tied to the rails, just waiting for it to run over me.... a helpless damsel in distress silently screaming to be rescued.
I was kind of pathetic...

"Hey, we don't have to go if you're not up for it," Chase assured me. His voice stayed calm and soothing, completely out of place from the atmosphere waiting for us inside.

"No, it's fine," I said quickly, hoping to shake off my own fears as much as his worry over me. "It's just been a while since... you know... I've been around all this." I gestured vaguely at the house and then jumped out of the car before I could let myself think about this any longer. My hand ripped out of Chase's in the process and after slamming the car door I stayed put until he could join me.

When he rounded the car and held out his hand to me again I took it quickly, breathing in the comforting warmth of Chase's skin over mine. I offered a confident smile that I did not feel and tried to push away all my worry. I just needed to remind myself that I was hanging out with Chase and nothing more. There would be no unnecessary drama tonight, no fights, or breakups or out of control drinking. Phoenix would only throw a completely relaxed, chill party. Nothing like the night of the accident.

A shiver wracked my body, but I fought it down. I found as much strength and control as I could, pulling on the set of skills I saved for when Nix was around and then walked up the little sidewalk to Phoenix's front door. Without knocking we entered the thrall and were immediately entrenched in party. The faint smell of casual narcotics drifted through the air and red plastic cups covered every available surface. A couple of kids I recognized from lunch but didn't really know were playing the Wii in the living room and there was intense, but good-natured shouting coming up from the basement. The kitchen was through the living room and dining room and that was where Chase led me, never letting go of my hand, never letting go of me.

We weaved through sweaty, drunken bodies and came up for air in a relatively empty kitchen. Phoenix turned around from the counter looking surprisingly sober although he was currently holding a bottle of cheap vodka in one hand and a two liter of Sierra Mist Cranberry Splash in the other.

"Ivy!" Phoenix bellowed. "You made it!"

"Hey, Phoenix," I called over the loud music pumping from an iDock on the counter.

He tilted his head to Chase and then wiggled both beverages at me with lanky arms looking all elbows and knees. I shook my head, "No thank you."

"Chase?"

Chase shook his head to decline and then brushed his hand across the dark gray Formica countertop testing it to see if it was sticky or not. When he was satisfied that it wasn't he leaned against it and pulled me next to him. I rested with my hip gently next to his, he was taller than me so mine fell a little below his, but the pressure of his body against mine helped ease the tension I felt creeping into my neck. His hand left mine to snake around my waist and I worked to keep a smile off my face when his hands splayed strong and confident against the thin silk of my top. Chase felt natural, easy. He was thoughtful and careful. I liked that. I liked that so much. But there wasn't much between us other than physical attraction and a little bit of easy banter.

If things were different I could get to know him, take things slow and actually let myself fall for him.

But things weren't different and I could never let myself go down that path again.

Not ever again.

"Not drinking tonight, Phoenix?" I asked. He had made a drink mixing the two liquids in his hand but then passed it off to the first girl who walked through the kitchen on her way to the backyard. She thanked him with a slight slur and droopy eyelids. She was for sure going to be puking that same drink up in no time.

"No thanks," Phoenix grunted. "My parents condone the parties, but they don't have to clean them up. I need to stay sober so I can make sure nobody gets sick on the furniture or carpet. Plus there's the hookups that have to be broken up, the breakables that need saving and the noise level that has to remain neighborhood friendly."

"Really? You always stay sober at your own parties? It's like you're babysitting everyone. That doesn't seem fair," I sympathized with the host.

Chase gave a soft laugh, "Phoenix always stays sober, it doesn't matter whose party we're at."

Phoenix winked at me before grabbing another plastic cup. He walked over to the freezer to fill it with ice and then with soda and soda alone. "Some of us like to have fun the old fashioned way," he explained. "And I'm not the only one."

"You too?" I asked Chase, craning my neck so I could look him in the eyes.

He just shrugged in response; I felt the movement of his shoulder against my back. His hand around my waist gripped my hip and pulled me closer to him. His body felt warm against me, his hand sturdy, holding me possessively to him.

"Well, don't I just feel like the worst kind of heathen," I grumbled. "If you guys don't like to drink, then why have these parties?" I asked, completely dumfounded.

More shrugging. Was it too much to ask for complete sentences?

"Is it a popularity thing?" I pressed.

"It's more like, everyone knows my parents are super relaxed about this kind of thing so they all expect me to have them. If I don't announce a party, one inevitably happens anyway just because people start to show up and then they call their friends and more people show up. If I invite people over, I have more say over when they happen. Plus, I usually wait for my parents to be out of town so that if the cops ever show up at least they won't be charged for allowing minors to drink and smoke. Also, I need to arrange for my sisters and brother to go somewhere for the night."

I gaped at Phoenix. "How very responsible of you, but it seems like a lot of work when you don't even want this trouble to begin with."

"That's not true," Phoenix defended and gestured around the house with two outstretched arms. "I like having people over. I like having parties. I just don't like to lose control."

I stood quiet long enough for our silence to be interrupted by violent retching coming from just outside the back door. I shot Phoenix a doubtful look but he just grinned in response.

"Okay, maybe I don't like the cleanup part, but at least that was outside. My mom has enough flowers, they destroy my allergies anyway,"

Phoenix's eyes were glinting with mischief and I couldn't tell if he was being serious or not.

"Really?" I asked unable to keep the skepticism out of my tone.

"His Zen is genetic. You should meet his parents. You could rob them at gunpoint and they would still ask you to dinner and make sure you got everything valuable in the house," Chase explained and I wondered if that was true.

"Which wouldn't be much," Phoenix laughed.

"The weed has to be expensive," I countered and then wondered if that was appropriate.

Phoenix just grinned wider, turning his happy face into a cartoon. "True. Very true. They could always take the drugs."

"But then again you just give them away at your parties, so why bother with the gun?" Chase spoke up.

"Better to get them out of my house then have my little sisters find them," Phoenix's expression finally turned grim and I realized that maybe these parties were part of protecting his family.

If that was the case then I could understand his motives.

I had my own little sister to protect.

"Well, well, well if it isn't our boy Fred," Phoenix's smile came back in full force and he reached out a hand to do the boy-hand-shake thing with Ryder.

"Fred?" I asked before I could stop myself.

Ryder turned his eyes on me and held my gaze for a long moment before answering. I felt like he was drinking me in, absorbing me into his reality. I shivered against Chase, not sure how I felt about the raw intensity Ryder always looked at me with. It was unnerving and made me feel vulnerable and exposed. I decided that I absolutely hated it.

At the same time, I loved it.

"Sure, Fred," he responded, his voice low and a bit gruff. "And Shaggy," he nodded at Phoenix. "And Scooby."

I felt Chase's chest vibrate with laughter behind me.

"Shaggy makes sense," I snapped my head toward Phoenix. "You look exactly like a Shaggy."

"Groovy."

"But you smell way too good to be a dog, sorry," I looked up at Chase. His eyes twinkled down at me, his expression soft and sweet. "So that makes you, Daphne?" I asked Kenna when she trailed into the kitchen, two of her friends on either side.

"Yep!" She grinned at me and then threw her arms around Ryder's waist. "We're auditioning for a Velma. Ivy, you in?"

"I'll think about it," I said pensively. "I look like a lumpy pumpkin in orange, but it could open all kinds of doors for me as a private eye. So, yeah... maybe."

"You do understand becoming Velma means you have to have friends?" Ryder warned with a note too close to serious for me.

"I have friends," I grumbled. I leaned back into Chase, inhaling his warm comfort.

"Boyfriends," one of Kenna's friends snorted.

"Boyfriend," Chase corrected and then looked down at me to make sure it was okay to say that. I waggled my eyebrows at him flirtatiously, but felt my heart turn five shades darker with the knowledge he wouldn't be for long.

Kenna cleared her throat and tried to cover for her rude friends. "Ivy, do you know Blair and Reagan?"

"Nice to meet you both." I tried to be charming and friendly and.... nonthreatening, but there was no way a friendship with any of these girls stood a chance.

"Whatever," Reagan, a girl with rich chocolate shoulder length layers and a spattering of freckles underneath artsy, green glasses sighed. She didn't even seem like the snotty type. She totally came off as the nose-in-a-book-wouldn't-hurt-a-fly type. It was me. I brought out the worst in all of humanity. "Ready, Ken?"

"Where are you ladies off to?" Ryder asked looking Kenna directly in the eye. A weird kind of tension filled the room and it made me wonder if the happy couple had been fighting earlier.

"The backyard," Kenna replied sweetly, kissing Ryder's jaw line.

"Are you kidding me?" Ryder did not even try to conceal his irritation and I had to assume the backyard was generally the worst of the partying.

"Relax, Ryder," Kenna whispered sharply. "Blair just wants to find Hayden and then I'll come back in."

"Whatever, Ken," Ryder wiggled out of Kenna's arms. Kenna's pretty face scrunched irritably and she turned her back on him in a gesture of dismissal. Ryder turned away from her too, but straight to me. The tension in the air grew thick and ugly and settled a heavy silence over us until Ryder broke it. "Ready?" he asked, his gaze holding mine fiercely.

"F-for what?" I was afraid of the answer, his eyes had melted into gunmetal pools of intensity and I didn't want to be caught in the crossfire of whatever was going on with him and Kenna. I hated that he put me between them, like he was using me to get back at his girlfriend. At the same time, this was the first time I had been used against another female. I mean, guys had left girls for me, sure, but never with the intention of going back to the relationship. And even now I knew Ryder had no intention of leaving Kenna for me. This was innocent.

Well as innocent as trifling manipulation went.

I was used to way worse behavior than this.

"Austin Powers? Remember? We have to make sure your sins against humanity are absolved?" The teasing tone was back in his voice but he was studiously ignoring Kenna and her friends like they weren't even there. Kenna rolled her eyes and pushed her friend Reagan through the kitchen and to the back door. Her silky black hair floated in waves around her slender shoulders. She was somehow prettier when she was mad, her green eyes alive with a fire that was usually dimmed and subtle.

"Uh, sure," I answered inarticulately. "Ryder thinks my life isn't complete until I watch this dumb movie," I explained to Chase who was watching me with mild amusement. "Up for it?"

"First of all, Ryder's right. You *need* to watch this movie, it's absolutely essential to your present and future happiness. And I am up for it, but first I need to find Nick Barrett and rip him a new asshole." Chase kind of mumbled his last sentence while staring out the window over the kitchen sink. Something had apparently caught his attention because he was letting me go and almost sprinting out the back door before I could ask him any questions.

I gave a curious glance to Phoenix but his attention was on the backyard too. "That little shit," he mumbled and flew off after Chase.

"What in the world?" I turned to Ryder.

"Nick Barrett's the only good keeper we have and he's missed the last three indoor games. Chase is one of the captains and it looks like he's about to find out why." Ryder explained. He hardly glanced in the backyard. I would have loved to turn around to find out what was going on, but Ryder had hypnotized me with one of his paralyzing looks again and I was helpless against his power.

"Soccer stuff?" I clarified since I kind of felt like Ryder was speaking a foreign language.

"Yep. Let's go," Ryder commanded and then turned his back on me. "They'll come up and find us when they're done."

"Up?" Somehow Ryder had reduced me to one word replies. I was turning into a caveman.

"To Phoenix's room."

123

And then he was gone, through the kitchen, the dining room and to the staircase in the living room that led to the bedrooms. I gulped loudly but no one was left to hear me. Released from Ryder's hold I glanced in the backyard to take note of the heated argument between Chase, Phoenix and a scruffy Jesus-impersonator with long hair and barely filled in facial hair, who I could only assume was Nick Barrett.

"Let's go, Pierce," Ryder called from halfway up the stairs.

I gulped again but obeyed. Shouldn't someone besides me be concerned that I was going to a quiet bedroom with Ryder alone? I mean, right? I could not be trusted. Not at all.

A million different excuses ran around in my head, all vying to be the first one spoken out loud. But instead of doing the right thing, the smart thing, I snapped my mouth closed and followed Ryder up the stairs and said a quick prayer that Chase would follow soon.

Chapter Sixteen

Phoenix's room was the last room down of four, just after a bathroom and linen closet and completely overstuffed with furniture. A single bed, two dressers, a tattered love seat, an old school plywood TV stand and box TV set that I wasn't even sure was in color and then a battered oak desk with swiveling computer chair. The door to the walk in closet hung open, revealing a space a quarter the size of his bedroom, an enormous amount of clothing for a guy, or really anyone, hung haphazardly on plastic hangers and a full and obviously well-used drum set. Posters of bands from the eighties till now were tacked up around the fake wood paneling and the door frame was decorated with ticket stubs I went ahead and assumed were from concerts.

I pressed my lips together, trying to hide my equal disgust and intrigue in the space. My first instinct was that the room was filthy. I spun around so I could take it all in and decided it was cluttered but clean. Ryder bent down to fiddle with the DVD player and I walked into the closet to better inspect Phoenix's drum set.

I was a musician of sorts. Not like Ryder and Phoenix, not like in a band kind of musician. But my mother had followed the traditions of our circle and I had taken piano and singing lessons since I could walk and talk. Nix firmly believed music was in inherent part of what made us and so I had been classically trained in both.

I wanted to hate my lessons, hate my skill…. my talent another reminder of what my life dissolved into. I was a showpiece, a trophy wife, a worker bee if gender roles were reversed, sent out into the world to make money and bring it home to our king. I shuddered at the analogy.

But I decided a long time ago that I couldn't hate music. Even though it represented every ancient curse I wanted to run from, it was as much ingrained in my soul as the desire to live was. And it had become an escape. When I played the world disappeared behind me, melted into the recesses of my mind and I existed in a way that I normally didn't.

Music felt like something I could control, my fingers went where I wanted them to, commanded the keys and created something beautiful. When everything else in my life felt out of my control, this was the one thing I owned. And something I *needed* to keep breathing. I had to be careful that I never used it along with the curse, but that wasn't a problem for me since I despised the curse more than anything. More than even Nix.

"Is this where you guys practice?" I teased when I felt Ryder behind me. I stood just inside the doorway to the closet; the space was big but cramped with the drum set taking up so much room. Ryder's heat was on my back, his breath floated over the nape of my neck.

"Just Phoenix," Ryder answered softly.

I ran my forefinger over the cold, sharp metal of the high hat. I stepped forward a little to separate myself from Ryder and then tapped my fingers on the underside of the cymbals so they made that brassy sound I kind of loved.

I felt Ryder completely still behind me, as if he were coming to some kind of incredible revelation. He suddenly reached forward and grabbed my forearm, spinning me around to face him. Crippling fear and anxious hope sprung up inside me simultaneously and I lifted my gaze slowly to his, hoping... well, I didn't know what I was hoping for.

His eyes weren't on my face though. They were staring down at my upturned wrist. With the hand that held me in place, his thumb moved back and forth across the inside of my wrist, rubbing gently at the skin. His expression was so fiercely intimate, so intensely determined that even though I knew what he was doing, what he was trying to see I couldn't stop him.

I needed to stop him, and now. But I couldn't make myself move away from him, I couldn't make myself hide the dangerous truth that would ruin everything for me if Nix found out. And out of all the dangerous reasons to snatch my hand out of his grasp, I was also partly stunned. After being so very careful to conceal the hidden word, I couldn't even fathom how Ryder saw through the thick concealer or how I missed even the smallest piece to cover.

Just under the base of my thumb, the black ink had been left exposed. How Ryder knew there would be more, I had no idea. The revealed marking could just have easily been a pen scratch or dirt smudge. Maybe it was the delicate scrawl or the greenish tint that gave the tattoo away, but either way it reinforced the idea that if you wanted to keep a tattoo hidden, the wrist was a really stupid place to put it.

The pressure of his thumb increased as he worked to rub away the cover up. Slowly the thick cream distorted and more of the full piece revealed itself. Ryder paused for a moment, transferring my hand to his other while he wiped his thumb against the collar of his black t-shirt. The cover up left a pale smudge where his collarbone was hidden under the fabric of his shirt and a shot of lust pushed through me. His eyes met mine as he transferred my hand back and continued to rub at the tattoo, exposing pieces of it with every swipe of his thumb.

His eyes were liquid silver, depthless and raw with perception. He was seeing a part of me no one had seen before, save for the poor tattoo artist I manipulated into marking a minor. Ryder discovered a piece of me that was intended only for me, a piece I never planned on sharing with *anyone*.

Finally, Ryder released me from his stare and his gaze traveled slowly, so slowly, from mine to my wrist. "Blackheart," he mumbled the word like a curse. Or a caress.

The word hung in the charged air between us. The small, fancy script looped around itself and created a pretty effect to the terribly ugly word.

"Blackheart," I concurred quietly.

"What are you, a pirate?" he tried to joke, but even he couldn't crack a smile. His voice strained over his words, his expression tight with some knowledgeable instinct that should have terrified me.

"Something like that," I answered without meaning.

"What else do you have?" he took a step closer to me. My breathing hitched in my lungs until it stopped completely and I instinctively took a step back until my back was balanced on the corner of the door frame.

"Why do you think I have anything else?" I gasped.

"You didn't want anyone to see this," He reached down without looking and took my wrist back in his strong grasp. His entire hand circled around the bone there and his fingers easily overlapped each other. I felt fragile and small with his hand so possessively on me, covering the hideous word now that it was exposed. "And it means something, even if you're not going to tell me what it is. Instinct tells me this is not your only secret, Ivy."

His words were like pin pricks in my carefully armored skin and I felt myself pull my wrist from his grasp, even reluctantly. I could have used my other, free hand, but the severity of the moment demanded I use this hand, some symbol of confession I didn't even fully understand myself.

I gripped at the hem of my shirt as if it weighed a thousand pounds instead of the delicate silk it actually was. Ryder's gaze fell immediately to the action and slowly, ever so slowly, arguing with myself the entire time, I pulled my shirt to just below the underwire of my bra. My stomach was completely exposed to Ryder's full stare, but, even though I was still trying to talk myself out of it, I trusted him. I trusted him to see this.

I trusted him to see more of me than anyone ever had, both physically and figuratively.

I looked down at my exposed stomach and quickly licked three of my fingers and rubbed at the second tattoo that ran across the ribs on my left side. I had to wet my fingers several more times to remove the concealer completely but eventually the words were revealed.

Ryder's own hand came up deliberately as if he were afraid to frighten me, as if I were a wounded animal he was trying to sooth. He brushed his fingers across the identical cursive script almost reverently. His brow furrowed deeply and I wondered what emotion was playing out in his head. Confusion? Pity? Lust?

Only it wasn't lust. Not by a long shot.

"My soul is free," he whispered into the silence with the reverence the phrase was meant to hold. "My soul is free."

He repeated the words and my heart expanded at the incantation. The words I had chosen so carefully held the deepest meaning of my existence. I loved the way they sounded out loud, how they fell out of his lips and off his tongue with care.

"What do they mean Ivy?" he asked while his hand fell back to my wrist and his thumb rubbed once more along the word that was inked there.

"Nothing really," I lied so obviously I was shocked when he simply waited for me to say more without calling me on my bullshit. "They're just reminders. Things I need to remember."

Ryder looked back down at the words on my stomach and wrist and when his eyes met mine the silver had been turned to gray granite, intense with anger and frustration and something that looked like…. concern. "And why do you need to remind yourself that your *soul is free*?" He bit out the words making them sound like he was dragging them across rough gravel. The reverence fell away and left only hatred for words he didn't even understand.

I mashed my lips together, afraid to answer him, afraid the truth would come pouring out of me eager to divulge every last sordid detail of my f-ed up life. The thought was so ridiculous, the action so close to completing itself that I burst out into laughter before I could burst into tears instead.

"Ryder, seriously, they're just words. Just little sayings I thought were…. whatever. I don't really have a cool story or anything. I was drunk one night in Arizona and bored and I convinced this guy to ink me. It's no big deal. Honestly, I kind of regret it," I rambled. I took a step away from Ryder and began straightening Phoenix's hanging shirts and jeans nervously.

"You were drunk during rehab?" Ryder pressed skeptically.

My mouth snapped shut when I realized I said Arizona out loud and that Ryder had correctly associated the time with my "rehab."

"And I don't believe you regret it," he accused, reaching for my hand again but I stepped out of his range, putting the drums between us.

My shirt fell back down to cover my stomach and a surge of panic zipped through me with my tattoos exposed. My mind spun with all the ways Nix could find out about them. Why was my generation constantly documenting their lives for the world to see? If I was tagged in some candid shot online, my life would be ruined in a strangled heartbeat and the random Facebook friend would have no idea how they sent me to my death.

Not that I had that many Facebook friends to brag about....

But still.

"You don't regret it," Ryder pushed, his expression flashing with determination. "Otherwise you wouldn't cover them up so carefully. Why do you need to cover a tattoo that your shirt already covers, Ivy?"

"You wouldn't understand," I bit out. I could explain this. Or I could brush it off like it was nothing. Or I could just walk away; remove myself entirely from this situation. Which is what I wanted to do.... but what was exactly not happening.

"What does the word 'blackheart' mean?" he changed his tactic, his voice softly begged with me to open up. He reached out his hand to me, stretching it across the void between us.

I melted, I couldn't help it. Nobody had ever cared enough to interrogate me like this, to get to the bottom of something I could possibly be *feeling*. "What do you think it means?" I tested a bit desperately.

"Because of all the guys?" he guessed accurately.

"How would you know?" I countered, trying to put him on the defensive, still not ready to make myself so vulnerable. Although, I was fighting a losing battle. If Ryder kept trying, kept putting all of him into these questions like this, like he wanted to know every single intimate detail about me, I was bound to give in. I felt raw from his investigation, completely rubbed down to the bone. Exposed.

"People talk, Ivy. *Especially* about you. All I have to do is listen," he explained gently. I winced at the compassion in his tone, at the pleading in his eyes for me to trust him. "Is that about Sam? Do you think you have a black heart because of Sam?"

I physically shuddered at his interrogation. How dare he! How dare he bring up Sam and assume that's where all my messed up issues came from. Sam was just the frosting on a screwed up, pathetic, life-ending cake. "Don't talk about Sam. You don't know anything about him," I ground out through clenched teeth. I wrapped my arms around my waist tightly, holding myself together, trying to protect everything hurt and broken inside... trying to protect Sam. Or at least his memory.

"I know he was the one driving that night, Ivy. I know he was the one drinking, not you. I know you can't blame yourself because he wrapped his car around a light post and sent himself to the hospital," he paused to let his words settle in. My chin started quivering before I registered that I was on the verge of crying and I looked up desperately at him, silently begging him to stop. "You do not have a black heart because some seventeen year old kid was stupid enough to drive intoxicated and recklessly ruin his life."

There was a full minute of silence between us as I tried to digest those words.... listen to them.... really *hear* them. But I already knew the truth. *Knew* it. There was no lying to myself. I had been over this same argument a million and thirteen times before, always trying to convince myself of the same thing.

"I know all that," I said so softly Ryder took a step forward to hear me better. "But here I am today. Walking. Going to school. Going to more parties. With *Chase*. And there will be more boys. After Chase. And after the guy after that. And I get to graduate high school. And live my life. And I won't look back at him, not ever. Not Sam, not Chase, not the dozen guys before them, or after them. I have to get out of here.... I have to." I paused for breath, to get something into my lungs, anything to keep from passing out. And then I announced with a tiny gesture toward myself, "Blackheart."

"Ivy, that-"

Whatever Ryder was going to say was cut off abruptly when Chase, Phoenix and Kenna walked into the room noisily. They called out our names and were laughing about something that happened downstairs.

Ryder held my gaze though, not turning, not even acknowledging them. Quietly, so only I would hear he said, "That's only true if you believe it, Ivy."

I nodded like his words had some deep impact on me, but the truth was I did believe it. All of it. Because it was true. His psychobabble was completely lost on me. But I didn't want to invite any more conversation with Ryder about it, so I turned my expression thoughtfully sad and just nodded.

Ryder let out a frustrated sigh, apparently my act wasn't Oscar worthy by a long shot.

"Ryder-"

He cut me off, turning his back on me. "I'm not going to tell anyone, Ivy."

He was disappointed in me.

But at least he knew the truth. At least his eyes were completely opened to the vapid, black hole of emotional trauma that I really was. Still the strong wave of his angry disillusionment punched me painfully in the stomach.

Ugh. *Ryder.* Why did I care so much?

"I was showing Ivy your drums," I heard Ryder announce after he left me alone in the closet.

I stood there battling with myself whether I could leave the closet and face the others or if I would need to pretend sickness so I could get Chase to take me home. I wanted to believe I was brave enough to face everyone, but I wasn't. I was weak, and selfish and....

"Hey, you okay?" Chase asked from the doorway. His happy, all-American face was pinched with concern. He glanced quickly over his shoulder as if gauging if he should confront Ryder or not.

"Actually, I'm kind of hiding," I admitted, realizing my decision as I said it out loud. "I'm sorry, this party is a little more than I can handle." I looked up at Chase from under my lashes and prayed for undeserved compassion.

"Do you want to go home?" he asked, chivalrous as ever.

"Do you mind taking me?"

"Not at all," he offered me a comforting smile. "Maybe you need to talk about it?"

"Maybe," I relented. "Maybe in the car."

He smiled down at me and I stepped into him, forcing him into a hug. I knew I wouldn't talk about this and I knew this was the best I could give him. His comforting arms helped ease the raw pain Ryder had ripped open and I relished in the easiness that came with Chase. I wasn't getting attached to Chase and that thought made it easier to inhale. I would be able to break up with him, even if the idea felt very similar to giving my favorite pet away. And though it would be difficult, it was doable. And that thought made it easier to exhale.

See? Blackheart.

I was right all along.

Chapter Seventeen

Thoughts of the night before attacked my emotions as I sat motionless in the passenger's seat of my mother's Escalade. We drove silently on the way to our Sunday visit with my little sister.

Usually I was dying to see Honor, make sure she was okay, and make sure the curse wasn't destroying her life... But last night replayed in my head like a destructive addiction.

How could I have been so stupid to let Ryder see my tattoo, first of all?

And then how could I have let his words affect me like that?

Blackheart. He *knew* better. Everyone knew better! Even people that didn't want to see the truth, that preferred ignorance is bliss and all that, *knew* better.

I was a borderline sociopath.

There wasn't an excuse in this world that covered my long list of sins. And that list would only lengthen unless I got the hell out of here.

"When we get there," my mother's melodic voice cut through the silence, "you need to be on your best behavior. I am not going to put up with any of your antics, Ivy. You *owe* me."

I wanted to ask, for what? Instead I nodded meekly, "I know. I'll be on my best behavior."

"Better than your best behavior," my mom pressed.

"Okay, yes. Better than my best."

I thought that promise would be enough to pacify her, but she had too much experience in all of this. "I mean it, Ivy. You have no idea what you put me through last spring. You have no idea what you put Nix through! And God, Smith was so concerned about you; it was like you were *his* daughter. He immediately blamed me, of course. Until I explained about the accident and what happened to that poor Sam Evans." She said *poor Sam Evans*, but I would have had to be deaf not to hear the smile in her voice... the excitement. "Still, Smith was so concerned about you, so worried. Honestly, it was a little sickening. I don't know what happened to him. There was a time when he adored me. He bought me that Tiffany necklace. You know the four karats one? Just because! He bought me that gorgeous piece of art *just because* and now look at him! I swear it was those cancer drugs. They screwed with his mind. He's not right. He shouldn't have Honor. Who knows when he'll turn on *her*? Then what? She's my daughter and I'll be damned before I let anything happen to her."

My mother rambled on and on like that until we pulled through the gated driveway of Smith Porter's gigantic West Omaha mansion. He was filthy rich, like more money than God loaded. It was what drew my mother to him in the first place, but he somehow clawed his way out of hell *and* my mother's greedy fingers. He must have been a monk in a former life, or Mother Theresa or something because to defeat stage four brain cancer and the curse was like legend status.

Maybe he was a super hero.

Honor certainly thought so, which made me immediately fall in love with him. Any man my mother hated and my sister loved was basically a saint in my book.

My mom pulled the car to a stop in front of the pillared front entryway of his huge modern estate and we exited the giant SUV in silence. My mother preferred demure-classy-Ivy over all other options and so I obliged her. She had the power to take away these visits and making sure Honor stayed as far away from our mother as possible had become my life's purpose.

Or one of them. Making sure I got far away from our mother was the other.

"Smile, Ivy," my mother commanded through her own plastic expression. "Look like you love me."

I obeyed and kept smiling as we were welcomed into the house by Smith himself and led to the drawing room. Okay, it wasn't actually the drawing room, but that's what it felt like. Smith had a whole household worth of servants but he preferred to answer the door himself when my mom was around. Personally I didn't think he trusted her around *any* man, even ones that worked for him.

Obviously he was smart.

"Ava," Smith greeted her coolly. He didn't even hold out his hand to her. Where in most of these pretentious circles people greeted each other with kisses or at least a handshake, Smith stayed as far from my mother as he could. It annoyed her to no end. "Ivy, it's so good to see you back home and healthy," he smiled down at me, bringing me into a hug. Another thing that would annoy my mother.

I let it happen. Smith was like the fun uncle I never got to have. He was devilishly handsome in that refined gentleman kind of way, with short, cropped blondish hair infused with streaks of gray although he was still in his early forties. He had a classic jawline and strong nose, and his eyes were deep brown but lightened when he laughed. I could so easily see why my mother had chosen him. And the best part about him was his easy going personality except when it came to everything Ava Pierce.

"Ivy!" my little sister squealed from across the room.

I wrenched out of Smith's grasp to open my arms just in time to catch her. She wrapped her stick thin arms around me, squeezing me until I could barely breathe. But I wouldn't have pulled away for anything. Tears pricked the backs of my eyes as I held her close, inhaling her unconditional love. She was like this mini version of me, with deep auburn hair and bright green eyes and perfect flawless skin. Her freckles spattered the bridge of her nose too, but scattered over her cheeks and one just to the corner of her eye. And she was untouched by our world, completely innocent.

I prayed every day that she would stay that way.

"I missed you so much," I confessed into her hair. My voice was full of emotion and I didn't even try to hide the catch in my throat.

"I missed you too," she squeezed me tighter, stepping on her tip toes so she could get a better hold. "Did you get my letters?"

"Yes, sorry I couldn't write back. They wouldn't let me," I explained hoping she didn't think I had blown her off.

"I know, mom told me. She said it was part of the therapy," Honor whispered but not from fear of being overheard.... from just plain fear. "You're better now? You're not... um.... depressed anymore?"

Ha. The million dollar question.

"No little one, I'm not," I lied. I hated lying to Honor, but sometimes it was necessary. I couldn't have her worrying about me. I couldn't give my mother something to use and lord over her. If my mom thought she could convince Honor I would be safer and healthier with Honor at home with us, she might just leave her dad to help me.

"Alright, Ivy. I would like to see Honor too," my mother's voice attacked our embrace and I could feel the rage pouring out of her in waves. She had seen the opportunity too and was furious I gave it away.

Honor tightened her arms around me once more and then released me. I watched her walk away and step into my mother's cold arms and shivered. I glanced up at Smith who was watching Honor with a barely restrained flight instinct. Anyone could see his desire to grab his daughter and get as far away from her biological mother as humanly possible. I wondered if maybe it *was* the chemo drugs that flipped the switch in his male brain. Is that what happened to Ryder too? Especially after our conversation last night, I was convinced my curse held no power over

Ryder. But then why not? Was he sick as a kid or something? Maybe a drug addict in years past, and the drugs had done a number on his brain?

Except he was way too perceptive for his own good. It definitely wasn't an intelligence thing.

Grrr. I hated how much he consumed my thoughts, how invasive just thinking about him felt. He was this absolute enigma in my life and I had no idea what to do with him.

I wasn't even sure I wanted to do anything with him.

I glanced up at Smith, wondering if there was a way to ask him about his time in the hospital. Maybe he had some insight that would be useful. He turned to face me when he felt my eyes on him and held my gaze. He tilted his head toward the hallway in a gesture asking if I would go with him. I nodded just barely in response, shocked that he was willing to leave Honor alone with my mom.

"Ava, I'm going to show Ivy a book I've been reading about depression. I think it will really help her," Smith declared in his rich voice that usually commanded board rooms and was right now bending the force of nature that was my mother to his will.

"Why, Smith?" my mother asked coyly. "Are you struggling with depression? I'm sure my lawyer would love to hear the details."

"Not at all," Smith replied with a firm hint of irritation lacing every word. "This is for Ivy. It has nothing to do with me."

"Fine," my mother sighed as if it was the greatest inconvenience ever. Although her pretend irritation was all a lie, I could see the greed light her dead eyes, her fingers practically shaking with the opportunity to manipulate and brainwash Honor.

I followed Smith out of the room, across his open foyer and down a short hallway. He opened the door to his study and let me pass before looking surreptitiously into the hallway as if on look out. When he was satisfied we weren't followed, he closed the door quietly and walked over to perch his hip on his massive mahogany desk.

"We don't have much time. I don't trust your mother alone with Honor for more than a few minutes," Smith explained quietly.

"I feel the same way," I lowered my voice as if my mother had super hearing or something.

"First, tell me, are you okay?" Smith's steely expression met mine. He was truly concerned. *For me.*

The realization took my breath away. Nobody was really concerned about me. Everyone, even kids from school, assumed my "rehab" was an excuse to escape the aftermath of Sam's accident. But now Smith and

Ryder in less than twenty-four hours. I felt the ground shift beneath my feet, or maybe it was less physical... maybe it was more like a shifting inside of me, like my soul opened a little bit to the outside world.

"I'm okay," I answered truthfully. Both in his question and my answer the subtle hints of what "okay" meant were obvious to both of us. Okay for me was all very relative. I was okay because I was alive and not currently being physically abused. I was okay because I was back home near Honor and able to keep a close eye on my mother. I was okay. But at the same time I was so far from being okay it was sickening.

"Good," Smith grunted gruffly. He paused for another moment, stealing a glance at the door. "Ivy, if you ever need anything, I mean anything, money, a place to stay, a plane ticket, *anything*, you let me know. Alright?"

"Alright," I nodded my head for extra emphasis. It was nice to know Smith wanted to help; it was even nicer to know Smith understood that I needed help. But, I couldn't under any circumstance take him up on his offer. And he knew that. It would have terrible consequences for Honor. If my mother ever found out, her lawyers would go straight for his jugular which had thus far been protected by innocence of action. But it was nice to know he cared and that he saw a need.

"Alright," he repeated, his voice never lost the refined hard edge that I was sure had been a key factor in all his success. "I called you in here because I've been talking with your father's attorney. When you went away," his voice broke for a moment and I stood up straighter, ready to bolt from the emotion that poured out of him. This scenario felt so dangerous my arms grew goose bumps and my breathing became erratic. "Listen, I know what your mother's like. I would never be able to forgive myself if something happened to you. I don't know details of what your life is like living with her, but I know damned well that my own daughter will never find out. That makes me very concerned for you, understand?" he softened his voice and started talking rapidly so I only nodded. I didn't want to interrupt him; he needed to get whatever this was out, quick. "Your father set up a trust for you that is available to you once you are eighteen and have graduated high school. The original language made it clear this money is meant for your future, so you can go to whatever college you wish or simply have access to it once he deemed you were an adult. However, there is some language that would suggest the money be made available to you immediately if the court ruled you were in danger."

His words hung in the air as if the world stopped moving, as if time completely stood still.

When he could see that I was speechless he continued, "It would be difficult for a court to decide you were in danger unless there was absolute evidence. I'm guessing you don't have concrete evidence of physical or verbal, even emotional abuse or even threatened physical abuse?" I shook my head in defeat. "Well, I didn't expect it to be that easy, don't worry. With your permission I would like to continue talking to your lawyer. I approached him on impulse after I learned you were sent for treatment. But I think he and I might be able to work through this and make your fund available to you before graduation. Would that be alright with you?"

I wanted to agree, I wanted to beg him to do whatever he could. I would even pay for it; he could take whatever he wanted from my inherited millions. I just needed enough to disappear, he could have the rest. But that's not what came out of my mouth, "I.... I have to say no. Smith, thank you so much for being so concerned about me. But I'm fine. I was sent away for what happened with Sam Evans, not because of anything else. But I'm better now. I'm fine." Even I heard how flat and lifeless my words sounded.

"Ivy, I have a lot of money. Whatever I work on will be kept completely private, completely secret," he promised. He was pleading with me, desperate to get me to agree. And I wanted to, I wanted to so bad.

"Smith, I can't," my voice broke and I shot nervous glances at the door every ten seconds. "Don't worry though," I was quick to assure him when I watched his face fall. "I have a plan. I swear to you I will be fine."

"I know you will, kiddo," he stood up from his desk and put a strong hand on my shoulder. "If you change your mind though, call me first thing."

"I will," I lied. I wouldn't change my mind and if I did the minute I dialed Smith I would remember Honor and hang up. I moved to the door and sprinted out to the hall as if the devil were chasing me. Smith's offer was way too risky to even consider.

And walking back into the great room where my mother was cuddled on the couch with Honor whispering all kinds of treacherous secrets into her ear I remembered why. Smith needed to stop playing my savior and focus on his daughter. My mother was a ruthless witch and she would do whatever she could, anyway that she could, to rip his happiness apart and steal everything of value from my little sister.

In two years, when I graduated high school and finally had the access to the trust I needed, Honor would be thirteen. She would be old enough to understand some of what went on in my world and why she needed to stay away. As long as she believed me, as long as Smith kept his umbrella of protection firmly over her, she would be safe.

Besides, by then I would have run out of time. At eighteen I could no more protect Honor than I could myself. I would be an adult, fully responsible to the circle, fully in the custody of Nix.

I allowed myself one long shudder of fear, reminding myself of my goal and why I needed to deny Smith any help he offered. And then I joined my sister on the couch. I would relish this time with her, cherish it and adore her. My freedom had a countdown clock attached to it, but so did my relationship with my sister.

I guessed it was true what they said, you couldn't have it all.

Or, in my case, any of it.

Chapter Eighteen

Monday morning was the worst mornings of all. And this particular Monday morning was worse than most. The sky was overcast and cloudy, dripping with freezing rain that reminded everyone winter was close. The trees were almost completely bare, save for the last golden leaf that hung on, desperate not to die. The sidewalks were drenched with puddles and mud. And Central High loomed above me, void of even shadows this morning.

The building usually beamed like a beacon of refined beauty. Once the state capital building, it had sharp lines and aristocratic architecture. It stood directly next door to the gleaming white and pink marble of the Joslyn Art Museum and together the buildings were joined in aged beauty. They broke up the cold, heartless skyscrapers of downtown and forced sprawling lawns in an otherwise jungle of concrete and stone.

"I suppose I should go inside, huh?" I grumbled inside the warmth of Exie's car.

"Do you want an umbrella?" Exie asked around a sip of her latte.

"Do you have one?" I turned back around to face her.

"Uh, no." She shook her head causing her golden hair to shake out around her shoulders. Her blue eyes contorted into confusion.

"Then why did you ask if I wanted one?" I laughed. Exie had this incredible ability to take my mind off my problems and forget myself for a while.

"It just felt right."

"It just felt right?" I repeated and mashed my lips together before I could ask any more questions. This conversation was not headed anywhere logical.

"Yep," she grinned at me. "Who's that with your boy toy?" Suddenly her expression was serious, scheming.

I followed her gaze and then worked at trying to swallow. "Uh, that's Ryder Sutton."

"Mmm," she purred.

"Yeah, isn't he all clichéd bad boy?" I tried to joke, tried to hide the notes of panic that were racing through me, pounding at my heart, tightening the bones that caged my lungs into vice grips of jealousy....

"Sure," Exie agreed without paying much attention to me at all. "I'll walk you in, yeah?"

Crap.

Honesty was so not my thing.

"Hey, Ex, he uh, it's not that he's off limits or anything, but he kind of has a girlfriend," I explained weakly.

"I guess that's not surprising," she murmured. "He's delicious."

I laughed, unable to stop myself. "Is he a boy or a candy bar?"

"Maybe both?" Exie laughed too and then silence fell between us for two beats. "Ives, if you want him, just say so. You can trust me, you know? Besides, I was mostly just admiring from a distance anyway."

I smiled at my friend because she really was a friend. Somehow I had thought our relationship completely a design of the cosmos without any real attachment, except for a kind of predatory protection for each other since we were going through the same thing. We were more though. There was an actual foundation to our friendship, real love between us.

It was the first time in my life I had been loved. Truly, deeply, genuinely loved. Even if it was all in the friendship form, I realized how rare those emotions directed at me were. And I drank them in; I closed my eyes and let them settle over me.

"No, it's not that. He's just different. He doesn't seem even a little bit fazed by me. He's like Smith. He sees through it all," I explained.

"How?" Exie gasped and then narrowed her eyes on Ryder as he talked and laughed with Chase and Phoenix at the top of the stairs in front of the school.

"I have no idea. I've wondered if maybe he was sick as a kid, maybe he went through what Smith did. I keep meaning to ask him if he's ever had cancer but somehow it keeps slipping my mind."

"I can't imagine why," Exie whispered.

I relaxed into the seat a little, relieved to be able to talk to somebody about this. "I make him mad all the time. It's like I was born just to piss him off." I laughed at the thought, how absurd it was to think he was the only male I could make mad besides Nix. "And he's constantly making fun of me. And not in the flirty way, like he actually thinks I'm stuck up."

Exie snorted unladylike. "I've got to meet this guy. And Sloane too! Sloane would *die* to see someone make fun of you."

"He actually works at Delice. We could go get coffee after school?" I didn't want to acknowledge the happiness that suddenly ping-ponged around inside of me. How messed up was that? I could have any guy I wanted.... literally. But that thought left me utterly dead inside. The one guy that wanted nothing to do with me however? Yeah, he somehow brought my body to life.... gave me emotions and everything.

I was so screwed up.

"I am so all over this!" Exie squealed with excitement. "I'll clear it with Sloane and call you."

I jumped out of Exie's car and into the dreary day, but the weather no longer dampened my mood. I waved goodbye to my friend and headed up to meet with my…. other friends. Weird. They were surprisingly happy to see me. Even Kenna. Well…. kind of Kenna.

I fell into the school routine easily. I hadn't been in school for six months, but somehow the constant schedule, the forty-two minute class periods, the bells and hall passes felt easily natural. And I felt thankful for that.

I liked to learn, I liked to study. I even liked to take tests. College would have been exactly where I wanted to go next, but there was no way that was in the cards for me. It was escape or enter the trade. Or worse, take Nix seriously and join his household.

I was wrapped up in those thoughts as I took a pass in English and headed toward the bathroom. I loved school, but that didn't mean Mrs. Wade didn't grow excruciatingly monotonous.

"Ivy Pierce," a nasally valley-girl voice called as Amber walked out of a stall to my left.

"Hi Amber," I said softly. I recognized the ugly bitterness she was throwing off her in waves.

"It's because you're easy," she said matter of fact, while washing her hands.

"Excuse me?" I asked in a pathetically quiet, meek voice. The thing about high school girls was they could be the best friends you ever had with the fiercest sense of loyalty or your worst enemy with the flick of a switch. We were emotional creatures, I understood that. But every girl was hard-wired with animosity against me already, born leery of me, waiting for me to betray them. Maybe I already crossed a line with Amber and didn't remember it, or maybe it was one of those crush things there was no way I could have known about… and it probably wouldn't have mattered anyway if she had a crush or not. Or maybe she just recognized the enemy inside me that I was to her. It didn't really matter though, because obviously Amber had it out for me.

Exie would have told her to mind her own business. Sloane would have figured out just what buttons to push and dated whoever meant the most to her.

Although, apparently I was already doing that.

I cowered in fear.

The truth was, girls scared me.

"You're easy," she repeated slowly as if to a child. "Their fixation. Why guys won't leave you alone. It's not like you're all that pretty. It's just that you're easy and boys have short attention spans."

I thought about Sam and his attention span, how it had ultimately led to the car accident. I thought about Chase and how he didn't push me to spend time with him or be something I wasn't. I thought about Ryder and how devoted he was to Kenna. Some boys were interested in one thing; I had known enough of that kind to not be completely naïve. But I also knew some of the other kind now and so with deafening clarity I saved my self-esteem.

It also helped that because of the curse I knew I was pretty. So she could suck on that one.

"I'm not easy," I replied stubbornly. Because I wasn't.

In return she cackled at me. Honestly, she cackled.

"Please, everyone knows what a skank you are," she rolled her eyes in the mirror at me and headed for the hand dryer.

"They're wrong. I'm not a skank." This was the most I had ever stuck up for myself since being sent away and I didn't even really know why I was trying. She was welcome to believe whatever she wanted about me. In fact, Nix preferred the rumors even if we were ordered to hold on to our virginity until he could line up a worthy buyer.

"That's not what Sam Evans told everyone the night of that party," she countered bravely.

That was enough to snap any calm resolve that remained. "You need to stop with that," I snapped. "You don't know anything about Sam, so stop using him to make your points. Sam loved me. *Loved* me." Well, not me. Sam fell in love with the curse, but Amber didn't need to know that. "So stop putting words in his mouth when it's so unfair that he can't defend himself."

"And look where that got him? Paralyzed and brain dead. Nobody could love you now, not after what you did to him. Now you're nothing but a used up hag," she turned on me with biting cruelty, her eyes burning orbs of hatred. "*You're* the reason he's not here to defend himself!"

And she had cut right to the most vulnerable vein.

My breath stuttered in my lungs as I tried to suck in enough oxygen to remain level headed. Hot tears pricked at the backs of my eyes and I wanted to curl up into myself and die, or at least weep. I repeated to myself that she didn't matter, that she didn't matter to me. I was stronger than this.

But I wasn't. And all of the broken, shattered pieces of me came crashing down in a suffocating deluge of weakness.

The bathroom door opened and laughing girls walked in completely unaware of the impending mental breakdown I was just seconds away from. I couldn't even look up to see who the happy girls were, my eyes focused on the dirty drain and broken porcelain sink I needed to hold me up. My knuckles turned as white as the sink basin as I held on for my life.

"Ivy, what's wrong?"

Kenna.

She was exactly the last person I wanted to witness this tragic side of me.

"Amber, why does she look like she's about to burst into tears?" Kenna demanded of my attacker. A soft hand rested on my shoulder as if to comfort me and surprisingly it did. I lifted my eyes to meet Amber's ashamed gaze in the mirror. She quickly fixed her expression to innocence and shrugged one shoulder casually.

"What did you say to her?" Kenna ground out and then thought better of rehashing Amber's accusations. "You know what? Never mind. You're a bitch. You've always been one and that isn't going to change. It drives you *crazy* Chase is happy with Ivy, but jealousy is an ugly color on you. Just leave her alone, Amber. She doesn't need your drama and neither do I."

Amber struggled to swallow against Kenna's tirade. I watched her throat work to finish the action, while her eyes glossed over with tears. She silently turned around, tugged at her shirt to make sure it was in place and then left the bathroom. I didn't have any trouble believing Kenna's words had hit home.

I realized slowly how popular Kenna was. It wasn't that before I left I was oblivious to her social status, but while I had my own agenda, popularity never really mattered to me. Besides Kenna seemed like one of the nicest girls ever, in the history of girls. She tried to befriend *me* for God sakes. Or at least she put up with me.

And now she was sticking up for me. The whole scenario felt surreal.

Nobody should be sticking up for me. I was the lowest of the low, the worst of the worst. I had one agenda and one only and it was completely selfish. But in the last three days more people had come to my aid than I thought existed in my life.

I wasn't alone. Not by a long shot.

But now what was I supposed to do with that realization? Besides my girls, I couldn't take anybody with me and there was nothing on earth that could persuade me to stay.

"Thanks," I mumbled to Kenna who waved me off like it was no big deal.

"Don't worry. She *is* a bitch. It's not like she doesn't know it. She's just not used to being told the truth," Kenna laughed and then turned to primp and preen in the mirror.

I smiled in response but didn't offer anything else. Suddenly and very inexplicably I felt bad for Amber. Which sucked since she made me feel like the worst kind of awful.... but still. I didn't deserve this kind of attention from Kenna and their friendship didn't deserve me getting in the middle of it. At the end of all this I was gone, out of here. There was nothing long term between any of us, and besides Amber couldn't even really be blamed. She hated me for good reason. Especially if she had a thing for Chase...

I sucked in a deep breath and snuck another peek at Kenna.

I couldn't identify anything going on between Ryder and me, but either way I knew without a shadow of a doubt that Kenna should not be defending me. She should be defending her relationship. I promised myself at least four times a day that I wanted nothing to do with Ryder, but the guilt seeping into my bloodstream and pumping through my heart with crackling clarity begged to differ.

"Are you going back to class?" Kenna asked me while her other two friends waited for her by the door.

"In a minute," I whispered, still trying to put the broken pieces of myself back together.

"No worries," she grinned a carefree smile and then met her friends at the door. "See you later, Ivy."

"Yep," I croaked and went back to gripping the sink. I looked up and met my watery green eyes in the mirror. I looked over my silky auburn hair, the reddish gold highlights were really coming out now that my hair had a chance to heal from the poor dye jobs I was obsessed with right before I was sent away. My skin seemed paler than normal but still held that milky-porcelain-perfection all the women in our circle kept. I was beautiful.

But empty.

And I didn't deserve any of this.

Chapter Nineteen

"Oh lord, I'm so nervous!" Exie squealed as we crossed the street to Delice.

I rolled my eyes. "What do *you* have to be nervous about?" I demanded over the clicking sound of our heels against the wet pavement. The sky hadn't stopped spitting since it opened up yesterday morning and the constant drizzle made even my hair frizzy and wild.

"To meet him of course!" she exclaimed dramatically. "I just hope he's everything I want him to be! Last night was so anticlimactic that if he's not there tonight I might die. Seriously, I might just die!"

Sloane laughed delicately from the other side of Exie and I threw her a "what the hell" look just for good measure. "He had band practice last night, or that's what Phoenix told me today. So he should definitely be here tonight. But, honestly, I don't understand why you're so worked up about this, Ex? It's not like I'm ever going to date him or anything. I'm just mildly curious about why he seems so.... impenetrable."

"Oh honey," Exie groaned. "I'm not sure there is a man out there that is.... impenetrable. In fact, I'm pretty sure they are all very aware of how.... penetrating they can be."

Sloane snorted this time, not at all delicately. Even I couldn't stop the smile from appearing on my face.

"You sound like my mother!" I laughed. "You're so gross."

"But accurate," Exie giggled.

"I just don't understand the fascination with him," I paused at the door to Delice, holding my hand firmly on the handle so they couldn't muscle their way by me.

Sloane let out an exasperated sigh and explained, "Let's start with the fact that you have never once, *not once*, been even curious about a boy. But you're so much more than curious, and don't even try to deny it. You are protecting him like the fiercest kind of guard dog, which is also completely uncharacteristic. We know he's hot and that you're attracted to him. And then throw in the fact that he isn't the least bit enslaved by the curse, I mean, come on, Ivy, it doesn't take a genius to figure out why you would be so fascinated by him. But don't take that the wrong way; it's okay that you're into him. I promise that it is. Just because the curse has repressed us, doesn't mean we have to live in bondage to it. You deserve a free life, a free *love* life."

"Plus, he's hot, Ivy! *Look* at him!" Exie practically swooned right here on the damp sidewalk. Her eyes glazed over and her lips parted slightly as she took in his extremely messy dark hair and full lips. He looked like he just crawled out of bed after hours of making out or something even more lascivious, and his tough, overly masculine hands were working the cash register with practiced, confident movements. He had a black apron folded in half and tied around his waist that accentuated how narrow his hips were, and he was wearing a gray cardigan over a faded red t-shirt that made him look more college-hottie than high school-bad-boy.

Sloane sighed again only this time it was in complete adoration for the boy on the other side of the glass. She pushed by me and walked into the coffee shop with an intense presence that demanded she be noticed. She had never looked more like Snow White in my opinion than tonight, with her long, almost black hair tumbling over her shoulders in soft waves, her glossy red lipstick and soft pink blousy mini dress.

A pang of jealousy clenched my gut and I hated how frumpy and unkempt I felt next to my two gorgeous friends. Exie followed Sloane and the two of them made their way up to the counter while I watched them like a creeper from through the door. I wanted to drag them back outside and explain to them that I hadn't meant *my* fascination with Ryder, I meant theirs.

They were wrong. There was no fascination on my part. None at all. Only a desire to protect something outside the realm of our world.

Sloane had waged a completely unnecessary argument against me.

I hoped.

Because even now something was fluttering in my stomach and I refused to name the emotion that drugged my senses and narrowed the entire scope of my vision just to him. He was looking at me through the glass now while my friends made fools of themselves gesturing for me to come inside.

The corner of his mouth kicked up into a crooked smile and his face softened into an intimate kind of secret between us. He tilted his chin, silently telling me to join them inside. The movement was so subtle but so commanding my hand was reaching for the door before my brain registered what it was doing.

I was starting to hate those subtle movements he seemed to command so carelessly but received the most immediate results with. As the warmth from the coffee shop blew into my face and tugged me inside I decided that Ryder must have some kind of mind control power to get everyone to obey those casual movements. Or at least he had one over me.

It would explain so very much.

And then there would be nothing to be worried about.

Only, there was no such thing as that kind of mind-control power. So whatever was happening between us had to be something even more unexplainable.

Or at least on my end. With a whoosh of exhaled breath I entered the coffee shop and made my way to the counter.

"Hey, Ryder," I threw a smile at him. In a weird play of power I wanted to be the one that spoke first.

"Hey, Ivy," he echoed in only a slightly teasing voice. "Caramel macchiato?"

"Yes, please," I dropped my eyes to the counter, hiding a wider smile.

"Have a seat ladies. I'll bring these out to you when they're ready," Ryder directed with his gravelly voice.

"How much is it?" I asked, reaching for my purse.

"That's alright, I'm using my employee benefits."

"Oooh," Exie cooed. "Employee benefits! Do all of your friends get these *benefits*?"

Ryder's small smile turned into a full on grin and he turned his focus to my best friend. I immediately felt the loss. "Sure, and friends of friends."

"Sweet!" Exie exclaimed in her screechy girl way.

"Mmm-mm. I want to pay," I argued.

"Not a chance, Red. Go sit down," Ryder countered with restrained force. He wasn't going to be argued with. I wondered if I had offended his pride, but when I looked up and met his stare a shock of some emotion rocked my body leaving me breathless. His steely gray eyes were daring me to defy him. They were filled with cocky arrogance and something more... something like possession, like it was his entitlement in life to pay for my coffee.

Losing the battle easily to that kind of resolve, I simply nodded and followed my giggling friends to a table. I was used to Nix's male-dominant tactics; they were like the slow poison sucking away at my life. Nix wanted to control, to force me to serve. I loathed the prideful power that was Nix.

But Ryder was something so different, so.... gentle. He was pushy and domineering and a complete Neanderthal. But his feelings came from a place of sweetness, and with a desire to protect.

When Nix ordered me around I felt like a caged animal.

When Ryder ordered me around I felt.... turned on.

Oh no.

This was so not good.

"Ivy, he's so yummy," Sloane murmured, her eyes glittering with appreciation for the male species.

"Right!" Exie squealed in an exaggerated whisper. "I told you!"

What was with my friends and look at all guys like they were *edible*? Possibly we should have ordered some croissants too to curb their obvious hunger....

"But you're right," Sloane continued, her tone dropping with disappointment. "He's so not affected by us at all. It's kind of eerie actually."

"But kind of nice?" I posed the statement as a question even though for me it was like balm to open wounds. I knew without a question how healing it felt to be around Ryder, to feel how unimpressed with me he was.

That was sick, right? There had to be something wrong with me.

"So are you going to...." Sloane hesitated and I knew what she was getting at but I didn't even want to hear the question out loud. "I mean, Chase is almost times-up, right?"

"I'm not, no way." I growled. "He will never get anywhere near Nix, or my mother. Could you imagine?" My voice dropped to a whisper as if the axis of evil could somehow overhear me.

Sloane nodded with approval, her worried expression turning back to one of respect. Exie just smiled at me with this enormous grin that ate up half her face.

"What?" I asked, narrowing my eyes at her.

"Nothing," she said but kept smiling and now her eyes seemed to be holding a secret.

"Exie, what?" I demanded.

"Nothing," she sighed contentedly. "I'm just... I'm just happy for you."

I snorted. "I just told you, I'm not-"

"I know," she rushed quickly. "I know you're not. But can't I be happy for you anyway?"

"Whatever," I laughed and then Sloane joined in.

Three coffees were set down in between us and I felt the presence of Ryder's overwhelming presence looming over me. He pushed the hot cups around the table, sorting out the different orders to their owners and then returned the smiles that Exie and Sloane were drowning him in.

"Ivy, scoot over. I'm taking my break with you guys," Ryder commanded and this time I didn't argue.

Well, I didn't argue until I scooted over. "You're so demanding," I accused.

"What?" Ryder shrugged. "Isn't that why you're here tonight? To introduce me to your friends?"

I choked on a sip of hot macchiato and then set it down hard enough so that it splashed over the sides of the red ceramic cup. "Geez, cocky."

He returned my snide comment with a proud smile and his eyebrows rose as if challenging me to contradict him. "Well, *isn't* that why you're here?"

"Psht. No," I denied adamantly. I turned my focus to cleaning up the coffee spill with the thin napkins that sat on the table. "We were just thirsty. Don't be so full of yourself."

"I'm not full of myself," he argued.

"Oh really? Then why assume we came here just for you?" I chanced a look at him, hiding half my face with my lifted shoulder. He stared met me straight on, his gunmetal gray eyes lit with amusement.

"Because you're friends *said* that's why you are here," he answered as seriously as he could.

"My friends? What?" I gasped. "I don't have any friends. At least not anymore."

"Ives, we so did not say that's why we're here," Exie shook her head, blonde curls swinging wildly around her shoulders.

"Sloane?" I raised my eyebrow at her. She was more of a straight shooter and the moment her shoulders sagged I knew they outed me. Wenches.

"I think it was more like, we might have said, um, how excited we were to finally meet him is all," Sloane answered in a small voice.

"Finally?" I squeaked.

"What they said was that they had been waiting a very long time to meet me and couldn't believe how much better looking I was in person," Ryder corrected in a smug tone.

I shrunk into my seat, praying for an earthquake that would open the ground beneath my feet and swallow me whole. That was possible right? A freak earthquake and quick demise? Ugh.

"So how long have they been waiting to meet me, *Ives*?" Ryder asked in a softer tone, but none the less dangerous.

"Since yesterday morning," I winced as the confession came out of my mouth. "Exie saw you yesterday when she dropped me off at school. So, obviously enough time for her to get worked up about meeting you." I shoved sarcasm into each syllable as I spoke, but it was only a weak attempt to salvage what was left of my pride.

"Wow, yesterday morning, huh?" Ryder pressed, addressing me only. "You must have given her a pretty nice impression of me to get Exie so worked up."

I peeked up at him, hating how he was lording this over me, but he was looking at Exie and sharing some kind of secret smile with her. Instead of mortification, jealously bloomed bright and fast inside my chest and soon my cheeks were painted red with the emotion. There was no end to how this boy affected me.

"I told her you had a girlfriend," I snapped before I could stop myself.

Great now I sounded jealous too.

Ryder's smile only grew. "I do have a girlfriend." He turned his attention back to me and held my gaze this time. "So why are you and your friends here?"

I took a breath and tried to come up with an appropriate response, er... excuse, but the gray of his eyes had melted to silver and I couldn't think straight. He tilted forward a little, closing some distance between us and waited for me to speak.

"For coffee," I finally whispered after what felt like an eternity of silence.

"For coffee," he echoed in a velvety voice.

More silence stretched out between us while we continued to stare each other down. We were bordering on inappropriate by now, but there was something about him that drew me in. He stared at me like an equal, like he could look away if he wanted. Like it was his choice to fall into this tractor beam between us.

And that terrified me. And then I felt like the worst person ever.

"I really like Kenna," I announced and then sat up straighter.

"Good," Ryder snapped out of his daze and cleared his throat trying to come back to himself. "I like her too."

I barely heard him. "I've never really had like a *girl* friend before..."

"Hey!" Exie and Sloane interrupted together.

So I amended my statement, "At school. I've never really had a girl friend at school before. But Kenna has been really, really nice."

Ryder stared at me for another thirty seconds, his expression turning to quizzically annoyed. And then he swung around to look at my two friends who were also giving me the evil eye. "Exie, Sloane, it's been... fun. But I have to get back to work now. You ladies should come with Ivy Wednesday night. I'm in a band and we play the Slowdown for their smaller house shows. You'll get a chance to meet Kenna, my girlfriend.

You already know Ivy likes her, so I'm sure you both will too. Have a great night."

He stood up and stalked around the corner and to the back room, ignoring his coworker as she tried to welcome him back from his break. I shivered against the completely unnecessary words that still hung in the air over us. What was that all about? He had seemed polite to my friends, but there was a hardness to his tone that even I couldn't ignore.

I took a quick breath and met the curious stares of my friends. "I don't know what that was about," I admitted before they could start the twenty questions. He was going to be back out here in a second and I didn't want to get caught in the middle of a discussion about him.

"Ivy are you still doing that concert thing?" Sloane demanded instead. Her eyes were pained and her mouth set in a grim line. "I thought you quit."

"I quit because I was out of state," I reminded her softly. "I've only been back once."

"Because you've only been here for one Wednesday," Exie lectured in a snippy voice.

"It's not like that," I said weakly. "I'm not like that." When they both continued to stare hard at me I mashed my lips together, wetting them quickly and then launched into an explanation. "It's my only thing. It's the only thing that's mine. And they won't find out, I swear. I couldn't.... I wouldn't let them send me back, *I swear*."

They were both oppressively quiet as they took in my explanation. Exie refused to meet my eyes, staring down at the napkin she was shredding apart in her delicate fingers. And Sloane was regarding me with her shrew eyes. She was hot in like the Sexy Secretary way and right now I could feel every ounce of her brain power as she tried to pick me apart.

"We're not worried about them sending you back to Arizona, okay?" She reached out her hand and laid it gently on mine for just a brief moment before retracting it immediately.

"I know." And I did know. If I was still a problem there was only one place I would go. And I was afraid I was already on my way. "I won't get caught. I promise."

"You won't get caught because we're coming with you," Sloane decided with a smile.

"We are?" Exie's face lit up and she was back to her bubbly self again. "Yay! A concert!"

Chapter Twenty

We stepped into the Slowdown just as the first band took the stage. The lead singer threw out a welcome and they launched into an amateur version of soulful blues. I smiled. This was perfection every single time. And even though I dressed to impress instead of my usual unimpressive emo digs, I felt great to be back here.

This place was like home base for me, safe, familiar, and so ear-spitting-loud. The far side of the room, where the main stage and pit were, remained blocked off with a thick curtain. The stage lights that lit the smaller stage were bright and blinding, hitting us as soon as we walked through the door. The bar area was packed but the rest of the floor stayed less filled out and felt a bit empty. I could feel Exie and Sloane assess the concert hall with skeptical eyes and almost laughed at their stiff posture.

The music was subpar, and the audience completely teenage grunge meets hipster chic. But that's what I expected, hoped for. To put it simply, this was so not their scene. It probably shouldn't have been mine either, except the anonymity of the place held that mysterious freedom I longed for.

"This is the place you're always sneaking off to?" Exie asked in a horrified whisper.

"Hey, it could be so much worse. Have you ever been to the Sokol Underground?" I shuddered at the thought. While above ground, the Sokol had this old school twenties steampunk vibe to it, the Underground had devolved into something absolutely gross. Decades of spilled beer, sweat, blood and decay had worked the opposite of miracles on the below ground concert hall.

"I'll have to take your word for it," Sloane drawled.

I didn't get it. This was a relatively new building and completely classy. Granted the clientele was different than we usually hung out with, but it wasn't like creepsville or anything. I glanced at the bar and noticed Neck Tattoos from last time and took a breath of relief. At least I wouldn't have to explain my addiction to water.

"Ivy!" a muffled voice called out from across the room. My eyes zoned in on the voice and saw Phoenix waving wildly at us. He stood above everyone else in the room and surrounded by his fellow band members and Kenna. Ryder wasn't with them though and I couldn't stop my eyes from roaming around the small space searching him out.

155

I quickly shook my head and waved back, I didn't really have any right to try to find him here. He wasn't mine and I was with somebody else. Okay, I was a cruel witch, but not a cheater. I took another quick breath and then grabbed Exie and Sloane's arms. "Come on, I'll introduce you to Scoob and the gang."

"What?" Sloane asked.

I didn't repeat myself, just kept dragging them through the thin crowd. They so did not fit in here, with their four inch stilettos and designer outfits. They were gorgeous, and drew every eye. But they were uncomfortable which threw off their curse a bit. Thankfully. Although Sloane would be more than welcome in a place like this tonight.

"Sloane, Exie, these are Chase's friends," I introduced by a general wave of my arm. "Guys, this is Sloane and Exie, um, my friends." I laughed a little at my solid introduction. Everyone was looking at each other, sizing the respective strangers up and that only built on the levels of awkward stretching between the two groups.

Kenna especially had the bitch-look going on. She was the only girl in the group though, so that could be understood. I smiled at her, trying to reassure her that they were as cool as me... which let's face it, was not all that reassuring.

"You made it," Ryder swooped in from around the corner wearing a huge grin for my friends. Immediately tension started to melt between everyone. "Red, did you introduce everyone?"

"Yes," I smiled back at him, happy with the attention he gave me.

"No," Exie cut in, equally happy to see someone she knew. "She said these are Chase's friends. We don't even know which one is Chase."

I flushed bright pink while Ryder laughed at me. "Okay, let me do a better job then. Exie, Sloane, this is my beautiful girlfriend Kenna. This giant over here is Phoenix, this is Hayden, Hudson and Cole. We're all in the band together."

"Sugar Skulls," Phoenix piped up giving Exie an extra-long look.

"Where's Chase?" Sloane asked, clearly dismissing all the boys in front of her. The hard-to-get-vibe was her signature and so ingrained in every one of her actions I wasn't entirely sure she knew she was doing it anymore.

"He couldn't come tonight," I explained before Ryder could take over for me again. It seemed important that I knew where my boyfriend was in front of this crowd. "He has a big test tomorrow, so he's at home studying."

"Bummer," Exie pouted.

"Lame," Phoenix booed and then shot Exie a look like they had just connected over one word responses.

"I thought he was in the band?" Sloane's eyebrows drew down in confusion.

This brought out hysterical laughter from Ryder and Phoenix.

Ryder explained, "Chase avoids this place as often as he can. He's completely tone deaf."

"Oh," Sloane sighed. At the same time I realized Ryder knew more about Chase than me. Which wasn't that hard to believe, because I had known Chase for all of one week, still it was annoying coming from Ryder.

We all fell into an awkward silence after that and it seemed to stretch out into the next three poorly performed songs.

"So this band is... good," Sloane commented dryly.

Phoenix snorted like he was offended. "Do you really think so?"

"Why? Do you know them?" Sloane asked carefully.

"Yeah, they're a bunch of tools. Totally sold that they're the next big thing," Phoenix shook his head with disgust.

"So you're better than them?" Exie asked slowly.

"Well, I mean..." Phoenix stumbled, clearly not used to being as cocky as his band mates.

"We're better than them," Hayden jumped in, not at all uncomfortable with being arrogant. He appraised Exie with hungry eyes and I felt the strongest urge to step in front of her and sacrifice my own body to save hers from whatever perverted thoughts were happening in his head.

"I guess we'll be the judge of that," Exie sighed.

I burst into laughter, knowing she was just kidding, but nobody else seemed to get the joke. She shot Phoenix a wink and he kind of stumbled backwards, not sure what to do under the pressure of the flirtatious winky-face from Malibu Barbie.

"She was kidding," I explained to the group when they all just continued to stare at her.

"No seriously I was," Exie agreed. "I know you're good. Ivy hasn't stopped talking about how *amazing* you are all night."

"Really?" Ryder asked in true surprise. He stepped back and cleared his throat as if he was as shocked by his question as everyone else was.

I blushed a deep red and turned around to the bar. I was first of all, not used to blushing so much and second of all, not going to wait around to embarrass myself more.

Sloane followed me, showing how uncomfortable she was. "Are you okay?" I asked as we found a place at the bar.

"Yes," she answered in a clipped tone.

"What are you ladies drinking tonight?" Good old Neck Tattoos asked with a smirk.

"The usual," I replied casually, careful to keep any tones of flirtation out of my voice.

"Alright, water on the rocks," Neck Tattoos confirmed, clearly disappointed. "And for you?"

"I'll have a vodka-"

"Uh-uh," I cut her off before she could continue. "*Rehab* remember?" I hissed fiercely and pointed at my chest. "I need you to be a good influence on me tonight." I caught her eye and held it, willing her to make the right decision. We were used to having alcohol thrown at us. Even in public we didn't have trouble procuring said libations... but these people thought the worst of me already and I didn't want to add to the rumor mill.

Which was an anomaly in itself.

Sloane sighed long and suffering, "Alright. Water on the rocks it is."

"Thanks S, you know I love you!" I wrapped my arms around her waist and gave her a squeeze.

"Sure, Ives. You just hope they're better than this band." She said with no enthusiasm whatsoever.

We walked back over to the band and Kenna. Exie eyed our tumblers of water with greedy eyes and I could immediately tell she assumed incorrectly.

"Yum!" She reached excitedly for my drink and her eyes lit up expressively. She grabbed it and drank from it before I could warn her discretely.

"Oh that's-" she stopped confused when the taste of cold water touched her tongue. She stared at me, silently demanding an explanation.

"Water," I finished for her. "It's water."

The band on stage finished a song and the room filled with the sudden quiet that came in between sets. They started to tear down their instruments while our group waited for something to happen between Exie and me.

"Obviously, it's water," She laughed, covering for her misguided expectations. "I mean, you did just get out of rehab. What else would it be?"

I winced. This was so awkward.

Thankfully Ryder corralled his band together and they went off to make music. Kenna stared at me like I betrayed her after they were gone so I sucked it up and tried to play nice.

"Is he going to dedicate another song to you?" I asked, hoping a little flattery would go a long way.

"He usually does," She smiled at me tightly. "So you girls don't go to Central, right?"

"Nope," Sloane mimicked her uncomfortable smile. "Brownell Talbot."

"We have to wear uniforms," Exie rolled her eyes. "They're so awful."

"I can imagine," Kenna laughed carefully. "We don't have to wear uniforms, but our school doesn't have air conditioning. It smells like a gym locker half the year."

"That it does," I agreed with a tiny shudder. I missed the warm months this year thanks to my extended vacay in therapy, but spring would be terrible.

"So how do you guys know each other, then?" Kenna moved in so that we formed a tight little circle. It was almost comfortable.

"Our moms all know each other," I explained before they had a chance to jump in.

"Cool," Kenna commented but then the music started with a strong guitar rift from Ryder and all conversation got lost to the music.

The band was incredible as usual- and most of all Ryder. Not that I was really surprised, and even though I had just seen them perform a week ago, his stage-presence was still mesmerizing. I forced myself not to be completely lost to his lyrics, or him.

I couldn't help it though and looking around at the captivated audience I could tell I wasn't the only one. Ryder sang with intense heart and raw honesty. His eyes squinched shut while his hands worked his guitar with absolute practiced skill. One hand kept getting yanked through his hair in a kind of nervous gesture that made it stick up outrageously in the sexiest display of terrible hair I had ever seen.

He was perfection as a musician. Everything the audience could hope for. And when the set decrescendo-ed into an acoustic number with only him and his guitar we all sat with bated breath and transfixed eyes.

"This is a song I wrote recently," he started, his voice echoing in the mic while he looked down to adjust his guitar. "The band hasn't had a chance to play it together yet, so it will be just me. But it's uh, about chocolate croissants and coffee." He laughed at himself, the sound gruff and warm in the microphone and the audience laughed right along with him. I swallowed back a strong wave of panic and forced myself to look casual.

"Is that something special between you two?" I asked Kenna, hoping I was wrong.

"I guess," she shrugged. "I get one every time I visit him at his work."

"Oh, that's cute." A wave of relief washed over me, I almost stumbled back from the force of it.

But then Ryder started singing about a black-hearted girl that never let anyone get close.

Damn him.

Chapter Twenty-One

Sugar Skulls finished up their set on just the right note. The small crowd went wild with whistling and clapping and Kenna beamed with happy pride next to me. Her boyfriend and his band played an incredible set. She was practically glowing with the raw sentiment Ryder sang with, and still blissing from the solo song she assumed was about her. I thought the song was actually kind of insulting and if I were her and thought the song was about me, I would have been pissed.

Actually, I knew the song was about me. And I *was* pissed. I couldn't move on from Ryder's solo number, the words were like razors on my skin with how exposing they felt and the emotion he sang with haunted me. The way his voice sounded husky and pained against the lyrics to his song, how his eyes shut tighter every time he sang the word inscribed on my wrist and then when his song was over how they refused to meet mine, how they looked everywhere but at me.

I had to be wrong about him. There was no way he could write a song about me and not be affected by the curse. And the song was obviously about me. Granted it wasn't like he sang a love song... it was almost the anti-love song. His rough lyrics about a girl that hated boys and herself more, her black heart infecting everyone she touched, how even though he wanted nothing more than to get away from her, he still found himself pulled to the place her black heart bled.

Yep, sounded pretty accurate to me.

Slowly the band started to pack up their instruments. The music venue was officially closing down for the night, and so house music came on over the speakers. The smaller-than-normal crowd was subdued after such an emotional performance by the band and left in a kind of ripped-apart stupor. Thanks to the emotional response Ryder demanded, everyone's souls were shredded by the set tonight, not just mine.

"I've never seen them play like that before," Kenna observed excitedly after we stood around quietly for a few minutes.

"Sorry, that's my fault," Sloane mumbled and I could tell just by looking at her how bad she felt.

Exie and I knew she would influence the room before we came tonight, but none of us expected this kind of reaction.

"What was that?" Kenna asked, not hearing her at all.

"I said, Ivy was right, they are *really* good," Sloane brightened her expression and gave Kenna a winning smile.

"It's Ryder, he's *so* talented," Kenna bragged. And she had every right to. Even without Sloane to add to his talent, he possessed something incredible every time he stood on stage.

"And so is Phoenix, oh my gosh, he's like the most talented ever!" I squealed. He walked up behind Kenna and I shot him a huge grin.

"What is this?" He smiled back. "Are these my groupies?"

"So, can I get your autograph?" I gave him my best valley-girl impression and stuck out my hip.

"Depends," he answered slyly. "Are your friends looking for some too?" He waggled his eyebrows at me so I knew, even though we were joking, he was interested.

As if I didn't know before that he was interested.

As if it was some foreign concept that a male would be interested in one of my female friends.

"Exie is," I smirked, throwing her to the wolves.

She looked over at us having missed the entire exchange.

"Exie..." Phoenix smirked. "Sexy Exie?"

That got her attention...

"Oh my gosh, Sexy Exie? That is *so* clever. How did you ever come up with something so original? I've never heard that in my life. Please say it again. Go on, say it again," she demanded flatly.

I bit back a smile because Phoenix looked so overwhelmed. It wasn't his fault guys had been using that nickname for Exie for as long as she could remember.

"Say it again. Come on. *Say it*," Exie taunted Phoenix further. The poor guy was cowering. This huge, gangly man-child was honestly cowering.

"Uh... Sexy-"

"Don't! It's a trap!" I shrieked, not even willing to put up with her wrath tonight. I shook my head at Phoenix and gave him my scary eyes. "You know better. Do *not* poke the beast."

"Girls are confusing," he said slowly with a shake of his head.

"Don't worry, Phoenix, Exie is going to forgive you because you just met her," I turned my serious eyes to my friend and demanded silently that she give him another shot. He wasn't like the guys we normally met and he certainly wasn't trying to impress her just to get in her pants.

She had to see that. He was probably the most innocent high school boy ever.

"Fine," Exie relented. "I'll forgive you, Phoenix, but no more Sexy Exie jokes, yeah?"

"Yeah," he breathed out a sigh of relief but with Exie's startling blue eyes fully focused intently on him, he never really relaxed. "What about Sexy Rexie jokes? Are those allowed?"

I cringed, waiting for Exie's reaction, but she simply shrugged and said, "I don't get it."

"Empire Records? One of the greatest movies from the 90's? Maybe of all time!" Phoenix's face widened in surprise as the three of us shook our heads, completely in the dark for most movies made in the 90's…. let's be real. "First Ivy hasn't seen Austin Powers. Now this! It's like not humanly possible *not* to have seen these movies."

"Nope, sorry," Exie smiled, turning back into her charming self. "I haven't seen either of those."

"Yikes, Ives, that was a close one," Sloane mumbled into my ear while Phoenix jumped into the cliff notes version of Empire Records and then started dancing…. "Exie almost went apocalyptic on your new friends. Entertaining, yes. But oh so dangerous."

"No kidding," I grumbled. "You have to help me keep an eye on her. No more outbursts."

"What is he *doing*?" Sloane looked over at Phoenix with open curiosity while he wiggled his hips at the same time he shook his outstretched knee and sang into a pretend microphone.

"I have no idea," I blinked a few times just to make sure this was real.

"It's from the movie," Exie giggled. "Some character named Lucas?"

Kenna walked over from where the rest of the band was hanging out and smiled at us. "Hey, we're all headed over to Amsterdam for some late night doner kebobs. You guys want to come?"

"Yes, curry fries!" Phoenix whispered excitedly while pumping his fist like a goofball.

"You're such a dork," I laughed, feeling surprisingly light after the concert tonight, even if I was going to have to get to the bottom of Ryder's solo-song-disaster. Inconspicuously of course. I so did not want Kenna finding out her boyfriend wrote a song about a girl he apparently didn't even like.

"Ives, you promised. You said you would be a groupie and do groupie things. Uh… some groupie things," Phoenix reminded me, circling his abnormally long finger in my face. "You're a Sugar Skulls fan for life now; you're obligated to hang out with us after shows."

"Ugh, you're right," I pretended to be annoyed. "I do love curry fries though, so maybe it's worth my eternal devotion."

"Oh me too," Sloane groaned.

I shot her a look completely surprised that she actually ate fries. I thought I was the only one that cheated on my diet. Maybe I wasn't the only freak after all.

Maybe our mothers would send us all away.

At least we'd have each other.

We walked over to join the rest of the band while they gathered the last pieces of their equipment and headed for the exit. My cell phone vibrated in my pocket signaling a new text message and since Exie and Sloane were here with me I knew there was only one other person that would be trying to get ahold of me so late.

And it was not Chase.

I groaned before pulling out my phone to check the message.

Where are you? Nix is here. Home. Now.

My mother had this unique way of texting that reminded me of old school telegrams. In my head, after each phrase ending with a period, I would mentally say "stop." Where are you-stop. Nix is here-stop. The war is over-stop. And so forth and so on.

"I've got to go," I announced to no one in particular, but everyone turned around.

"What? Why?" Exie asked a bit desperately which made me think she actually had a fun time tonight.

"I got a text from my mom. She wants me home," I explained. My friends would understand. If my mom called me home, it was not to spend time with her.

"Bummer," Sloane agreed. "Mom was out tonight and my curfew was forgotten.

"Hey you guys can still go. Why not? Just drop me off first and then you can meet up with everyone." I gave my friends my brightest smile and hoped they wouldn't give up on this night of normalcy just because of me. Plus, they would be able to have a better time if I wasn't there.

"Okay, we could do that. If you're cool with it," Sloane asked Exie, not wanting to drag her to something she didn't want to go to, but I could easily tell they were both kind of dying to go.

It wasn't often that we had the chance to hang out like other normal kids. We were either attending social functions in our circle, or on dates. And we hated both activities.

"I could hang," Exie replied, hoping to maintain her careless attitude.

"And I could take you home," Ryder offered from a little ways away. "I actually have a curfew, unlike everyone else, so I have to head home anyway."

He looked at Kenna and shrugged his shoulder casually, like it was no big deal. She narrowed her eyes just the tiniest bit but returned his slightly beseeching look with a casual double-shoulder shrug. I didn't shrug at all because it was a *big freaking deal*!

"Uh, it's okay, they don't mind," I scrambled to get out of this.

"Yeah, but it's way out of their way. This way they don't have to cross Dodge and then backtrack," Ryder argued.

I blushed beat red. Why did he have to make so much out of this? "Really, they don't care. Do you girls mind?" I pressed frantically, but when they refused to meet my eye and offer me immediate reassurance I stopped thinking of them as friends and started referring to them as traitors.

Traitors of the worst kind.

"See? It's no big deal, Red. It's just a ride," Ryder said more forcefully. I knew I lost this battle, that I would have to agree, but his commanding tone proved he was just bossing me around again and after that little stunt with the song I really wanted nothing to do with him.

"Fine," I gave in to get the attention off me and for no other reason. "Thank you."

"Alright, now that *that's* settled," Hayden broke in with his usual arrogance. "We have to go now or they will be closed and I won't get my falafel, damn it."

That broke the silent spell that had fallen over our group while Ryder and I argued awkwardly. Everyone turned to leave, falling back into their loud conversations. I let everyone pass by me while I weighed my options and reviewed the bus schedule in my head.

Once outside in the chilly late October air I searched the street for any sign of public transportation. Unfortunately, this part of town had fallen eerily quiet. Tucked to the north of the busiest part of downtown, and filled with shops that all closed earlier, even pedestrian traffic didn't exist. No bus in sight, not even a cab to overcharge me for the ten minute drive.

"Bye, Ivy, I'll call you later?" Sloane waved while walking toward her vintage BMW.

"Better let me call you," I sighed.

"Oh right. Nix," she bit her lip thoughtfully while her expression pulled down into sympathy.

"I'll be fine," I forced a smile.

"I know," she said quickly.

We both knew these were lies. She very well knew I would not be fine.

"Bye, Ex," I shouted after her. She waved me off, still distracted with conversation and Phoenix.

"So, are you ready for this? Because I don't think you are. I don't think you are ready for the awesomeness that is the..... Bronco!" Ryder called enthusiastically from behind me. I heard his hands hit against hollow metal in a slow drum roll that echoed in the empty night air.

Swallowing against a sudden onslaught of nerves, I turned around and came face to face with the ugliest POS ever created. Or maybe it couldn't even be considered a creation. Maybe it was something more like leftover volcanic ash, or demon vomit.... granted, a lot of rusted blue and gray demon vomit, but demon vomit nonetheless. This was not happening.

"You're joking, right?" He had to be. There was no way this thing could start, let alone safely drive me home. Pathetic didn't even come close to describing this sorry excuse for a vehicle. Rundown didn't even fit in the same synonym family. No, this car, SUV... uh, whatever you were supposed to call it was the reason all those global warming activists attacked motor vehicles. The Bronco as he called it, was a dilapidated piece of machinery born from maybe the eighties? What pieces of the car weren't covered in rust were painted in a shabby gray or pale blue, one of the headlights dangled precariously from its empty socket, both side mirrors hung at unnatural angles and the hood was crumpled and squished like an accordion. I felt my mouth sag open and my eyes widen in shock.

"You're in love aren't you?" Ryder beamed at me, waggling his eyebrows while brushing a gentle, loving hand across the hood. "She's my baby."

"*She* is not a baby. She's like your grandma.... on hospice care," I commented dryly. "Pull the plug, Ryder. It's not humane to keep up the life-support at this point."

"Don't be rude. She's safe, I promise. She's just a little rough on the eyes."

"She's deadly on the eyes. I feel like I'm going to turn into a pillar of salt any moment now," I laughed a little. This was kind of fun. I had never ridden in a junker before. I didn't even know anybody who owned a junker before this moment.

"You're a comedian tonight," Ryder drawled, clearly unimpressed with my sense of humor. "Besides, it's what's inside that counts."

He let his hand trail up the hood as if he was actually apologizing for my cruel words and opened the passenger side door for me. The gesture tore my mind away from the sorry excuse for transportation and to how he leaned against the door, waiting for me to climb in. He was actually being kind of sweet…. even though I just insulted his car. Part of me wanted to panic that he thought we were more than we were, even while part of me swooned at his thoughtful chivalry. But most of me instinctively knew this was just the kind of guy Ryder was. He dressed like a bad boy, even had an attitude and a terrifying car to go with it. Also, there were the arm tattoos. But he wasn't one. He was good all the way through his spotless soul. Just another reason to keep him way, way out of my life.

And definitely enough reason to convince him never to write a song about me again.

"Thank you," I murmured while I climbed into the surprisingly clean interior. The outside might have been made out of more rust than paint and appeared to be more skeleton than healthy body, but his upholstery wasn't torn or ripped, there was a newer cd player where an older radio had clearly been ripped out and behind the front bench seat the rest of the interior had been stripped down to make room for transporting band instruments and equipment in a comfortable and efficient bed.

I waited for Ryder to buckle up and pull out of his on-street parking spot before bombarding him with fury. Gentleman or not, he should never have written a song about me. "No more songs about me, Ryder. What the hell were you *thinking*?"

"Uh-"

"I'm serious. How dare you! Kenna actually thought that song was about *her*. And I wasn't going to be the one tell her differently. But if I were her, I would have found that really insulting since the song was *mean*. Did you know that? It was mean! Is that really what you think about me?" I demanded wildly.

"Ivy, calm down," he ordered in his superior-I'm-more-of-an-adult-than-you-are voice. Which of course, was no way to get me to calm down. "Yes, the song was about you, but it wasn't… All it was… Okay, I was just inspired by your tattoo. That's all. There's no hidden message from me to you, if that's what you're getting at. I just thought your tattoo was kind of cool and it gave me this great idea. I sat down with my guitar and the hook just came to me, Okay? I thought you would be… flattered." He stuttered through his apology, keeping his eyes locked on the empty one way streets of downtown. I should have taken this opportunity to cut all ties with him. Not that I would punish him for the song much longer anyway, although I was taking a serious hit to my self-esteem, but because clearly he was too attached to me. And I didn't need that.

"It's just, you scared me," I whispered. The words felt stupid in my mouth even as they fell into the air between us. I couldn't explain my fears for our friendship and I sure as hell couldn't explain my feelings. I just hoped he would let it drop.

"Scared you?" Ryder glanced over at me, his charcoal eyes darkened to black in this light and his eyebrows pulled together in concern. I wanted to be honest with him. I wanted to tell him the truth.

See? Dangerous.

"I like you," I admitted out loud and then realized what that sounded like. "Shoot. I mean, I like you as a friend. You're a... friend. And I don't have many of those. I just don't want to jeopardize what we have here."

"Oh you mean the constant bickering and fighting? Me either. I love that," Ryder half laughed, half winced.

"Yes," I smiled at him. "I don't get to do this with anybody else. Nobody else... fights with me."

They control me. Or they use me. But I wasn't about to say that either.

"And me writing a song about you is going to change that? You know it wasn't like a love song or anything, right?" Ryder asked, his gravelly voice deep with concern.

"Please, I know that. You practically called me an evil bitch on stage to a room full of people. I am perfectly aware of how lacking in love that song was," I rolled my eyes even though he was watching the road.

"So what's the problem?"

Before I could stop myself I opened my mouth and spewed... truth. "I just want to make sure we *stay* friends. If you haven't guessed, I have kind of an... f-ed up home life. And... if we were anything more, anything like... together, I would have to give this up. Not that we would be or anything. I mean, not that you're interested. But as long as we remain just friends, it doesn't really matter. Friends is fine. But *never* anything more."

"Ivy, I only like you as a friend," he promised with heavy tones of sadness.

"This isn't reverse psychology, Ryder," I snapped, angry that he thought this was my plea for attention. "I'm serious. I can be friends with you but nothing more. You might not like me now or even ever, but I just want you to know if there is ever anything between us, I mean, even the smallest spark I am walking away from you immediately. There can't be anything, *ever*, or I will never see you again."

"Okay, yeesh. I got it! It's not something we need to worry about right now anyway," he said carefully. He glanced over at me again, but I was too embarrassed to look at him to see what his expression was doing now. Finally, after several long minutes he asked quietly, "What about Chase?"

I took even longer to answer, digging deep for courage. This would be a lie, but a necessary one. "Things aren't really working out for Chase and me. He's a really nice guy and all, but-"

Ryder fell back against his seat like I knocked the wind out of him. His jaw turned to stone and his hands gripped at the steering wheel angrily. When we pulled up to the full block-long circular drive in front of my apartment building Ryder threw the Bronco into park and looked over at me.

His narrowed eyes were calculating and made me shrink under their intensity. He was pissed. So much more than pissed. There was a muscle ticking in his jaw and his intensity radiated off him like heat.

"You know I'm going to have to tell him," he finally announced with deadly calm. "He's my friend. And he *likes you* Ivy."

"You don't understand," I mumbled weakly. And he never would.

"I guess I don't," he grunted. "Want to explain it to me?"

"I can't," I practically whimpered.

Never before had I felt this bad. Well, except for Sam, but that wasn't until the night of the accident, until after our relationship screwed up his entire future. But this had to be worse. This was judgment, cold, hard and final. I didn't even need to go through the whole "stay away from me" speech. Ryder would have no problems keeping his distance after this conversation.

"Blackheart?" he mumbled into the awkward silence.

"Blackheart," I confirmed. He finally got it at least. Well, his song proved that he understood, but now he *got it*. The truth would settle into whatever left over good thoughts he had about me and ruin them.

"I wanted to be wrong." His words were soft and sad in his voice, but dug into my heart like a dagger.

"But you weren't," I mumbled. Unwanted tears started to prick at the backs of my eyes and I willed myself not to show emotion in front of Ryder. He couldn't get it. He *wouldn't* get it, if I was honest with myself. Nobody could.

A sharp rapping on the window caused us both to jump in our seats. Ryder's window was being assaulted by angry pounding and I leaned forward so I could see around him, see why somebody was so desperate to get our attention.

"Shit," I groaned. "Shit. Shit. Shit." Not very ladylike, I know.

Ryder rolled down his window to address the angry man standing outside. "Can I help you?"

"Ivy?" Nix demanded, panicked and mad as hell. "What are you doing in this car? Are you okay?"

I bit back a thousand sarcastic remarks. Of course a car like this would startle Nix. He probably thought the driver was some homicidal maniac trying to kidnap me. Or he sensed the difference in Ryder from wherever the hell he was before now and had to come investigate what was up.

Or maybe he just saw me with another guy and transformed into the possessive psychopath he really was.

Had he been waiting for me? Or was this a coincidence?

"Uh, Nix, this is my friend Ryder. He gave me a ride home tonight," I explained in my softest, most patient voice ever. I shot Ryder a calming smile and willed him to return it.

"I hope this car is safe, young man," Nix turned his blindingly handsome face on Ryder and his voice turned cold and authoritative. Nix was just crazy enough to believe Ryder would be his competition and if I didn't separate them soon, Nix would also be holding a verbal pissing contest. Not really fair for an ancient douche bag to go up against an innocent-vaguely-naïve-high-school-kid... But that was Nix. Nothing stood in the way of what was his.

"Absolutely," Ryder answered. "I would never intentionally hurt Ivy, Sir."

I bit back a groan and then had to sit on my hands to keep from slapping them over my eyes. I could not watch this. This was going to end badly.

First the song and now this? I was not sure the night could get worse.

"Well, since you're her friend, why don't you join us upstairs for a while? Ivy's mother and I would love to get to know one of her school friends better. Especially one she trusts to drive her home."

Ryder sent me an encouraging smile, probably hoping he was doing me a favor. Holy hell, he probably thought Nix was dating my mom, or some father-figure in my life.

I was wrong. *So wrong.* This night could definitely end worse.

And why was Ryder suddenly being nice to me? I so wished he would have just told me to piss off and then left me on the sidewalk.

"Sure, I have a few minutes before curfew," Ryder answered with a friendly-love-me smile, totally the polite gentleman.

Oh, no! He was actually going to try to win Nix over.

Cheese and rice, this was going to be a disaster.

Chapter Twenty-Two

The elevator ride to the apartment was silent and awkward. I felt Ryder trying to catch my eye while Nix stared straight ahead, his jaw tight with agitation. I simply watched my shoes, unable to bare Nix's frustration or Ryder's curiosity.

"This way," Nix instructed once the elevator doors opened.

We followed dutifully behind. Ryder cleared his throat, still trying to get my attention.

"This is a really nice building, Ivy," he announced, no longer trying to be discreet. Not that he would see a reason to be anything but normal.

"Thanks," I mumbled. My body was rigid with anxiety, my stomach flipped riotously as I waited for the blade to drop on this guillotine.

"My dad and I live in a loft downtown, but it's an older building so it's not nearly as nice," Ryder went on.

Nix opened the door to the apartment and held it for us. "Is it one of those with all the exposed brick?"

Ryder sounded more confident when he answered, "Yes, it is. My dad loves the architecture downtown."

"I do too," Nix replied sounding deceptively friendly. "I recently rented one off thirteenth."

"Ours is closer to tenth, but we looked at ones over there," Ryder explained. I met his eyes then and he sent the question of who Nix was through his stare.

"Ava," Nix called out when the door closed behind us. "Ivy brought a friend."

My mother appeared in the foyer with a plastic smile on her face. Her eyes darted to Nix when she realized my friend was a boy. I looked back to the ground completely ashamed of the situation for everyone.

"I'm Ava, Ivy's mother," my mom introduced herself to Ryder casually. "You are?"

Ryder took in my mother with widened eyes. She was gorgeous as ever, with her auburn hair down and soft around her shoulders, and a tight pencil skirt and silk blouse. She was perfection and Ryder could easily see that. "I'm Ryder Sutton. Ivy and I go to school together."

"How nice," my mom murmured, narrowing her forest green eyes just a bit. "Why don't you come in?"

She turned on her heel and led us all to the delicate dining table. Nix sat down and the rest of us followed suit, except for my mother who disappeared into the kitchen to make drinks.

"Ivy is going to have a glass of water," my mother announced from the other room. "Would you like one, Ryder?"

"Yes, please," Ryder called back.

"So what class do you have together?" Nix initiated conversation. He was pushed away from the table with his legs crossed in that masculine way very virile men can pull off. One hand rested on his bent knee, while his other arm draped over the back of my chair. My nerves were strung tight this close to him, but even more so because of Ryder watching me from across the table. It was like he thought he would finally get his answers here. I had just admitted to a bad home life not ten minutes ago and now he had a front row seat to find out why.

Except he wouldn't get answers tonight. Just more questions.

Probably starting with why he thought I lied to him.

"We're not actually in any classes together," Ryder answered.

When Nix stayed silent, obviously waiting for more, I volunteered some information. I knew it would cost me later, but I would have done anything to break up the tension radiating at my back. "I'm dating one of his really good friends, Chase."

"So you're a senior?" Nix pressed, like he knew all about Chase. A shiver slid over my skin while I wondered exactly what he did know.

"Yes, he is," I answered quickly.

"No, I'm not," Ryder corrected. My head snapped up to meet his eyes then. I realized I always assumed he was a senior but had never confirmed whether that was true or not. I felt really stupid. "I'm a junior like Ivy."

A fire of indecision spread through my veins. I had been assuming he would graduate and leave after this year. I hadn't realized how much I was looking forward to being away from him and all the confusion he brought with him. At the same time, unexplainable joy followed quickly in its wake. We would be together for another year. And even if our friendship ended after Chase and we never talked again I knew just being in the same school as him would mean something to me.

"Honestly, we're only friends through Chase," I said quickly, hating how callous I sounded. "Ryder was just nice enough to give me a ride after mom texted."

Ryder looked at me like I just shot his puppy, so I sent him a pleading look not to say anything differently. His gaze intensified at the same time his mouth pressed into a grim line. This was important. He needed to leave.

My mom came back in the room and when Ryder stayed staring at me instead of looking at the perfection that was my mother, I felt Nix tense

172

next to me. Men weren't supposed to be able to help but look at my mother.

"What do your parents do?" My mother asked, feeling the same absence of attention Nix noticed.

Ryder accepted his glass of water from my mom, and then explained, "My mom passed away when I was a baby actually, but my dad is a professor at UNO."

"Oh how sad," my mom gasped with the appropriate amount of sympathy even though I knew she felt none. "Did Ivy tell you her father also passed away when she was a baby?"

"She did," he answered simply.

"Really? Ivy isn't usually so open about her past," Nix's tone was clipped and reprimanding and I felt every one of my privileges slipping out of my grasp.

"It's just something we have in common," Ryder replied more politely than ever. My eyes flickered over to him and I could tell he was just barely holding onto his control. Something set him off and I had to wonder if it was me or Nix.

The iciness of controlled anger settled into the atmosphere around us. I hated having Ryder here, having him face my mother and Nix. This was a place I didn't want anyone to see, least of all him. And when his expression turned from fury to wild concern I wanted to push him out the door and make him promise to never have anything to do with me again.

At the same time I wanted him to never leave.

"Ryder has curfew," I blurted suddenly. "He should probably go."

I stood up before anyone could challenge me and walked straight for the door, hoping Ryder would follow. I pulled frantically on the handle and held it open until he made his stunned appearance around the corner. He was leaving, but it didn't look like he was happy about it.

"I'm going to walk him to the elevator," I called when he was finally through the doorway.

I shut the door behind me and grasped his wrist with a shaking hand. I needed to act normal, act like everything was fine. Even though it wasn't. I needed him to believe that it was.

"Hey thanks for the ride," I tried to smile while I tugged him along to the elevator.

"No problem," he answered slowly. "Hey, Ivy, is everything-"

My apartment door opened and Nix filled out the doorframe. He didn't say anything, just watched us from the end of the hall. I slammed my finger into the down button as soon as I was in reach and released his wrist before Nix could make anything of it.

"I'll see you tomorrow at school," I said in way of goodbye.

"Sure, Red," Ryder answered, finally taking the hint. "I'll see you tomorrow."

And then he stepped into the elevator and was gone.

A breath of relief whooshed out of me and I felt like I could finally turn back and face Nix.

"One boy at a time, Ivy. You know the rules," Nix scolded before I could even get through the door.

"He's not…. I swear, it was just a ride," I promised. My voice was shaky, my eyes unable to meet his. Which wasn't fair since it *was* just a ride on his part. I hated that it felt like more to me.

The door closed with a bang behind Nix and startled me. I ignored the way my heart hammered in my chest and the goose bumps rose on my arms. I went back to my place at the table and sipped from my water as if nothing happened.

"Ivy," my mother started.

"Mom, I haven't even broken up with Chase yet, please don't start," I begged.

"Is he always like that?" she asked, ignoring my statement.

"What do you mean?"

"Is he always so composed?" she clarified calmly but I watched her eyes dart nervously to Nix.

"He's really shy," I lied. I wasn't sure how else to explain his lack of interest. They could never know about his immunity from the curse. Never. Better to play up my mother's insecurities anyway. "He's also pretty oblivious. The first time I met him he didn't see me until he crashed into me."

"Crashed?" Nix asked noticing my word choice.

"With two cups of coffee," I smiled weakly. *Please buy it. Please buy it. Please buy it.*

"That's not what we're here to talk about anyway," my mother's tone was sharp and to the point. "We want to know what Smith took you into his office for the other day. And before you deny it, I know you went in there. I watched him close the door."

I mashed my lips together, sliding them back and forth while biting painfully into them until they felt bruised and swollen. I knew these questions were coming, I just didn't think she actually saw us go in there. She was way too sneaky.

"He had this book on depression he wanted to give to me," I replied carefully, slowly. I had practiced this answer in my head a hundred times since Sunday. This interrogation was inevitable, but it didn't make me any less nervous. "But I said no thank you. I didn't want him to think my condition was worse than it is. He was just worried about me."

Nix sat thoughtfully for a few moments while my explanation digested between us all. His dark eyes narrowed in thought and his sculpted eyebrows pulled together. My mother sat demurely to my left, swirling her martini nervously. She tried desperately to wait for Nix to speak, to respond first, but her own self-doubt couldn't hold her back.

"He was worried about you?" she echoed in the same casual tone I used. "Worried that you were still battling with depression? How sweet."

"What else did he say, Ivy," Nix demanded, knowing there was more.

"He thought maybe," I paused. This was dangerous ground. But what else could I do? "He thought maybe mom had something to do with why I was sent away."

I cleared my throat while that grenade settled.

"Smith," Nix growled.

"Damn that man," my mother echoed.

Like *Smith* was the villain. She married him to get knocked up, take all his money and then watch him die. And Nix orchestrated the entire plot.

"What did you tell him, Ivy?" Nix asked, his eyes flickering up to mine. They were fierce and demanding. They were eyes that would not be lied to.

"I told him the truth," I began and forced myself to control the tremble in my voice. "I told him I went away because of Sam."

More pause. Nix looked down into the depth of his scotch glass and seemed to simply watch the oversized ice cube melt. My mother's gaze flitted between me and her employer and I wanted to roll my eyes and demand she grow a backbone. I was her *daughter.*

But she wasn't afraid of me.

Not like she was afraid of Nix.

"Did you tell him what happened with you and Sam Evans?" Nix finally asked.

"No, not specifically," I answered quickly.

"Have you told anyone what happened?"

"I, uh, no. Kids at school assume the accident was my fault. But everyone knows it was a drunk driving thing. There's a.... a, uh, can at school for him," my voice was a whisper, weak, tremulous and delicate.

"A can?" Nix asked in a gruff voice. He was impatient with me. I had failed him. I had failed him in lots of ways, but tonight he was frustrated with my weakness.

"They take donations for his recovery. He will be wheelchair bound for the rest of his life." I sucked in a breath, feeling as though my soul was being scraped across broken glass. The empty remains of my heart lay shattered on the floor and I continued to drag my fragile soul back and forth until I was left bleeding and desperate.

"Ivy, we're not still here are we?" Nix suddenly demanded, standing abruptly from his chair. "Sam chose to drive after drinking. Hell, Sam chose to drink as much as he did. You cannot keep blaming yourself for his poor decisions. And when I think about what could have happened to you, how he could have hurt you...." His expression broke for just the briefest second and I saw actual emotion behind his perfect façade of control. My breath stuttered in my lungs at the thought he would actually care what happened to me. "It's time to get over it. Grow up, Ivy. Be an adult for once and put the blame of this unfortunate situation where it belongs. No more sulking. I mean that, no more." he finished on a growl and then stalked into the kitchen where he threw his still half-full glass into the sink. The glass shattered against the stainless steel, the sound of splintered shrapnel breaking up the shock he left behind.

My mother simply stared at me, unsure what to do with Nix's show of emotion or my still-obvious trauma.

"Ivy," Nix's voice was gravel and rocks when he returned and leaned against the wall. "The boy that was here tonight, he would be a good choice for you next. He will give you a bit of a challenge. You need that. How long have you been with the other one, the one you're with now?"

"Not even two weeks," I mumbled.

"Give it two more," Nix commanded. "And then the other boy."

"He has a girlfriend," I pleaded desperately. "They are in love. I couldn't.... I'm friends with her too."

His eyes darkened with anger until they were black orbs of fury, sucking the light of the room into their depths. "Don't be ridiculous," he hissed. "This isn't a discussion. You know that. I have business in Greece for the next two weeks. When I return, my apartment will be ready. I've decided to stay until this group of legacies graduates. You have two weeks to find a way to deal with all of this. I don't want to see any traces of this when I return. Am I understood?"

I could only look up at him for a few seconds, hating him with every fiber of my being, with every molecule and atom I was made with. "Yes, I understand," I finally answered, meeting his stare at the same time my fingers traced along my ribs where a tattoo that meant more to me than anything else in this world was etched. "I'll be better, Nix."

"Ava, don't disappoint me," Nix turned his attention to my mother who audibly gasped at his words. "I'm leaving her in your hands. I want her perfect again. Do your job as her mother for once in your life."

She nodded pathetically, barely able to meet his intense eyes.

"Good," he finally growled and then pushed off the wall.

My mother and I sat perfectly still long after the door slammed behind him. Neither of us could meet the other's eyes or get up to move around. He was everything in both of our lives. We both bent to his will, followed his commands.

The difference between us couldn't be more obvious. My mother resigned herself to this life a long time ago. There was no other existence for her.

And for me? This was the only existence I refused to live. I would play my part. But Nix would not rule over me forever.

I decided to call Smith in that moment. He offered help and I would take it. Things could always get worse than they were now- but not by much. And that was a risk I had to take, because if I waited much longer I wouldn't be able to leave. I wouldn't be able to piece back together all of the broken pieces that ceased to make a whole person. There would only be the ghost of me that remained.

A ghost, just like my mother.

Chapter Twenty-Three

"Ivy," Ryder called before I could even step foot inside the building.

Damn it. I hoped my whole plan to arrive late and leave early, avoid even eye contact with him and ignore all people completely would work out in my favor. Apparently, Ryder came prepared this morning, verbal guns blazing and all.

"What?" I grunted. I knew this was coming. Obviously he would have questions. But it didn't make me any more excited to deal with them.

"You need to talk to me, Ivy." He leaned against one of front doors waiting to attack me. His arms crossed over his chest pulling his faded blue long sleeved t-shirt tight across his biceps, his jeans hung loose and torn at the knees and thighs. His black combat boots went untied and still damp from the constant fall drizzle outside. And his hair, oh good lord, his untamable hair. His wild, bed-head hair stood up haphazardly in every direction. The dark brown locks going straight up only to fall over at the tips and tell the story of a hand being dragged through them in frustration, or anger, or…. desire.

Energy rushed through me at the sound of my name on his lips. I paused in the doorway, without consciously deciding to stop. He had that kind of control over me. He called to me. Intoxicated me. He was becoming so much more to me than I should have ever let him. And yet my eyes were locked to his even while I screamed internally at my legs to move.

"About what?" I shrugged one shoulder and waited. I was hoping if I could pull of indifference maybe he would chicken out.

"Who is that guy?" his deep voice demanded, even while I watch his tongue wet his bottom lip and his jaw clench with some kind of raw emotion I couldn't identify.

"What guy?" I whispered, forcing my eyes back to his.

"Stop it, Red. Just stop." I winced against his harsh tone and his gray eyes immediately softened.

"I can't," I shook my head desperately and then glanced down the hallway nervously.

"You told me we were friends last night. You. *You're* the one who told me we were friends. Let me be your friend," he pleaded in the softest voice I had heard him use.

I tilted my head so that I could inspect my Tory Burch flats and the hot pink skinny jeans that were basically painted on my legs. I could kick myself right now. Keeping Ryder at a distance did not mean declaring a relationship with him even if it was of the platonic variety. And it certainly didn't mean including him in all the twisted intricacies of my life.

"Ivy," he breathed. He took a step forward and very gently slipped his fingers into the hand hanging limply at my side. "I'm not going to do or say anything that will get you into trouble. But I need to know that you're alright."

The warmth of his fingers spread through my body like liquid heat, infecting every inch of me. I felt every small connection of his skin to mine, the pads of his fingers, his joints that bent to curve around my hand, the heel of his hand as it pressed into mine. I closed my eyes against the sensation. The feeling was so profound, so all consuming that it intensified until my fingertips tingled and my toes curled. I closed my eyes and prayed this was all that Ryder was, just a rush of feeling, of sensation, that the only pull I felt to him was the rush.

But even I wasn't that good at lying to myself.

"Are you in trouble?" he whispered.

"No," I felt myself answer. "He's just a friend of my family. He... he's overprotective of me. That's all."

I made myself look up at him and meet his penetrating gaze. I mashed my lips together and begged him to drop this.

"I just want-" he started, but didn't get to finish.

"Oh, good you found her!" Phoenix called from down the hall. He was walking toward us from the same classroom I knew Chase was in and I instantly felt guilty. I pulled away from Ryder immediately, breathing easier with the small distance. "So have you asked her yet?"

Ryder shook his head, his expression pulled into masked pain. He smiled at Phoenix as he approached with a large wooden hall pass swinging in his hand, but his eyes stayed hard granite, pinched in the corners and he raked his hand through his already tousled hair as if he were trying to pull it from its roots.

"Ask me what?" I braved, ignoring the way my voice cracked and tremble.

"Your friends spilled your secret last night, Ives," Phoenix announced somberly and I felt all the breath leave my chest in a whoosh of panic.

"What do you mean?"

"About the you know," Phoenix's brow turned down to concern before he mimicked playing the piano, his fingers wiggled animatedly in the air. "Exie said you could seriously play."

"Oh, the piano? Um, yeah, just a little bit," I answered. My breathing returned to normal, but this secret was no less dangerous.

"They said you were super talented," Phoenix pressed.

"I don't know about that. I've been playing most of my life though," I answered truthfully. I embraced the distraction from Ryder's intense focus and line of questioning.

"So you'll play for us then?" Phoenix asked so casually I almost didn't catch the weight of his words.

"What do you mean? For Sugar Skulls?" I asked a bit hysterically.

"Yeah, we're looking for a keyboardist," Phoenix's eyes lit up with excitement and expectation while Ryder stilled to stone next to me. "We need you, Ives."

"No, I don't think you do," I backtracked quickly. "I've only ever played classical. I wouldn't even know how to go about playing with you guys. Plus, it will mess up your whole look if you add a girl. It's cool that you would think of me, but honestly, I would be more work than it's worth."

"Don't be so modest, Red," Ryder chided with a challenge. "I'll help you out, help you get the feel of playing with a band. It will be good for you. Expand your horizons and all that."

I cleared my throat nervously. "My mom probably isn't going to be okay with it."

Phoenix's entire body sagged with disappointment. His eyes pulled into huge, cartoonish versions of sadness and his lower lip slipped out into the most pathetic pout. "Aw, Ivy, we need you. Come on, don't you want to help out your friends?"

"It's not that. I mean, I would if I could. But you guys probably have lots of practices, plus the gigs and I don't think I can commit to all of that right now. Don't forget, I've never even played in a band before. I've never had to try to play with anyone. It's probably outside of my skill set. I just don't want to disappoint you guys, that's all." I hurried through my list of excuses trying to convince them to look elsewhere but I went wrong somehow. They only seemed to grow more determined the farther down my lame pile of excuses I got.

"How about we just start with one song, yeah?" Ryder asked just a fraction more gently but it was enough to break down my resolve. "You play one song with us and decide from there."

I hesitated, wanting to say yes, but needing to say no.

Phoenix looked at me expectantly, the energy in his body slowly building again until he bounced with the restrained excitement. "Come on, Ivy, we *need* you." he pleaded with me, his hands pressed together in prayer position.

I opened my mouth to say yes when the office door flung wide and Mrs. Tanner hauled her large frame through the narrow space and gasped in horror at our little pow wow. "What is going on out here?" she snapped, her beady eyes falling immediately on me.

"Hall pass!" Phoenix held up the awkward wooden board with an abrupt swing of his arm and started walking backwards toward his classroom. "Check you guys later."

I waved at Phoenix limply and waited for Tanner the Wench's wrath. I leaned back against the wall Ryder was resting on and worked my expression into bored. Not that I wasn't feeling the sharp pangs of panic, but it was more important to piss Mrs. Tanner off than anything else in the world.

"Where's your hall pass Ivy Pierce?" Mrs. Tanner snapped.

"I don't have one. Yet," I clipped the "t" sharply just to get under her skin.

"Ryder? Please don't tell me you're abusing your office aide privileges with *her*," Mrs. Tanner asked desperately in a high shriek.

Before he could even speak, a pang of guilt punched me in the stomach and I knew I had to salvage what was left of Ryder's reputation. "Not to worry, T. Ryder wouldn't be caught dead helping the likes of me. He's smarter than that, aren't you Ryder?" But before he could answer I pushed off from the wall and walked purposefully toward my locker located on the opposite end of the hall. "He was in the middle of sending me to you."

"You're not getting a pass from me," she laughed bitterly and shook her head, gray tinged hair flying.

"That's what I told him," I tossed my thumb over my shoulder and rolled my eyes for her benefit. "I'd much rather take the detention than have to deal with you this early in the morning anyway."

"Careful little girl or it will be worse than a detention," Mrs. Tanner hissed.

I mashed my lips together dramatically and then zipped them closed with my forefinger and thumb before walking on. I didn't even bother to stop by my locker. I shoved my cropped jacket into my backpack on my way to class and didn't slow down until I had been reprimanded by my Government teacher and slid to safety in the seventies era desk.

My heart hammered in my chest, pounding out my guilt and shame for including Ryder on the rollercoaster I lived on. He was crazy to spend more time with me, to ask questions about my life. So much could happen to him, to me…. to us.

And yet my hand still vibrated with little tingles where he touched me.

The morning of classes was a blur of movement and confusion. I knew I went to all of my classes, and walked through the halls to get there, but my mind stayed busy with thoughts of Ryder. *Always* Ryder. I went over his song, the car ride home last night, his interaction with Nix and then again this morning over and over and over until I felt a little bit crazy. The constant argument of whether he was drawn to me because of my curse or that I was completely misreading his intentions warred back and forth in my head until the voices felt like they were screaming at each other.

By the time I walked into lunch I gave up trying to declare a clear winner and gave into the fuzzy haze of exhaustion instead. I avoided the buffet line completely and wandered over to Chase, hoping to extract the easy warmth he readily gave out. The rest of our little group was stretched out on the long benches, munching away at their meals, completely blind to the turmoil spinning inside me.

"Hey," Chase murmured against my hair before he pressed a kiss to my temple.

"Hey," I sighed right back, leaning into him. Instant relief settled over me and I felt myself take my first full breath of the morning.

That is until I lifted my eyes and accidentally met Ryder's disapproving stare from across the table. His granite eyes were back and colder than ever. He shook his head slowly as if I didn't feel bad enough from the look he sent me. His eyes shifted to Chase for just a second before coming back to me. His message was clear.

Just last night Nix gave me a direct order to date him for two more weeks. But Ryder was right. I couldn't keep stringing Chase along. I couldn't treat him like this. Not when he had been so great to me. A shaky breath vibrated through me and I pulled my courage together.

Knowing Nix was out of the country might have helped too.

"Hey, can we go somewhere?" I asked in a subdued voice so only Chase could hear.

"Sure," he smiled down at me until he noticed my expression. "Everything okay?"

"Let's just go somewhere," I stood up quickly and fled from the cafeteria with all of its prying eyes. I felt Chase close behind me but didn't turn around until we had slipped out a west side door that faced the art museum. The drizzle had stopped for now, but the gray October sky promised more rain to follow. The grass between the school and marbled art museum was brown with the threat of winter and soggy and slick with mud.

"Ivy?" Chase asked when I kept my space from him outside and crossed my arms.

"Chase," my voice faltered before I even started with the hard stuff. "You're really great-"

"Oh, no," he sighed. He ran his hands over his face roughly and then had to push his dirty blonde hair out of his eyes. "I'm not going to like this am I?"

"I jumped into this too soon, I think," it felt weird being truthful with him. But this *was* the truth. I was breaking up with Chase for all the right reasons, even if I would have done the same thing for the wrong ones. "I'm just not ready for any kind of relationship. Not even a slow one."

"You're breaking up with me before we were really ever together?" Chase turned his back on me and pressed two palms against the rough stone of the building like he could push through it.

"I just don't want you to think that this was you or anything you did," I rushed to offer promises. "This is all me. I'm just still… broken," I admitted lamely. My voice filled with emotion and my lungs felt closed off and drowning with dread, but between the two of us there was nothing. I didn't know Chase enough to really be upset about it. The only emotions I felt were selfish and shallow. I felt bad for letting him down and guilty for letting the curse pull him in only to push him right back out.

"What is that? An *it's not you, it's me speech*?" He looked over his shoulder at me. His cheeks red with frustration and his eyes shifted to hard blue orbs of anger, but he was a good enough man to treat me gently.

"No," I swore. And then hated the lie. "Okay, maybe?"

That earned me a small crack in his surly demeanor and he smiled at me. "I really like you, Ivy." His words were a harsh whisper of declaration.

"No, you don't," I whispered back. "You think you do. But you deserve someone who can give you everything, who can give you a complete version of a relationship." The truth hurt as it came out of my mouth, like it was barbed and prickly and ripped from my throat. It settled into the air like weights pressing against my chest, oppressive and suffocating.

"What if I would rather have you?" Chase turned around so he could face me again. He brushed away the leftover gravel on his hands against his pants. His gaze was piercing, demanding.

"You can't have me, Chase."

We stared at each other for a few moments while he accepted this truth. There was no real connection between us; our interest in each other had barely been two weeks long. Still, the curse was hard to walk away from. That was the whole point.

Sailors to their graves and all.

"Does anyone get to have you, Ivy?" he asked somberly. His blue eyes were the deepest I'd seen them, dark rises of ocean waves.

I shook my head and looked away.

Nope, no one got me. And I planned to save all mankind by keeping that true.

"When you're, um, not broken anymore?" I lifted my eyes to meet his very serious ones. "Think of me?"

"When I'm not broken anymore, Chase, you will be the first person I think of." My throat was thick and coated with emotion and not even because of Chase.

Because I knew there wouldn't be a time when I wasn't broken.

Only a time when I would be free.

Chase shot me one more of his adorable grins and seemed to accept his defeat with grace. "Ivy," he nodded as way of goodbye.

"Goodbye Chase," I forced a smile back and then watched him slip back into the building.

I stood outside in the damp air, the chilly wind coasting across my arms and face. I had no energy to face the halls of high school again after that. I felt emotionally drained and empty. Another breakup was just a reminder in the long list of reasons my life would never be what it should be. Born into this world, I was already a slave. And unless I worked out my own freedom, I would remain a slave until the day I died.

My phone chimed with a new text message. I pulled it out of my jeans pocket and didn't recognize the number although it was local.

Thank you for that.

For what? Who is this?

For Chase. Ryder.

Freaking Ryder.

How did you get my number? I wasn't exactly surprised that he had it. But still.

Your file.

You have access to my file? What the hell…. I kind of wanted to strangle him at this point.

Not why I'm texting. Band practice tonight. I will pick you up. 7.

But I just broke up with Chase.

And I still need you.

My heart started pounding fast and hard in my chest and even though the rational part of my brain screamed he was only talking about the band, I couldn't help but repeat that phrase over and over and over. *I still need you. I still need you. I still need you.*

And even though I knew this was the opportunity to run, to cut ties completely with Ryder and that entire circle of friends that deserved more than knowing me…. I could take on the wrestling team. Or band geeks. Or drop out of school today and save everyone the hassle of dealing with me. My fingers were typing out my response before anything logical and sane registered. Instead the rush of those words were all that I felt.

I still need you.

That's what sealed the deal.

Fine.

Chapter Twenty-Four

"My cell number is not in my file," I declared irritably when I climbed into Ryder's death trap that night.

I had been waiting on the stairs in front of the circular drive in front of my apartment building for fifteen minutes and I was cold and a little bit damp. Even though Nix was out of the country and my mom was off on a date, I hated the idea of Ryder stepping foot in my building again. I wanted him nowhere near where the Queen of the Damned, aka my mother, resided. Nor did I want him caught on security tape entering the building. And even though I was extremely annoyed with him for making me do this stupid band thing... Okay, I was annoyed because he made me *want* to do the band thing... I wasn't stupid enough to draw attention to him twice in one week.

Did I really think Nix checked the security tape of our building whenever he was away, which was usually most of the time?

No.

Well. Maybe.

I wouldn't put it past him.

It was a risk I was not willing to take anyway.

"It's not?" Ryder asked completely innocently. He shot me a crooked smile from the driver's seat of his Bronco, not even calling attention to the fact I didn't say hello. I kind of liked him more for that. He wasn't all about being polite. He could just roll with anything.

"No, it's not."

"Oh," he said thoughtfully while pulling onto Farnam. He ran a hand through his wild mess of hair, making it stand up on its ends. "Huh."

"Huh," I mimicked in an exaggerated tone.

"Okay, Phoenix gave it to me," he admitted without looking at me. His profile was shaded by the evening darkness, only spotlighted every once in a while by a streetlamp or stoplight. I could make out just the barest scruff along his jaw line, not enough to hide the way his neck muscles moved when he swallowed nervously. He probably had the sexiest neck alive. Which was weird of me to think. Right? How sexy could a neck be? It had to be the Adam's apple, or the pronounced muscles... Or the way it connected to his broad shoulders.

I blinked to work myself off of that bizarre thought train.

"And how did Phoenix get it?" He was hiding something, I could feel it. My fingers itched to get to the bottom of this, although I had no idea why he was creating so much mystery.

"He got it from Chase," he breathed on a whisper like he was hiding it. I shot him a meaningful look that demanded he finish his story but he just kept his eyes on the street ahead while he turned left at the next block and then left again so that he could head east on Harney.

"When?"

Ryder didn't answer.

"*Really*, after I broke up with him?" I demanded in a tone full of accusation.

"Ivy, you guys were never really going out," Ryder was so carefully controlled, so condescending that I had to sit on my hands to keep from smacking his arm.

Granted I wouldn't have done much damage.

"Fine, we weren't really going out. That doesn't mean rub it in the guy's face," I huffed.

"Why is that?" Suddenly Ryder was staring at me. His gray eyes piercing through the darkness, pinning me to my seat. The car was stalled at a stoplight so he just sat there, staring at me, and waiting for me to answer. "Chase has known you not even two weeks and as far as I know you guys never..."

"We didn't," I rushed to explain away the doubt in his voice. At least sex would explain somewhat of an attachment to me. There wasn't enough air in the car, not even to breathe. I reached for the hand-roll to crank the window down but stopped myself before I could follow the impulse through.

"Then why the devastation? Why the despair? Couldn't you have walked away friends? What did you say to the guy to break his heart?" The light turned green, but Ryder just kept staring at me.

"It's green," I whispered.

"I know," he snapped back and pushed his foot down on the accelerator too hard. The Bronco lurched and groaned but hardly picked up any real speed. "Seriously Ivy, what did you say to Chase to crush him so badly?"

I took three long breaths, trying to find my equilibrium. I'd never had to answer these questions before. Usually, if I stayed in the same dating circle, whoever I moved onto next was just grateful I chose them. Yes, it was sick and destroyed friendships. But I didn't have a choice. It was what I did.

What I would do if I didn't get out of here.

Ryder demanding answers for my behavior wasn't fair. It wasn't. He had no idea the kind of pressure I was under. Or what my mother expected of me.

My own *mother*.

I scratched at my wrist tattoo that was back to being carefully covered up. It was burning like the tattletale it wanted to be.

"I didn't say anything!" I all but shouted. "You don't know anything about us, Ryder, so you have no right to say those things!"

"You must have said *something* though," Ryder pushed, not caring at all that I was upset. "You broke his heart! After two weeks, you managed to *break* his heart!" His hand rammed through his hair, and his jaw ticked with frustration.

There it was. The words that had been spoken so many times in conjunction with me. The words that haunted me. Chased me in my sleep. That never gave me a moment's peace. I broke his heart. After one freaking week, he was broken.

Just like everyone else before him.

Just like Sam.

Just like me.

"You know who I am, Ryder. It's not like it's this great big secret!" My voice was reaching a screeching pitch now, I was all but hysterical. "You've seen the tattoo. You've heard all the rumors. Don't act so surprised just because it plays out in front of you. Let's not forget, you're the one that begged me to break up with him."

Ryder pulled the Bronco over to the side of the road, parallel parking with disgusting ease. He didn't even have to try more than once. He just pulled right into the tight spot and turned the car off.

Abruptly the air became silent between us. There was no loud groan of the engine, no traffic whirring by alongside us. There was only us, in the quiet of the front seat, bathed in the light of the streetlamp overhead.

"Ivy," Ryder started, but his voice was low and careful.

"Don't Ryder. Believe me, there is nothing you can say that can make me feel worse. I didn't want to hurt Chase, okay? I *like* Chase. I think he's great. Just because it was never going to work between us, didn't mean I wanted to hurt him." I stared out the window desperate to avoid Ryder's intelligent eyes or scornful expression. He parked in a long line of cars parallel with the Gene Leahy Outdoor Mall to my right. The trees drooped in autumn death in a perfect line spaced exactly apart from each other. The hills and hills of grass that broke up the downtown industrial-ness in a five city-block long park were brown with the injury of frost-filled nights and barren of the people that usually occupied them during the spring and summer months.

"And there was no way to be more gentle with him? I get that you have your hang-ups, but Ivy, really, there had to be a better-"

"Stop it," I bit out. "You don't know what you're talking about. I was as nice as I could be."

"I'm sure you were," Ryder said in a pacifying voice that really pissed me off. "But maybe if you had just thought-"

"Enough," I shrieked. "You weren't there. You weren't. And you don't know what was said. Besides that, Chase isn't some breakable doll. He's going to be *fine*. Stop treating him like he's fragile. Have more respect for your friend."

"Is that what you think? You think I'm coddling him? You have no idea what you do to men, do you? You have no idea how you affect them!" he was shouting back at me, enunciating certain words with anger and gripping the steering wheel like he wanted to rip it off.

His emotion infuriated me, and he had no idea. He just happened to press every single one of my buttons and he probably expected an apology. Only the thing was, I couldn't even be mad at him. He shouldn't be punished for being right. And he certainly shouldn't be punished because I was cursed.

"You're right," I gave in. Suddenly I was very tired. "I should have handled things differently with Chase."

I watched Ryder open his mouth and then close it out of the corner of my eye and didn't know what to make of his eventual silence. He just kept staring at me, like he could see through me, all the way through me. And not in the way that made me feel like I didn't exist, but in the way that made me feel like I very much existed. Like his stare could reach every single piece of me I tried to hide, tried to tuck away. Like his eyes were super powered and he had no issue with finding every single vulnerable place inside me and shining his bright, brilliant silver spotlight on every last nook and cranny.

"Chase is my friend," Ryder finally settled on the obvious. "But so are you, Ivy. If you want to talk, I will listen."

I swung my head around to finally focus on those unsettling grays.

"I can't-"

"I didn't ask that," Ryder cut me off, his expression fierce and hopeful all at the same time. "I won't ever ask more of you than you can give. But if you want to, I am here for you."

I don't know what my face looked like, or what emotion he watched cross my face because honestly I didn't even know. My blood grew hot with the multitude of them, my skin prickling with something. I felt like my wires were crossed, like my heart knew something my brain didn't because it was pounding in my chest with painful purpose. I shook my head as if to remind myself not to say anything to him, not to even hint at the real purpose.

But I found the words bubbling up before I could stop them; they swam their way to the surface and made it all the way to the tip of my tongue before I could even register what a terrible idea this was.

"Ryder, what you don't know is... there's actually a lot you don't-"

Banging on Ryder's window scared the ever living hell out of me and a blood curdling scream wrenched from my mouth, covering whatever terrible truth I was about to confess.

"What are you guys doing in there?" Phoenix shouted through the closed window, his voice muffled by the glass.

Phoenix. *Good grief.*

My heart beat more frantically than ever against my battered rib cage, and sweat formed at my hairline and lower back. Holy hell, that reminded me of Nix the other night and I was fairly certain I nearly died of a brain aneurism.

"I'm sorry," I panted out of breath. I clutched a hand to my neck and cleared my throat nervously. "I'm really sorry."

Ryder looked at me with concerned shock before finally rolling down the window for Phoenix. "Was that necessary?"

"Sorry, Ives," Phoenix apologized sheepishly. "I didn't mean to scare you."

"It's fine," I waved a dismissive hand, but I was still out of breath. "Honestly, it is. I just wasn't expecting you."

"Are you okay?" Ryder faced me again, his eyes gentled with worry.

"Yes, seriously, I am. I just scare easily," I tried to laugh, but let's be real, I sounded a little deranged. Yep, we were never visiting this conversation again. Obviously, this was the universe's way of warning me.

"You want to go get started?" Ryder asked in that same patient tone. "If you're not up for it, I can just take you home."

And I knew he would. If I wasn't up for this, Ryder would let me go.

I both loved that and hated it at the same time.

I didn't want him to let me go.

"I'm up for it."

And I was. At least for tonight.

Chapter Twenty-Five

I followed Ryder and Phoenix across the street to a standalone brick building with two floors of apartments on top of a small-ish, independent bank. The building was quaint and kind of adorable. There were boxes for flowers hanging out of every second and third story window, but they were empty now because of the season. There was another standalone brick building directly to the east of it, but it was larger and a lighter shade brick than Ryder's and to the west a block down was the Holland Center, a gorgeous modern performing arts center made of steel and glass.

We entered Ryder's building through a side door using a keypad access and came immediately to the stairwell. The building was absolutely quiet and dark, the only disruption our footsteps echoing off the tile floor as the sound got lost in the open stairwell.

We climbed the long flight of stairs in silence, while Phoenix beat his drumsticks against anything that got in his way: his jean-clad thigh, the bannister, the steps in front of him, Ryder's back, my arm. There was obviously a song playing in his head, but he was the only one that could hear it. And in the fast flicking of his hands holding the sticks, I realized where all that contained energy was channeled too. Even though his fingers were constantly moving with rhythm his face was calm now, placid and relaxed. It was like this outlet for him completely sedated him, but in a way that was all creative genius.

At the top of the stairs, Ryder opened the heavy metal door with another key and led us into his apartment.

I was honestly surprised to walk directly into his living space, I expected there to be... I don't know, more to the upstairs. Instead, Ryder's home consisted of the entire third floor of the building. The loft space was mostly open and heavy with industrial design. There was an incredible round concrete table that took up way more space than I could imagine necessary for a family of three. And there were these rusted looking metal chairs that were clearly one of a kind. They had high narrow backs, but wide seats that were fit almost like old tractor seats, maybe? Weird. The kitchen was darker tones of concrete, and mixed with a 1950's inspired collection of appliances. The living room was dark, worn leather couches and a mixture of recycled wood turned into a low coffee table and unique end tables. The living room also faced the street-side windows and was completely devoid of electronic entertainment. Doors to what I assumed were either bedrooms or bathrooms broke up the wall space around the room and I couldn't help but wonder which one led to Ryder's.

"What do you think?" Ryder asked in a quiet, self-conscious voice.

Phoenix's drums suddenly burst through the apartment in random thuds and thumps of energy. While he warmed up I couldn't bite back the smile.

"I love it," I answered. I did love it. I loved the scattered newspaper covering the coffee table, the forgotten about coffee cups still sitting in front of pushed out chairs at the table. I loved the smell of some kind of spicy dinner that remained in the air, Ryder's indoor soccer gear piled in a messy heap by the door. I loved that this place felt like a home. I loved that his home was lived in. "Where did you find all this…. stuff? Who did your dad hire?" I laughed taking in the ginormous table. That must have been insane to move up three flights of stairs and through the narrow door.

"Hire? You mean a decorator?" Ryder's face was scrunched up in confusion. I nodded though, wondering absently what my mom would think about all this. "We didn't hire anybody. My dad has a soft spot for student art and my uncle is big on the whole Renew, Reuse, Recycle thing. Together, they created this…. mess."

"Mess?" I barely held back my offended gasp.

"Yes, Ivy. Mess. This isn't a decorating scheme. This is Goodwill meets the Habitat for Humanity Restore shop and has a love child with every starving artist in the city. It's definitely a mess." Ryder laughed at my expression and I had the urge to smack his arm again.

"Fine, if it's a mess, it's a beautiful mess." I conceded.

"My dad will be so happy to hear that." He shook his head at me and then walked over to the corner of the living room where Phoenix was still beating away at his drum set.

While Ryder pulled out an acoustic guitar and plugged it into his amp I looked down at my royal blue knit dress that stopped mid-thigh and my designer wedge boots. Then I thought about my worn out Chucks in my closet at home and decided something very crucial. I wasn't either of those people. I was this person. Whoever lived in this house, that's who I was.

And for a moment I felt this overwhelming peace, like suddenly I knew exactly who I was and what I wanted out of life. And surprisingly it was more than just escaping.

Suddenly I didn't just want freedom, or escape.

I wanted a house, and people to love.

And someone that loved me.

But then the sounds of guitar strings being tuned broke through the incessant drum beats and I forced myself back to reality.

I shuddered at my thinking because this wasn't an abstract daydream, I *knew* the person that lived here. It was weird that I wanted to be him.

Or have his life.

Or be a part of his life.

No. No... I just wasn't used to being in a happy home. High school house parties were hardly the testament of a loving, doting family and any other time I was invited into a house was with someone from the circle.

So, that's all this was. Nostalgia. Nostalgia for something I didn't know.

"Hayden and Cole are coming later. And Hudson can't make it tonight," Ryder explained when Phoenix finally stopped messing around. "We thought you could try it out with us first, Red, and then when you're comfortable with the rest of the band."

"Sure," I mumbled trying to get back to business. "I don't think it will make a difference, but whatever you want. Do you at least have sheet music? I mean, I'm not good enough to just make something up." My tone was impatient and abrupt. Panic flashed like strobe lights inside me and the unsettling feeling of wanting something I could never have seriously messed me up. This was more than uncomfortable, this was terrifying.

"No one expected you to be," Ryder's voice had that patient, gentle tone again, like he knew I was going through something just standing in his living room.

Damn him.

I wasn't fragile. I lived through a lot of crap. I faced dangerous situations sometimes. Like real danger. He didn't need to treat me with kid gloves.

"So, sheet music?" I pressed.

"It's over on the counter," Ryder gestured with his chin and I dutifully walked over to get the small stack of loose leaf music.

"Is Kenna coming tonight?" I heard Phoenix ask in a muffled voice once my back was turned.

Ryder didn't respond, so I almost turned around to ask the question for Phoenix again when Phoenix's voice made me stop and pretend to fiddle with something on this side of the room.

"Why not?" Phoenix's voice dropped lower, almost so I couldn't make it out.

Ryder replied with something I couldn't understand from here and my curiosity peeked further.

"Why do you think that?" Phoenix asked, outraged. I heard Ryder shush him and I imagined his angry eyes shutting Phoenix right up. "You're crazy man. She would never."

More of Ryder's mumbling. Phoenix made a half grunt, half scoffing noise and then suddenly banged his drumsticks down onto the head of his cymbal. The loud crashing broke up whatever they were talking about and practically burst my inner eardrum.

"Well, Ivy, you ready? Let's get to this," Ryder commanded suddenly as if the cymbal crash never happened.

Or maybe Phoenix did that all the time and Ryder was just used to it. I was not used to it and half expected my ear to be bleeding.

"Sure," I answered unenthusiastically.

I walked over to where a decent Korg was set up facing the drum set. There were about a million buttons on the top of the instrument and the plastic keys were narrow and not enough octaves long. I struggled to hide my grimace at the foreign instrument while I placed my fingers into and an easy C chord and pressed down. The sudden loudness of the triad made me jump and release the keys. The sound immediately stopped, nothing resonated afterward, nothing happened, there just wasn't sound anymore.

"You've played a keyboard before, right?" Ryder asked deadpan.

"Oh yeah, lots of times," I lied but sounded obvious enough that I didn't feel guilty about it.

I ignored the look Ryder and Phoenix were giving each other and took a breath to settle my nerves. I fiddled with the volume button, turning down the sound so it wouldn't rival Phoenix's cymbals and then pressed down on the same chord again. The keys were lighter than I was used to, there was no weight to press into, no heavy feeling of accomplishment. It was just... easy.

With my fingers pressed down, I wiggled them around a little, getting used to the width of each key. When I finally felt like I could wrap my head around the plastic feel of the keys, I lifted off and began moving my fingers in quick scales up and down the shortened octaves. After a while, I flexed my fingers, loving the warm feeling tingling in each joint.

"Wow, you're really good," Phoenix commented in awe.

"Phoenix, I was just warming up," I sighed, a bit exasperated.

"Fine, let's hear it then," Ryder commanded in his gravelly voice. I looked up and accidentally caught his eye. He was staring at me intently, waiting for me to wow him. Only... I didn't want to wow him. I wanted to walk across the room and kiss him. Like attack him with kisses.

What the hell?

Obviously, those psychotic thoughts were enough to get me to move my ass. Instead of Ryder's mouth, I attacked the keys, throwing myself into Piano Concerto by Tchaikovsky. I immediately ran out of keys on the small set of octaves, so I switched to something more contemporary. I ended up not really having the range for that either, so I improvised.

"That's beautiful," Ryder commented. He walked across the small practice space and stood hovering over me while my fingers moved nimbly up and down the cheap plastic keyboard.

"At times," I murmured and then hit a section of harsh, discordant notes.

Ryder laughed softly at the broken, mismatched chords being played before they were switched back to light and airy and sweet again. "What is it?"

I lifted my gaze from my fingers to meet his silver eyes without realizing it. "Romance," I heard myself say out loud in an embarrassingly breathy voice. I cleared my throat and focused back on my hands. "Jean Sibelius."

My fingers danced and flew, crossing over each other and then crossing back. I didn't have a pedal, so the piece sounded choppy and broken up and the very low notes and very high notes were absent, leaving much to be desired, but the captivating melody was there. And I was there, caught up in the music, lost in the swell and intensity as the melody carried us through what I pictured real life romance to be like, easy at first, passionate, consuming, difficult as real life set in, confusing, infuriating, discontented and then back to the best notes, the best sounds and ending with both hands on chords that complimented each other, that made the other whole.... that finished each other.

My fingers lay heavily on the last notes because once I removed them I knew the music would be gone. That it would be quiet again. And even as the last of the sound faded away I stared down at my tense fingers waiting for it.

Ryder placed a hand on top of my own. I stared at the way his tanned, masculine fingers contrasted with the pale ivory of mine. His thumb moved against mine in a sweeping gesture of comfort. "You're incredible," he whispered gently.

I mashed my lips together, forgetting everything else in the room. I lifted my eyes to meet his and the breath caught in my throat. His eyes were liquid pools of silver, intense and exposed all at the same time.

"You're really incredible, Ivy," he whispered again once he had my attention.

"Thank you," I meant to reply but was only capable of mouthing the words.

Finally my fingers lifted from the keys and whatever was left of the faint sounds disappeared completely. Phoenix started clapping obnoxiously before he stood and started whistling for me. "Holy shit, Ivy, that was insane."

I blushed, realizing I had never just had fun playing for anyone before. My mother used my talent to impress dates or Nix. Nix used this to intimidate other legacies. And I hadn't taken private lessons in three years.

"Thanks guys," I breathed, all of a sudden embarrassed.

"You're like a musical ninja," Phoenix bounced over, staring at my hands like they were aliens.

"Definitely a musical ninja, Red," Ryder agreed with a smirk on his lips.

"Yes!" Phoenix exclaimed suddenly. "The ginger ninja.... the Ginga Ninja!"

I burst into laughter. The ginga ninja? Was he serious?

"We'll make t-shirts," Phoenix continued, bouncing on his toes. He was like a human version of Tigger. "You can thank me later."

A loud buzzing interrupted our laughter and Phoenix looked up sharply at me and then swiveled his head to Ryder. "I'll get it," he announced. "It's probably just Hayden and Cole."

Before Ryder could remind him this was his house, Phoenix disappeared out the door and into the stairwell.

"Don't you have a button up here to let them in?" I asked with my eyes on the door.

"They probably need help with their equipment," Ryder explained. His hand on mine again drew my attention back to him. When I faced him he wasn't laughing anymore, his expression completely serious. "I like it when you laugh, Ivy," he admitted in a low voice.

I stood there breathless and frozen. His gaze delved into mine, capturing it, holding it hostage and the heat from his hand scorched my skin wherever it touched me. The keyboard still separated us, but that was the only thing separating us. Other than physical contact, I felt completely drawn into him, Ryder, like he encapsulated all of me, every hidden, secret part of me. And I was helpless against him.

No.

I chose to be helpless. I *wanted* this.

Wanted *him*.

Which was crazy. These feelings were *crazy*. If Ryder had feelings for me there was only one explanation for them. The curse. Always the curse. And even if I could make arguments day and night to why he had never been affected by it before, the truth was that I would always doubt myself. Always. If I acted on my own feelings and there happened to be something between us, I would never be able to trust it.

I would never be able to trust him.

There would never be a way to know that his attachment to me was not because of the curse.

And so I needed to stamp these thoughts and feelings down immediately. If not sooner. If not yesterday....

His tongue ran across his bottom lip, and his gaze dropped to my mouth. I just talked myself out of this, so I should move.

Now. I should move *now*.

My breath returned to my chest in fast, heavy pants. My chin tilted up without my permission, like a sunflower to the sun.

Ryder's gaze heated to desire, his eyes hooded with heavy lids, his mouth opened. He leaned forward, we were just inches apart. Just three inches. "Ivy, I-"

The door to the apartment exploded open with the sounds of banging equipment and three loud boys laughing about something completely grotesque. Ryder and I broke apart immediately, his hand removed from mine, his attention back to his guitar. We avoided each other's gazes and my blush was definitely back.

I might like this band thing.

I might like this circle of friends.

But that could never happen again.

Ever.

Except when I caught Ryder looking at me not four seconds later, I quickly remembered that you were never supposed to say never...

Chapter Twenty-Six

I followed the sheet music religiously. It was the only way I knew how to play. To be honest, it was a bit embarrassing that I didn't have the creative ingenuity to just improvise. Especially when that seemed to be what everyone else was doing.

Especially Ryder.

I knew he was talented, but he didn't have to be the smart kind of talented that made everyone else feel stupid.

I took private lessons for eight years. *Eight.*

He apparently picked up his dad's guitar at twelve and turned into a prodigy.

Ugh.

"I can't do this," I grumbled at the end of the millionth play through. It was this melancholy ballad with a pretty piano melody that played above everything else. Ryder's voice sang rough and raw about a lonely girl with eyes that saw everything and a heart that felt nothing.

As soon as Ryder started singing the lyrics I shot him a sharp look, but he shook his head to deny it. Since then I had been living in a world I liked to refer to as blissfully ignorant. Although, others might have called it denial. Still, if he said it wasn't about me, then who was I to disagree? Also, I didn't want to be the girl he was singing about. She sounded sad, and alone and…. empty.

And I wasn't empty.

Mostly, I was just…. afraid.

Of so many things.

"You were better that time," Ryder called encouragingly after the last notes of the song drifted off to nothing. "You were uh, more on time."

I blushed immediately, a deep red that painted my skin. I could feel the heat in my face and across my collar bone, but there wasn't anything I could do about it. I wasn't used to being bad at something. "This is so different than what I'm used to."

"You're doing really well, Ivy. Ryder's a bastard," Phoenix encouraged from behind his drums. His hairline and the collar of his shirt were damp with sweat but he never stopped twirling his drum sticks. If he wasn't throwing his entire body into the song, then he twirled them between his long fingers while he waited for the next one to start. He looked extra gangly perched upon the tiny drum stool, but this was exactly his element, exactly where I could tell he felt most alive.

"Thanks Phoenix," I smiled at him and his whole face lit up. The curse was extra hard to control when music was involved, but these guys seemed to be okay. Besides, all my frustration and failure probably obscured whatever elevated affects swirled around in the air.

"I didn't mean that you weren't doing well, Red," Ryder immediately put in and I could tell he felt bad for all of his "helpful" tips that had been fraying my nerves for the last two hours. "I was just trying to say that was the best you've sounded. I get that this isn't easy for you."

"It's fine, Ryder," I offered politely. "I get that this is your thing. I don't want to mess it up for you. But I did tell you this would be a problem. I won't be offended if you guys don't want me after all."

"We want you," Hayden piped up quickly. "Ivy, *I* want you at least."

Ugh, that so sounded like an innuendo coming from him.

"Creep much, Hayd?" Cole grunted. I could tell Cole was just as interested in me as Hayden was, but his shy nature and quiet personality kept him from turning into stalker material.

"Shut it, Cole," Hayden grumbled.

"Why don't you both shut up and leave her alone?" Phoenix's voice rose above both of them.

Okay, and this was my cue to leave.

"Actually, I have to get home before my curfew," I announced cavalierly. "Sorry to break up practice."

Everyone gave a whine of disappointment but backed away from the fight that was about to break out. Well, everyone except Ryder sounded disappointed. I chanced a peek at him, but he was already looking at me, eyes narrowed, expression tense. His hand was half way through his hair and tugging at the roots.

"I'll just take these," I picked up the sheet music and then tapped them against the smooth top of the keyboard so they all lined up together. "I can practice at home on my real piano and hopefully next time…. uh, if there is a next time…."

After a long, awkward few moments of silence Ryder finally relieved my tension, "See what you can do at home and then we'll try again in a few days. Maybe you and I can just get together and see if you can hear the guitar melody a bit better."

"Sure, sounds great," I smiled but there was no enthusiasm in my voice. Ryder had to have been able to tell, but he just kept looking at me like he was waiting for me to come clean about something.

The band began to pick up various pieces of equipment and instruments and pack them away. I glanced at the microwave clock in the

202

kitchen desperate to be away from all this competitive testosterone, hating that these guys felt a contest over me and then hating that I felt disappointed Ryder wasn't trying to join in.

I stood awkwardly outside of the practice area, since I didn't know how to put anything away and my only task was picking up my sheet music. I tried not to stare at the band, but it was difficult. They were kind of fascinating with how much care they took with each piece of equipment or how cruel they were to each other... but in a funny, happy way.

Boys. They were so different from girls.

I felt like I was a National Geographic photographer observing African lions in their natural habitat. Honestly, all I needed was a pair of cargo khakis and a British accent.

The male drummer turns to face his natural enemy, the male bass player. They eye each other for a while before the second guitarist jumps in with a harsh quip about the bass player's frayed skull cap. This is the opportunity the drummer has been waiting for and he pounces on the bass player until he alone emerges victoriously-

"What are you thinking about?" Ryder broke into my thought train so suddenly I nearly jumped out of my skin.

"Nothing," I squeaked.

"Really? Because you have this really deep-in-thought look on your face," Ryder remarked honestly.

The blush returned. "Um, are you going to take me home or should I call someone?" I changed the subject before he could ask any more questions, but I also really needed to know.

"Actually, is it alright if Phoenix takes you? I was working earlier so it worked out, but it would be easier for me if he took you. You're right on his way," Ryder explained.

See? No curse. If he felt the curse, no way would he send me away with another guy.

"Sure, that's no problem," I replied with so much energy Ryder shot me an offended look. "I mean," I faltered a little, "whatever works for you."

"Uh-huh." His eyes narrowed on me. "Are you okay with taking Ivy home, Phoenix?"

"Huh? Oh sure! Yeah, it'll be fun, won't it Ives?" Phoenix grinned at me with this huge, boyish smile and I had to fall in love with him just a little bit more. The feeling made me instantly want to text Exie and make up some excuse for her to meet me at my apartment just so she could run into him again. But then I quickly squashed it. Exie's rules weren't exactly the same as mine, but Nix still ran the show in her life. A relationship with anybody would eventually be terminated and I didn't want to do that to Phoenix. Or Exie.

"Yes, we will!" I gushed. "But can we go soon? I really do have a curfew I have to be back for."

"Sure. I've got everything packed up so we can just take off now," Phoenix started walking toward the door, shooting Ryder a peace-out over his shoulder.

Peace out?

People still said *peace out*?

Fifteen minutes later, Phoenix pulled up to my apartment in his beat up El Camino and told me how amazing it was to have me in the band for about the millionth time. He had been gushing nonstop since we left Ryder's and I couldn't even get one word in to remind him that I hadn't played good at all. In fact, I was almost positive I was going to destroy their entire reputation and fan base.

But that wasn't something Phoenix could comprehend right now.

"Are you sure you guys don't know *anyone* else that can play the piano? I mean there has to be *somebody*." I turned in my seat, determined to help Phoenix remember somebody else that could fill this role.

Phoenix looked at me for a beat. No, not looked, Phoenix examined me, took in everything about me with a lucidity I had never seen him use before. "Sure, there are other people that play, we could have asked others."

A breath of relief whooshed out of my lungs and I felt a huge burden lift off my shoulders. "Oh, good."

"But Ryder wants you." Phoenix continued, not noticing my reaction at all, despite this new found clarity. "I think he thinks you're a troubled teen. That you need like, an outlet or something."

Harsh laughter ripped out of my mouth. The statement was both true *and* ironic. And annoying. "He thinks I need an outlet?"

"Uh, yeah," Phoenix mumbled, realizing he might have said something he wasn't supposed.

"He thinks I need an outlet? For my troubled behavior?" I ran through it again, just to make sure I had all the facts correct. Anger built inside me quickly the more I repeated the words in my head. "What does Ryder think will happen if I don't have an outlet?" My voice rose to an angry screech and Phoenix flinched a bit. "Does he think, what, I'll turn to

204

drugs? Drinking? I'll hurt someone again? What does he think will happen, Phoenix?"

"Uh...." Phoenix glanced at my apartment entry nervously before daring to meet my eyes. I didn't mean to make him feel bad, but this was ridiculous. "I don't know, Ivy. I just know he's really worried about you. He cares about you. We all care about you."

All of the dangerous energy left me in a rush of defeat. I slumped against the frayed maroon upholstery of the El Camino and slammed the back of my head against the head rest. People were not supposed to care about me. This was not supposed to happen. I had a checklist.

1. Follow the rules.
2. Keep my head down.
3. Graduate.
4. Get the hell out of Dodge.

How did things get so messed up?

"Are you going to quit?" Phoenix braved, his voice gentle and soothing.

"No," I gave in. This was a mistake, a huge mistake. But I couldn't walk away from these people. I shouldn't involve them in my life, and I certainly shouldn't expect their feelings for me to be real... But I couldn't walk away from them now. I cared about them too. "But I'm not this, this person Ryder's made me out to be, okay, Phoenix? I'm just fine, really."

"If you say so, Ivy," Phoenix shot me a sad smile. "But, uh, before you go... I've been meaning to ask you about, um, Exie?"

Despite the mood I slipped into, I couldn't stop smiling at Phoenix. "Yeah? Exie?"

"Is she like, with anybody?"

"Um, not that I know of," I encouraged. Even though I knew she actually was with somebody, but not somebody that mattered and she was probably plotting their breakup already anyway.

"So she gave me her number, but I didn't know if she, you know... should I call her?" he asked so adorably nervous I couldn't help but laugh a little.

"Yes, Phoenix. If she gave you her number, you should definitely call her." I was actually impressed with him. Exie did not just give out her number to random people. Even a lot of the guys she hooked up with didn't get her cell number. Of course they also didn't last more than a couple days. And I was hoping Phoenix would last for more than that. Exie had a chance at some happiness with Phoenix and I just wanted her to have that, have some happiness, for at least a little bit.

"Thanks Ivy," his huge grin was back, lighting up his entire face. "See you tomorrow."

"Yep, thanks for the ride," I climbed out of the car and all the way up the stairs, through the glass doors and to the elevator. This night turned out weird, fun, frustrating and…. just weird all the way around.

I didn't know if I would ever find my equilibrium with Ryder.

The door to my apartment was open when I got off the elevator and a shot of nerves zapped through me. *Shoot.*

As the elevator doors quietly closed behind me my mother appeared in the doorway. Her bronzed red hair hanging loose and wild around her shoulders, her usually bright green eyes were dulled and anguished in the corners and her mouth was pressed into a grim line as she watched me approach.

Although our apartment building was not entirely full yet since it opened a few years ago, this floor was. However we didn't know any of our neighbors. It was dangerous to get to know people where we lived, the curse was unpredictable and we preferred to live without the drama. Besides, my mother was a selfish creature and making friends was not necessarily a top priority for her.

Her priorities started with making money and then only became variables of that.

Because we didn't know our neighbors and didn't care to know them, I knew I was safe until the door shut behind me, but walking down the long hall with her eyes so hatefully turned on me was intimidating.

To say the least.

"Where have you been?" she snapped as the door clicked closed behind me.

She hadn't moved, except to allow us privacy. Still framed in the doorway, her hands had moved aggressively to her hips and her eyes narrowed into slits of fury.

"I was out with Chase," I lied. Blatantly.

She seemed to chew that over for a minute before deciding that was an acceptable response. She forced a breath out and a wave of whisky hit me. Then she wobbled on her feet and I knew this was bad.

She never drank whisky. *Never.*

Lady's only ever drink delicate drinks. Save the hard stuff for the boys.

Still, when things went badly for her, she hit the sauce. And hard.

"Are you okay, mom?" I asked before thinking better of it.

"Of course, I'm okay," she bit out, her relaxed eyes instantly tensing again. "Have you gained weight?"

I opened my mouth, closed it again and then opened it. "Um, no, I don't think so."

"Oh, well maybe you need to drop three pounds anyway, Ivy," her tone was that pretending kind of care. A sick feeling washed over me and settled in my stomach. "You're coming into womanhood and you don't want that extra weight to settle in unflattering places." I just nodded slowly. Three pounds felt like too much to me. I already barely ate. But mom wasn't finished, she continued with "Did you dye your hair again?"

Her question caught me off guard. "No, not since I dyed it back." I touched the end of my golden red hair and then held it up to the light. Before Sam I had gone through this super rebellious phase and dyed it black. It wasn't so much this desire to get in touch with myself as it was to send a big F you to Nix and my mom. Of course it backfired when Sam crashed his car into the streetlight. But at the time I had felt pretty badass.

Now I knew better. Pissing off Nix and my mom only intensified their efforts to break me. The new game plan, to simply slip away in the dead of the night, was my only hope.

"It looks darker. Oh, god, I hope this isn't how it stays. You probably ruined it when you dumped all that black poison on it." She took a step forward and grabbed a chunk full of my hair. Her fingers closed around a fistful of it, near the roots and she yanked it toward her. I winced a little when biting pain shot across the base of my neck and up to the crown of my head.

"Ow, mom," I whispered.

"Oh, did I hurt you?" she let go of my hair with so much force I stumbled backward. "Did I *hurt* you Ivy? God, you're so pathetically fragile," she waved her arms around as if to demonstrate the whole of me. My heart constricted into a tight ball in my chest. This wasn't the first time she made this speech, nor would it be the last. Still, the wounds were always fresh, always just as painful. And the worst part about everything she was saying, was that it was all true. "Do you know what I was doing at your age, Ivy? Do you have any clue? I wasn't running off for six months of spa treatments, that's for goddamn sure. I had my priorities straight. I believed in my future. I was *loyal*. I have no idea how you are even my child. I was Nix's choice too once, his trophy. I've been where you have, but the difference between me and you is that I treated my responsibilities with respect. I became the person I was supposed to be. I embraced my destiny. I need to get your sister back, she will know better. She will *be* better."

Angry tears pricked at my eyes, hot and ready to spill over. "This? *This* is who you were supposed to be?" I gestured at her with my hands now, at her black silk pants, and lavender halter top, at her outrageously expensive shoes, to her Cartier necklace and earrings. "I don't want your destiny; I don't want your responsibility. It's so sick and disgusting that I can't even stomach what you do. And I hope to God, Honor never comes here, never has to live through what I've lived through. I hope she *never* sees what kind of monster you really are." The words were out before I could stop them. Our faces registered the shock at the same time. And while I stood there staring at her dumbfounded, she recovered first by slapping me across the face.

The sound of her palm hitting my cheek resounded loudly between us. My mouth hung open stupidly, while the tears finally slipped out the corners of my eyes to my cheeks and then dripped carelessly off my chin. I brought a shaking hand up to my face and held it gently against the still stinging skin.

"Don't ever speak like that to me again," she growled in a hoarse voice. "How dare you."

I closed my mouth with a clap of teeth hitting teeth, but I refused to apologize. This might be the dumbest thing I had ever done, but I wasn't going to apologize.

"Go to your room," she snarled viciously at me. "I'm calling Nix. I'm sure he will be so happy to hear how his therapy worked out for you."

My chin trembled as her words hit me, the full realization of what I'd done finally settling over me. *Damn it*. So much for keeping my head down and just getting through this.

"You think you are so much better than me? So much better than everyone else! I will make damned sure that this is a lesson you learn from Nix. He can show you your place because I have no more patience for you." She didn't even look like herself. Her eyes were crazed and psychotic, her face screwed up with rage. In the motion it took her to slap me her hair became wild and out of place, her shirt a little off center and her eye liner smudged in the corner. She was a mess and suddenly unwanted pangs of sympathy flooded my veins like ice. I didn't think I was better than her; I just wanted a better life. "Go to your room, Ivy. I'll call for you if I need you."

I didn't say anything; I just turned on my heel and obeyed. Once the door was closed and locked behind me I collapsed on my bed in a heap of despair. The tears didn't stop for a long time, they fell in relentless puddles mixed with snot and more emotions than I knew what to do with.

Eventually I fell asleep with my mother's threats and accusations rolling around in my head.

And Ryder's.

And when I finally fell asleep it was only to dream of a troubled teen that couldn't escape the ugly role life had dealt her. She never escaped. She never knew another life than slavery and submission.

Worst of all she never knew love. Not from her family, not from a man. And not from herself.

Chapter Twenty-Seven

The next morning was a blur of emotional dysfunction. I didn't want to stay home where my mother was lurking, but school seemed like not the answer. Still, I went.

Even though I knew I could still sit with Chase and his friends, it seemed like such a heartless thing to do. I didn't mind remaining friends with Chase, and I apparently couldn't get rid of Ryder and Phoenix, but the day after we ended it, seemed a little sudden to flaunt that in his face.

So after a morning of mindless classes I found myself wandering around the band room. I used to come here a lot, before Sam. Well, and during Sam. There are never any classes over the lunch period in this wing of the building, so it's nice and quiet. But there is a hallway off the tiered band room filled with practice rooms and those are occupied a lot over lunch.

I love the muffled sounds of all the different instruments colliding in the hallway. The sounds individually could be beautiful, or strained or awful, but together, in the hallway they were complete chaos. It's how I pictured the definition of "cacophony." Not that I said that word often, but still, this hall was what a cacophony of sound.... sounded like.

But today everything was silent and still. I was alone. Which seemed fitting, since in my head I was anything but alone.

I walked all the way to the end of the hallway where it ran into a brick wall and entered the last small practice room without a sound. There was a piano set up on the far wall, and one extra chair besides the piano bench with a metal music stand in front of it.

I contemplated calling Exie or Sloane and opening up about how unhinged my mom was, but they had their own maternal problems. Besides, I wasn't really sure what to do with it all. She had never been the most in-touch mom, especially lately. But she had never hit me before.

I shivered in the damp room and let the silence wash over me. It was so loud, so deafeningly quiet that my ears rushed with the absence of sound and my skin felt physically oppressed by it.

Suddenly I couldn't take it anymore, the soundlessness, the thoughts in my head, none of it. I yanked the piano bench back and slammed my body down. My fingers were flying up and down the keyboard before I could catch my breath.

Loud, pounding melodies that were meant to be sweet and slow, or fast, feverish classical pieces that I butchered until they were unrecognizable even to my ears. I pushed my fingers into aching numbness. My back stiff and my neck pained. Still I ferociously attacked the piano until I was sweating and exhausted.

Finally, out of breath, I slumped back and dropped my hands to my lap.

"Frustrated?" a gravelly voice came from behind me.

I screamed in response, completely surprised. I whirled around on the bench, the smooth wood making it easy to spin around and face Ryder.

"*What* are you doing here?" I gasped. My heart still beat frantically in my chest and my hands flew to my hair which I knew was disheveled and frizzy.

"Looking for you," he said simply. His eyes swept over me with something hidden in them. He made me nervous. There was something different about him today, even from last night. Something I couldn't place. Like he was lighter today, weighed less or something. But not in pounds... like he wasn't tied down to gravity today, like he would just float away at any given moment.

And at the same time he was more intense, more.... intent with me.

"So you had to scare the bejeezus out of me?" I demanded. I slipped my hands under my thighs and rocked forward so that my hair covered my flushed face.

"I didn't mean to scare you, Ivy," he said patiently. "Sorry. It's not like I snuck up on you or anything, you were just making a lot of noise."

I laughed a little hysterically. And then it turned into more laughter. Good grief, maybe I was the one that was unhinged.

Ryder walked over to me and held out his hands. I retrieved mine from under my thighs and slipped them into his and let him pull me up. We were just inches apart when I was standing, our bodies so close together I could feel the heat from his chest and then his minty breath fan over my hairline.

"Someone's here to see you. They're in the office," he explained.

"Is it my mom?" I asked in a small voice. I could just imagine what she was doing here trying to pull me out of school. And then panic set in, what if she was here to take me to Nix. What if I ran out of chances and last night was the final nail in my coffin?

Oh, no.

"No, it's not your mom," Ryder answered.

"Is it Nix?" I whispered, full hysteria setting in.

"No, it's not. I'm not sure who it is. Tanner just caught me in the hall and asked me to find you since you weren't in class yet." Ryder must have seen something in my eyes because his grip on my hands tightened. "Ivy, are you okay? Are you expecting someone?"

"No, I'm not," I tried to relax. If it wasn't my mom or Nix, I had no idea who it could be, especially who would come visit me at school. But as long as it wasn't one of them, I felt a little bit safer.

"Ready then?" He asked, although he made no effort to move away from me.

"Sure," I nodded my head and he finally stepped back.

As we left the still empty music hall, I asked, "How did you know I would be back there?"

"I didn't. I looked everywhere else I could think of first and called your cell. I actually thought maybe you decided to ditch today. But then I remembered you took all that sheet music, so I thought maybe you went to practice, since you weren't at lunch."

"Oh."

"But you weren't... uh, practicing." Ryder slanted his gaze at me, taking me in, all of me in, in just a quick sweeping gesture, but still my skin felt hot from his attention.

"No, I forgot about the sheet music, honestly. I was, um, it's like therapy," I admitted. "I was expressing some frustrations."

"No kidding," Ryder chuckled. "I hope they're not all about the band. Because we'll take this slow. I don't expect you to play next week. And seriously, Ivy, you don't have to do it if you don't want to."

"No, I want to," I was surprised by my own conviction. My mom would kill me if she knew I was in Ryder's band. It was okay to spend time with any kind of boy. And technically it was okay to go to concerts, although my mother might have disapproved of what I wore. But it was in no way okay to associate myself with a boy band. Or any kind of band. My talents were strictly cultivated to enhance my beauty and nothing more.

Gag.

"I want you to, too," Ryder admitted.

"Hey are you alright?" I asked, intuition niggling in my stomach.

"Why wouldn't I be alright?" Ryder asked softly.

"I don't know," I admitted with honest humor. "I just had this feeling that you needed to talk. But maybe I was wrong."

Ryder stopped in front of the office door and turned around to look at me. He ran a hand through his hair but paused half way through with his elbow suspended straight up in the air and his head dipped as if he were deep in thought.

"Maybe I do need to talk," he started and I could tell he was nervous.

"Okay," I whispered, probably more nervous than him.

"Um, okay," Ryder took a deep breath, and then blew it out slowly. "Kenna and I, we, uh-"

"Ivy, get in here," Mrs. Tanner's shrill voice broke through the spell Ryder placed on me. "They are waiting for you! What on Earth are you doing out here? Ryder Sutton, get to class right now before I write you up."

"Yes, ma'am," Ryder smiled dutifully, gave Mrs. Tanner a playful salute and then squeezed my bicep before leaving me alone with the wicked witch of the west.

"Principal Costas is waiting for you in his office," Mrs. Tanner explained with as much disgust and impatience as any one human being was capable of.

"Thanks, T-dog." Not because I thought I was clever, only because it would annoy the ever living hell out of her and that was one of my main goals in life.

"And Ivy?" Mrs. Tanner called right before I reached Principal's Costas's office door.

"Ryder's a good kid, with a strong future ahead of him. He doesn't need the likes of you poisoning his life." When I remained calm and still, she pressed, "Do you understand?"

"More than you know," I mumbled, feeling the poison she referred to spreading from my heart to every living part of me.

She made a feminine grunting sound but didn't push the issue further. So I raised my hand and knocked on the Principal's door. Antonio Costas was one of the youngest principals in Omaha. Early thirties with a young family and a reputation for being a hard-ass with heart, the parents of Central adored him.

He in turn, being male and notwithstanding Ryder's super powers, adored me. Where other students were asked to face their consequences head on, or make mature choices, I was disciplined with swats on the hand and threats to call my mother that he never followed through with.

Not that he minded calling my mother. Please, he was male after all. And she was…. my mother. But I tried to spare him the embarrassment of groveling at her feet since he had snot nosed toddlers and a high school sweetheart waiting for him at home every night.

Not that he was an unfaithful man. It wasn't his fault.

He was actually a really good guy and because I couldn't blame him for his reaction to my mom or me, I respected him.

Principal Costas opened the door and greeted me with a huge smile. "Hi, Ivy, I'm glad you could finally join us."

"Thanks," I returned the smile. My eyes fell immediately to the guest in his office, a woman I didn't know.

I followed Principal Costas into the office and swallowed back a lump of nerves when he closed the door behind him. He was a good looking guy for a teacher, young, in shape with tanned, olive skin by birth. But his most attractive feature was the confident happiness he evoked. He was always pleasant and kind, but there was an air about him that made you certain you never wanted to disappoint him.

Principal Costas gestured to the remaining vacant chair in his dated, but well-maintained office. I sat down next to the mystery woman and shot her an uncertain glance.

"Ivy, I'd like you to meet Mallory Hunter," Costas explained.

I smiled at the attractive blonde in her early thirties. She was wearing a sharp, black skirt suit and screamed polished hard-ass. Her returning smile was tight, but there was a soft pity about her expression I didn't entirely understand.

"Ms. Hunter is a lawyer on behalf of your father's estate, as I understand," Costas explained. "Smith Porter called earlier this morning to arrange this meeting. I am going to give you time to…. talk."

Principal Costas put a reassuring hand on my shoulder and then left his office quietly. I gulped back some awkward nervousness and then shifted so I could face Mallory Hunter head on.

"Hi, Ivy," she greeted soothingly. She held a folder in her lap, and there was an expensive brief case at her feet.

"Hi," I said simply and then curiosity got the better of me. "Do you work for Jared?" Jared T. Artero was the lawyer in charge of my father's estate and my trust. We talked every year around Christmas time because he was my father's friend as well as legal advisor and he liked to make sure I was okay. I looked forward to talking to him because I liked to make sure my money was okay.

"Not exactly," she smiled brighter and I could see that it was her method of placating me. "I'm here on behalf of Smith Porter. Actually I work for the sister firm of Arnold, Terkoff and Blane. My firm is Hastle and Crimmens, but Catarina Arnold is my mentor."

"Okay, so I'm really confused," I grimaced. What did she just say?

"Catarina Arnold is employed by Mr. Porter, she is also my boss. Well, indirectly. As I understand this, your situation is very… precarious. Smith brought me in to ensure nothing could be directly linked back to him, Catarina or Jared."

"Ah." Well, Okay, that made sense. And if my mom ever started asking questions I would just have Mallory recite that entire jumble of words. She would be confused immediately.

"I've met you here, because I understand your home life is intense?" Mallory had this way of punching her point. She would pause dramatically and then say her point with enthusiastic curiosity. I bet her tactic worked well with indecisive juries. "Smith has expressed concern that you might be facing abuse. As you know if you are in verifiable danger, it is possible for you to acquire the full amount of your trust early. Verifiable danger can be defined as any kind of abuse, emotional, physical or verbal with recorded evidence or life-threatening circumstances that you are capable of involving the police or FBI in. Can you claim either of these conditions?"

My mother slapping me flew to the forefront of my mind, but then again it wasn't that awful. It was just a slap. It wasn't like I had to be rushed to the emergency room or anything. The mark was completely gone by morning, no evidence or scars left behind. What did verbal abuse even mean? My mother was harsh at times, callous and unfeeling always, but was that actual abuse? Had I suffered anything that could be proven in the court of law other than a messed up sense of reality and unrealistic expectations?

"I don't have anything I can prove," I finally admitted. "I'm not even sure Smith is entirely justified in involving you. There's no abuse happening in my life."

Not yet anyway. And by that time I'll be eighteen, I'll be an adult. So it won't matter.

"I was afraid of this," Mallory's face filled with more pity. "Smith and Catarina are very good friends of mine. I've taken this case as a favor to them. And I'm working with Jared, who seems to share some of the same concerns as Smith. Unlike Smith, Jared respects your mother, thinks the world of her actually, but he has shared some of your father's dying words and I understand why Jared feels the way he does."

My father's dying words? What did that mean?

I opened my mouth to ask, but she continued. "There might not be anything to share with me now. There might never be. But I don't think Smith would have gone to all these lengths if there wasn't something going on."

After several moments of charged silence I finally settled on, "You're right. I can't prove anything, but I need my trust early. I need it *now*."

"Alright, then that's what we will work on. I won't call you, or contact you in any way other than here at school. And I'll visit again in a month. If

216

you can record anything you think is useful on your phone. Or if anything happens take a picture of it immediately. If conditions worsen for you, get ahold of Smith as soon as possible. Does that work for you?" She raked her eyes over me in a way that screamed I was her client and nothing else. Pity maybe? But there was no sympathy behind Mallory Hunter's expression.

Still, it was obvious she kicked ass in court.

"Yes, that works for me," I agreed feeling like I was signing away something very precious. Like my soul.

Which was ridiculous. If anything, staying was so much worse than leaving for that same thing.

"Alright, then. Ivy, thank you for your time. I'll be in touch," she stood then and stretched out her hand. I echoed every movement and then bit back a smile at her firm handshake.

She was just so.... professional.

"Thank you, Mallory," I gushed not meaning to. I actually meant to return the professional air of civility, but suddenly I found myself near tears. Partly because Smith had disregarded everything I said. But mostly because there was hope that I hadn't felt in a really long time. Hope I hadn't felt in maybe ever.

Chapter Twenty-Eight

Three pounds my ass. Literally... maybe that's where the three pounds were hiding. But I honestly gave losing them a legitimate run for two full days. And nothing happened. Not even a half of pound. Not even after I peed first thing in the morning.

Now that it was Saturday and I was practically faint from hunger I decided to screw it. Okay, so two days didn't exactly equal the strongest effort ever, but chocolate croissants were calling to me from across the street. Fresh, warm, gooey ones. With a caramel macchiato to drink.

I could always start again tomorrow. Right? Right.

I rushed through a shower, only shaving my calves and ankles, leaving my thighs for a different day. Small rebellion, but well worth it. I blow dried my hair, hot rolled, then brushed it out to erase all previous efforts and painted my face with the usual regimen of makeup. My mom wasn't going to wake up this morning and do a leg check on my dedication to shaving, but she for sure would check out my face in one second flat if I didn't take cautious care. And if I intended to sneak out for chocolate croissants I needed to be extra careful.

After the beauty routine, I dressed in a pair of turquoise skinny jeans, white scooped neck tank top and a sheer oversized white cardigan. I slipped into some red wedges and threw on the required amount of jewelry to complete the overdressed outfit. But bases covered and I was ready to go.

As long as I didn't spill chocolate on my shirt, I would probably get away with this too.

Mom hadn't talked to me since she shut me up by slapping me across the face. So... I had that going for me.

I slipped out of the apartment and across Farnam without incident. Once I gained some distance from my happy home, I found myself breathing easier, taking in the crisp coolness of the late October morning, and even smiling a little.

This morning felt like a reprieve from everything, from my mom, from Nix, from school, from... me. That same everything felt easy. And for a moment I forgot about it all and just looked forward to breakfast.

Until, I opened the door and saw him waiting for me next to the counter.

Ryder.

And then nothing felt easy.

Not even breathing.

He stood with his hip leaning against the counter, in casual conversation with another one of the college girls that worked here. He turned back to smile at me, as if expecting me any moment and then winked. He was dressed in the nicest jeans I had seen him wear, boot cut and dark washed and his black button up shirt was rolled to the elbows. His hair was in all its voluminous, coarse, in-desperate-need-of-industrial-strength-conditioner glory.

The butterfly in my stomach must have mated sometime during the last thirty seconds because suddenly there was a storm of them viciously attacking my insides. Nervous energy rushed through my body, completely disorienting me. My brain went all fuzzy, like everything intelligent and coherent was suddenly abducted by aliens. My fingers actually started to tremble, like I had a crack addiction and I was jonesing for a hit and my lips adapted a will of their own and curved into a smile without my permission. Actually, completely against my direct orders!

I was a mess. And a puddle of goo. And a nervous wreck all at the same time!

Was this honestly what it was like to have a crush on a boy?

Because if so I hated being a girl.

And loved it at the same time.

Good grief, this was confusing. Now to round this multi-personality-riddled problem out, I just needed to act cool and not trip face-first over my feet.

No problem.

"Morning, Red," he greeted with a deep, rough voice that hadn't recovered from sleep yet.

"Good morning," I replied politely, faltering a little on my way to the cash register.

"I was hoping to catch you here," he admitted, and his mouth curved up into a reserved smile.

"Yeah?"

"Yeah," he echoed and then turned to his friend working. "She'll have a caramel macchiato, extra hot. And I'm ready for my order too now. Thanks Gwen."

I finally made it to the counter and contemplated forgetting the croissants altogether with how sweet Ryder was being, but then my stomach growled loudly and I knew I needed to eat something.

"Hungry?" he turned to face me, and crossed his arms against his chest. The movement pulled his shirt tight at his biceps and shoulders and

I had the strongest urge to run my fingers against the creases in the fabric and smooth them out.

"Mmm-hmmm. I could eat like five croissants this morning."

"Good to know," Ryder's face broke out into a bigger grin, his gray eyes sparkling until they turned into shiny silver. "But I have a better idea."

"Than chocolate croissants? You can see why I would have my doubts," I took another step forward so I could press my hands against the cool glass of the counter and lean forward. I looked back at Ryder over my shoulder, noting how close we were. I was having fun flirting with him, I could admit that. But I also had to admit I needed to stop myself soon. It wouldn't do any good for him to actually start returning these feelings.

"Come have breakfast at my house," his voice dropped to a rumbling timber.

For a few moments I was stunned into silence, only the sound of the espresso machine whirring in the background, the soft tickling of ceramic dishes being used and melodic hum of conversational voices interrupted the shock that froze all of my thoughts.

"I can't," I mumbled finally. I dropped my gaze to the counter, to my hands, to the cash register, to *anywhere* but Ryder's face.

"Yes, you can," he pleaded gently. Always gently with me. Always careful.

I shook my head quickly. "No, thanks, it's sweet of you to offer."

"It's not sweet of me to offer," Ryder laughed harshly. "It's against my better judgment to offer. But come anyway."

"Well, now you've convinced me," I groaned. A moment ago my thoughts were all vibrating and fuzzy with confusion, but leave it up to Ryder to bring me right back to reality.

"Here you go," Gwen interrupted Ryder's ready response. She handed Ryder a drink carrier full of four large coffee cups. The scent of fresh, hot caffeine permeated the air around me and I instantly took a step forward to inhale a good whiff.

Ryder slid a twenty and a five across the counter and winked at Gwen.

"This is way too much," she smiled at him.

I forced my expression to remain the same and hide the jealous monster that lurked just beneath my calm surface.

"I know," he shrugged. "Think of it like a bribe. I'm holding her," he gestured to me with his elbow, "coffee hostage. If she decides not to come with me, do not serve her under *any* circumstances. We clear?"

"Sure," Gwen laughed. "We're clear."

My mouth dropped open in surprise and I shot Gwen an imploring look. She looked me over, not in a very kind way and her expression became steel.

"Are you serious?" I gasped more to Ryder than to Gwen, but she shrugged her shoulder as if there was nothing she could do. "Ryder, make her serve me coffee." I whispered harshly when he started to walk away and Gwen disappeared through the door that led to the kitchen. "Ryder!"

"Not a chance, Red. If you want this delicious, amazing-smelling macchiato, you better move your ass." He didn't slow down and soon he was out the door while I stayed staring after him.

I decided he was right, so I hurried after him and my kidnapped coffee. "You know, I could always just go to Starbucks if I get desperate."

Empty threat.

"Yep, you could," he admitted, but didn't look back at me.

I let out a long suffering sigh, but in the end I let myself in the passenger side of his Bronco parked on the street. He handed me the carton of coffees, shot me a huge grin and then started the car.

I held the coffee in my lap with both hands and tried not to move one way or the other when his arm rested on the back of my seat, just above my shoulder blades while he backed out. There was warmth in that movement that I was almost desperate to lean into and at the same time the clawing need had me eyeing the door handle and contemplating my chances of diving out of the car before he could put it in drive.

In the end I just remained still- absolutely still.

When the Bronco faced east on Farnam he removed his hand from across the seat to deal with the gearshift and I released the breath that had been bottled up inside me.

We were quiet on the way to Ryder's house. Just the sounds of the radio, top forty surprisingly, and Ryder's soft humming filled the car. I glanced over at him several times but his eyes were focused on the road and his jaw didn't give anything away, except maybe he felt more relaxed than I did.

Ryder parked parallel from his building and then shut the car off. He stayed still for a few moments while the engine wound down and I didn't dare move from the car before he did.

"Hungry?" he finally asked, tilting his cocky grin to face me.

"Do I have a choice?" I grunted, working up my best martyred-victim-expression.

"It's going to be good, I promise. But before we go in, I wanted to warn you that my uncle and dad will be there," his grin faltered, leaving behind some nervous embarrassment I didn't quite understand.

"You kidnapped me to meet your family?" I bit out, suddenly furious. "Ryder, what the hell is Kenna going to say? What is your *dad* going to say? This is so weird. You should have asked me first."

I counted the four coffees before we left the café, but some part of me held out hope they were just extras. And I had been so blindsided by his desire to take me with him that I hadn't really thought through what breakfast with his family meant.

"Probably I should have asked you first," he shrugged off whatever embarrassment was there before and replaced his expression with a determination that sucked the breath from my lungs, "but you wouldn't have come. And Kenna won't care that you came for breakfast. Promise. We're friends Ivy. Stop reading into everything I do. I just want to be your friend."

I thought over everything he said and convinced myself he was right. Friends. We were friends. But then a thought flashed through my resolve and I blurted out, "Your dad and your uncle! I mean, I have this effect on... uh, parents. Parents *really* love me. It's just this talent I've always had. Actually with all adults. So um, if your dad seems to really like me, then you should know it's just my natural charm."

I wanted to smack my hand against my forehead and groan, but I smiled instead.

"Natural charm?" Ryder laughed. "Yeah, you're really oozing with it." He rolled his eyes but then shot me an encouraging smile. "There's no need to be nervous, Ivy. My dad likes everybody."

I grimaced. "I swear, I'm not nervous. I just want you to be...." I coughed, trying to get the ridiculous words out, "aware of my... parental charm."

"Sure, I'm aware," Ryder chuckled and unclipped his seatbelt, "of your parental charm. Tanner gushes about it all the time."

A laugh bubbled up in me before I could stop it by pretending to be offended. "Fine," I sighed and unbuckled too. "But don't say I didn't warn you."

Chapter Twenty-Nine

We met on the driver's side of the car and walked across the street together. He led me around the building and punched in the code for his door. Holding it open, his hand landed on the small of my back when I walked by. A shiver rippled through me at his touch, but I ignored it.

At the top of the stairs, I waited for him to open the door again and then inhaled deeply at the heavy scent of bacon frying and bread baking. Deep, rumbling male laughter filled the air and paused at the sound of the door.

I walked in and turned to the kitchen to meet Ryder's dad and uncle. There was at least twenty years between them, but the resemblance was obvious. Ryder's dad, the older of the two, was very cool-professor with gelled hair, turned up into messy spikes and thick, black hipster glasses. He was classically handsome though too, with the same chiseled jaw line as Ryder and those silver-gray eyes that could be so unnerving. Ryder's uncle Matt, seemed sandwiched between Ryder and his dad in the timeline of the Sutton Male Lifespan. I pictured the evolutionary timeline with Ryder representing the primitive ape and Ryder's dad the full grown man. Matt fit somewhere in the middle of hunched over primate with less hair and elongated thumbs.

Matt slouched over the stove, hip pressed against the counter, wooden spoon in long, slender fingers. He had extremely messy bed head hair, long to his chin and sticking out in every way. He was wearing glasses too, but they were thinner framed and did even less to conceal the flash of silver behind them. His face was covered in several day stubble and his worn white t-shirt and sweatpants revealed the same broad-shouldered, narrow-waist build Ryder carried.

"Ryder, is this your friend?" his dad asked from the kitchen. He smiled over at us and then took a sip of his orange juice while he waited for Ryder to respond.

"Yep," Ryder nudged me forward and I found myself walking to the kitchen counter and setting the coffees down. "Dad, Matty, this is Ivy Pierce. Ivy, this is my uncle Matt, and my dad, Dr. Nathan Sutton."

"Nate is just fine," he laughed at his son and then extended his hand beyond his breakfast glass.

I took a few steps forward and accepted his hand shake. He had a strong but friendly grip and his eyes still twinkled from laughter. I sucked in a breath and met his gaze, but nothing except openness seemed to look back at me. No lust. No desire. No unwelcomed interest.

Whew. "Hi, Nate," my voice trembled beneath nerves and I prayed no one else noticed.

"We've heard a lot about you, Ivy," Matt called from next to the stove and I turned to meet his outstretched hand.

"Oh, no," I groaned dramatically.

"All good things of course," Matt was quick to reassure. I took his hand, and he shook it but his eyes were fixed behind me for a long moment before they flickered down to meet mine. He cleared his throat and something changed in his expression before he quickly added, "It's always nice to meet one of Ryder's *friends*."

I stopped, but just barely, from rolling my eyes.

"It's nice to meet you too," I said politely.

Ryder clapped a hand on my shoulder and pulled me out of the kitchen a little bit. "Alright, let's let Uncle Matt get back to breakfast before he burns everything." Matt waved an annoyed spatula in the air, but winked at me before turning back to the stove. Ryder leaned in closer and spoke with a softer tone, "Grab your coffee."

And then he reached around me so that his arm slid across my side and the weight of his chest pressed into my back. I froze. He plucked his coffee from the carrier all the while I counted the places our bodies connected and then he was gone, along with his warmth. I cleared my throat and focused harder on the three remaining cups trying to decipher which one was mine.

"Could this be it?" his dad reached forward and picked up one that had "macchiato" scrawled across the top.

I looked up at him a bit dumbfounded but managed a small nod. He handed me my cup and I quickly turned around to hide my deep blush from him.

Ryder stood over the keyboard, messing around with the melody to the song he wanted me to play with him, so I assumed breakfast also meant practice. That was fine with me. As long as I had a reason, any reason, not to obsess over my feelings for Ryder or analyze every stupid move, touch or word he was responsible for, I could survive this morning.

"You're still set on making me join the band?" I asked through gritted teeth.

"Absolutely," he grunted, not even a little bit amused with me. He moved out of the way so I could take my place behind the keys and then took my coffee from me. I let it go with heavy regret and watched him set it down on a bent back music stand. "Besides, I think you're pretty face on stage will help draw a bigger crowd."

"You have no idea," I mumbled. I wondered if Ryder was serious, if he really thought I would. A defeated feeling settled over me and I felt deflated.... lost and alone again. He hadn't meant to, but his words were a cold dose of reality.

"That's it," Ryder snapped his fingers in front of me. His tone suddenly stern frustration and I glanced up just in time to see his eyes flash with anger. "We're going to have a talk later, Ivy. I'm not doing this anymore."

"Doing what?" I gasped. His words were spoken quietly and for my ears only, but his tone was unmistakably cold.

"My dad and uncle are *staring* over here," he whispered fiercely. "At you," he finished on a snarl in case I didn't already assume that was what he meant.

"So?" I forced myself to remain casual.

"I'm not playing games anymore. I want to know what's going on."

"Nothing is going on," I sighed and then pretended to be confused. "You're scaring me."

That was my go-to self-preservation phrase. I had a perfect success rate with that. Decent guys *never* wanted to be the reason for female distress. And Ryder was probably the most decent guy I knew.

My tone was all bored confusion, but only because that was how I had been taught to behave. On the inside my heartbeat pulsed in my ears, loud and banging, and my breath whooshed in and out like a vacuum. Ryder's gray eyes were granite and steel with determination and a huge part of me didn't believe I could get out of explaining it this time.

And the other small part of me didn't want to get out of it.

I wanted to tell Ryder my secrets.

I wanted him to know me.

"Do not play games with me, Ivy," Ryder growled, low and rough. And then he softened, his eyes almost pleading, "You can trust me."

I held his gaze and panicked. Honestly I couldn't trust anybody with my secret, not even him. But that wasn't the point since it didn't matter if I could... I wanted to trust him. I wanted to let him in. And that terrified me. Tearing my eyes away from Ryder, my fingers moved against the keys but they pounded out loudly in the now quiet loft, so I paused to adjust the volume with shaking fingers. The music, now barely above a whisper, seemed easier today and my fingers moved to the haunting melody Ryder composed.

"You sound better today," Ryder admitted in a more normal tone. "Do you feel more comfortable with an audience now?"

227

"I feel more comfortable with the keyboard," I explained, ignoring his small jab.

"Do you think you can keep the melody strong if I start playing along? Or is that going to mess you up?" Ryder asked with a sweetness that had been absent not just two minutes ago.

I shrugged a shoulder but stayed focused on the sheet music in front of me as my right hand soared upward and heightened emotionally(or would have if the keyboard weren't so inflexible) while my left hand harmonized in chords.

From my peripheral I watched Ryder walk over and pick up his guitar. He slung it over his shoulder and immediately his fingers found home on the used guitar strings. He plucked out a few tuning issues that I did my best not to pay attention to and then walked over to me with a silly grin on his face.

He looked over my shoulder and studied my music for a long time before strumming out a chord that fit exactly right. And then he was off into the lead guitar piece that clouded all of my concentration and forced me to ignore him completely just so I could remember middle C.

We actually started to make music together. After the other night and my obvious failures this felt kind of.... nice. Ryder, the talented rock star, covered my mistakes easily. But I was starting to make fewer mistakes anyway.

I had natural talent in all things musical, but any accomplishments on the piano were achieved by hard work and tons of practice. So even though this wasn't more than complicated harmonies, I still had to work at it. And I had never played with anyone else before.

After about fifteen minutes and the fourth time through the song, we actually started to sound really good together. Plus, I could hear the guitar a bit better, and because I was familiar with the song I was taking over on my own. This felt awesome.

"Alright Simon, Garfunkel, time to break for breakfast," Matt called out from the kitchen.

Ryder smiled at me over his guitar, "That sounds good."

"Yes, it does," I admitted.

I stood back from the keyboard and grabbed my now cold coffee while Ryder set his guitar down and slipped his black pick into a pouch filled with others of all different colors. I hesitated long enough so Ryder could lead the way to the big concrete table where a huge spread of scrambled eggs, bacon, sausage, rolls, gravy and bowl of fruit were laid out.

"Wow," I admired. "This looks incredible."

"Thanks," Matt beamed.

I sat down next to Ryder, and then accepted the frying pan filled with eggs from his dad. He had to stand up and reach across the table to give it to me and I had to do the same. I accepted the weight of the heavy pan and immediately added some to my plate before passing it to Ryder.

Ryder looked at me for a moment, hands filled with hot frying pan and serving spoon, before he dug a huge spoonful out and added it to my plate. My mouth gaped open with chagrin and I whipped my head around to say something about women's rights and knowing my own body but he wasn't looking at me and I didn't want to make a scene in front of his dad and uncle.

The food continued to be passed around and soon my plate was heaping with homemade goodies. I had never even had biscuits and gravy before. I'd seen it on other people's plates, but you can eat a great breakfast without ever being subjected to that kind of greasy calorie fest. I would have passed on it altogether, but Ryder lifted a ladle full of gravy to dump *all over* my plate, eggs, bacon and all, so I took back the spoon and added it myself. Now the thick, white gravy was mixing with my fresh cut cantaloupe and pineapple and I wasn't sure exactly what to do.

"So Ivy, tell us a little about yourself," Ryder's dad, Nate, asked from over a fork full of eggs.

I felt the attention of everyone in the room like a blinding spotlight. I hated questions like this, and Ryder stayed so still and quiet next to me I realized he was just as interested in what I was going to say as his dad. If not more interested…. he was no help at all.

"Um, I'm not sure what to say," I admitted. "I go to school with Ryder at um, Central. And I'm a junior…. I've never had a breakfast like this before, it's really incredible. I can't believe you eat like this every Saturday."

Deflecting the attention from myself to the food worked and everyone laughed at the insane amount of food on the table.

"Well, it's not *always* like this," Matt spoke up. "Ryder begged for the works this morning. I think he was trying to make a good impression."

Ryder jerked at his uncle's words and gave me a sheepish, embarrassed smile, "I just wanted to make sure there was something you liked. It wasn't a big deal."

"Oh, no it wasn't a big deal," Matt covered, realizing he had said something that made Ryder and me uncomfortable. "I'm just giving Ryder a hard time." His easy grin was one I had seen on Ryder's face probably a hundred times in our short friendship and I didn't even think about it, I just returned it.

Nate cut back in, probably hoping to take the awkward attention off his son, "So you play the piano well, Ivy. Are your parents musical?"

"It's just my mom," I offered casually. "And she does play. It's kind of a tradition in our family. She made me start when I was really young."

"That's great," Nate nodded along. "I always appreciate when a parent takes solid interest in their children's musical educations. She probably loves the band then? A practical use for all that talent, it's got to make her proud."

Unease filtered over my skin and I dropped my eyes to the plate of food I hardly touched. "Actually, my mom doesn't really understand anything but the classics. I was classically trained with Bach and Mozart, she hates anything composed beyond the nineteenth century, save maybe for Sibelius."

"Really?" Nate practically choked on his breakfast. "So she never let you play anything jazz? Blues? Contemporary?"

I hid a smile and shook my head. "Nothing current. And especially nothing jazz."

"Just for the piano though, right?" Nate pressed and he seemed more like Ryder than ever before. "You've heard Gershwin? Duke Ellington?"

I gave him a blank look although I had heard the names before and his entire body sagged with the news. Ryder chuckled next to me and put a reassuring hand on my knee under the table. My heart started pounding double time at the small contact, but he simply squeezed my knee cap and then removed his hand like it was no big deal. Because it wasn't a big deal- at all.

"You'll have to forgive my brother," Matt interrupted. "He's a bit of a fanatic when it comes to contemporary music."

"No kidding," Ryder groaned.

All three men broke out into big smiles then. I shot Ryder a questioning look and he rolled his eyes before explaining, "I'm named after a Van Morrison song."

"Oh," I said like that explained everything. "What song?"

"Rough God Goes Riding," Ryder tried to pretend like the song was annoying, but I caught the reverent tone to his voice as he spoke the title carefully.

"I've never heard of it," I confessed.

"But you've heard of Van Morrison before, yeah?" Nate asked while his hands gripped at the table nervously.

230

"I mean sure," I laughed at his reaction, "I've heard the name before." Even though I didn't even know if Van Morrison was one man or a full band.

Nate winced dramatically. And Matt burst into good natured laughter. "It's alright, big brother. Look, Ivy's managed to escape the regurgitated pop bullshit culture her whole life and she seems to have turned out just fine."

I turned to Ryder for some clarification. "Where my father obsesses over everything current and cool to the point he can karaoke to Gaga, my uncle shuns society as the harrying work of the devil," Ryder paused dramatically and then finished with, "Except Tarantino films. We all find common ground with Tarantino."

"Well, that's the good Lord's work, right there," Matt grunted in approval and then shot me another wink.

"And I don't obsess," Nate defended. "I am just fascinated by the constant evolution of society. Music is continuously changing, growing.... moving, even if some think backwards. Human creativity is so interesting. And take your mother and me for a moment, how different our tastes are, our values. There is something in that, something worth studying."

I sat spellbound, loving every word as it fell out of his mouth. He was so opposite of my world, so different and rebellious from anything I had been taught. In the circle you like the same thing everyone else likes, the same thing everyone else has liked forever. There are no individual opinions or tastes, there's just what we always did, what was expected of us, what was commanded of us. Nix decided. Or our mothers decreed.

"I had no idea these guys were such hippies, I swear," Ryder laughed and then pushed away from his plate. His arm went around the back of my chair and his fingers tapped out an unheard rhythm against the metal.

"Don't let him fool you, Ivy," Nate's silver eyes twinkled at me from behind his glasses. "He's proud of his old man."

"Yeah, yeah," Ryder rolled his eyes. "Now please enough questions. I brought Ivy here to eat, let her *eat*."

Nate and Matt grinned at each other sharing some secret that didn't need to be said out loud. I chose to ignore them and Ryder's hand as his fingers accidentally brushed across the top of my shoulder. I looked down at my plate and dug in.

Everything was amazing. I sighed happily as I shoveled the food into my mouth, not caring if I looked like a pig. My mother would have been so proud.

Or probably the opposite of proud.

Nate and Matt included Ryder in their conversation that seemed to jump all over the place without any clear direction. They talked about Matt's classes this semester and I learned that he was older than most to be going to traditional university. But he had spent four years after high school traveling the world and then another two years after that working in Colorado just so he could afford to have a place to sleep, eat and snowboard as often as he wanted to. He finally moved here when Nate accepted the position at UNO and decided to start taking his life seriously. This was all shared in casual clips and phrases that I pieced together myself. I also learned that Ryder's dad not only taught music but also shared his love for soccer and he and Matt played in an indoor league together. Nate hated Omaha in the winter, but loved it summer through fall. He was disgustingly proud of both his brother and his son and had long ago decided that wherever Ryder wanted to go to college, he would just apply for a job there to both take care of tuition and stay close to Ryder. There was also a healthy mix of politics, upcoming plans for the week and a discussion about Batman versus Iron Man weaved in.

By the time Matt stood up to start clearing the plates, I had never laughed so hard in my life. I hopped up to help with the dishes, but Ryder reached for my hand and tugged me back down. I landed half off my chair, my legs pressed into Ryder's, his hand still gripping mine.

"This is always my job," he explained in a soft voice. "If Matt's offering, let him do it."

"Okay," I agreed. This close to Ryder, with so much of our bodies touching, I felt breathless, disoriented.

"Do you have time for a walk?" he asked, his thumb brushed a line across the palm of my hand and his knee pressed harder against my thigh. I felt slightly jostled as his knee bounced furiously up and down, connected so tightly to me.

"Yes," I answered before I bothered looking at the time.

A crooked smile broke across his too handsome face and he met my eyes and held them for several moments. Neither of us said anything, or moved, and then everything quieted around us, or at least I felt like it did. The sounds of dishes clinking together in the sink ceased, his father and uncle's voices faded away and then there was only my breathing and his as our chests lifted and fell in harmony.

"Okay, let's go," he breathed and then tugged me to my feet.

"Okay," I heard myself say. And then I was following him out the door and ignoring every single rational protest that was screaming inside my head.

Chapter Thirty

We didn't walk far, just up the last flight of stairs and to the roof of the building. The concrete roof was flat and littered with gravel. The wind whipped, chilly and crisp across our faces. The sun was bright and warm this morning, in constant battle with the dropping temperatures of autumn.

Ryder let go of my hand when we were alone on the roof and walked to the far side. I followed. I didn't have a choice but to follow. I was in way deeper than I wanted to be- than I should be.

He turned around once he reached the shoulder-high wall barricade of the brick building. The tall wall kept us from having a great view of downtown but over the top of it I could see the trees from the mall all turned brilliant fall shades of orange and red and yellow and I could see the tops of all the biggest buildings, First National, the Holland Center, The Double Tree Hotel.

"I want to know, Ivy," Ryder said simply in a way that seemed relaxed but sincere.

Tears pricked my eyes immediately. Whatever I said about Ryder, whatever I wanted to believe…. I liked his friendship, I *valued* it. And I liked him. This conversation was the beginning of the end. The death of everything beautiful between us.

"No you don't," I whispered. "I promise you, you don't."

"Tell me," he demanded, taking a step forward and gripping my hands in his.

"Tell you what?" I turned my head, afraid to meet his eyes.

"Ivy, don't," his voice grated against my heartstrings, rough and violent, demanding and authoritative. And it was like my entire being responded to him, like my soul sat up straight and my blood buzzed attentively in my veins. He pulled at me.

And that terrified me.

"Ryder I can't… there is nothing to tell," I argued.

He took a step forward. "I want to help you. I want to be your friend, but you have to let me."

This did not feel like friendship.

I turned my head away and avoided his eyes some more. This tactic wasn't really working, but I wasn't strong enough to leave him, so it would have to do.

"Okay, then start with Sam. Will you tell me about Sam?" That damn voice. I regretfully looked up and the soft, pleading tone of his voice trapped me. Paralyzed me. And then bewitched me. "Please, Ivy. Help me understand."

I hesitated for as long as I could, for an entire two minutes, and then I caved, "Sam Evans... we dated last year. He was a senior and I was a sophomore. But, um, he was on the basketball team and I was kind of working my way through dating them all." A blush flooded my face and for the first time what my life represented and the expectations Nix and my mother had for me *humiliated* me.

"Ivy, it's okay, you can trust me," he swore in a way that I had no choice but to believe him.

I pulled some courage from places I didn't think I had, and cleared my throat. "By the time Sam and I started dating, I had already been through the point guard, the center and some of the second string. I was tired of dating.... tired of, just tired of it all. And I really liked Sam. He was nicer than some of the other guys, more laid back. He didn't... he wasn't always pushing me." I cleared my throat again; a little surprised I admitted that much. I couldn't *bear* to look at Ryder, I was too embarrassed but I felt his body tense until he was rigid and every muscle was hard. "Um, anyway, Sam and I clicked in a way that I hadn't ever clicked with anybody before and I don't know. When it was time to break up with him, I just couldn't. I liked him, like really *liked* him. So we dated for a while, almost four months. But things started to get serious and I wasn't ready for that. He wasn't really ready for that either, you know? But he thought he was. And then, it was spring and he had this scholarship to play basketball out of state, but he started talking about staying here and giving it up, just to be close to me. I didn't mean to do that to him, to ruin his life. I just liked being around him, I just wanted a little bit of a break from the constant wannabe date rapists and... I just... For the first time, Sam saw me, really *me*, not the pretty package I'm wrapped in and I was selfish with that." A tear slipped down my cheek but I was too wrapped up in the ugly memories to wipe it away. "But I couldn't let him give up his *scholarship*. Or stay here for *me*. He needed to live his life, and he wouldn't.... couldn't see that. So I broke up with him. I had to, I mean it was time. But he took it really, really hard. And then we were at this party. We didn't go together, but we ran into each other there. And he was drunk, like really, really drunk. But when he saw me.... He just broke. I *broke him*. And then he stormed out of the party, so I chased after him; I mean I couldn't let him drive like that. But he was bigger than me and I called for help, but everyone there was pretty much toasted. And anyway, I jumped in the car with him, thinking I could, I don't know, convince him to stop, or pull over

234

or something. But he was pissed, and so… *hurt*. He just took off and before I knew it we were on the wrong side of the road going like seventy-five and then… and the next thing I knew I was in the hospital. I had buckled my seatbelt, but Sam had not. No one else was hurt, he crashed into the median and the car flipped and rolled eventually into a light pole, but it was late enough that there weren't any other cars on the road. Sam was thrown from the car on the first roll, but the car landed on top of him. He's in a wheelchair now, and he won't be able to talk ever again, or walk again. He'll never be able to play basketball again." The tears were streaming now, huge, messy rivers of tears that mixed with snot and ran down my face. I wiped at my face with my sleeves and makeup and wetness stained the white fabric.

Ryder let me hiccup a sob one time before he pulled me against his chest and wrapped his arms around me. One hand tangled in the back of my hair, pressing my skull against his breastbone, and the other hugged me around the waist so that there was absolutely no space between us. More sobs burst from my lungs, like lava from a volcano and they came in a torrential downpour of emotion I wasn't prepared for.

Emotion I promised myself was buried away.

"Ivy, what happened to Sam is *not* your fault. He should never have been driving and he should never have tried to medicate his pain with alcohol. You cannot blame yourself," Ryder ordered in a hoarse, pained whisper.

"Yes, I can," I snapped, the sadness abruptly replaced with anger. "You have no idea. Everything was my fault. *Everything*."

Ryder pulled away from me and tried to look in my eyes, but I ducked my head away. I was ashamed and ugly with emotion.

Finally, he settled on, "Why is it your fault, Ivy?"

"Because of who I am!" I screamed at him. I was tired of his calm, placating tone. He couldn't sooth me, not this. This was pain he couldn't take away. "Because of what I do! I destroy lives. That's my whole purpose. Sam, all the boys before him, Chase, you! The crash was my fault. If he never would have met me, he would have been safe!"

Ryder met my fierce emotion with his own angered conviction, "Why Ivy? What does his crash have to do with you? What does who you are have to do with any of it?"

"It's crazy," I let out hysterical laughter that came out rough and course in my winded lungs. "You'll think I'm crazy."

"I already think you're crazy," he admitted and this time my laughter was less crazed and more genuine.

"Siren. I'm a, uh, I'm a siren," the words rushed out of me in a waterfall of truth I would never be able to take back. Ryder let go of my arms and took a step back, completely shocked, or stunned, or... I didn't know. I couldn't imagine being told something as crazy as that for the first time. "I told you, *I told you* that you would think I was crazy. And it is crazy! It's completely f-ing nuts."

"What do you mean you're a siren?" Ryder bit through my hysterics with a cold, demanding order.

"Greek mythology? Zeus, Mount Olympus? Gods and goddesses, nymphs, muses... sirens? I am a siren," Sanity started to return to me once the truth was out there. And shockingly my breath came easier and my shoulders straightened out. Whether Ryder ever believed me or not, I felt better knowing I came clean to somebody. "It's all true, Ryder. All of it. Well, okay, not all of it. Not in the context you read about it at school. And Mount Olympus isn't like some reference to heaven, it's just a normal mountain. But the rest of it is somewhat true."

"I don't understand, Ivy. Is this like, a, uh, uh, metaphor?" It was like he was begging me to say yes, his entire body bent forward, his eyes pleading... he needed me to say yes, that this was all just one big giant metaphor for life and I wasn't completely insane after all.

"No, it's not a metaphor. Ryder, this is truth. Or at least my truth, what I've lived with my whole life. But you have to look at it differently, like it's not this exaggerated fairy tale that you're taught in school. The legends are embellished to pander to their egos, but for the most part.... they're true. And our society, it's not like it was way back in the day. I mean, there are not that many of us and we all just kind of blend into the rest of humanity now. But, the guys, the attention, Sam's *crash*.... It's because I'm a siren. That's what I do to men."

"Explain it to me slower," Ryder growled out and I couldn't tell if he was starting to believe me or not.

"Men feel attracted to me because they can't help it. I've been cursed since birth by this.... genealogy. I don't have a choice about what I do to guys, it just happens. And the more time I spend with any one guy, the deeper the connection for me they feel, the harder it is to get away from. That's what happened to Sam, he spent too much time with me until I destroyed him and then the crash? That was just like the end of the road with someone like me. The ultimate closure," I laughed bitterly.

"The crash was on purpose?" Ryder gasped, gripping my forearms in his strong hands.

"No!" I quickly reassured. "No, it wasn't on purpose, but it wasn't necessarily avoidable either. I mean, that kind of stuff hasn't happened in a really long time. We don't lure sailors to their graves anymore or anything like that. For the most part, whatever elevated evolution we possessed back in the day is mostly gone by now, but then the crash with Sam happened and my circle, um, my little sect of people like myself look at it like a sign, like a good sign of things to come."

"You *want* to be able to hurt people?" Ryder's grip tightened on my arms, and I winced a little. He immediately dropped my arms and turned away like he couldn't stomach looking at me. I couldn't let myself hope that he believed me, that he wouldn't cut off all communication with me after this conversation, but I had to keep talking, I had to make him understand I wasn't like them.

"No, not me, I'm *not* like them. I *never* wanted to hurt Sam, to hurt *anybody*. I don't want this life. But I was born into it. Right now, I don't have a choice. But I have this trust fund. I'm planning on…. You are planning on going to college, or whatever and I'm, I just have to get *out*."

Ryder let that sink in, his breathing was deep and measured and his eyes smooth silver in thought. Finally he looked up at me, his jawline tensed with some kind of emotion I couldn't figure out. "Suppose I…. suppose I believe you. Who's Nix?"

"My um, godfather," I explained but that didn't really explain anything.

"No way, Ivy. The way that guy looks at you, how he acts around you…. it's like he's trying to own you. Like you're his *possession*. Who is he? You've been honest with me this far." His words cut at me like razor blades, but he was right. I had been honest this far.

"In the big perspective he's Poseidon's nephew. I wasn't lying, he really is my godfather. But he's also my mom's boss. And he'll be mine too one day. I mean, if the trust fund plan doesn't pan out."

"And by boss you mean what? What does your mom do?" he questioned me with enough resentment that I wondered if he was starting to get it.

"My mom, um, all of us, once we reach a certain age are required to work, to contribute to the general fund. We're raised and groomed to be these perfect women, so that we can use our natural charm to entrap men. Marry them, take their money, destroy their lives or what's left of them and move on. Or watch them die if we're really talented and are good at picking them."

"And Nix?" Ryder asked again.

"He's in charge of it all," I half shouted in exasperation. "He sets up the meetings, or flies in to assess our work. He controls my mother's life. And mine. He, he wants me to date you. You're supposed to be my next... conquest," I shuddered at the word. "In high school we date for practice, it's like training. We're not actually allowed to sleep with anybody, not that I would or anything, but our virginity, it's like part of our initiation."

"Oh, my god," Ryder spat out with so much hatred and disgust that I cringed. "You're in the sex slave industry. You're a goddamn sex slave."

"What?" I shrieked because I hadn't figured he would jump there that fast. And despite all my truth telling, all the honesty that I spewed like vomit, I still couldn't admit that fact out loud. It was too ugly, too pathetic. "Didn't you just hear me? I have to *keep* my virginity. I'm not like a prostitute or anything."

"No you're not, not yet. Don't you see how sick this is? How *twisted*?" And he really did look like he was going to be sick.

And it was the look on his face more than his words that finally broke me, "Yes, Ryder! Damn it, of course I do!" I crumpled against the building, pulling my knees to my chest and wrapping my arms around them. I dissolved in to tears again, the weight of everything pressing down so tightly I couldn't breathe.

"Oh, hell, Ivy," Ryder's voice cracked and he slid down the wall next to me. He put a solid arm around my back and when I didn't shrink away he pulled me against him again.

I wept into his chest, more ugliness and brokenness than I knew what to do with. When the reality of my life passed, new hysteria broke out at the realization I just included Ryder in my screwed up world. He wasn't supposed to know any of this and I had all but written him a manual.

"Hey, it's going to be alright, we're going to get you out of this," he soothed into my hair, his lips pressed against my head. "My dad can help. We can go to the authorities. Maybe not tell them everything, but enough so that they know you're in trouble. Child Protective Services can help. We will get you out of this."

My head snapped up, my eyes cleared. I hadn't thought this through enough to realize Ryder would, *of course*, want to help. "Ryder, we can't go to the police, are you crazy? First of all, this is nothing like what you see on TV. This is highly protected and nothing is done illegally. Nix owns several corporations; he's a world renowned businessman. So the local police aren't going to be able to find anything dirty on him. And as far as my mom goes, or any of the other women in our circle, by the time they get involved they go willingly. It's like a cult. I belong to a cult. Only,

238

religion's not really part of it. Trust me though. I wasn't in rehab for six months; I was in intense behavior modification. It was supposed to fix me because I felt bad for what happened to Sam. My mom has legally married every man she's been with. She's legally inherited their fortune or won it in a divorce settlement. The authorities can't do anything for me. And I'm not being abused."

Ryder's jaw locked in thought. A muscle kept ticking in his cheek and for just a moment I felt relieved to have someone share my same frustration. But then the hopelessness caught up with me again and I spiraled back to the pits of despair.

"Okay, if there's nothing legal we can do, then we'll just get you out of here. Your trust fund, right? Why can't you take that now? Matt has friends around the world from when he went traveling, they would help you. Or at least house you for a while. I could even go with you for a little bit, help you get set up," he sat forward, excited by his solution and I *loathed* being the one who had to destroy those hopes. I knew, firsthand, what it would feel like.

I shook my head first, my eyes filling with tears again. "I've already thought something like that through. Right now my trust is untouchable until I'm eighteen and have graduated high school. Those conditions are unbreakable. Trust me, I've looked into it," Although I didn't want to get his hopes up so I refrained from telling him about Smith and his secret team of lawyers. "And besides, even if I could get to it now, I wouldn't leave. I have a sister, half-sister really, Honor. She's only eleven and I just can't leave her yet. I mean, I will one day, I will, but not yet. I want to protect her as long as I can."

"She lives with your mom?" Ryder asked, looking sick all over again.

"No, she lives with her dad. She's…. He's special. I mean, he was one of my mom's marks, years ago. Not just for his money, but because she wanted another child too. But he was supposed to die. He had stage four brain cancer. He somehow survived and then, when he recovered it was like he was immune to the whole Siren thing. He's not affected by my mom, by any of us. He has custody of Honor. And he is protecting her for now; he barely lets my mom see her. But everyone in my circle wants my mom to have custody, obviously, so Honor is *not* safe. Nix will do anything to get her."

"He's immune? Has that ever happened before?" Ryder asked carefully and I could see a light go on in his eyes.

"Just one other time that I'm aware of," I answered quietly.

"With me?" He clarified like he knew the truth already.

I nodded, afraid that the spell would be broken. "With the coffee, in the hallway.... I mean, you didn't feel anything did you?"

Ryder thought about it for a while and then replied, "Just irritation. *Lots* of irritation."

I rolled my eyes but let out a soft laugh. "You're so obnoxious."

"That's what was with my dad and uncle?"

I nodded again. "That's what's with everybody."

"But it's not like they were worshipping at your feet," he argued. I recognized his desire to stand up for those he loved, to make them appear strong and capable. Nobody wanted to be helpless against a force they couldn't control.

"The pull gets harder to resist the longer you're around me. And sometimes, with stronger personalities, it takes longer to be affected. Weak men feel my pull even before I'm near them. But some, very strong men, can subconsciously resist for a while. For everybody but you, and Honor's father," I explained. "As long as you're being honest. As long as you really don't feel *anything* between us."

"That's why you warned me before? About falling for you?" His voice was soft and understanding.

"Yes," I agreed simply.

"We'll figure this out, Ivy," he promised. "You're not alone. You have me, you have friends. We will get you out of this."

"Thank you," I whispered against the biting wind. And meant it for so many more things than his promise.

The sun had dropped from its morning high point to the other side of the sky and I shivered against the temperature that had also dropped. Ryder pulled me closer and we sat in silence for a while until I pulled myself together. He helped me wipe my face clean of makeup and then stand to my feet.

"I need to get home," I said through a throaty voice. "My mom is probably wondering where I am by now."

"I don't want to take you back there," he growled in a primal, protective voice.

"It's okay, Ryder, I have to go at some point," I tried to make my voice sound light and casual, but neither of us were convinced. "Besides, Nix is out of town right now. My mom is almost harmless when he's not around."

"Nix? The pimp-slash-conman?" Ryder snarled.

A laugh bubbled out before I could stop myself, "Yes, my pimp-slash-conman."

"You'll be alright?" he asked while he rubbed a hand up and down over my back.

"Mmm-hmm, I'll be alright." And I would be.

"Then I agree to take you home," he offered magnanimously. "But only if you text or call me the second you are not alright, okay? For any reason, for anything. Real danger, or emotional or anything, Ivy. Promise me you'll call."

"I promise." I closed my eyes and savored the moment before Ryder led me down from the roof and through the stairwell back to his car. I had never had anyone I could count on before. Even if I never used Ryder's number as a distress call, his offer would mean more to me than he would ever know.

Finally, *finally*, he felt like the friend I kept convincing myself he was.

A real friend.

Chapter Thirty-One

I walked as quietly into the apartment as I could, trying not to make a single sound. But it was a wasted effort because she was waiting for me. Her posture was absolutely perfect, her arms crossed elegantly across her chest so that her freshly manicured nails lay undisturbed. Her brilliant red hair cascaded over her shoulders in loose waves and her slinky outfit clung to her like a glove. She was perfection except for the scowl twisting her face into sheer disappointment.

"Where have you been?" She hissed.

"Chase took me to breakfast this morning," I mumbled. I needed to fess up about breaking it off with him, but not yet, not until I had anybody besides Ryder to use.

"You went to breakfast... looking like that?" She sneered openly at me. "You look like hell, Ivy! Have you been *crying*?"

"No, I, uh-"

"Spit it out," she commanded in clipped tones. "And I swear, if this is about that Sam kid again, I will call Nix this instant and make him come clean this up. I cannot *handle* this anymore." Her voice was bordering on screeching and she was red in the face. This was so not behavior my rational, cold, distant mother would normally condone.

"Mom, chill," I broke in before she really got hysterical. "I broke up with Chase this morning. It's not a big deal. I just felt bad. That's all. This isn't about Sam." Not entirely.

She paused at my interruption, sanity returned to her face and she visibly calmed down. "You broke up with him? I thought Nix gave you a timeline?"

"I had to, I didn't want to drag things out and then..." I paused not wanting to use Sam as an excuse. It was on the tip of my tongue, the lie, the reason... but it seriously made my stomach turn.

"Alright, Ivy, I get it," she rolled her eyes at me. "We do *not* want a repeat of your meltdown." She visibly shuddered, "Can you imagine how embarrassing that would be?"

"I can imagine," I said on a bitter laugh.

"Enough of your sarcasm. You need to get ready. We're expected at Thalia's in an hour and a half." She started walking to the kitchen but paused to give me another once over. "Does that give you enough time to become presentable?"

"Yes," I sighed. Thalia was Sloane's mother and I was more than ready to spend some time with Sloane and Exie, especially after spilling my guts to Ryder. But an evening with the circle of women without Nix present, meant I had to be. This wasn't a dinner party, this was a gossip session and my mother fully expected me to participate.

Bleh.

An hour later I was showered and beautified and ready to go. I hung out near the entry way, straightening the kitchen and wasting time while I waited for my mother to do…. whatever it was she needed to do before we left. She made a big deal about being there on time but if Nix wasn't waiting on her, my mother was under the impression that she needed to make everybody wait on her.

Including me.

Finally she walked into the kitchen looking the same as when I left her. Her dress was made by a different designer, but basically the same style and her hair was maybe fluffed, but that was it. She gave me a scathing, calculated glance before I received the nod of approval. Ugh, and we were just going to dinner with other women!

A Town car was waiting for us when we reached the ground floor, heaven forbid my mother drive. And then we were silent until we reached Sloane's sprawling midtown home. I realized when the car stopped in front of Sloane's house that Exie's mother, Echo, hadn't thrown a party in a while.

There was only a second to contemplate that before my own mother was rapping her knuckles against the black painted door and Thalia was welcoming us with her wide, fake smile and perfectly coiffed black hair.

"So happy you could finally join us," Thalia cooed, referencing my mother's inability to be on time.

"So are we," my mother echoed without any enthusiasm. Technically we were all chained to the same destiny, working for Nix, but somehow my mother and I as sirens held a higher rank of respectability than Exie or Sloane's family. It had something to do with our ability to bring in the cash.

Basically because we could be bigger sluts than them, we were worth more.

Disgusting, right?

"The girls are in the dining room, Ivy," Thalia mentioned over her shoulder before she escorted my mother to the kitchen where a fresh cocktail would be waiting for her.

I left them without a word and worked my way to the dining room. I didn't meet anyone on the way so I had to assume this was a small gathering. Hopefully the party was contained to my mom and me, Exie's family and Sloane's family. All women, so it was bound to get catty after a while, but it was better than performing for middle-aged men and pretending I was interested the entire night.

Especially after talking to Ryder. There was this rebellious freedom pulsing through my veins tonight and I knew I couldn't be trusted to behave.

He had lit something inside me, something that demanded to be set free. But the rational part of my brain warned that it was still too soon. That until my trust fund was available I still had a part to play.

"Well, hey there gorgeous," Anaxandra called as I walked into the dining room. The long French vintage table, set to accommodate all of us, shined with polish and pretty cornflower blue patterned China.

"Hey," I smiled. I held back my disappointment at seeing Anaxandra and Evaleen already seated with Exie and Sloane. I wanted a few minutes alone with them so I could tell them about Ryder, but now was obviously the wrong time. "So what is this? Dinner with the families?"

"The families" was what we called our inner circle, a reference to the mob. Not that we were the mob, although there were definite connections, but in this area of the country, my family, Exie's and Sloane's were the top of the pyramid.

"Organizational," Evaleen confirmed.

"Strategic and logistical," Sloane added, rolling her eyes.

"So we'll be here for what, the next twelve hours? Hope your mom ordered lots of alcohol," I groaned.

"Did Ava tell you nothing about this?" Evaleen asked suspiciously.

"We're not on the best of terms right now." I avoided their eyes and focused on finding the right chair.... far enough away from the adults that I could actually enjoy dinner without being obvious about ignoring my mother.

"Why not? What happened this time?" Anaxandra gasped. She was the one who taught me how valuable my mother was. Our mothers were our only allies in this world. Where a friend's mother would only view me as competition for her own daughter, it behooved my mother for me to do well. Ava always treated me like royalty before Sam and my six month exile; I was her crowning jewel, her legacy. But now I was this dark cloud over her carefully plotted parade.

If I cared before, I didn't now. Ava's only motivation for treating me well before had been purely political and manipulative. Nothing she did for me was done out of something as simple as mother-daughter love.

245

That thought was only laughable. And now that I knew the difference, now that I *knew* the truth, I didn't miss her attention, or her affection.

"Who knows," I sighed.

"How can you be so casual about this, Ivy?" Anaxandra snapped. "You need to fix whatever is broken and fast."

"Ana, let her be," Exie spoke up for the first time, tossing her golden curls over her shoulder. "Whatever's going on with her mom is her business, not yours."

"We look out for each other," Anaxandra defended and I saw a spark of the old her flash brightly. "Ava will throw you to the wolves if you're not careful," her voice dropped to an earnest whisper and her eyes pleaded with me to take her seriously.

"She's right, Ives," Evaleen leaned forward with critical eyes. She dressed to kill tonight, which surprised me a little since this was just a girls' night. Her chestnut hair was lifted off her neck in an intricate updo that piled on top of her head. One lone strand of long hair had slipped out and curved gracefully around the back of her neck. Her dark eyes were beseeching at the same time they were cunning and her perfect, rosebud lips were pressed into a frown. "You're the firstborn, that means she has an entire other child to turn her attentions to if you screw up anymore."

"Maybe in other families, but not so in mine," I divulged. "Honor is in no way ever leaving Smith. He has her on complete lockdown."

"How is that possible?" Anaxandra hissed.

"Plus, it doesn't matter how Ava feels about Ivy," Exie spoke up conspiratorially. "Nix wants her, so she's safe."

"Shut up!" Eva gasped. "Nix wants you? Like he wants to take you?"

I blushed a deep, revealing red and stared intently at the flower pattern on the ivory China. "Uh, yeah."

"When?" Ana demanded.

"After I graduate," I whispered.

There was silence at the table then as we all absorbed this information. A pain shot out from my chest and pierced every piece of me. I recognized the feeling as debilitating fear, the kind of fear you couldn't pretend didn't exist or ignore or runaway from. This fear reared up and made itself known, promised more and never, ever let go.

Tinkling, forced laughter came from the hallway and as if on cue we all sat up straighter and put hands to our hair to make sure it was in place. Our mothers entered the room as one unit, smiling and beaming at each other. Their cold gazes assessed us at the table like they were robots sharing the same brain. When they finally decided everything was as it should be they joined as at the table, sitting together at one end so they could continue their business.

Dinner was served as soon as they sat down. A hired team of caterers brought out cold soup and small bread platters that went untouched. I never understood why so much food was ordered for these events, when these women barely ate any of it. Even I knew better than to snatch a dinner roll even though I had been eyeing one for the last twenty minutes.

During soup the conversation was mostly lulled to topics like the weather for traveling, winter break destinations and new purchases. The salad course was next and discussion deepened to subjects like education beliefs and local elections, which was mostly important for how the courts ruled over Honor and my mother. The third course, prime rib cut into tiny little strips and served over a creamy risotto intensified the dialog further and we began to discuss the politics of our circle.

"So, Ava," Thalia began, "Nix is planning to stay in town for a while, is that right?"

Echo jumped in, "I heard that too. It has something to do with Ivy, doesn't it?"

"Nix wants her," my mother answered proudly. Her eyes lit up for the first time all night, and a real smile played at the corner of her lips. "He's asked her to join him after graduation."

All other conversation stopped at this point and we all turned to my mother. Anaxandra, who happened to be sitting next to me, put a hand on mine under the table to reassure me. This surprised me more than my mother's forwardness. I thought Ana was completely converted to the dark side, but maybe not.

"And she agreed of course?" Thalia's cool gaze pinned me to my chair, daring me to deny anything. The wicked queen to her daughter's Snow White looks, she had all the beauty Evaleen and Sloane did except she was aging and she knew it. The wrinkles in her laugh line and looser skin had turned her cruel and greedy.

"He hasn't asked me formally, yet," I clarified even though I knew it would cost my mother. "He just mentioned it at dinner once." I tore my eyes from Thalia's triumphant stare and noticed the sky had gone completely dark outside. We had been here for hours and there were still hours to get through yet.

"He intends to take her," my mother spelled out with force. "We've had several conversations about her."

"Won't that leave you without a legacy?" Echo asked and the note of laughter rang out in the room. These women were so catty; I could feel the few bites I allowed myself for dinner threaten to reappear.

"I have Honor," Ava returned serenely.

"And if Smith always keeps her? If she is never allowed out of that house?" Thalia scoffed. "What then?"

"Honor will be my legacy; there is no question about that. Nix wants Ivy enough that he will make sure I get Honor," Ava promised self-confidently.

A jolting shiver washed down my back and I was sure I would be sick for a few moments. Eventually the racking nausea slowed and I looked up in time to watch my mother smirk at her supposed best friends. "Honor will never go with you," I spat in a hushed tone before I even registered the words were being said.

Oops.

My mother's scathing glare swept towards me and I summoned every ounce of courage I possessed to sit up straight and stare her in the eyes. A collective intake of breath could be heard around the room and then everything was silent while my mother's rage grew until I could feel it pouring off her in waves.

"What a strong spirit you have, Ivy," Thalia broke the charged silence with the backhanded compliment. "No wonder Nix wants to add you to his collection."

Strangled laughter erupted in Ava and her restrained fury turned her eyes wild. "My daughter? Strong spirit?" more crazed laughter. "You forget that this is the same child that needed to be sent away after her breakup. One broken heart and she's a mental case! Nix is saving us all from the disaster she brings with her. She is a tragedy waiting to happen. No, Ivy has always been too weak for this world, too *weak* for anything of worth."

"Weak?" I choked on the word; it felt vile and repulsive in my mouth. I had survived this long, made it this far with *her* and with *him* and she was calling me weak! I felt the presence enter the room behind me and pause in the doorway, but I was too emotionally involved to stop myself now. "No, not weak. I have a *soul*. That may be a weakness to you, but it is not to me. I have common decency, some f-ing standards and you call that weak! Of course I don't fit in; I'm trying to be a *good person*, to be *better* than this life you force me to live."

I jumped at the sound of the next voice, even though instinct warned me he would be there.

"It's not about being a good person, Ivy," Nix calmly soothed from behind me. I felt his voice grow more placating as he walked into the dining room. Every head swiveled around with mouth agape to stare at him. He was picture perfect in his pressed suit and shiny shoes, but his tie was absent and the top button of his white oxford was undone. He fiddled with one of his cufflinks and then continued, "You should be concerned about my expectations for you, my desire for you. You're mother's right, the rest is weakness, not anything else. And definitely a waste of time."

"What isn't a waste of time, Nix?" I asked with more contempt than I felt. Not that I didn't feel hatred but it was being severely overshadowed by fear at the moment.

"Money, Ivy. Money is never a waste of time." His hands rested on the top of my high-back chair and I straightened out my spine just to keep from shrinking beneath his powerful presence.

"Oh, that's right. Because money makes the world go round, right Nix?" I held his gaze bravely. As desperately as I wanted to look away from his dark, relentless eyes I wouldn't allow myself to show the weakness they accused me of.

Nix's smooth, solid façade cracked at my words, anger flashed in his expression and I felt his grip tighten against the chair all the way down to my toes.

"No, Ivy," he barked out at me. "I make the world go round. *Me!* And it would behoove you not to forget that." He reigned in his temper and smoothed out his features and it was like a tornado had been destroying the room around me and then suddenly sucked through a window. The calm after the storm was as eerie and deadly as the storm itself and I shuddered despite my resolve not to show fear. "Eva, call a cab for Ivy. I want her out of my sight for now."

With that last command he turned his back on me and stalked from the room. The entire room stayed still even with his absence until Eva finally reached for her cell phone and followed his orders. I had been banished for the rest of the evening. And even though a pit of absolute terror started to grow in my stomach and spread roots to my heart and lungs, I was thankful to be excused from this gathering. If I continued to misbehave like this I knew I would have to face discipline, but I couldn't stop myself.

I just didn't want to know what that meant for me.

Chapter Thirty-Two

This time the ride to visit Honor was more tense than normal. My mother hadn't talked to me since last night at Sloane's, except to tell me when she was leaving for Honor's. She hadn't left it an option to decline, but I didn't plan on it anyways.

We pulled up to Honor's and went through the same routine as always. She walked with me to the front door and raised her hand to knock, except at the last minute she pulled back.

"Ivy, I'm not mad at you for last night," she allowed calmly. "Regardless of how you feel right now, you need to know that I am not your enemy. I am your ally. I have your best interest in mind. If you don't want to go to Nix, I'm trying to understand that, but then you and I need to work together. Alright?"

I thought over her words for a moment, not really accepting them, but knowing I needed to appear to. She was right in that if worse came to worst she was my only supporter in staying away from Nix.

"Alright, mom," I conceded. "I'm sorry for my behavior last night and recently. I just, what happened with Sam scared me. And I'm over it now, I *really am*," I lied, "But I guess I'm a little…. I don't know, like gun shy or something. Okay? I'll try to be better though, I promise."

"Oh sweetheart, I understand," she cooed and then drew me into a stiff hug before I could wiggle away from her. "I know you'll try harder. I know you won't embarrass me again."

She gave me an air kiss while I kind of stood there stunned. Eventually she let go of me and turned her attention back to the door. She pressed the doorbell with a long French nail and then waited tranquilly for Smith or one of his assistants to open the door.

It was the assistant this week, a twenty-something woman probably straight out of MBA school. They all clamored to work with Smith, to learn from the master of business. But Smith would only let women work for him. Not because he was some pervy womanizer, but solely to protect his life and Honor. He would never trust a man in his house.

The assistant didn't say anything to us, just moved out of the way and allowed us to enter. She silently turned on her one inch practical pump and led the way down the hall. Smith's assistants were generally all the same. Not that he had a type, but mainly because he required a dress code. Hair pulled back tight, pant suit or skirt suit and low heels. They all looked like uniformed flight attendants from the fifties, but I kept my opinion to myself.

In the sitting room, we were alone for a few minutes. My mother made herself at home, flinging herself onto one of the couches and crossing her legs impatiently. I paced around the room nervously. I felt itchy in my skin after the makeup session with my mom outside and anxious for her sudden compulsion to forgive and forget. Was she putting on a show for Smith's benefit or was this something more sinister? Was Nix doling out the punishment so she felt like she could let go? Or was this really a gesture of maternal instinct, possibly her first one ever?

"Ivy!" Honor squealed from the doorway. She bounded across the space between us and threw herself into my outstretched arms. Whatever nervous energy was there before disappeared with my sister so close and so happy to see me.

"Hey, little one," I whispered into her hair. "How are you?"

"So good," she exclaimed and then pulled back from me. She wrapped her long auburn hair around her hand a few times and then lifted it off her neck. She twisted around at the waist until finally I noticed the two blue sapphire studs in her ears.

"Oh my gosh! You got your ears pierced!" I screamed high and loud enough for any eleven year old to be proud of.

"I know!" She was so ecstatic, she dropped her hair and grabbed on to my forearms so we could dance around and shriek at each other.

Honor had wanted her ears pierced forever, for as long as she could talk. Mom pierced mine when I was a baby and so Honor grew up fascinated by the pretty things hanging from my ears. She started bugging Smith about it two years ago. He resisted for, well, since then, but something must have happened between last week and this one to get him to cave.

"Let's see, darling. Come show me," my mother commanded from her perch on the couch.

Honor stopped jumping around with me immediately and walked over to our mom to show them off. Smith stood in the doorway smiling at me.

"What did she do to convince you?" I asked with a smug smile.

"What didn't I do?" Honor sighed dramatically and then plopped down next to mom. Ava extended her thin arm across the back of the couch and Honor snuggled right in. I ignored the picture of pure evil wrapped around perfect innocence and tried to school my expression into anything but the disgust I felt.

"She had to receive all A's this quarter and she volunteered at some of my charitable causes," Smith explained in his dignified voice. "She had to earn them, but she worked very hard. I am very proud of her."

252

"Plus, there's a dance next weekend," Honor's whole face lit up in expectation.

"But we haven't decided if you will go, Honor," Smith reminded her with gentle authority.

"Have you been asked by a boy?" It was my mother's turn to get excited. These were exactly the signs she was looking for, more reason for her to want to possess Honor.

Honor blushed deeply, from the top of her hairline to her ankles. "Yes, but daddy says I can't go with a boy. If I go to the dance, I'll just go with friends."

"What is his name?" my mother pressed, ignoring Smith's scowl.

"Ava, she's only eleven. She's too young for this, do *not* encourage her." Smith growled.

Usually Smith and my mom tried to hide their utter hatred for each other, but this would definitely be a volatile issue. My mom kept her easy smile and started to run her fingers through Honor's hair. It was a soothing motion that she used to do to me when I was a child, her trick to lull me into trusting her. I wouldn't let her do that with Honor.

"You can't keep her locked in a tower her whole life, Smith. It's not like she can't meet the boy at the dance. If she really wants to go with him, she'll find a way," my mother's smile turned smug. She knew she was planting ideas into Honor's head.

From the way Smith's face heated up and his hands clenched viciously, I started to think he knew it too.

"Honor, are those the only earrings you have? Or did Smith let you pick out another pair for when your ears are healed?" I asked quickly.

"Daddy let me pick out *two* pair," she gushed. She sat up out of our mother's arms beaming again.

"Will you show them to me?" I took a step toward her and extended my hand.

She leapt from the couch and attached herself to me. I gave my mother an apologetic smile, but she just waved me out of the room with a roll of the eyes. At the doorway I chanced a glance back at Smith who was looking at me with an unreadable expression. He didn't hold my gaze though, fury twisted his features and before we were to the staircase Honor and I could hear them arguing heatedly.

Honor's room was a princess palace. Decorated in all white and soft pink, there was an enormous canopy bed fit for royalty with matching dressers, vanity and night stands. A huge dollhouse took up one entire wall, extending even higher than Honor could reach and another wall displayed floor to ceiling bookcases with a moving ladder connected to the ceiling. Smith seriously spoiled his little girl.

But she was so lucky to have her father.

Fate balanced life out for her in this way. Because as lucky as she was to have Smith, she was as equally unlucky to have our mother.

So what did Fate give me? Where was my equalizer?

Or maybe I didn't get one. Maybe life stepped in and decided a balance wouldn't have done any good. I would be this same rotten, black-hearted witch with or without a representative from the good side.

"Is it because Tyler asked me out?" she whispered when the door closed behind us. The earrings were forgotten in the wake of the crestfallen expression painting her face.

"No, absolutely not," I rushed to pull her into a hug. "They don't agree, that's all. It has nothing to do with you. I promise."

"But it does have something to do with me," she whimpered.

"No, it doesn't, sweet pea. Your father loves you very much is all. He wants to protect you. And mom... Mom doesn't always know what's best for you, Honor. She sometimes... sometimes she wants bad things for you."

This was the most honest I'd ever been with my little sister. She was too young to see the evil creature that was Ava Pierce, and I didn't want her to end up resenting me or Smith because I pushed her too hard. And now I wondered if I had made a mistake when she looked up at me with shimmering eyes and a deflated expression.

"Does she want bad things for you too?" Honor whispered, the horror in her face making her green eyes shine with tears.

I was momentarily stunned. Maybe Honor was more perceptive than I gave her credit for. Not really knowing how to respond, I just hugged her tighter and said, "Hey, don't worry about me, okay? I'm just fine. It's you we have to worry about. With these newly pierced ears Tyler's not the only boy we're going to have to worry about."

I regretted the words as soon as they left my lips.

"Ivy?" Honor asked in such a small voice that I closed my eyes against the sudden anxiety I felt for her. "Tyler's not the only boy. Lots of boys asked me to the dance, but Tyler's the only one I liked enough to think about going with."

"Oh, really?" I closed my eyes tighter, but this time against tears. I hated that she would have to go through this mostly alone, and without any idea of why this was happening to her.

"Don't you think it's weird?" she asked truly perplexed.

"Was it a lot of boys?"

"All the boys... In my class and in seventh grade," she confessed in that worried tone again. "But I didn't tell daddy that."

Oh no. I could not let her get away with that. I walked her over to her big bed and sat down with her so that I could face her. "Hon, don't keep that kind of stuff from your dad, okay? I know it might seem embarrassing, or it might be hard to tell him the truth, but he really does want what's best for you. He won't get mad at you; it's not anything you did wrong, okay? He can probably help you, make it easier for you."

She nodded along, seeming to understand how important it was to be honest with Smith by my freaked out tone.

"Ivy, is something happening to me?" she whispered in that frightened little voice again.

"Honey, no! Why would you think that?"

"Because... because it's not just the boys. It's the girls too," she admitted and then looked away.

"What about the girls?" Suddenly there was ice in my veins. I remembered what middle school was like for me away from Sloane and Exie, completely on my own. It was *awful*. Girls were cruel, and the boys were relentless.

"They stopped being nice to me," she croaked. Her chin trembled and then a tiny little tear slipped from the corner of her eye. I wiped it away quickly with my thumb and then held her face in my hands so she was forced to look at me.

"Honor, there is *nothing* wrong with you. You are perfect and special and wonderful. No matter what anybody else says, or does, you have to know that is true about you. You are the one that decides how you feel, okay? You make you matter. And I think you are the greatest eleven year-old in the universe and my opinion matters too." She laughed at that with a watery smile. "I love you, okay?"

"Okay," she mumbled, throwing her arms around my neck. "I love you too!"

And then my eyes were brimming with tears.

A knock at the door and Smith walking into the room tore us apart from each other. Smith looked back and forth between us before deciding that whatever had caused the tears must have been a good thing because his face softened and a sweet smile turned his mouth.

"Honor, your mother would like to spend more time with you before she goes," he instructed. Honor stood up and gave me one more confident smile before disappearing into the hall.

I stood up too, wanting to follow her before my mother got her alone again. Smith stopped me with a raised hand though and asked me to wait.

"Mallory talked to you this week?" he whispered.

I nodded and then stole a glance at the door just in case my mother suddenly appeared.

"Please let her try," he begged in a rumbling whisper.

"Okay," I said quickly. "I told her okay."

Smith immediately relaxed, his face smoothing out to happy. "Good, Ivy. That is good."

We both moved toward the door before I said, "Have you thought about homeschooling Honor?" My voice was as quiet as I could make it without having to resort to smoke signals to communicate with Smith.

"After last week, I'm seriously considering all-girls school," he sighed. Smith ran a rough hand over his face showing me how much he realized this problem was going to cost him.

"Please don't do that. It would crush her," I pleaded. I grabbed onto the sleeve of his navy blue oxford and gripped it tightly. "All-girls could be... could be rough... Could be traumatizing. It would push her right to my mother."

He thought over my words carefully, taking them in, chewing on them and then visibly deciding that they were helpful. "Homeschooling? You really think I need to remove her from society completely?"

"No," I answered quickly. "Not completely. But enough so that you can keep an eye on her and help her mature. She will *never* be like my mother. She has you. It won't happen to her. But it won't stop either, what happened last week will never stop. She has to learn to.... handle it."

"What is this Ivy? What has its claws on my little girls' life? On your life?" Smith's voice broke on his last question. I could see how sickly worried he was for Honor, how desperate he was to protect her from our mother and everything she represented. "Is it something I can stop?"

"It's uh," I obviously couldn't reveal my secret twice in the same weekend. "It's just bad genetics. Honestly, Smith. Just think about homeschooling, please?"

He nodded his agreement and before he could ask me anymore questions or before my mother spent one more second alone with Honor, I bounded down the steps and rejoined my family.

Homeschooling, although dreadful, would protect Honor. And right now that was my only goal in life. I wondered how different my life would be if I had someone to protect me.

And then I thought about Ryder and how desperate he was to help me.

So maybe my bad did balance out after all.
Maybe I did have someone special looking out for me.

Chapter Thirty-Three

The next day at school I felt this weird mixture of strong hope and eternal despair. My situation was depressing. Nix was scary as all hell. And he was back early from Greece. My future loomed bleak and ominous on the horizon.

But Ryder gave me this smile when I walked up to the school this morning that was secret and meaningful and…. possessive. His eyes grazed over me from head to foot as if he were searching for something physically out of place. And then his powerful silver eyes met mine and held them, connected me to him and transferred some of his indomitable strength to me.

I could smile then. Breathe again.

And it was because Ryder knew my secret and decided I was still worth friendship.

We hadn't actually spoken to each other yet today. He was with Chase and Phoenix in front of the building and I wanted to avoid all things Chase for a while. But just knowing Ryder supported me, made getting through the monotony of the day easier, made *everything* easier.

Between fifth and sixth period I found myself alone in an upstairs bathroom. I was kind of just wasting time and messing around with my hair when three girls walked in laughing loudly. They were giggling about boys and parties over the weekend. I recognized them instantly, cheerleaders that used to hang around Sam and the other basketball guys. Maybe they still did, I avoided the entire basketball crowd like a death sentence.

There laughter evaporated when they noticed me, their expressions puckering like someone had sucked all the oxygen from the room. And maybe someone had because I was finding it hard to breathe again. The shortest girl, also the ring leader from what I remembered lifted a slender finger and circled it around slowly, pointing at me, marking me.

"Well, look who it is," I thought her name might have been Cammie snarled.

A taller, thicker girl, who was maybe Jayla, huffed out a bitter puff of laughter. "Heard you were back, Ivy. I also heard you were making your rounds on the soccer team now. *Slut.*"

"*Whore,*" Cammie quickly reinforced their nasty sentiment. So we obviously would not be sharing our grief over Sam today.

"Why did you even come back?" The third girl asked with so much pain and loathing that I almost forgot my own problems with hers glaring so achingly bright. Her name was Cassandra, and she was drop dead gorgeous. Perfect mocha skin, long silky black hair, the darkest, deepest black eyes. She was prettier than me. Smarter than me. And had been dating Sam for two entire years before I showed up.

Before he broke up with her for me.

I sucked in an ugly, ragged breath and willed myself to meet her eyes. "I didn't have a choice," I admitted with not even a hint of strength or poise.

Cassandra bit out a bark of laughter. "Well, isn't that just nice for you."

Cammie took a step towards me. She was tiny and petite but packed with muscle. All these girls were. And even though I wasn't helpless if it came to a fight, I knew without a doubt I wouldn't fight back. This was a punishment I wanted, I felt like I deserved and I was going to take it.

"You shouldn't have come back," Cammie threatened in a menacing voice. "Nobody wants you here, nobody wants to watch you ruin someone else's life. You're a cheap skank that destroys people. You make me sick."

My heart started hammering in my chest so loud I was positive they could hear it, hear my fear and self-loathing. Hot tears stabbed at my eyes and I shut them quickly to stay that weakness. I didn't mind being the target for all their insults, or even their punching bag, but crying in front of them seemed too pathetic even for me.

The bathroom door opened and surprise of all surprises Kenna Lee walked in. She had her purse in her hand and seemed to be in a hurry, but when she stumbled into the trinity-of-hatred she paused. Her head snapped back and forth between them and me.

"What's going on, Ivy?" she asked in a hesitant tone.

Damn it, why did this stuff always happen in the bathroom? And why was it always freaking Kenna Lee?

"Nothing," I whispered, but even I heard how tragic I sounded.

"Cassandra?" she questioned instead.

"We're just leaving," Cassandra said in a bored tone. She looked me up and down one more time, taking in all of me, my hunched shoulders, my nails dug painfully into my palms, my hair that seemed to be everywhere at the moment, my forehead that had started to sweat and my wild eyes that couldn't escape the guilt and shame for what had happened to Sam. "I hate you," she confessed in a mean, ugly voice. "I have *never* hated anyone like I hate you." She paused for several moments, seeming to compose herself. "But he still asks about you. Not…. he can't…. it's in his eyes. It's how he watches the door. The least you could do is pay him a visit. Ease his suffering some."

Her words floored me. I felt like she just punched me in the heart. The wind was knocked all the way out of me. I stood their trembling, shaking from head to toe while she and her friends gave me one more disdainful look and then they turned as one unit and left the bathroom.

Kenna disappeared into a stall and all the while I stood there staring at the door, not able to move or react. She reappeared in front of me. She washed her hands and then pulled some paper towels from the dispenser without saying a word. While she dried her hands she looked me over with the kind of pity that was reserved for abused circus animals. Like her shame for me was so strong it bordered on disgust.

"Ivy, this is the second time I've rescued you in a bathroom," she sighed, sounding somewhat exhausted. "So you've made some enemies? So what? Life goes on. It has to and you can't stop it. Learn to stand up for yourself for God's sake."

I jumped at her words. There was a time not that long ago that I knew how to stand up for myself. I knew exactly what I was and even if I didn't want to accept my future, I could at least accept my reality. But now? Now the guilt ate away at every good, strong piece of me until I didn't want to stand up for myself, until I wanted someone else to tell me exactly what I already knew.

"You're right," I mumbled instead. No need to belittle her efforts.

"Listen, it's not like... Okay, you and me are never going to be friends, right?" I nodded weakly, hating that her words were truth. "But, I care about Ryder. I mean, even though- I care about him despite how we ended things. I just don't want to see you hurt him, alright? Can you at least try to be gentle with him?"

"Wait." My heart slammed against my chest and then dropped to my stomach. "What?"

"Oh, I thought Ryder would have told you. I thought Ryder had a thing- I guess, never mind." Kenna looked thoughtful for a moment and then waved her hand in the air as if swatting away the idea.

"Ryder broke up with you? And you thought it was because of me?" I squeaked out, feeling suddenly very sick to my stomach. The world kind of reeled around and my vision started spotting. This was very bad news.

"What?" Kenna asked abruptly. "No, I broke up with Ryder. I had a thing- Hayden and I have been talking for a while and I didn't think it was fair to Ryder." She looked at me closely. "Although I don't know why I'm telling you that."

"Oh," I started, feeling completely disoriented.

"Sorry, he always said you guys were just friends. But I don't know, I had a feeling it was more." Kenna looked thoughtful for a moment before straightening. "Guess, I was wrong."

"Uh, yeah, we're just friends," I confirmed, feeling a little flattened. Which made no sense. "Um, can I ask when you guys broke up?"

She looked at me sharply and then the pity was back. Oh great, she thought I had a thing for Ryder. Good grief.

"It was the beginning of last week, like maybe Tuesday?"

"But I saw you guys sit together at lunch every day?" I demanded. A righteous anger was building up inside me, I felt lied to. Manipulated.

"We're still friends, Ivy. Not every break up ends badly," she patronized but then shot me a sidelong glance. "At least for me."

"Huh," I mused, ignoring her jab. "I thought you guys, I don't know, I thought you were really into him."

"I did too, but I think I was more into Ryder the musician," she confessed, her lips pouting thoughtfully. "You know what I mean? Ryder as the boyfriend can be…. boring."

"Boring?" I snorted. I never once remembered feeling like Ryder was *boring*. "Uh, so Hayden, huh?"

She smiled this ridiculously huge grin and I wondered if it was a special talent of Kenna's to look like she was in love with every one of her boyfriends. "Mmm-hmmm. He's not nearly the rock star Ryder is, but we get each other, you know?"

"Sure, I know," I nodded slowly. I didn't really know, but I could pretend. "Well, um, thanks for intervening. Again." I smiled at her, hoping to convey my gratitude. But after our weird conversation about her ex and current boyfriend, the confrontation with Cassandra felt almost forgotten.

Almost.

"No problem, Ivy. Just maybe… maybe you should avoid the girls' bathrooms while you're at school from now on," her eyebrows furrowed in concern and I wondered if she had a point.

"You make a good point," I sighed and then left her in the bathroom.

Weird. That was so weird.

Chapter Thirty-Four

"Are you sure you don't want some company?" Exie called from the driver's seat. "I could use some caffeine." She smiled at me knowingly, daring me to turn her down.

"No thanks," I smiled confidently back, like this was no big deal, like I wasn't blowing off my friend so I could interrogate Ryder until he turned blue. "I need to get to the bottom of this."

"I'm sure he wants to get to the bottom of this too," she winked at me and I rolled my eyes but then slammed her passenger door.

I watched Exie drive away, thankful she was willing to give me rides again now that Chase and I no longer had the carpool thing going on. I pivoted around and marched into Delice full of determination.

Ryder was wiping down the counter with a white rag when the bells over the doorway signaled a customer. He looked up from his task and when his eyes met mine they lit up in that shared secret again. He smiled at me, friendly and casual and I about snapped.

The café was empty now. The workday hadn't wound down yet for the surrounding businesses and school had been out for a half an hour so either it was too early for kids around here, or they had already been through on their way home.

"Hey, Red," he called from the counter. I couldn't see anyone else working with him and wondered if his boss trusted him alone with the store. "Caramel macchiato?"

I paused midstride, trying to ignore the shiver that slid down my spine because he knew my drink. Not that he hadn't already ordered it for me a couple times, but it was just so thoughtful... so... No. This was exactly why we needed to have this little chat.

"We need to talk," I barked and planted my hands on the counter.

His forehead wrinkled and his eyebrows drew down in concern. "Okay, let's go," he walked over and held the gate open that separated everything behind the counter from the rest of the store. He motioned for me to walk through and a little confused I did. He closed the gate behind me, and then led me along to the door that opened to the kitchen and office.

When the swinging door stopped moving behind us, he turned to face me, putting two gentle hands on my biceps. We were surrounded by stainless steel kitchen appliances and counters, everything was shiny and cold to the touch. Everything except Ryder's warm, gentle hands searing my skin even through the material of my shirt.

"Why didn't you tell me you and Kenna broke up?" I demanded out of breath.

His forehead smoothed out for a second and then wrinkled in the opposite way when his eyebrows shot up towards his hairline. And then a smug smile turned the corner of his mouth.

A soft laughed rumbled out of him and he shrugged a careless shoulder. "I didn't think it mattered."

"It matters," I argued stubbornly.

Ryder took a step closer, closing some of the space between us. The air around us changed, from casual to intense in just a moment. His breath fanned over my face, a mixture of strong coffee and spearmint. His gray eyes heated to pools of liquid silver and his tongue made a small sweep across his bottom lip.

"Why?" he whispered, his voice coarse and raspy. It coated the sound as it hit my ears and pushed me a step forward, a step into his arms.

"It just does," I explained without explaining anything.

"Yeah?" he asked, his voice that same sexy growl.

My body heated to a liquid fire. I felt burning hot and tingly and so lost at the moment I didn't know what to do. My heart hammered in my chest loudly, pounding and furious. My fingertips buzzed with anticipation and my eyesight had narrowed so severely that anything beyond Ryder's face felt fuzzy and far away.

All of a sudden the space between us was filled, brimming over with emotion and tension. There had been some of that before; the space between us had *never* been empty. But now it was completely full. Atoms and particles and molecules and whatever else occupied the space between zinged around in a wild frenzy, charged with the growing *something* that enveloped everything separating us.

"So it matters to you that I'm single," he dropped his head to just a breath away from mine. I shivered, a quick, jerking motion that propelled me the rest of the distance to Ryder's body.

He caught me, like he was expecting me and in the next moment his mouth was on mine. One hand slipped around my waist pulling me impossibly closer to him, the other sliding up to cradle my neck in his huge hand. His lips pressed against mine so gently, so impossibly careful that I barely felt the soft fullness of them.

I was frozen, hypnotized, I couldn't have moved for anything, not even to intensify the kiss even though that's all I wanted. And while he seemed to hesitate in indecision, I struggled to step out of my decision. I screamed every argument at myself I could think of, every truth and lie I had been convincing myself of ever since we met. But the most sincere truth, the most base, primal, real truth I could admit to myself was that I *wanted* to kiss him; I wanted this more than *anything*. More than freedom.

And in the same instant I admitted that to myself, Ryder seemed to come to a conclusion of his own because his lips moved against mine. Delicately at first, and then demanding, hungry.

He *devoured* me.

Possessed me.

And I let him own me. There was no fight against him, no will or resolve left to do anything except give myself up to him.

I opened my mouth and let his tongue in, let it sweep along mine, so sweet at first, so achingly tantalizing that I felt myself moan into his mouth. A blush heated my neck and began creeping its way up my face, but there was no time to be embarrassed because the sound seemed to flip a switch in him and then all of his inhibitions were gone and he pushed me against the cold metal of the refrigerator and consumed every piece of me.

His arms imprisoned me to him, his fingers splayed against my skin, pressing into me as if I would evaporate if he didn't hold on to me. His mouth was relentless against mine, nipping, licking, sweet then rough, gentle then bruising. I made more sounds, desperate sounds of need that he matched with low groans of satisfaction.

The hand on my back tugged at the hem of my shirt and then slipped under so that the heat of his palm scorched the sensitive skin of my spine. I bucked forward, and my arms tightened around his neck.

This wasn't a kiss. This was an epiphany. My moment of clarity.

My salvation.

Ryder's hand left my back and reached down to cup the back of my thigh. With one swift movement he lifted me off the ground with that one hand, his bicep straining tightly under my grip. He brought my body up and I instinctively wrapped my legs around him. He sighed his approval and then took a stumbling step forward. We tilted off balance, dizzy and upended with desire. He adjusted my weight with his other hand and I clung to his biceps to keep ahold of him. With another stumbling step, he set me on the edge of the metal counter. My legs stayed around his waist and he pushed into me, keeping no distance between us.

His lips left mine to explore my jawline, my neck, my collarbone. I dropped my head back to allow him more room and I closed my eyes so that they wouldn't roll in the back of my head.

"Ryder, I whispered against his teasing kisses.

He worked his way back up my neck, his tongue sliding sensually over the sensitive skin of my earlobe and then he started to work back to my lips. His fingers grasped my hips, digging into my flesh and holding me in place. I was thankful for his tight grip, thankful that he was holding me in place because I was positive that without his hands supporting me I would have slipped off the counter, slipped out of reality and just floated away.

I tightened my legs around his waist, bringing him as close as possible; hating that anything was separating us, even the clothes we were wearing. His hands jerked my waist forward in response, as if I could get closer, as if I would allow anything between us.

Through our haze of lust the front door of the café chimed, alerting us that someone had walked in. The faint, distant sound seemed to affect us both simultaneously and we pulled back immediately. Ryder was three steps away before I could blink my eyes open. But the cold reality that washed over me like a bucket of ice forced me to ignore the heartbreaking feeling of emptiness that accompanied the space between us.

We stared at each other for a few moments, neither sure what to say. Ryder's hair was messier than usual, tussled and wild from our minutes of passion. His lips were swollen and more sensual than ever and even though I refused to acknowledge them his hands were trembling just barely at his sides.

"Ivy, I-" he started but I cut him off with a wave of a hand.

He was the first guy friend I had ever had. Maybe the first real friend I ever had. I couldn't ruin that.

I wouldn't ruin that.

"We, that was, um," I fumbled through some lame excuse, but my brain was still addled from the desire still pounding through me. Damn it. This was frustrating; I just needed to think of something.

But Ryder beat me to it, "Do *not* read anything into that," Ryder raised a firm, authoritative voice at me.

"Uh, okay," I agreed, my brow wrinkling just a little and the irrational urge to giggle bubbling up into me.

He seemed just as desperate as I was to keep things platonic between us.

"That was *not* a kiss," he reiterated and this time I did laugh.

"It wasn't?" I questioned with a smile lifting the corners of my mouth.

"No, definitely not. It was... it was, uh, an experiment." He ran two hands through his already riotously mussed hair. "I just wanted to see if it was as repulsive as I thought it would be."

266

"And was it?"

"Yes. Definitely," the only tell that he was lying was the way his eyes heated again, as if we were dangerously close to repeating the "experiment" right this second. "Actually it was much worse. You're a terrible kisser."

The impassioned moment was instantly defused and I burst into laughter. "Thanks for the critique."

"That's what friends are for," he smirked at me, casual, lazy and back to normal.

That's what friends do. Exactly. Just friends.

I took a big breath and hopped off the counter.

"Okay, I should," he pointed toward the café. "Right."

And then he was through the swinging door and I was alone. I heard his polite tone, muffled but recognizable, ask for the customer's order. I took the moment to smooth out my rumpled clothes and pull my tangled hair into a low, side ponytail. I pressed my lips together, hoping they weren't nearly as swollen as Ryder's had been, but I kind of knew that was asking too much. And then I nonchalantly left the kitchen and walked behind Ryder through the lift-gate counter.

"Ivy?" a disturbingly familiar voice asked from in front of the cash register.

"Nix?" I turned around and faced him straight on. "Hey, what are you doing here?"

"Afternoon pick me up," he gestured toward where Ryder was swiping his credit card and shooting me a sideways glance. "What are *you* doing here?"

What was I doing here, damn it? I hadn't anticipated this. "Um, Ryder and I have a project we're working on. I was just going over some of the notes with him."

"Are you finished with him?" Nix asked, his dark eyes impossible to read.

"Huh?" My mouth dropped open at his question and the blush was back crawling up my neck and giving me away.

"With your project? I want you to have coffee with me," he commanded and I just nodded my head in response.

"Sure," I finally choked out. "Ryder and I are done."

Nix turned back to Ryder, "She'll have a caramel-"

"Macchiato," Ryder finished on a snap of possession. I shot him a pleading look that he definitely ignored. And then when Nix held out his card again, Ryder declined him. "She actually already ordered, I just hadn't made it yet."

Nix took this in with a clipped nod and then walked over to a table. He waited for me to follow and sit down before he joined me. He unbuttoned his gray suit jacket and loosened his tie just a tiny bit for comfort. I recognized all these gestures as him getting ready for serious business.

Nix cocked his head in the direction of Ryder and lifted a thick, black eyebrow at me.

"Just following orders," I mumbled.

His eyebrow descended back to its resting place and his face smoothed out in acceptance of my lie. "I'm glad I caught you here," he admitted in a low voice. "I was just coming over to talk to you."

"Yeah?" I asked. My stomach erupted in nerves. Not nerves like the butterflies Ryder gave me, unless these butterflies had strapped razor blades to their wings and were flying about with the sole intention of shredding me from the inside out until I bled to death.

"It seems you have a few things to learn, Ivy. I didn't want to have to do this, but I'm sending you on a job." His eyes were pure authoritative arrogance. There was nothing there but cold decisiveness. This was a lesson he decided he needed to teach me. And he was right, if he really thought I was going to stay with him. I needed to be broken, bridled. But because I knew that there was no way in hell I would ever stay with him, a shudder convulsed my body and I gripped at the table so tightly my knuckles turned white.

Nix, noticing my reaction grunted a short puff of air in disapproval. "You brought this on yourself, Ivy. I would have been happy to have trained you…. personally. But I cannot ignore your disruptive behavior or your disrespectful attitude. So you're going on a job tomorrow night with Anaxandra and Evaleen. It's nothing you won't be capable of, just a friendly dinner with some colleagues of mine."

An escort. I was going to be an escort.

"Nix, I am *sixteen*," I hissed frantically. My nails bit into the underside of the table, and if I put any more pressure on them, I would rip them off.

"Ivy, it's dinner. That's all. Trust me, I would not ask more of you than that. Do not forget that you are *mine*." His words were a heavy bark of an order before his eyes flickered to Ryder who was setting our drinks down on the table.

"Thank you," I mumbled, ignoring Ryder as he tried to catch my gaze. I couldn't acknowledge him in front of Nix, not after this conversation, not after what happened in the kitchen.

268

Ryder disappeared back behind the counter but I could feel his concentrated stare as he watched us.

"Let's take these to go," Nix stood with his coffee. "We have more to discuss."

I obeyed. What else could I do? I was still a prisoner. Still chained to this Godforsaken life.

I dared a quick glance at Ryder on my way out, before Nix got to the door and held it open for me. I expected to see anger and revulsion staring back. I expected Ryder to be righteously pissed. But instead his gaze was soft and steady. He narrowed his eyes in an expression of support and he tilted his chin down as if to promise that everything would be alright.

If it had been fury staring back at me the shame would have overcome me, and left me useless.

But his silent show of support had the opposite affect and instead of soul-eating guilt I could stand up straighter and square my shoulders. I would live through this.

I had Ryder, I would be just fine.

Chapter Thirty-Five

I looked at the clock for the hundredth time in the last five minutes and regrettably noticed only five minutes had gone by. Unable to sit still any longer, I stood up and started pacing the foyer. Smoothing out invisible lines on my campy black satin cocktail dress, I looked up to gauge Anaxandra and Evaleen.

They sat unmoving, with legs crossed and hands neatly folded in their laps, like they had done this plenty of times before. Hell, maybe they had.

Technically they weren't supposed to be assets yet, but you couldn't tell that from the way they shot bored looks around the hotel lobby or sighed impatiently. They looked like pros sitting on the plush bench seat, their slinky stilettos dangling from their toes, their tight skirts riding up just a smidge too high and exposing mile long legs. Eva's stems were ivory porcelain underneath her silk pink off the shoulder dress. Her long chestnut hair hung down to the middle of her back, straight and sleek. And her lips were glossed and kept strategically away from bangs that slanted over one eye. Ana was just as gorgeous tonight, with her messy blonde braid hanging loosely over one shoulder and her bright blue strapless dress the exact color of her eyes. They were minxy perfection.

And I was a jumbled ball of nerves.

My palms were sweaty, my knees were clammy, my dress felt suffocating and too small. My hair was in this really intricate knot thing on the back of my head, with some faux bangs swept over my forehead, a lot like Eva's. My bottom lip wouldn't stop trembling, so I was forced to bite on it which in turn dissolved my lip color a half hour ago. And my hands were convulsing.

I was not supposed to be here.

I had plotted my entire life to get me out of this exact situation.

And for opening my big mouth one too many times, I had been punished by my worst fear.

I absently wondered if Nix knew that. If somehow he had actually seen into my soul and doled out punishment accordingly. Even if he would have taken me two years earlier, it would not have compared to the torture of getting paid to be some old man's arm candy.

Sex slave industry. Ryder had been right.

Only instead of kidnapping and an unwanted addiction to drugs, my mother had given birth to me for the sole purpose of passing on her legacy. Her whore legacy.

I shuddered as the reality, more than ever before, sunk in.

"Would you stop?" Eva finally snapped. "You are making *me* nervous. Just sit down!"

I let out a rush of breath but obeyed. I sat on my hands to keep them from spreading the shakes to the rest of my body and then stared down at my feet. I tried to remember the words of comfort and encouragement Ryder had whispered to me all day. Immediately this morning he started drilling me about Nix's "assignment" and because he already knew more than he should, I told him everything. I laid out my evening for him in exact terms, to give him an idea of what I would face and myself peace of mind because someone else, someone normal, wholesome and *good*, would know where I was tonight. Because he would be concerned about me. *Thinking* about me.

"It's alright, Ivy," Ana put a comforting hand on my back. She was a little awkward since my dress was backless down to my lowest vertebrae and it was weird with the skin to skin contact of her hand. But she was maternal and sweet and I sank into her tranquility. "This isn't a real job. Think of it like…. riding your bike with training wheels."

I thought about that for a minute and then said, "I was never allowed to ride a bike, training wheels or not."

There was a moment of silence before Ana said, "Me either,"

"Too risky for scars," Eva added.

"Ugh, what kind of pathetic childhoods did we lead?" Ana groaned and then all three of us burst into laughter.

"How about another analogy that doesn't remind me of why I'm in therapy?" I asked, but already I felt more relaxed.

"Okay, how about this?" Ana seemed to think about it, "You've been on dates before? Lots of dates, I bet, right?"

"Yes."

"Well, just think of this like a date. A date with a man you don't really like all that much, but you still have to finish out your commitment. He's not going to try anything; he's not even going to get further than a goodnight kiss. Most likely, these are some business colleagues of Nix that just want to have some company while they're in town. We meet them, we go to dinner, maybe out for drinks after, and then we part ways. There's nothing to it. You'll be fine."

Only nothing about this felt fine. I was a junior in *high school*. I shouldn't be here with a business colleague of Nix.

And I sure as hell shouldn't be kissing them goodnight.

The very thought of kissing sent me back to the Delice kitchen with Ryder. It had been a mistake. A horrible, awful, delicious... wonderful mistake. One that would never happen again.

But even as I swore to myself I could never slip up like that again around him. I mean, it was all my fault, wasn't it? I was the one stupidly attracted to him. He was just a guy reacting to his baser instincts. And I didn't mean because I was a siren. Because he was a teenage boy and I basically climbed him like a tree and assaulted his mouth. But then again, he had even commented immediately on how it had been an experiment. So...

So, even as I swore all that to myself, I hated, absolutely loathed the idea of cheapening that moment of blissful perfection by kissing a middle-aged pervert goodnight.

"This must be them," Eva commented and sat up a bit straighter.

Three young guys in expensive, well-tailored suits strolled into the lobby of the hotel looking like they could buy this place with a swipe of one of their credit cards. They were younger than I thought they would be, which initially seemed great, but on closer inspection of all things douchy realized that age might have been better than cocky arrogance in this case. Where an older gentleman would have been considerate and grateful to have my attention, these mid-twenty pretentious a-holes would demand it while filling my head with every vapid self-honoring detail they could think of.

Still, now that they were here, I felt better. Just a little more relaxed.

"Drew?" Eva asked, pretending to be shy. She swiped at the bangs that had fallen into her eye and smiled her award winning I'm-a-saucy-sexpot smile.

"Yes," Drew, the tallest of the three guys smiled hugely in return. He was tan, with overly glossed hair and giant white teeth. While he was handsome in that "Ivy-league-I-do-a-sport-like-rowing" way, he was also so obviously full of himself I wanted to choke on the vanity. "And you are?"

"I'm Eva," she smiled at him again and held his gaze before she extended her hand. "And these are my friends, Ana, and Ivy."

"Blake," Drew gestured to the guy to his right. Blake stuck out his arm and took Ana's. He had the long, lithe muscles of a runner; I could see them even through his charcoal suit. His hair was shorter than his friends, closely cropped so there was no expensive product to maintain the stray strands. He was better looking than Drew on close inspection, more mysteriously handsome than classically. Except his eyes were almost too enigmatic, too haunting. They were dark brown and roaming. Even though Ana clearly marked him as hers, his eyes floated over Eva and me, drinking us in with an obvious air of approval.

"And this is Taylor," he gestured to the man on his left who reached out a hand to me.

Taylor smiled at me shyly, lifting a dark eyebrow as if asking me a question. I held out my hand and he took it in his firm grasp, pulling me forward a little while he shook it. I stumbled in my heels, stepping right into his chest. I looked up at him from under my lashes, hoping to convey that I was embarrassed about tripping. He looked down at me with dull green eyes that weren't upset at all we were standing so close.

Taylor had longer hair than his friends, the top layer falling right to the corner of his eyes. He didn't seem to notice though, or be bothered by it while he held me close to him, totally invading my personal space. His face was tanned and sculpted, with only a few wrinkles in the corners of his eye and thick ones that crinkled with his forehead.

"Nice to meet you, Ivy," he murmured smoothly.

"Nice to meet *you*, Taylor." I smiled my practiced smile, the one I turned on when it was necessary to perform. His dull eyes twinkled in return.

"Shall we go?" Drew interrupted our too-long greeting.

Thankfully.

Taylor turned skillfully, somehow managing to keep hold of my hand while tucking it into his elbow. He kept a tight grip on it, not a painful one, but one that felt awkward and forced. One that I knew I couldn't break free from.

Ana and her date, Blake, led the way to the dining room that was just around the corner and we fell in step last. Taylor trailed a little, separating us from the other two couples.

"You are truly a stunning creature, Ivy," Taylor's words were clipped and enunciated perfectly, like speaking was an art form for him. He didn't have the smooth, sexy sound that came out of Ryder's mouth, but I could tell he was used to being listened to. Used to giving orders.

"Thank you," I offered in return and then coughed to cover my nerves.

"I love this dress, it fits you perfectly," he continued. A blush crept up my neck; it was awkward to keep talking about my looks. And although I had been in this place before, with guys my own age, I was not anxious to repeat the experience.

"Thank you," I repeated. "Again." A moment of silence stretched out between us and I found myself quick to fill it. "So how do you know Nix?"

Taylor looked straight ahead, his jaw clamping together before he cleared his throat and seemed to put himself back together. "Drew and I run one of his smaller subsidiary companies. We're originally from the south, but while he is relocated to the Midwest, we'll be coming up here often to visit."

"Ah, so Nix is your boss?" I clarified.

Which was apparently a mistake. Taylors hold tightened on my hand until he was squeezing it roughly, his short nails biting into my skin. "Do you have a problem because I work for someone?"

We were stopped in front of a table set for six. The other two guys were helping Eva and Ana into their seats while we stood in front of the table looking like a fighting couple.

"No, not at all," I gushed quickly. "I just wanted to figure out the connection, that's all." And now I just wanted to get my hand out of his, before he dug his nails all the way to the bone.

"Well, now you know," he ground out bitterly. He yanked my arm from the crook of his elbow and let go of my hand with such force that I fell into a heap on my chair. I hit the seat hard, and bumped my tailbone on the corner before I was able to right myself and sit up normally. I wanted to stand up and slap him for his abuse, but this was part of the job.

Taking it.

And so fighting back the tears of frustration and pain, I reached for my napkin and laid it across my lap just so I would have something to do. I ignored looking at the palm of my hand so I wouldn't have to see the damage he did to it.

But when I pulled it from the napkin, I noticed the blood smears on the white linen. Not wanting to smear blood on anything else, I dropped my hand to my lap and pressed it into the unsoiled fabric. So what if I couldn't use a napkin again tonight. I just wouldn't order salad or anything all that messy, which also kind of sounded fantastic at this point.

Thankfully dinner was less eventful, at least to begin with. The men, for the most part, ignored us. We ordered drinks- a water for me since I didn't want to risk being carded, how embarrassing. We picked at our meals and let the men discuss business, politics and sports around us.

Anaxandra gave me a sympathetic look when Taylor insisted on keeping his arm around the back of my chair. I didn't mind his arm so much as his hand kept reaching out and pinching my shoulder whenever I would slouch over. My mother raised me with perfect posture, but occasionally I would lean forward to take a bite of my meal, eggplant parmesan, although I hadn't touched the noodles. Whenever I would, his

275

hand would subtly clamp down on my clavicle, press down and then pull me back until I was in a posture he approved of.

It was starting to weird me out.

And then when the plates had been cleared, Eva stood up to go to the bathroom. I set my napkin down, careful to hide the blood stains, as if to stand up with her. I mean, wasn't it a universally known fact that women went to the bathroom together? At the very least in pairs? But before I could stand up, the full weight of his arm was pressed down on my shoulder, telling me to sit tight.

I sighed and went back to staring at the table, watching the small votive candle flicker in the dim lighting of the Liberty Tavern. Eventually, the bill was paid, by Taylor, who insisted that this was his treat and we were on our way to after dinner drinks.

I had to assume Nix explained that I was underage and wouldn't be able to go anywhere they carded. Not that I didn't have my fake ID with me, I did. And not that I wasn't used to charming my way through bartenders and bouncers, because I was. But warning bells were ringing in my head that I should not at all give another man attention while Taylor arranged for me.

He did *not* seem like the type that played well with others.

The whole underage thing turned out to be a null point anyway, when to my horror, instead of leaving the hotel to drive somewhere else, the men led us over to the bank of elevators. Anaxandra and Eva were cozy and friendly, draped on their dates' arms, but I remained stiff and cautious next to Taylor.

Even though I hadn't had anything to drink at dinner, everyone else had plenty and Drew and Blake were more than a little tipsy. Ana and Eva seemed relaxed enough; even though I could tell they were still very much in control.

Taylor on the other hand... he was clearly on his way to inebriated, but instead of getting loud and goofy, he held on to me tighter, pressed me against him harder. His arm was snaked around my waist with his fingertips digging into my side uncomfortably. And he had me pulled against his body so that my side was pressed firmly against his. It was awkward to walk that way, and I was obnoxiously off balance.

Not to mention he reeked of beer.

Once we were all piled into the elevator, he gripped me tighter, wrapping his whole arm around my waist and then burying his face in the crook of my neck and collarbone.

He made a sexual grunting sound and then inhaled loudly. "Damn, girl, you smell so good."

I mumbled my thank you and then tried to wiggle out of his hold. We were in the back corner of the elevator and even though I wasn't exactly in danger, I was extremely uncomfortable and I desperately wished Ana or Eva would pay attention to me. They were busy flirting with their own dates, who had gotten very handsy themselves after dinner, so they were dealing with their own problems.

"I cannot wait to get you alone tonight," Taylor murmured against my skin. Everything went motionless inside me, petrified with fear. Even my lungs stilled and my heart stopped completely.

"No, I don't think we're supposed to be alone," I fumbled through an excuse. "I uh, I don't think that's a good idea."

"Sure it is," he growled, digging his fingers into my stomach and wrapping his other hand around my shoulders so I was effectively caged against him. "It's a great idea. A fantastic idea."

I let out a shaky breath and placed my hands over his, the one that was bruising my abdomen. "Please let go. You're hurting me."

The pressure let up, just a little bit. "Say it, Ivy, say it's a good idea."

I shook my head in response, trying to fight back big tears that were threatening to spill. His fingers went back to jabbing my skin and I would have doubled over if his arm across my chest hadn't kept me locked in a standing position.

"Say it," his voice was deadly quiet, just a whisper in my ear. But the ugliest, most dangerous whisper I had ever heard.

"I would love to be alone with you," I forced out. But no. No I did *not* want to be alone with him. I wanted anything *but* to be alone with him. His fingers lightened against my stomach and shoulder and I used the moment to take a deep, steadying breath.

I had to get out of this.

I wasn't exactly sure what the protocol was here. Last night, Nix made me understand that it was my duty to make my date feel welcomed and at home. I was supposed to be the perfect date, have no expectations on the man and allow him to relax completely with a beautiful woman on his arm.

But surely this was not in the contract. There had to be some kind of code that I could use to warn Anaxandra and Evaleen that my date had gone bad. *Really* bad.

The elevator doors finally opened on the top floor and we all poured out of the closed metal box. Drew and Eva started down one way while Blake and Ana walked along with us.

"See you in the morning, dude," Blake called out to Drew who just laughed hysterically in return.

I looked over at Ana until I caught her attention. We were side by side with the boys on the outside talking about stupid things above our heads.

"I can't do this, Ana," I whispered fiercely.

"He knows not to push further than you'll let him, Ives. It's in his contract. You have got to relax," she bit out back at me.

"I can't. Ana, please, help me get out of this," I begged as silently as I could. A treacherous tear escaping down my cheek. "Please."

Taylor's pull on me was abrupt and painful as my body slammed back into his. I didn't know if he had heard me or not, but I felt like a worthless ragdoll against the strength of his arms.

Ana must have seen the fear in my eyes or the forceful way he was treating me because suddenly the annoyed look on her face turned to concern.

"Hey, why don't we party together for a while?" She suggested coyly. She turned in Blake's arms and played with the top button of his open oxford. "It could be fun. Just a few more drinks? Maybe play a little poker?"

"Strip poker?" Blake asked with hooded eyes.

"Sure, strip poker," Ana cooed back. "Ivy loves strip poker, don't you Ivy?"

I opened my mouth to announce how much I loved strip poker, anything was better than being alone with Taylor at this point, but he beat me to it.

"That's alright," Taylor said in a cold voice. "Ivy and I are ready to be alone. But you two go on and have fun now."

Taylor stopped at the door to his room and pulled out the keycard that would open it. Blake laughed at Taylor's brazenness and pulled Ana along to his room. She gave me an anxious, apologetic look but let him drag her along.

Then the lock clicked open and Taylor was leading me into his room. He didn't bother to turn on the lights so as soon as the door shut behind us we were lost in complete darkness. His hands had never left me and were now holding me in place, both of them firmly on my waist.

"You, you, y-you should know that I'm actually underage," I stammered. "I'm only sixteen!"

My voice was a desperate cry, my breath stuck in my throat.

"You better be," he sneered, and then pushed me forward. My foot caught on something, a suitcase or desk leg or something and I stumbled forward and fell on my knees. My hands caught my fall, but then his polished shoe came down hard on my backside, propelling me forward so that I flew face first into the carpet. The rough, hotel room carpet burned against my face and I cried out in pain and fear. "I wanted someone young, Ivy. You're exactly what I was hoping for."

Chapter Thirty-Six

I laid there on the carpet, hands clutching the short, tough fibers, *freaking* out. I mean, I had a meltdown like seven months ago, but no emotions I ever felt compared to the fierce terror that momentarily froze me to stone.

He *wanted* somebody underage?

Nix sent me into this situation *knowing* that?

Oh. No.

Oh, no no no no no no.

I ordered my brain to think of an escape plan, to find a way out of this, and to do it now! But before I could even think about moving, his hand was tangled in my hair and yanking me to my feet. I cried out again at his tight hold and the way he ripped my head back in order to get me to bend to his will.

Once I was standing again, he turned me around to face him. He placed his huge palm against the curve of my face very delicately and looked into my eyes like he was a gentle person. The effect wasn't placating or relaxing but sickening and my chin started to tremble under the intensity of his gaze. His face was bathed in the dim light from the half open curtains behind us. My eyes had adjusted to the darkness of the room, but all I could see were the sinister, evil lines of the man holding me in place. The same hand that was caressing my face so gently suddenly pulled back and then slapped me. *Hard.*

I bit my cheek as a result, the coppery taste of blood mixing with the extra saliva from the desire to vomit. Holy hell, what was going *on*? How did I get to this place in my life? How did I get *here*, where someone was beating the hell out of me for their *sick entertainment*?

"You can't- I'm Nix's. Nix wants me for himself," I shouted out in a desperate plea. No desperate wasn't even the right word. There *wasn't* a word that could convey how badly I wanted to get out of here. How afraid I was of this man.

That threat was met with a harsh, gunshot of laughter. It pierced the dark, silent room like the very sound of it was *raping* the quiet. I had to get out of here. Now.

"I'm not going to have *sex* with you, Ivy," he taunted me, making it sound like I suggested something inhumanely vile. "Nix wants me to teach you a lesson, to *discipline* you. Trust me if I wanted to get off by sleeping with you, this would have gone completely different. I'm actually a fantastic date."

His explanation caught me so off guard I was rendered completely speechless. This was actually part of my punishment? Nix had arranged this?

Cold, frantic dread settled in the pit of my stomach and a hopelessness so strong, so consuming I almost decided to take this willingly and get it over with. What else was there? I had no reason to fight, to try to get out of this. If I didn't take this punishment now, Nix would just find another way.

A huge part of me had been so distressed over protecting my virginity, especially when I thought the man was going to rape me that I hadn't really given much thought to the other physical consequences that would come out of this. But now that my virtue was safe from this raving lunatic, the rest of the real fears that he brought with him descended on me and the tears started to fall in huge, sobbing drops down my face.

"Don't *cry*," he growled. "Don't be so *weak*." His palm smacked across my face again and my neck snapped back from the force of it. He caught me with his other hand before I could fall, and his fingers dug into my neck until I felt the hot blood streaming down my neck.

"Stop hitting me," I screamed, suddenly so furious, so *angry* that this man kept assaulting me. Surprisingly I had pictured myself being attacked lots of times before. Usually it was in the context of working for Nix one day far in the future and stopping some sick pervert from making me do something I didn't want to. In those scenarios I was always this super-powered badass that kicked the ever loving crap out of my assailants.

In reality I wasn't turning out to be the Kung-Fu master I imagined.

I took a step back, giving myself some space from him. He matched me, step for step until my back was to the wall, half on solid plaster, half pressed against the edge of the window frame. I tilted my chin in an act of defiance and made myself look for an opportunity to go for his junk.

In hindsight and in the profession I was supposed to be planning to go into, a few self-defense classes might have been a good idea. Still, there was promise in good nut-shot.

"There really is something special about you," Taylor's voice dropped to a husky murmur.
"I've been around sirens before, but it's like, it's like you really set something off." His hands clenched my biceps, almost so that the entire circumference of his thumb to middle finger touched. It was agonizing and chilling but then he let go and started to rub my biceps, up and down with ice cold palms. I just stood their frozen, waiting for my opportunity to

strike. His hands moved from rubbing my arms, to my shoulders and then across my collarbone to my neck. "Say please."

"What?" I croaked.

"Say, please don't hit me anymore," he ordered, his voice still deceptively calm.

"Please don't hit me anymore," I echoed and then braced myself for the hit.

He smiled at me, his lips twisting to an unsettling imitation of happiness. His hands wrested at the base of my throat, his fingers wrapping around my neck until they touched in the back. His eyes intensified right before he struck, they went from dull to blazing just a fraction of a second before his hands clamped down and together, choking the life out of me.

My instant reaction was pure surprise. I tensed immediately and began to scratch and claw at his hands as they shook me by the neck, blocking my air supply. Then there was panic, pure panic. Not the kind that causes panic attacks, which are a slow buildup to the real deal, not even the small kind that shoots razors down your arms and makes the hair stand up on the back of your neck. No real, unadulterated panic that blinds you, that cuts off all rational, clear-thinking thought and thrusts you into the heart of fear.

My throat was making these gasping sounds, hoarse and deep bellied but I couldn't get any air, I couldn't suck in enough oxygen to get myself under control. And then my vision began to black out completely, first at the edges and then big black spots everywhere I tried to look. I kicked out with my right leg, hoping to land a good solid foot on his manhood, but I was too weak to get control of my appendages and too disoriented to cause any real damage.

Until a knock on the door caught us both off guard. First it was light, just a regular tapping sound. Even as I was being pulled under, I could make out the sound and recognized it immediately. Taylor cursed under his breath and loosened his hold on me just a little. And then the pounding was harder, more forceful until it was noisy banging.

Another stream of curse words flew out of Taylor's mouth but this time they were aimed at the door. He released his grasp and I slid down the wall to the floor, pulling the curtain with me so that it was straining on the curtain rod. I watched his footsteps cross the room but I was gasping for breath, barely able to hold myself up in a sitting position.

I took big, gulping breaths, willing my heart to slow down, willing my wits to come back. That opened door was my only shot to get out of here, my only shot to escape. As soon as he turned the door handle, I would make my move.

I started to crawl noiselessly toward him. My clutch lay abandoned on the floor and thankfully directly in my path. I snatched it up on my way. I wasn't very concerned about the designer bag or anything else in it besides my phone and my credit card if I needed to pay for a cab. My vision was starting to clear, and I had enough big breaths now that I felt the strength to run return.

Taylor yanked open the door, wider than I think he intended, but he was blind with bloodlust and unable to gauge his strength. And that was all I needed. I burst forward like a sprinter out of the blocks and bull-rushed his side, squeezing under the space just between him and the door. I ignored Blake's shocked look of surprise at seeing me bolt out of the room like a bat out of hell and just started screaming at the top of my lungs. The sound was piercing but ragged, shrill but scratching and raspy from the choking incident not forty-five seconds before.

I looked around for the exit, desperate and wild and I just kept screaming. I had to. And even though my lungs were burning and my throat so ready to give up, I willed myself to continue making sound, to fulfill this plan for escape. My vision was still hazy enough that it took way longer than it should have to find the stairs, but all the while irritated guests had started to step out of their hotel rooms to see what the commotion was about. I heard the suspicious sound of a door clicking shut and locking. Without looking I knew it had to be Taylor and Blake hiding away from the crazed girl who would rat them out to the police in a millisecond if they tried to follow me.

I leapt down the stairs, sometimes propelling myself forward by the railings so I could take five and six steps at a time. I never looked back, never glanced behind me, I was too afraid. A tiny, but present rational part of my brain announced that not a door to the stairwell had opened since I entered and only the sound of my feet echoed throughout the stairwell but I couldn't chance it. I couldn't take the risk.

Once I reached the ground floor I tore through the door and to the lobby. I spun in frantic circles, looking for Taylor or Blake or Drew. My eyes moved back and forth, frenzied in their search. They could have taken the elevator down; they could be waiting for me. But if I saw them, I would just start screaming again. I would just keep screaming until I drew so much attention to myself that someone called the police and they carted me away to an insane asylum.

I didn't care.

That could never happen to me again.

That was insane.

I wasn't. But that *was*.

Now I just had to figure out what to do. How to get out of here. I dug through my clutch and pulled out my cellphone with violently shaking hands. I scrolled to the first number on my call list, only because he had called tonight to make me promise that if anything went wrong I would call him, and so I did. I called Ryder.

"What's wrong?" He asked after the first ring.

"I need you," I sobbed. "I need you. You said to call if I needed you and I do. I *need* you."

People were starting to stare at me, to stop whatever they were doing and just gawk. I didn't know how I could stop them, or if I wanted them to. As long as they were looking at me, nobody was going to barge down here and take me back up to that room.

"I'm outside, I'm waiting for you outside," Ryder announced. That was the most wonderful news I had ever heard. Ever.

With numb feet and shaking knees I walked out the lobby door of the hotel and into the frigid fall air. The end of October was bitingly cold, signaling a snowfall soon and the presence of a looming winter. I was convulsing with shivers but I was certain those would have been happening with or without the cold air.

Ryder leapt from his Bronco that he had pulled front and center of the covered driveway. A valet was yelling at him to move his junky POS from in front of the Hilton Hotel, but Ryder ignored him.

Instead he sprinted to me, and opened his arms before I was even close enough to fall into them. I threw my arms around his neck and buried my face against his throat.

"I'm taking you home," he demanded and then picked me up like a child. One hand supported my back, the other slipped under my knees and he walked directly to his car. He deposited me in the front seat and then buckled me in before taking my face in both of his hands. "I knew this was bad news. I just couldn't... I wanted to be here if something went wrong." He reasoned for his being already present in the parking lot.

"Something did go wrong," I admitted in a croaky, harsh voice as if it wasn't obvious. "But I'm glad you're here."

Ryder pulled my face down and gave me a sweet kiss on the forehead before closing my door. When he turned around Blake and Taylor were just walking out the sliding doors of the hotel. They noticed me immediately in the passengers' seat of Ryder's car and pointed at me.

285

Ryder noticed them too unfortunately and I watched his body physically react to Taylor. It was like I could feel his stare fall on Taylor's outstretched hand that was bloodied and scratched from when he tried to choke me. I might not have ever gotten a good punch in or hit him back, but scratching his hands turned out to be its own form of karma.

Ryder's whole body tensed when he realized Taylor was the one that hurt me. It was like he followed that bloodied fingertip up the length of his arm and to his face and put the entire night together in his head. And then Ryder snapped.

He launched himself forward, onto Taylor and his fist connected with Taylor's face like a branch breaking off a huge tree during a lightning storm. I heard the crunch of bones from even inside the car and then watched the splurt of blood soil Ryder's face, hands and chest. My hand flew to my mouth and I gasped against the horror of the moment.

And then I just watched in trancelike fascination as Ryder cocked his arm back and delivered one punch after another. Ryder tackled Taylor with his initial hit and so with each subsequent one, Taylor's skull bounced against the hard concrete. There was blood everywhere, flowing in thin crimson rivers.

And even though Ryder was the younger man, and maybe not even equally muscled, he had the element of surprise on his side. And revenge. He was a man *possessed* by rage and retribution.

I couldn't move. I couldn't think. I just watched Ryder take out my pain on the man that inflicted it.

Blake tried his hardest to pull Ryder off, but it was like he was a machine with super human strength. Eventually the valet jumped in to help Blake and then the concierge. Someone called the police but by the time the ambulance and police cruisers pulled up, six men had stepped in to restrain Ryder.

I stayed frozen in place while Ryder was handcuffed and then shoved into the back of a police car. His hand swollen, mangled and bloodied. But his face was calm, satisfied... justified.

And I would be lying if I said I didn't feel those same emotions coursing through me.

Taylor was loaded onto a stretcher and the ambulance left immediately with sirens blaring. I barely heard the sound though. After everything that happened tonight, I had finally become numb.

I started to float through these events as if everything was happening to someone else. As if someone else's lungs were burning, someone else had finger length bruises across their neck, someone else had bloodied fingernails and black and blue marks painting their skin.

As if my entire life was happening to someone else.

I hated that Ryder was separated from me. *Hated it*. But in the same moment I also knew I would get to see him again because of what he'd done for me. And if he wouldn't have stepped in, I could very likely be back in that sick f-ing hotel room, with that sick f-ing bastard.

The cops approached me eventually, after everyone in the lobby and some from upstairs, pointed me out. They took my statement, in which the only thing I lied about was that I had been set up on this date by *my pimp*. I told them instead that I was here with some girlfriends and that we happened to meet them in the lobby.

And the only reason I lied about that was because nobody would believe me if I told the truth. Nobody would believe I was this stupid, watered down version of Greek mythology and fate had decided that I spend my endless existence whoring it up for the god of the sea.

Ugh. It sounded so crazy, even to me!

Finally Nix and my mom showed up. The police released me into their care and they loaded me into the back of Nix's tiny sports car. My feet were propped up on the seat so I had enough room to breathe and my mom and Nix sat in tense silence all the way home.

They had spoken briefly to the cops, but all they came away with was a stern lecture on keeping better tabs of their daughter.

Their daughter. Like they were this happily married couple and I was a wayward teenager.

Finally once we were on Farnam and five blocks away from the apartment complex, Nix spoke to me, "Ivy, I had no idea Taylor was so goddamned crazy. I *never* would have sent you in there, had I known what could have happened to you." His hands were white as they gripped the steering wheel so impossibly tight and his jaw muscle popped in and out while his teeth ground together in fury.

I was shaking, I couldn't stop. I wondered if I would ever stop.

I snorted, it was an ugly, accusing sound, but I was beyond caring. "Save it."

"What did you say?" my mother turned on me, her eyes glittering with anger and some unidentifiable emotion that I didn't even want to try to name.

"Taylor told me this was my punishment!" I screeched. "The minute he had me alone, he told me Nix set this up to punish me! Look at me! Look at me!" My voice was getting louder and louder, but it was still raspy from being choked and screaming so much.

And my mother did. She really looked at me. For maybe the first time in my life. Her eyes narrowed and then widened with horror. "Did you really ask him to do that to her, Nix? This was your way of setting her straight?"

"I didn't know he would go this far. I asked him to scare her, I did not ask him to physically harm her." When I snorted the second time, he grew impatient, "Listen, you're more valuable to me flawless, so don't think for a moment that I wanted him to touch your skin or your hair. He was obviously a loose cannon and I take that responsibility on myself."

"Obviously," I agreed with dry humor.

"How could you?" my mother hissed, turning to face Nix.

"Therapy didn't work," he answered simply and then shrugged his shoulder. And that was the only explanation we were going to get. That was the only explanation he had to give. He was in charge of us. He owned us. He could do that to me every night if he wanted to.

My mother faced forward again, arms crossed tightly across her chest. Nix dropped us off at the front door of our complex without so much as another apology. That was it, what he said in the car was as good as I was going to get and even after all the trauma of the night I was still going to have to see him on almost a daily basis. I was still going to have to serve him, answer to him.

Before I could successfully vomit after that my mother cut into my thoughts, "You're not going anywhere until those bruises heal, Ivy. I will not have people asking more questions about you. Do you understand? Not even across the street for coffee, alright?"

"Alright," I accepted this. I didn't want to go anywhere looking like this, like an ad for domestic violence.

"And Ivy?" she stopped me before I could get to my bedroom and strip all my clothes and then stand under the hot shower until I had brand new skin. I looked up at her, restraining what was left of my tears until I was in the privacy of my own bedroom. "I'm sorry this happened to you. It will not happen to you again."

I just looked at her. I couldn't even smile in response. I wanted to believe her, I wanted to trust her…. but she was my mom. So after an acceptable amount of stare-down I disappeared into my bedroom and accepted the fact that this was all the sympathy I was going to get tonight.

This was my life. I could cry it out in the shower, but the minute I stepped back onto dry ground I had to suck it up and move on.

Chapter Thirty-Seven

"Are you sure you're ready for this?" Exie asked from beside me on the sidewalk.

"Uh, no. Actually I'm pretty sure I'm not ready for this," I groaned, and then ran my fingers through my hair. Again.

"You don't have to go, you know," Sloane reminded me. "Your mom said that you could take a few more personal days."

"Yeah, right. Except my mom doesn't really know anything and I don't want to make summer school a permanent part of the summer calendar. Besides, Tanner might lynch me if I call in to school one more time with the same excuse."

"Lynch? Really?" Sloane rolled her eyes at me and then pulled me in for a two-air-kiss hug. We were so mature for our age.

"See you girls after school?" I asked as Exie received the same snobby goodbye.

"You bet," Exie answered enthusiastically. "But only if you bring Phoenix down here with you, I have a uh, band I want to show him on my iPod."

"You're so cute when you have a crush," Sloane laughed, but I had the feeling it was a sarcastic laugh. "See if you can't rustle up a man for me too, Ivy. I could use someone who's not a class-A douche."

"Sure thing," I joked. "I'll just punch it into my day calendar. Right between chemistry lab and American government."

"Don't be a smart ass," Sloane warned and then smacked my ass for extra emphasis.

"Bye girls, love you!" I called after them while they piled into Exie's car and headed off for their posh private school.

Even though they never said love you back, it had become our thing. Me saying it, them just.... receiving it.

Two weeks had gone by since I was attacked in that hotel room. My bruises were faded, my fingernails had grown back and my voice box had returned to normal. Still images of that night haunted me, terrorized me when I let it. And I never wanted to let anyone I loved, go without knowing it for a single day.

"Well, look who's back," the one person I was making an exception to that rule called from above me on the steps. "Hey there, Red."

"Ryder Sutton, when did they let you come back? Rumor has it, you were sent to the big house," I flirted shamelessly. Ryder had gone to jail, but was soon bailed out by his dad. Taylor never pressed charges and so

Ryder was only charged with some minor offenses and sentenced to some community service.

Thank God.

But then again, part of me knew Nix had something to do with it and the idea of Nix helping Ryder repulsed me.

Violently.

"Fun fact," Ryder smirked at me. "Tanner blames that on your terrible influence. Turns out your poison to a good boy like me."

"Huh, imagine that," I sighed. "And what do you say to that."

"I say it's less like poison and more like kryptonite." His steady gaze held mine and my heart thumped in my chest, responding to his words, even if I wouldn't let any other part of me. "Come on."

He held out his hand and I took it without thinking. If Ryder was going to hold his hand out for me, I was going to take it. Today. Tomorrow. And any day in the future.

He led me beyond the offices and down the main hallway, up the stairs and to the music wing of the school. I finally figured out where we were going when he entered the band room and started walking toward the practice rooms.

A few of them were occupied this morning, an advanced cellist, a beginning bass guitar and a struggling oboist. It kind of took all of my effort not to poke my head in and ask the dying duck to give it up! Music was just not in his cards. Not now, not ever.

Ryder stopped at the last practice room with nowhere else to go. He held the door open for me and I walked into the small space just as a cascade of butterflies let loose in my stomach.

"You're going to get me into trouble back here. I'm supposed to be in class," I lectured.

"Well good thing I'm the office aide and can write you a pass," he reminded me smugly. "Besides, we need to talk. I haven't seen you since... Well, it's been too long. I had to know you were okay."

My mother banned all communication from the outside world until I healed. I wanted to believe it was her motherly concern, but instinct told me she didn't want anyone else remembering what I looked like after they brought me home.

It was frightening.

I sat down, straddling the piano bench. It was unladylike and completely unattractive, but then maybe that's why I did it. I wasn't trying to attract Ryder. I was trying to do the opposite.

And feel the opposite towards him.

290

Until he sat down opposite me, mirroring my pose. He didn't look nearly as uncomfortable as I did. His long legs fit the piano bench better and okay, his crotch wasn't completely on display either.

Not that mine was, I was wearing jeans after all. But still.

"Thank you," I whispered to him when we were settled. He reached forward and took my hands in his, holding them in the space between us. "Thank you for... thank you for it all."

He heard my words and drank them in. "Sure, it's what friends do."

A small part of me wondered if he was belittling the situation as a defense mechanism, to deflect whatever real emotion there was between us. I thought about it for a minute, but decided to shake that off as vanity.

Ryder really was just a good friend.

"Mmm, not all friends." I clarified, not wanting to take away his heroics, both in what he did that night at the hotel and in what he went through to actually befriend me. "Besides, I'm not the easiest person to get along with," I admitted.

He leaned forward so that our bodies were closer, so that our lips were closer. "That *is* a good point," he agreed. "It's a good thing I only like you as a friend."

I looked up to meet his silver-gray eyes, the eyes of someone that was more than a friend, the eyes of someone that didn't think of me as a friend at all. If the last two weeks taught me anything it was how dangerous my life was, how inescapable my future was and I cared about Ryder way too much to involve him in all my bullshit.

"It's a good thing you don't like me more than a friend," I breathed out on a whispy breath.

"And why's that?" Ryder asked, his voice rumbly and gruff. "Why is it good that I'll never be more than a friend?" He looked down at our entwined hands and then up at me from under dark, sooty lashes. "Explain it to me."

Nervousness shot through me, setting every nerve ending on edge, but I sucked in a breath for courage and answered truthfully, "Because you know, you would never really be sure how you felt about me," I obeyed and explained it to him. "I'm all smoke and mirrors. There's nothing real about me. And you would be caught up in the game. Everything between us would always be fake... forced. Maybe it wouldn't feel like it to you, maybe you would be convinced that everything we had was real. But it would be the curse, just the curse. You would be in love with something you wanted me to be, not the real me. You could never love the real me," I sucked in a staggering breath and held it; if he told me how he felt, if he admitted more than platonic feelings for me right now, I was gone. To hell with waiting until I turned eighteen, to hell with my mom and Nix and sticking it out for my trust, I would leave tonight. I couldn't hurt Ryder. I *wouldn't* hurt him. Not after what he did for me. And not just the douche bag at the hotel. He also made me believe in friendship, in caring about somebody and being cared about in return. Falling for me was a trap and I would never involve him in the screwed up soap opera that was my life.

"Nothing I feel for you is forced or fake," Ryder confessed sincerely. His eyes turned into silver pools in the darkness, promising me truth, promising me authenticity and honesty. His words and the deep, hopeful meaning floated on the air between us; wrapped around me whole and sank into my skin before I could stop them. "Nor will it ever be."

The urge to flee was so strong and dominant that I thought it would propel me from the bench on its own but I couldn't make my feet move, I couldn't find the courage to leave him. It didn't exist inside of me. All my lectures, pep talks and hours of reasoning to give Ryder a better life, a life without me fell to the ground in a pile of ashes when presented with the challenge. I chose Ryder. And even though I hoped to keep him as a friend, I knew without a doubt I would always choose Ryder.

A flutter took off in my stomach, flapping wings of reluctant hope and distant excitement. My heart clenched in my chest, an unfamiliar pang of affection I was starting to associate with Ryder. Only Ryder.

"How can you be sure?" I challenged on a whisper, afraid my own voice would prove him wrong.

He smirked at me then, wicked and taunting, "Because I don't like you... at all. You can't fake this level of irritation. You could quite possibly be, the most obnoxious person I've ever met," He explained everything on a smile so that I know he was teasing me.

But that was also how I knew I was in trouble. I was falling for him and in every single way. I wasn't supposed to. Hell, I didn't even want to, not really. I didn't want the baggage, or the mess, or the unrequited feelings. But there it was. I was falling. And I couldn't stop it from happening.

The way he played his guitar... the way he drank his coffee... the way he didn't bother with his hair, the way he laughed at me, the way his silver eyes cut to me from across a room and he could determine in once glance if I was alright or if I needed to be rescued, the way he protected me from everything, even myself... but most of all the way he made me feel when we're together, when we're not together, hell the way he made me feel anything at all... the butterflies and blushing... the rush of it all. Damn it. I'd fallen for the rush.

"You are *such* a brat!" I rolled my eyes and leaned back, forcing our hands apart.

"Takes one to know one," he droned, still making fun of me.

"That was so clever and creative, I'm speechless," I teased. "So speechless. Did you make that up? How did you get so smart? I want to be like you when I grow up!"

"Alright, smartass, let's get you to class before Tanner hunts you down and performs the Spanish Inquisition on you." He stood up, legs still spread across the bench seat and reached for my hands again.

I gave them to him and let him pull me to my feet. We had another moment of staring into each other's eyes until he reached down and cupped my face in his hands. "I will never let something like that happen to you again, Ivy."

I knew exactly what he was talking about. And so I stayed quiet. Because knowing my life, knowing what Nix had planned for me, I knew there was no way for him to keep his promise. He didn't react to my silence, or try to argue his way into my belief system.

But he did close the distance between us and press an utterly heartbreaking, devastatingly sweet kiss to my lips. I just responded. There was nothing else I could do. I couldn't pull away, or even press back. I just let him kiss me and in doing so, take away some more of my pain.

"We're going to get you out of this," he promised.

And this time, I didn't know why or what changed, but I believed him.

"Okay," I agreed.

He took my hand again and then led me back to the main upstairs hallway. We walked quietly down the staircase and back toward the office. Just as we moved by the closest classroom to the main office, Phoenix and Chase emerged from the room, carrying that same stupid oversized wooden board.

"Well, look who decided to grace us with her presence again," Chase called out sarcastically and then nudged Phoenix in the rib.

I cringed for a second, even closing my eyes against the awkwardness, but after a moment I realized there wasn't really any weirdness going on. Chase sounded... just... casual.

"Ah, the Ginga-Ninja. How are you sensei?" Phoenix did his best impersonation of my Kung-Fu apprentice maybe...? And then turned to bow to me with palms pressed flatly together.

"Did he tell you, he's trying to make t-shirts of that?" Ryder laughed. He had dropped my hand a few steps back, but now he threw a friendly arm across my shoulder.

293

"Obviously that would be awesome!" I laughed too.

Mrs. Tanner stepped out into the hall at the sound of our raucous behavior and frowned at all four of us. "The prodigal daughter has returned," she grunted at me, leveling me with her angry-wench eyes. "Didn't I warn you about missing more school? Mr. Costas wants to talk to you about summer school, unless you're seriously considering doing us all a favor and just dropping out?"

"Sorry," I shrugged apologetically. That was not an option yet.

Mrs. Tanner's attention snapped up to the three boys that surrounded me, my three friends. "Don't you boys know better than to hang around Ivy Pierce? She's no good. She's going to get you all into trouble."

Surrounded by this loyal company I barely even felt the sting of her words.

Ryder looked back and forth between Mrs. Tanner and me and then said in a proud, raised voice, "It's too late for that. Ivy Pierce may be trouble, but she's exactly the kind of trouble I've been looking for."

I smiled at him for sticking up for me again and then my grin grew when Chase started clapping and Phoenix hollered a "Preach it."

Things were still bleak. But not nearly as desolate and depressing as they had been.

Besides, tragedies were always easier to face when you had friends.

Book Two in the Siren Series, The Fall, is available now.

Acknowledgments

First to my God, in the land that is plentiful and when I walk through the wilderness, may I always turn back to praise.

To my husband and best friend, Zach, you complete me. Just kidding! I love you. You are an amazing man, and none of this would have ever happened without you, or because of you. Plus you're a really good kisser.

To Stella, Scarlett, Stryker and Solo, I love you more than anything. This is all for you.

To my mother, Helen, I couldn't have asked for a better fan or supporter than you. Your encouragement, support and fix-it-texts mean everything.

To Jennifer "Nate" Nunez, you are a phenomenal editor and fantastic friend. Thank you for helping me make sense, (deleting my parenthesis) and putting up with every long email and run-on text. But most of all, thank you for making me laugh. I couldn't do this without you.

To Carolyn, thank you for catching everything else. I truly appreciate your editing eye and all the work you do. You are such a blessing in my life.

To Caedus Design Co, thank you for your vision. You see creative in a way I can't and have genius in a way I never could. Thank you for every cover and every design. I am in love with this one. But then again... I'm in love with *all* of them!

To Lindsay, Miriah, Bridget, Diana, Brooke and Ashley, you girls are the greatest friends. Thank you for your energy and excitement. Thank you for letting me talk about myself. And thank you for promoting me! You are true friends. You make me feel like a *real* writer and I can't thank you enough for that!!

To my Hellcats, Michelle Leighton, Georgia Cates, Shelly Crane, Amy Bartol, Angeline Kace, Samantha Young and Quinn Loftis, I am so beyond blessed to know you ladies. You are the greatest writers I know! Badass, rock stars that dominate this world. Love each and every one of you!

To Jenn Sterling, you inspire me daily. I am so proud of you and amazed by you! Thank you for your friendship and knowing when to call "Seahorse" when you see it.

To Lila Felix, one day soon we will share a table together. I'll bring the fire extinguisher; you just give me the signal. It's important we stick together! Also, thanks for being so awesome.

To Andrew James, thank you for creating real beauty out of this. Thank you for putting a soundtrack to my words. I didn't know what to expect, but what came out of long, confusing emails and your musical genius is so insanely good there are not even words to accurately describe. Thank you for I Believe and thank you for Blackheart. There have never been greater songs.

To Kristen, thank you for supporting this, and your husband. And thank you for playing Just Dance with mine!

And to the reader, each and every reader, thank you so very much for all your support, for buying this book and making it all the way to here. I cannot tell you how much I appreciate you and thank God for you!! I seriously have the most amazing fans ever. Thank you!

The Music

While I was writing The Rush, I had the incredible opportunity to work with Andrew James. He is a truly talented musician, based in Omaha. His sound is this raw blues that draws you in and makes you appreciate the authentic sound of genuinely good music. And because he's so awesome, he agreed to collaborate with me and this series and write some original music.

For The Rush, he gave Ryder a voice, and a sound and he took the concepts talked about in the book and brought them to life.

The first song released for The Rush is called I Believe and is available wherever music is sold, iTunes, Amazon, and Spotify.

The second song, Blackheart, talked about specifically in the book, is also available at all the above distributors.

If you enjoyed Ryder and Ivy I hope you take the time to check out the songs!!!

You can find Andrew James on Facebook at The Andrew James

Or on Twitter at @Andr3wJames

About the Author

Rachel Higginson was born and raised in Nebraska, but spent her college years traveling the world. She married her high school sweetheart and spends her days raising their growing family. She is obsessed with bad reality TV and any and all Young Adult Fiction.

The Rush is the first book in The Siren Series.

The Fall, the second book in The Siren Series, is available now. And the third and final book, The Heart will be released November, 2014.

Other books by Rachel coming out in 2014 are Bet on Me, an NA contemporary romance, The Redeemable Prince, the seventh book in The Star-Crossed Series and The Five Stages of Falling in Love, an adult, contemporary romance.

Other Books Out Now by Rachel Higginson:

Reckless Magic (The Star-Crossed Series, Book 1)
Hopeless Magic (The Star-Crossed Series, Book 2)
Fearless Magic (The Star-Crossed Series, Book 3)
Endless Magic (The Star-Crossed Series, Book 4)
The Reluctant King (The Star-Crossed Series, Book 5)
The Relentless Warrior (The Star-Crossed Series, Book 6)
Breathless Magic (The Star-Crossed Series, Book 6.5)

Heir of Skies (The Starbright Series, Book 1)
Heir of Darkness (The Starbright Series, Book 2)
Heir of Secrets (The Starbright Series, Book 3)

Bet in the Dark (An In the Dark stand-alone)
Bet on Me (An In the Dark stand-alone) coming October, 2014

My Zombie/Dystopian Novella Series:
Love and Decay, Season One
Love and Decay, Season Two

Striking, a co-authored contemporary romance

Follow Rachel on her blog at:
www.rachelhigginson.com

Or on Twitter:
@mywritesdntbite

Or on her Facebook pages:
Rachel Higginson

Keep Reading for an Excerpt from Rachel's new contemporary romance Bet in the Dark, a never before seen chapter from Lila Felix's Down N' Derby and a chapter from Shelly Crane's newest Wide Awake.

Chapter One

I blamed this on Kelly Clarkson.

On Kelly-Freaking-Clarkson.

The angry man standing across the kitchen island looked like he was about to throttle me. I had visions of large hands gripped firmly around my neck shaking me like a rubber chicken. His eyes flashed with frustration and I cursed Kelly Clarkson straight to the grave.

Things started out so good this morning, so unbelievably, unnaturally good. I should have known better. But at the time, I woke up in my bed to the powerful chords Kelly Clarkson belting through my radio alarm, and laid there for the length of the song just to let her words sink in.

Stronger.

In fact, I started to think Kelly Clarkson was a genius. And like maybe we were soul sisters that survived something awful, but came out on the other side of it stronger. I started to think maybe she got me...

Because the bed did feel warmer, and I dreamt in color again. I never felt lonely when I was alone anymore and really I was standing taller. Kelly Clarkson had it all figured out.

Well "was" as in the seriously past tense because with monster-man looming over me, pissed off and yelling about money he wanted and I definitely did not have, I wasn't standing taller anymore. I was shrinking slowly into what I assumed would soon be the fetal position.

But this morning, even as the warm sun sifted through my bedroom window and heated my exposed skin, everything seemed possible. I felt strong enough to get out of bed today and conquer the world- or at least the closest Starbucks and my Econ class.

Which come on, that's close enough, right?

And even though last week I missed a seriously important pop quiz in my post-break-up-cowering phase and now my grade was in some trouble.... and then it started raining and I happened to be wearing a white t-shirt and red bra. Who does that by the way? Me apparently, in my Kelly-Clarkson-gave-me-the-strength-to-be-a-skank-mood. And then even after I came home to my roommate on her way out, for what at the time she promised was just a bite to eat even though she was two months behind on her share of the rent, I believed today was the start of better things to come.

All thanks to Kelly Clarkson.

After setting my purse down on the kitchen counter because the entry hall table that I usually placed it on had been moved, I started to wonder if maybe Kelly Clarkson lied to me.

Well, okay, that's not exactly true. First I wondered if I was hallucinating. And then I ran through the possibility of being robbed, but my roommate's casual departure quickly negated that idea.

I blinked. And blinked again. And then blinked so hard tears formed in the corners of my eyes and I felt like I was trying to be the second coming of I Dream of Jeannie. If I willed all of my furniture and belongings to reappear, they would.

But they didn't.

And that was just the start of my disappointment.

Then there was the letter... The one calmly explaining my roommate had a clinically diagnosed gambling addiction and was thousands of dollars in debt. She explained that she had to sell the furniture, my furniture, to pay for rehab. Her family insisted on it. She had a real problem. A real problem. And I needed to understand that anything she had done to hurt me was her addiction and not the real her.

Well, her addiction wasn't going to replace all of my furniture.

Her addiction wasn't going to come up with the other half of my rent!

And her addiction really wasn't going to explain to the man across the kitchen yelling at me that no matter who he thought I was, I did not owe him seven thousand dollars!!

I picked up the handwritten letter of crazy with a shaky hand and held it out to him.

"What's this?" He paused in his tirade to take the half sheet of torn notebook paper. I noticed my Biology notes on the back of the paper for the first time. Seriously, she couldn't even use her own paper???

"Um, see? I'm not the one that owes you money," I sounded confident, but inside I was a trembling, terrified puddle. And on second thought, maybe I didn't sound quite so confident....

"Who's Tara?" he grunted after skimming the note quickly.

"My roommate," I said simply and then thought better of it. "My ex-roommate. She's moved on to group therapy and the twelve steps apparently."

"And who are you?" he asked carefully. His eyes swept over me in a way that made me feel like he had x-ray vision and suddenly I felt very vulnerable and very naked.

Okay, more vulnerable.

And not really naked.

But feeling more vulnerable was a hard emotion to feel since he elbowed his way in here not even ten minutes ago and started shouting at me and threatening all kinds of legal action and at times bodily harm.

"I'm uh, wait a second! Who are you? You're in my apartment!" I dug deep for some courage. I slammed my fists to my hips and tilted my chin in my best I-mean-business pose.

"Don't get cute with me." He sneered. I wanted to explain that I wasn't being cute; I was being tenacious but decided to stay silent when his full upper lip curled in frustration and his dark, chocolate brown eyes narrowed. "I'm the guy you owe seven thousand dollars!"

Ugh, he was still stuck on this! I cleared my throat and tried again, "How could I possibly owe you seven thousand dollars? I've never even met you before! I don't even know your name."

"You're really going to stick with this whole doe-eyed-innocent act?" he scoffed unkindly. He walked forward and placed two meaty hands on the kitchen counter slowly, like he was weighing his strength against a fragile surface. His broad shoulders tensed and stiffened and his entire body went rigid with frustration. I almost felt bad for him.

Almost.

But then I remembered I was not that person anymore. No more pity for people that didn't deserve it. No more sacrificing my time and money and energy for people that would just screw me over when they got what they wanted. This was the new me. The stronger me. The me that was soul sisters with Kelly Clarkson. The I-get-what-I-want-me! And right now, I seriously wanted this guy out of my life, or at the very least out of my apartment.

"I'm not innocent," I spat back with my arms crossed firmly against my chest and my hip jutting out. I realized that maybe that wasn't my best defense but I pushed forward. "And I'm not doe-eyed!"

His face suddenly opened up in some shock and his lips kind of twitched like he was holding back a laugh. "I can't believe this." He rubbed two hands over his face in a sign of exhaustion and turned his back on me.

With his body more relaxed I saw him almost in a new light. He was less macho-Neanderthal in this posture and more holy-sexy-back-muscles-batman. Obviously the disaster that was my last boyfriend did a number on me if I was checking out the confused hit man pacing back and forth in my kitchen. I mean honestly, fantasizing about what his back could potentially look like under his thin t-shirt was seriously clinical, right?

Maybe Tara wasn't the only one that needed medical observation and group therapy.

"I think there has been some miscommunication," I ventured, now that he was somewhat

relaxed. "You think I am someone that owes you money, but I am not. Do I look like a drug addict to you?"

He swung his head back around to face me. "You think I'm a drug dealer?"

"Seven thousand dollars is a lot of money," I sniffed.

"Yes, it is. And you think the only way to go that much in debt is by drugs?" His eyes widened in disbelief.

Now that he was even calmer I noticed his face wasn't necessarily menacing, but more chiseled and dignified. Actually when his dark eyes weren't bugging out of his head in rage, he looked more like a Calvin Klein model than Tony Soprano... And his hands weren't so much meaty as they were just large and connected to very defined arms. And okay, originally I was under the impression that his neck was the size of a redwood, but now that I was really paying attention it was more like just a very strong, carved out piece of art, attached to an equally and artfully sculpted body. And then to top it off, he had great hair. I just needed to admit that. He had amazing hair. Hair that I was instantly jealous of! Dark, rich coffee colored hair that matched his eyes. Short on the sides and just a little bit longer on top, it was stylish and trendy, not at all ex-military-renegade-private-security like I originally associated him with.

Wait a minute, I didn't think I liked that he was attractive... more than attractive, hotter than hot attractive. When I finally took in the scruffy growth across his jaw that partially hid too full lips, I wanted to roll my eyes. Who was this guy?

"Well, it's one of the ways," I huffed impatiently.

He cocked his head back, seemingly surprised with my answer. "I actually have no argument for that. You're right, drugs are one way to go into that much debt." I smirked at him, momentarily satisfied until I realized he was really a drug lord and he thought I was his client! A client that owed him money! "But that's not why you owe me money. I'm not a drug dealer."

Oh whew. Sure, I knew that.

"Okay, are you a bill collector then? Because I don't even have a credit card. Well, I have one credit card, but it's for emergencies only and I've never used it. Besides, it only has like a fifteen hundred dollar limit on it. And it's actually in my brother's name." I was growing more impatient the

304

longer he stared at me. It was like all of the anger that propelled him into my apartment to begin with had evaporated somewhere between drug dealer and bill collector. Now his chocolate eyes were lit with amusement and his mouth was doing that annoying twitching thing again. "And my roommate gets calls from debt collectors all the time. Phone calls- have you heard of those? You seriously did not need to come all the way over here; I could have explained this to you over the phone."

"I'm not a bill collector either."

This time I could tell he was laughing at me. The corners of his eyes crinkled with humor and he held his hands up, palms out as if to stop me from guessing anymore. But I wasn't finished. If he wasn't a hit man, drug dealer or bill collector but wanted seven thousand dollars from me that left only one option.

I gasped, "Oh my gosh, is this about prostitution? Oh my goodness, are you a pimp?" I shrieked and backed up three steps.

"What?" he burst out in a bark of confusion. "Are you into prostitution?"

"What? Me? Do I look like a prostitute?" I was back to being angry; narrowed eyes, hands cocked on my hips, scowl tightening my expression.

"Well, no, honestly, you look more like a missionary," he shrugged a casual shoulder and let his eyes travel over me.

"A missionary!" I spit the word out like it burned me. I clutched at my gray infinity scarf that covered my black and white cowl neck long sleeve tee. Okay, maybe it was a little conservative... but he seriously did not need to confuse modesty with missionary.

"Would you rather look like a prostitute?" He asked, his stupid dark brown eyes laughing at me.

"Why in the world would you think that?" I demanded. This conversation had the disorienting feel that we were going backwards instead of forwards and I started to feel dizzy from all the circles and the way his mouth quirked up when he was trying not to laugh.

Wait, scratch that. I was only dizzy from the conversation!

"Listen, honestly, I don't care what you are, I just want my money," some of his amusement faded and a wave of exhaustion flashed across his face.

"So this isn't about prostitution?" I asked, just to clarify. It was kind of important that this wasn't about prostitution.

"If you're not a prostitute and I'm not a pimp how in the hell could this be about prostitution?" he rumbled.

"Well, I don't know, I just need to be.... sure," I finished lamely.

He ran a hand over his face again and growled out a frustrated sound. Then he pulled his cell phone out of his pocket and checked the time. "This is taking up too much time. I just want my money and then I'll be gone. I won't bother you anymore. I promise. Although I strongly suggest that you stay away from anymore poker games. You are obviously not nearly lucky enough to be as careless as you are with your money."

That got my attention. "Wait," I held up a hand like I was asking him to stop his vehicle. But then I didn't know how to go on. Gambling? This sounded way too convenient... way too coincidental. A man comes to my door, demanding a seven thousand dollar poker debt minutes after my crook of a roommate robbed me blind and then headed off to rehab for a gambling addiction? "Okay, I don't know what you're talking about, but why don't you just tell me who you think I am. That might make things easier."

A smug smirk turned his mouth and he said with confidence, "Eleanor Harris."

That caught me off guard. Because he was right. "Um, Ellie," I corrected before he stuck to calling me Eleanor. Ugh! Even if he were here to murder me I would make him call me Ellie.

"Fine, Ellie Harris."

"Okay, you know my name, but you don't know anything else about me. Like for instance, I don't owe you any money!" I argued, still wondering how he knew my name.

"Alright, let's see, you're a sophomore, originally from farther up north. You transferred to La Crosse spring semester last year. You were originally at the University of Madison, but you wanted to be close to your boyfriend who turned out to be a cheating douche bag. He broke up with you two weeks ago for another girl and since then you've gone from being a straight A student with a nearly perfect attendance record to skipping all of your of classes, doing your best to fail out of school and now you've apparently acquired a gambling addiction with a side of pathological lying."

"What!" I would have made a terrible reporter. "I am not a liar! And I have never gambled a day in my life! And I'm not trying to fail out of school! A girl is allowed to take a few sick days after her three year relationship ends! How can you possibly know so much and so little about me at the same time?" This was possibly the most exasperating conversation I had ever had.

"I make it a point to know all my players, Ellie. Especially ones that come into the game waving money around like you did," he explained patiently with that same cocky smile on his face.

I had the strongest urge to smack him. And I had never, not in my entire life, ever felt like hitting anything before!

"Clearly you have me confused with somebody else because I have no clue what you are talking about!"

"That is not going to work on me!" the anger was simmering under the surface again, his eyes turning almost black with emotion.

"Okay, okay, okay," I backtracked quickly. "I can see that. So, just for fun, how about you explain to me exactly how I came to owe you all this money and then we can figure this out together. I want you to get your money just as badly as you do, I promise, alright?"

He seemed to think that over for a minute, his face relaxing back to movie-star-stranger instead of serial-killer-hit-man. It didn't take a genius to figure out which version I liked best.

"Alright, fine. We can do this your way. Especially if you promise you'll help me get my money," he said evenly and then waited for me to answer.

"Yes, I promise. I mean, I know I don't owe you the money. But if there is any way I can assist you with it, I'd be glad to help." What I didn't say was that as long as I didn't have to shoot, stab or bury somebody I would be glad to help. Really, I meant like a stern, authoritative letter I could put a stamp on and mail for him. Plus, these were mostly just empty promises until I could get him out of my apartment, lock the two deadbolts, slide the chain and then call the police.

"About a week and a half ago, you contacted me about joining the game. I had heard your name around campus and knew that your request was entirely out of the ordinary for you. So I started to ask around about you and that's when I found out you just got dumped. It made sense then, why you would want to play. Even if I didn't think it was a good idea, I've been dumped before, I guess I could relate in a way."

"You've been dumped?" I scoffed before I could stop myself. He was gorgeous, all testosterone and muscles, standing in the middle of my kitchen with his gray t-shirt, loose jeans and flip flops. Plus, he was more than just a little intimidating; I could hardly believe a girl found enough courage to break up with him.

He seemed to find this more amusing than anything and actually broke into an eye-twinkling grin. Yes, his eyes twinkled. I was so shocked by the expression I had to look away. He was more dangerously good looking than ever and a strange heat lit a fire in my belly. So I cleared my throat and pretended that never happened.

"Sure, I've been dumped," his smile turned wicked and I suddenly felt like he was laughing at an inside joke. "So I know what it's like to do something reckless after the heartache."

I snorted. "There wasn't that much heartache. Trust me. You were right when you called him a cheating.... uh, you know."

"Douche bag?" he questioned.

"Yes, that," I blushed a deep red. I wasn't a missionary. But okay, sometimes curse words made me uncomfortable. Which was kind of surprising since I grew up with three brothers that basically existed with "R" ratings attached to them: strong language, violent behavior and sexual content.

He actually let out a soft chuckle at that. I was becoming unending entertainment for this guy and I was suddenly hit with a flash of irritation. He didn't know me!

Although... he kind of did know me. Or at least a lot of random facts about me and it was definitely weirding me out.

"Anyway, when you proved you had the buy-in, I decided to give you a chance. I mean, who was I to judge your methods of coping, am I right?" he asked and actually waited for my agreement.

"I guess so," but an ugly foreboding feeling started to unfurl inside my chest and I suddenly found it hard to breathe.

"In fact, if you remember, I even advised you to hold back some since I didn't want to see you lose everything at once."

"And you advised me how?" I clarified, trying to piece this together. Except I wasn't even sure what he was talking about. Buy-in? Game? None of this was making sense.

"Private message," when I gave him a blank look, he continued, "online."

"Online," I repeated.

"Yes, online. But you didn't listen to me. And then you got in way over your head, lost and now you owe me seven thousand dollars." He finished arrogantly and I almost expected him to bow.

"I lost in a game of...." I prompted slowly, so afraid of the answer my hands had started to tremble.

"Five-Card-Stud." When I continued to just stare at him, he finally added. "Poker. Online poker."

"Oh my goodness," I winced. Suddenly the puzzle was pieced together and in front of me. I was going to be sick. I was going to be really sick. I reeled in a circle, desperately searching for a place to sit down, but all of my furniture was gone. Another wave of clarity rippled through me and my stomach actually lurched this time. I took off for the kitchen sink and gripped the stainless steel basin. I ignored the anal retentive voice inside me screaming about germs, not because I wasn't worried about them, but because thinking about them was making it worse. I choked on a gag and then dropped my head forward so I could breathe in and out deeply through my nose.

"You're not going to....? Are you going to be sick?" the guy asked from behind me. He didn't sound concerned, just really grossed out.

I waved an aggravated hand behind me, hoping he would get the hint and just leave. He didn't, or if he did he ignored it and instead walked over to the fridge and opened it. I heard him rummage through the practically empty appliance; my college sized budget didn't cover much more than a value pack of Ramen Noodles. I heard the telltale sign of a pop can opening and then the fizzy bubbles of ginger ale were tickling my nose.

He placed the can to my lips and then tilted it back before I could protest. I took a small drink and then stood up before he could force anymore down my throat. The carbonated beverage settled in my stomach and coated the nausea with something soothing.

Okay, that felt alright.

I took the can from his hand, my fingers accidentally brushing over his before I took possession and then sipped another soothing drink.

"That wasn't me," I finally choked out, squeezing my eyes shut.

"What?" he asked and I jumped by how close he was.

I took a step back, opened my eyes to meet his and said slower, "That wasn't me. I didn't place the bet, or play the game or whatever. It was my roommate, she must have... stolen my identity! I swear to you, not even an hour ago I found this note that said she had a gambling addiction and she was going to rehab. She owes me money too! "

A long, very still moment of silence stretched between us before he said, "She stole your identity?"

"Yes!" I squealed. Even I could tell how high pitched and annoying that was, but I couldn't help it! "And my furniture," I said with further emphasis.

"I was actually wondering about that," he said pensively.

"So you see? It's not me that owes you seven thousand dollars, it's her."

"But she's gone? To rehab? With all of your furniture?" His phrases sounded like questions, but they didn't feel like them. It felt more like he was trying the words out, rolling them around on his tongue and deciding whether or not I was lying.

"Yes!" I answered anyway, hoping he would believe me.

"You can see why your version of what happened is hard to believe," he sighed and if I didn't know better, or if maybe I wouldn't have slapped my hands over my eyes, I would have been able to assure myself there wasn't a hint of amusement in his voice, or the sound of him smiling. Those things were all products of my delusional imagination...

"Yes, I could see why, but it's the truth," I promised, struggling to peek from behind my fingers.

"Regardless of what happened, your name is still signed on my contract, you still owe me my money," he stated finally.

"Contract?" I croaked.

"Online document, your initials were used. Unless you have a way to prove to me that it wasn't you who signed the document, I have to assume it was. I mean, that's a lot of money. It's not exactly like I can just look the other way."

"But it wasn't me! I'm sure I can prove it, I just need... time," I pleaded, my head spinning with every kind of crazy thought to get out of this.

His hand went up to cup his chin in thoughtful silence for a while. His eyes roved over me again, taking in every piece of me as if to weigh it on his internal truth scales and decide whether to trust me or not. Finally, after several minutes of quiet, he said, "I'm a nice guy-"

"You're not a nice guy. You're a scary guy," I confessed honestly and probably a little frantically before I could think better of it.

A rush of laughter fell out of his mouth before he could compose himself, "You don't even know me!"

"You're right! I don't even know your name," I pointed out, suddenly realizing that should have probably been the first thing I found out.

"Ah," he stewed on that for a moment and then said, "Finley Hunter."

I gulped. "Finley Hunter?" Okay, the online gambling thing made sense now. Because Finley Hunter, a senior track star, rumored to go through girls like Kleenex's during flu season and ditch more classes than he attended, was also rumored to run an online on campus gambling site the university had no idea about.

"Fin," he smiled at me. "You can call me Fin."

"You are a nice guy," I drawled.

His grin widened to wicked trouble. "So nice, I'm not going to make you give me my money tonight."

"You're not?"

"No, I have a solution that will help both of us get what we want," he announced confidently.

"You do?" I asked dryly with so much less confidence at the same time I wondered what it was that he thought I wanted.

"Just don't forget, you promised you would help." The hard, authoritative look returned to his eyes and a shiver of nerves climbed up my spine.

I nodded because there was nothing left to do. I needed time to think this over, to hunt down Tara and strangle her until dollar bills popped out her eyeballs.

And now an excerpt from Down 'N' Derby, the third installment in the Love and Skate Series by Lila Felix

Chapter 2
Reed

The lady across the street made a grave mistake by opening her garage yesterday. I swore I saw at least eighty boxes of Girl Scout Cookies over there just waiting for me. And then she closed it. Doesn't she know my everlasting craving for cookies? I tried to get a stick from the yard and say "Comehereium Cookiosa" but it didn't work. And has she sent her daughters over here to sell them to me? No.

Freakin' Girl Scouts.

I'm in trouble. I'm in so deep that I'm looking through shit shaded lenses. If one of them looks at me point blank and asks whether or not I've heard from him, I'm dead. Because I don't think I could bold faced lie to them. Hiding something was one thing but openly lying to my family was another. I understood all of those months in which Falcon hid the house thing from me. It hurt my heart to lie to Falcon, to Nellie, to all of them. I justified it to myself saying that even if they knew where he was, he would still go through with finding his dad. But I knew the truth, I was a dirty liar. This whole thing was tough. Mostly because Falcon would be hurt beyond belief. But Mad made me swear. It's that fine line we all rode on. I would never expect Falcon to tell me Nellie's secrets. I'm sure those two gossipers had plenty of stories and I didn't expect for him to tell me a single one.

Mad was in Arkansas the first time he called me. It was the time he made me swear on my parents' dead souls that I wouldn't tell. I have this tiny black and white marbled notebook that I write down where he calls from and the phone number; then I delete it from my phone. God help me if Nellie actually takes the time to look at her phone records. The second time he called it was from Oak Grove, Arkansas. I snuck on my laptop and Googled the location. Nixon also called me once. He whispered, so I assumed Mad didn't know. They had made it to Missouri and were stopping for the night. I kept track of it for my sanity and for safety's sake. God forbid if something happened to him, I would at least know where he was last.

Falcon felt horrible. He blamed himself for Mad leaving. He gave Mad five thousand dollars as a graduation present and we assumed that was the money which funded his trip. He beat himself up about it more and more every day. I think Mad assumed we would all move on. I don't know how he could've underestimated how much we loved him. He was our clown and he made us all happy. Owen was the brawn, Falcon was the brains and Mad was the clown. He was just as important as anyone else. I cried for hours and hours on the night he left after Sylvia called everyone.

Falcon and I were supposed to get married in a month but without Mad, we both refused. It just wouldn't be right. Falcon would never vow to marry me without all of his brothers beside him and I didn't blame him one bit. No matter what Sylvia said or even what Mad said; he was Falcon's brother. My future husband held me as I cried for my wedding, for his lost brother, for Sylvia's heartache, for my best friend.

And Owen and Nellie—they had finally decided to start trying for another baby. But now that Maddox was gone, it was like our whole world stopped. Plus, she wasn't even sure she wanted to get pregnant ever again. But I was the only one who knew that.

Chase was practically comatose. He stood in the kitchen looking out of the window while Sylvia explained to us why Mad was gone. She started the story twenty years prior...

Expected Release Date: May 1, 2013
Catch Lila's antics here:
www.authorlilafelix.blogspot.com
Facebook: Lila Felix (author)
Twitter: @ Authorlilafelix

And now an excerpt from Wide Awake by Shelly Crane

A girl.
A coma.
A life she can't remember.

When Emma Walker wakes up in the hospital with no knowledge of how she got there, she learns that she's been in a coma for six months. Strangers show up and claim to be her parents, but she can't remember them. She can't remember anyone. Not her friends, not even her boyfriend. Even though she can't remember, everyone wants her to just pick up where she left off, but what she learns about the 'old her' makes her start to wish she'd never woken up. Her boyfriend breaks up with the new girl he's dating to be with her, her parents want her to start planning for college, her friends want their leader back, and her physical therapist with the hazel eyes keeps his distance to save his position at the hospital.

Will she ever feel like she recognizes the girl in the mirror?

Please enjoy an excerpt from Shelly Crane's new novel, WIDE AWAKE, available now.

Someone was speaking. No, he was yelling. It sounded angry, but my body refused to cooperate with my commands to open my eyes and be nosy. I tried to move my arms and again, there was no help from my limbs. It didn't strike me as odd until then.

I heard, "All I'm saying is that you need to be on time from now on." Then a slammed door startled me. I felt my lungs suck in breath that burned and hissed unlike anything I'd ever felt before. It was as if my lungs no longer performed that function and were protesting.

Then I heard a noise, a gaspy sound, and my cheek was touched by warm fingers. "Emma?" I tried to pry my eyes and felt the glue that seemed to hold them hostage begin to let go. "Emma?"

Who was Emma? I felt the first sliver of light and tried to lift my arm to shield myself, but it wouldn't budge. Whoever was in the room with me must've seen me squint, because the light was doused almost immediately to a soft glow. My eyelids fluttered without strength. I tried to focus on the boy before me. Or maybe he was a man. He was somewhere in between. I didn't know who he was, but he seemed shocked that I was looking up at him.

314

"Emma, just hold on. I'm your physical therapist and you're in the hospital. Your..." he looked back toward the door, "parents aren't here right now, but we'll call them. Don't worry."

I looked quizzically at him. What was he was going on and on about? That was when I saw the tubes on my chest connecting my face to the monitors. The beeping felt like a knife through my brain. I looked at the stranger's hazel eyes and pleaded with him to explain.

He licked his lips and said softly, "Emma, you were in an accident. You've been in a coma. They weren't sure if...you'd wake up or not."

Of everything he just said, the only thing I could think was, 'Who's Emma?'

He leaned down to be more in my line of sight. "I'll be right back. I promise." Then he pressed a button on the side of the bed several times and went to the door. He was yelling again. I tried to shift my head to see him, but nothing of my body felt like mine. I started to panic, my breaths dragging from my lungs.

He came back to me and placed a hand on my arm. "Emma, stay calm, okay?"

I tried, I really did, but my body was freaking out without my permission. And then his face was suddenly surrounded by so many other's faces. He was pushed aside and I felt my panic become uncontrollable.

I thrashed as much as I could, but felt the sting in my arm as they all chattered around me. They wouldn't even look me in the eye. That man...boy was the only one who had even acknowledged me at all. The rest of them just scooted around each other like I wasn't important or wouldn't understand their purpose, like it was a job. Then I realized where I was and guessed it was their job.

My eyelids began to fight with me again and I cursed whoever it was that has stuck the needle into my arm. But as the confusion faded and the air become fuzzy, I welcomed the drugs that slid through my veins. It made the faces go away. It made my eyes close and I dreamed of things I knew nothing about.

My eyes felt lighter this time when they opened themselves. The fluttering felt more natural and I felt more alive. I could turn my head this time, too, and when I did I saw something disturbing.

There were strangers crying at my bedside.

The woman caught me looking her way and yelled, "Thank the Lord!" in a massive flourish that had me recoiling. She threw herself dramatically across the side of my bed and sobbed. I shifted my gaze awkwardly to the man and waited as she stood slowly, never taking his eyes from mine. "Emmie?" When I squinted he said, "Emma?"

When I went to speak this time, the tubes had been removed. I let my tongue snake out to taste my lips. They were dry. I was thirsty on a whole new level and glanced at the coffee cup stuck between his palms. He looked at it, too, and guessed what I wanted. He sprung to set the cup down quickly and fill an impossible smaller cup with water from a plastic pitcher. I tried to take it from his fingers, and he must have sensed I needed help, because he held my hands with his and I gulped it down in one swig with his help. My arms ached at the small workout they were getting and again I wondered what I was doing there.

I made him fill it three more times before I was satisfied and then leaned back to the bed. I decided to try to get some answers. I started slow and careful. "Where am I?" I said. It felt like my voice was strong, but the noise that came out was raspy and grated.

"You're in the...hospital, Emmie," the woman sobbing on my bed explained. She smiled at me, her running mascara marring her pretty, painted face. "We thought we'd never get you back."

That stopped everything for me.

"What do you mean?" I whispered.

She frowned and glanced back at the man. He frowned, too. "What do you remember about your accident, sweetheart?"

I shook my head. "I don't remember anything." I thought hard. Actually, that statement was truer than I had intended it to be. I couldn't remember...anything. I sucked in a breath. "Who are you? Do you know something about my...accident?"

The woman's devastated face told me she knew everything, but there was apparently something I was missing. She threw her face back onto my bed and sobbed so loudly that the nurse came in. She looked at the man there. He glanced to me, a little hint of some betrayal that I couldn't understand was in his eyes, before looking back to the nurse. "She must have amnesia."

The nurse ignored him and took my wrist in her hand to check my pulse. I wanted to glare at her. What the heck did my pulse have to do with anything at that moment? "Vitals are stable. How do you feel?" she asked me.

How did I feel? Was she for real? I rasped out my words. "I feel like there's something everyone isn't telling me."

She smiled sympathetically, a side of wryness there. "I'll get the doctor."

I looked up at her. She was short and petite, her blond hair in a bun and her dog and cats scrubs were crisp. I watched her go before looking to the man again.

"I don't understand what's going on. Did I..." A horrifying thought crossed my brain. The gasp I sucked in hurt my throat. "Did I kill someone? Did I hit them with my car or something? Is that why you're all being so weird?"

The man's own eyes began to fill then. I felt bad about that. I knew it was my fault, I just didn't know why. He rubbed the woman's back soothingly. He shook his head to dispel my theory and took a deep breath. A breath loaded with meaning and purpose. "Emmie... you were in an accident," he repeated once again that I was 'in an accident'. Okay, I got that. I wanted him to move on to the part that explained the sobbing woman on my bed. He continued after a pause, "You were...walking home from the football game. Someone...hit you. A hit and run, they said. The person was never found. They left you there and eventually someone else came along and helped you. But you'd already lost a lot of blood and..." He shook his head vigorously. "Anyway, you've been here for six months. You were in a coma, Emmie."

I took in a lungful of air and uttered the question that I somehow knew was going to change my world. "Why do you keep calling me Emmie?"

He grimaced. "That's your name. Emma Walker. We always...called you Emmie."

"My name... Emma," I tasted the name. "I don't feel like an Emma."

He smiled sadly. "Oh, baby. I'm so sorry this happened to you."

The woman raised her head. "Emmie." She tried to smile through her tears. "Try to remember," she urged. "Remember what your favorite color is?" She nodded and answered for me, "Pastel Pink. That's what you were thinking, right?"

Pastel pink was the last color I would ever have picked. "Are you sure I'm Emma?" She started to sob again and I felt bad, I did, but I needed answers. "Who are you?"

"We're your parents," the man answered. "I'm...Rhett. And your mother is Isabella. Issie..." he drawled distractedly.

"Rhett?" I asked. "Like in Gone With The Wind?"

He smiled. "That was your favorite movie when you were little."

I closed my mouth and felt the weight bear into my chest. I wasn't me. I had no idea who I was. These people claimed to know me and be my parents, but how could I just forget them? How could I forget a whole life?

I tried really hard to remember my real name, my real life, but nothing came. So, I threw my Hail Mary, my last attempt to prove that I wasn't crazy and didn't belong to these strangers, however nice they may be. "Do you have some pictures? Of me?"

In no time, two accordion albums were in my lap. One from the man's wallet and one from the woman's. I picked up the first, trying to sit up a bit. The man pressed the button to make the bed lean up and I waited awkwardly until it reached the upright position. Then I glanced at the first photo.

It was the man, the woman, two girls and a boy. They were all standing in the sunlight in front of the Disneyland sign. The man was wearing a cheesy Mickey Mouse ears hat. I glanced at him and he smiled with hope. I hated to burst the little bubble that had formed for him, but I didn't recognize any of these people. The pictures proved nothing. "I don't know any of those people."

The woman seemed even more stunned, if possible. She stood finally and turned to go to the bathroom. She returned with a handheld mirror. She held the picture up in one hand and the mirror in the other, and I indulged her by looking. I have no idea why I was so dense to not understand what they had been implying, and what I had so blatantly missed.

I was in the photo.

I looked at the mirror and recognized the middle girl as the girl in the mirror. I took it from her hands and looked at myself. I turned my head side to side and squinted and grimaced. The girl was moving like I was, but I had no idea who she was. She looked as confused as I felt. I looked back at the picture and examined...myself. She was wearing a pink tank top with jean shorts. Her hair was in a messy blonde ponytail and she had one hand on her hip and the other around the girl's shoulder. One of her legs was lifted a bit to lean on the toe. Cheerleader immediately rambled through my head. I almost vomited right there. "I'm a cheerleader?"

"Why, yes," she answered gently. "You love it."

My grimaced spread. "I can't imagine myself loving that. Or pink."

It hit me then. Like really sank in. I had no idea who I was. I had forgotten a whole life that no longer belonged to me. I felt the tear slide down my cheek before the sob erupted from my throat. I pushed the pictures away, but kept the mirror. I turned to my side and buried my face in my pillow, clutching the mirror to my chest. My body did this little hiccup thing and I cried even harder because I couldn't even remember doing that before.

The man and woman continued to stand at the foot of my bed when the doctor came in. I looked at him through my wet lashes. When he spoke, his voice sounded familiar. "Emma, I'm sorry to have to tell you this, but it appears that you've developed amnesia from your accident. We'll have to run lots of tests, but the good news is that in more cases than not, the amnesia is temporary."

I jolted and wiped my chin clear of tears. "You mean I could remember one day?"

"That's right."

"Don't get her hopes up," I heard from the doorway and turned to find the man-boy. My heart leapt a little. He was the only person that I remembered. Well from when I woke up at least. He felt like some awkward lifeline I needed to latch onto. He shook his head. "Every case is different. She may never remember anything."

"Mason," the man yelled, making me jump at the volume of it, and shot daggers at him across my bed, "this doesn't concern you."

"She's been in my care for six months," he growled vehemently and then glanced at me. He did a double take when he saw me awake and looking at him. I had no idea what the expression on my face may have been, but he softened immediately and came to stand beside...my parents.

"Isabella. Rhett," he said and nodded to them as they did in turn. He was on a first name basis with my parents. He wasn't wearing scrubs like the nurse. He was in khakis and a button up shirt, the sleeves rolled almost to his elbows. His name tag said "Mason Wright - Occupational Therapy". He looked at me with affection that showed the truth behind his words. "I'm Mason, Emma. I've been doing all of your physical therapy while you've been...asleep."

"You look a little young," my mouth blurted. I covered my lips with my fingers, but he laughed like he was embarrassed.

He swiped his hand through his hair and glanced around the room. "Yeah... So anyway, I'll be continuing your care now that you're awake. You'll have some muscle atrophy and some motor skills that will need to be honed again." I nodded. "But, from what I've seen from working with you these past months, I'll think you'll be fine in that department."

"Working with me? Like moving my legs while I was asleep?"

"Mmhmm. And your arms, too. It keeps your muscles from completely forgetting what they're supposed to do." He smiled.

I wanted to smile back at him, but feared that I didn't know how with this face. Plus, my body was exhausted just from this little interaction. He must have seen that, too, because he turned to the tall man who had yelled at him before. "She needs her rest."

"I know that," he said indignantly. "However, the news crew will be here later on." He turned a bright smile on the woman that was supposed to be my mother. "She'll do an interview with them and tell everyone all about her ordeal. I'm sure you could even get a deal on a big story to the-"

My father spoke up, putting a protective hand on my foot. "You set up an interview with the press the day she wakes up...and don't even get our permission first?"

They all kept talking around me. Mason started defending me along with my parents. The man apologized half heartedly and I assumed he was the head doctor or some hospital head from the way he was acting.

My mind buzzed and cleared in intervals. I lost all track of time and eventually just turned to let my cheek press against the grainy pillow. My throat hurt from the tubes that had been keeping me alive.

Only to wake up to a reality that was more fiction than non.

My eyes still knew how to cry though and I tried to keep myself quiet as I let the tears fall. I thought I'd definitely earned them. Eventually the room quieted and the lights were turned off, all but the small lamp beside my bed. The phone on my bedside stand had a small list of numbers, for emergencies I assumed, but the name on the top of the card was what caught my eye. 'Regal City Hospice'.

Mason had been right. I wasn't even in a real hospital. They hadn't intended for me to wake up.

I wondered if that fact had put a kink in someone's plans.

End of Preview
You can find info on Shelly and her books at her website
http://shellycrane.blogspot.com/